CW00350444

# VLADIMIR OBRUCHEV

# PLUTONIA

**Fredonia Books**
**Amsterdam, The Netherlands**

Plutonia

by
Vladimir Obruchev

ISBN: 1-58963-561-2

Reprinted from the original edition

Fredonia Books
Amsterdam, the Netherlands
http://www.fredoniabooks.com

# CONTENTS

## AUTHOR'S NOTE

This description of a most unusual voyage to Plutonia, to an underground world of rivers, lakes, volcanoes, and strange vegetation, a world which has its own sun—Pluto —and is inhabited by monstrous animals and primitive people, may set the young reader wondering. Does this fantastic world really exist, he will want to know. Is there, somewhere in the Arctic ice-fields, an opening where one can go down into the underground void and explore it?

Many readers have written to me in all earnestness to ask when a new expedition to Plutonia was planned, and if it would be possible for them to join it and see for themselves all the wonderful things they had read about. They also wanted to know why the opening in the Arctic ice, leading to the underground kingdom, has not been found again.

I must say at the very outset that the voyage I have described in this book did not and could not take place, as there is no opening in the earth's crust through which it would be possible to penetrate to the earth's core and enter a void which does not and could never exist there.

This novel is science-fiction, its plot was invented for the purpose of introducing the reader to the animal and plant life of ancient geological periods in their natural surroundings. I decided to write the book after I had re-read as an adult Jules Verne's novel *Journey to the Centre of the Earth*. I was an experienced explorer by then and felt that his description of an underworld voyage was not realistic; besides, many new facts on the prehistoric inhabitants of our planet have been uncovered since the novel was written. For instance, the remains of prehistoric herbivorous and predatory reptiles of the Permian period have been discovered in the steep banks of the Severnaya Dvina. The bones of a large hornless rhinoceros called Indricaterium after the legendary beast Indri have been found beyond the Urals. The carcasses of mammoths which once inhabited the cold forest-tundra in great numbers have been found in the frozen wastes of Northern Siberia. In 1892 I found a tooth of a tertiary rhinoceros in the steppes of Mongolia, which proved that the Gobi steppes and deserts were not at one time part of the Khan-Khai sea bed, as had been supposed, but were dry land. As a result of this find, a large American expedition set out for Mongolia in 1923 and discovered the bones of cretaceous and tertiary amphibious and land reptiles and mammals which used to inhabit the Gobi Desert.

As the basis of my book *Plutonia* I have used a hypothesis which was discussed in foreign scientific writings of little over a century ago and which had many supporters. They asserted that the earth was hollow and that its inner surface was inhabited and illuminated by a small sun. This hypothesis set forth in detail in the chapter "A Scientific Talk," and defended by Trukhanov, the hero of the novel and organizer of the expedition to Plutonia, has long since been repudiated by science. Although we still lack an exact picture of the earth's core, we can guarantee that neither an inner sun nor an opening leading to the earth's core exists. I have, however, made use of this hypothesis as the basis of a science-fiction novel.

Recently Soviet expeditions exploring the depressions in the Gobi Desert in Central Asia have found immense graveyards of prehistoric land and lake reptiles and mammals there. Such depressions will yield invaluable material to science and to our museums and can be discovered and studied by young explorers on the earth's surface, not in an inner void.

I hope that this new edition of *Plutonia* will encourage young people to get to know more about the interesting science called Geology, which studies the composition and structure of our planet and describes the plants and animals that inhabited it in bygone eras, the changes they underwent and the way one species replaced another until the animal world produced a thinking being that became the master of the earth.

*V. A. Obruchev*

# A SURPRISE OFFER

Pyotr Kashtanov had just returned from his laboratory. The autumn term had ended; lectures and examinations were over. He was really looking forward to the coming three-week winter holiday, but had absolutely no intention of idling away the time. Kashtanov was a professor of geology at the University, famous for his voyages to Novaya Zemlya and Spitsbergen and his exploration of the Polar Urals. A vigorous middle-aged man, he planned to rest for a few days and then tackle the scientific article on the geological correlation of the Urals and Novaya Zemlya he was working on.

He was in his study, looking over the day's mail as he waited for dinner to be served. There were several scientific pamphlets, sent by their respective authors, and a catalogue of the latest German scientific literature. He finally noticed a large manila envelope, addressed in a small, even hand.

The professor had no trouble recognizing the handwriting of his various correspondents, and that was why the strange letter intrigued him.

He opened it and was amazed to read the following:

*December 1, 1913*
*Munku-Sardyk*

*Dear Professor Kashtanov,*

*I know of you as an experienced polar explorer, a person greatly interested in the geology of the Arctic. I am organizing a large expedition to the unexplored regions of the Arctic Ocean this coming spring. We will be gone a year or two.*

*If you are interested in the idea, and would like to join us, will you be kind enough to meet me at the Metropole Hotel in Moscow at noon on the 2nd of January, 1914, to discuss the matter in person. The other prospective members of the expedition will also be there at that time and date.*

*If the project is of no interest to you, will you be kind enough to inform me of your decision, by writing to the above address. In any case if you do come to the conference, your travelling expenses will be reimbursed.*

*Very truly yours,*
*Nikolai Trukhanov*

The professor laid down the letter and tried to recollect.

"Trukhanov? I'm sure I heard that name before. But where, and when? I think it was in connection with astronomy or geophysics: I'll have to check. This sounds very interesting. He's stuck away somewhere on the border of Mongolia and he's organizing an expedition to the Arctic Ocean!"

Kashtanov picked up the phone and called one of his colleagues, a professor of astronomy, who told him that

Trukhanov, since his graduation from university, had devoted himself to astronomy and geophysics. He had recently built an observatory on top of Mount Munku-Sardyk in the Sayan Mountains on the Mongolian border in order to take advantage of the clear air of Eastern Siberia during the cloudless days and nights of the long winters there. But where did the polar regions fit in? The atmosphere over the Arctic Ocean could certainly never compare to the clear air surrounding the observatory on Munku-Sardyk.

The professor of astronomy couldn't answer that question, and Kashtanov had no alternative but to wait until the 2nd of January to satisfy his curiosity. He had of course decided to go to Moscow.

## A CONFERENCE IN MOSCOW

At noon on the 2nd of January, Professor Kashtanov drove up to the Metropole and knocked on the door of Room 133, to which he had been directed from the desk. The door was opened and he found himself in a large, light room. There were several people there already, one of whom rose to greet him.

"You're as punctual as a clock, Professor," he said, shaking his hand, "in spite of the real Siberian blizzard outside! It's a good omen for the future. I'm happy you came—it's an honour to have you here. I'm Trukhanov. Let me introduce you to the others."

Each of the men rose, as Trukhanov introduced them:

"Semyon Papochkin, a lecturer in zoology."

"Ivan Borovoi, a meteorologist at the Central Physical Observatory."

"Mikhail Gromeko, a physician and botanist."

A large map of the Arctic was spread on a round table in the centre of the room. It was criss-crossed by heavy coloured lines to indicate the routes of polar expeditions over the past fifty years. The land discovered by Vilkitsky as late as the summer of 1913 had also been outlined on the map, to the north of the Taimyr Peninsula.*

When everyone was seated round the table Trukhanov began to speak.

"You can see from the map that five-sixths of the Arctic area between Siberia, Northern Europe, Greenland, and North America is covered by the routes of various previous expeditions. However, the recent amazing discovery of new land by Vilkitsky indicates that other important conquests are also possible. One must only be able to make use of the experience of one's predecessors.

"Expeditions headed by Sedov, Brusilov, and Rusanov are now studying the Kara or Barents seas, continuing the work started by the famous expeditions of the 17th and 18th centuries, which were headed by Pronchishchev, Laptev, Dezhnev, and Bering, and the expeditions to the extreme north of Siberia in the first half of the 19th century, headed by Wrangel and Middendorf. Vilkitsky has been conducting his research in the same area, and, no doubt, will continue his explorations. I have no desire to compete with him.

"My plans concern a different part of the Arctic," Trukhanov continued after a short pause.

"Look at this large white area to the north of the Chukotka Peninsula and Alaska—you won't find a single coloured line across it! The ill-fated *Jeanette,* locked in the ice, floated by to the south of this area. The last expeditions of Sverdrup and Amundsen were to the east of it, among the islands of the North American Archipelago.

"Somewhere in this white area there is at least one island, half the size of Greenland, which has not yet been

---

* It is now called Severnaya Zemlya.

discovered. Perhaps there may even be a whole archipelago there. See, here on the eastern side of the area, Crooker has charted the problematical land he saw from afar. To the south is Keenan's Land. Nansen does not believe in the existence of a large area of dry land in this part of the Arctic Ocean. Peary, on the other hand, is convinced that he saw the outline of a large continent to the north-west of Cape Thomas Hobbard. Harris, a member of the United States' coastal and geodesical survey team, is certain, from a study of the tides off the northern shores of Alaska, that the continent exists. By measuring the fluctuations in sea level in the Beaufort Sea he has proved that the tides come from the Atlantic Ocean, along the deep channel between Norway and Greenland, and then between the supposed continent and the shores of Alaska and Siberia, weakening all the while—and not from the Pacific Ocean through the narrow and shallow Bering Strait. If the continent did not exist, the tidal wave would cross the North Pole from the Greenland Sea to the shores of Alaska and Chukotka Land, without getting weaker or slower. Further evidence that the continent exists lies in the fact that the Beaufort Sea is unprotected from the west, and yet west winds increase the tidal wave and east winds weaken it, producing a difference of six feet in the height of the wave. Such a phenomenon is possible only in a narrow sea between two continents. The supposed continent is separated from the islands of the North American Archipelago by a narrow strait. If this strait were wide, the Atlantic tidal wave would then be able to reach the shores of Banks Island, where it would collide head on with the tidal wave which had come round this continent from the west and south, and the two tidal waves would then engulf each other. However, MacClure's observations off the west coast of Banks Island have confirmed the predominance of a tidal wave coming from the west out of the Beaufort Sea.

o, we should no longer doubt the existence of ıt or a close-lying group of large islands in this part of the Arctic, and it is now up to us to discover them and declare them Russian territory," Trukhanov said in conclusion. "I am informed that the Canadian Government is sending an expedition into the unexplored area from the east this coming summer. We can delay no longer. We must enter the same area from the south and south-west, from the direction of the Bering Strait.

"That is why I decided to organize an expedition to go there and am inviting you to join it.

"Now I'd like to tell you about my immediate plans. Construction was begun last autumn on a ship of the *Fram* type but improved in many ways on the basis of the latest practical experience. It will be launched this week and fitted out by the end of April. It will dock in Vladivostok on the 1st of May to pick up the members of the expedition. We'll weigh anchor the first week in May, set our course for Kamchatka, and put into Petropavlovsk to pick up a team of dogs and one or two experienced Kamchadals to handle them. If we can't get the dogs in Petropavlovsk, we can get them on the Chukotka Peninsula, in the Bering Strait, where we must stop in any case to stock up on *ukola* fish for the dogs and fur clothing for ourselves. From the Bering Strait we'll head north-east, making straight for the unknown land, instead of north-west as the *Jeanette* did. We shall try to penetrate as far as we can through the ice, but shall probably be unable to reach land by boat and will have to send out an expedition on dog sledges the rest of the way north. The expedition that sets out from the ship by dog sledges will carry supplies for a year in case it will be unable to return to the ship by autumn or in case the ship, which will be cruising along the southern shore of the land or the edge of the ice-field, will be unable to pick up the men before the polar night sets in. The ship will leave supplies at specified points along the coast so that the expedition can replenish its stocks if a second year ashore should unfortunately become necessary. If, towards the end of next summer, the ship does not return to a port that has telegraphic communication with Europe, a rescue party will be sent out the following spring to find the ship and pick up the members of the expedition.

"So you see," Trukhanov concluded, "although our goal is not the North Pole, our intention of exploring the unknown continent to the north of Bering Strait is no less difficult an undertaking. At best we shall return in the late autumn of this year, perhaps without even having seen the land we are seeking. More probably, however, we shall have to spend the winter on the ship in the ice-fields or on the continent itself and return a year or two from now. At worst, we might not survive. Each of us must bear this possibility in mind and arrange his affairs accordingly."

There was a pause, and each man in the room had a chance to weigh the situation and determine his own feelings about the expedition. Trukhanov broke the silence by saying, "If anyone decides, after hearing the plan, that it is impossible for him to take part in our expedition, I would ask him not to make our plans known until the beginning of May."

"If I'm not mistaken," Kashtanov said, "when you spoke of the expedition that was to set out by dog sledge you said, 'We'll send it out . . .' Does that mean that you yourself do not intend to take part in exploring the unknown continent?"

"Unfortunately, I won't be able to. I'll sail with you and remain aboard the ship. One of my legs was amputated below the knee as a result of an accident during a trip to the wilds of the Sayans. I have an artificial leg, and so, when it comes to expeditions over the ice, I'm doomed to a sedentary way of life."

"Who will go on the dog sledge then?"

"Everyone here except myself and the captain, plus one or two Chukchi or Kamchadals, five or six men in all. A study of all three realms of Nature is provided for, and our meteorologist has agreed to chart the longitudes and latitudes, apart from keeping a record of the atmospheric conditions. Right, Ivan?"

"Yes, that's right," Borovoi answered. "I think I'll be able to handle the problem."

"I don't expect anyone to give me an immediate answer," Trukhanov said. "I'd like each of you to think the matter over in private."

"When must we give you our final answers?" Papochkin asked.

"One week today, at the same time. I'm sorry I cannot give you more time to think the matter over, for I shall have to find another expert if any of you decline the offer. And then, I must be back in Siberia by the end of January to make arrangements about my observatory, as I shall be leaving it for quite a while."

A week passed. At noon on the seventh day the same company gathered in Trukhanov's hotel room. None of the scientists had declined the offer to join the expedition which, in spite of the dangers and hardships involved, had proved too tempting to resist. Trukhanov was jubilant and announced that such unanimity and lack of hesitation on the part of the members of the expedition should certainly guarantee a successful outcome. They discussed the plan again, and each member made suggestions concerning the specific scientific and personal equipment needed in his field.

The next day they departed in different directions to prepare for the expedition and to put their personal affairs in order.

# JOURNEY'S START

There were four men who had met according to pre-arranged plan on the Siberian Express leaving Moscow on the 20th of April. They were Professor Kashtanov, the zoologist Papochkin, the meteorologist Borovoi, and the botanist Gromeko, who had all come to Moscow from different parts of the country. Ten days later they were in Vladivostok.

They had the name of the hotel where they were to meet Trukhanov and they found him waiting for them when they arrived. He had come to Vladivostok a week earlier in order to see to the various purchases and receive the goods ordered previously. The next day, which was the 1st of May, all five of them went down to meet the *North Star* as it dropped anchor in the harbour.

During the next three days the ship was loading coal, lubricating oil, food-stuffs, scientific equipment, and the personal belongings of the members of the expedition, who went aboard on the third day.

Early on the 4th of May the *North Star* sailed gracefully

across Golden Horn Bay, cleared Donkey Ears by noon, and headed past Russian Island to the east. The five members of the expedition stood on the bridge and watched the city, spread out in a semi-circle on the hills behind the green bay, vanish from sight. The same question involuntarily arose in the heart of every man standing there: "Shall I ever see these shores or indeed my country again?" But the fresh ocean breeze and the slight rocking of the ship soon put an end to their melancholy thoughts.

The sound of a gong announced that lunch was being served, and the travellers took one last look at the narrow strip of their native land before going down to the mess.

They all went up on deck again after lunch to see Askold Island, the last piece of Russian soil until they reached Kamchatka. The *North Star* turned east after passing the island; the wind died down and the ship sailed smoothly over the light-blue waves of the Sea of Japan which stretched to the south and east as far as the eye could see. The dark outline of the Ussuri coast could be seen nine or twelve miles away to the north. When they had rounded Cape Povorotny at sunset, even this thin line quickly disappeared.

The ship took a sharp turn to the north-east.

"Which port are we making for?"

"Unless we get caught in a storm, we're not making for any port, but the barometer is high, and no storms are predicted as far as the Kuril Islands."

"What happens then?"

"Then the cold Sea of Okhotsk will probably have a few unpleasant surprises in store for us. It's an awful corner of the Pacific Ocean, and ships headed for Kamchatka usually get stalled in the spring and autumn fogs, sudden storms, and rain or snow. I think that will be the beginning of our polar conditioning."

The sea was calm; everyone had a good night's sleep and rested up after the excitement and commotion of the last few days ashore. The next day Trukhanov's prediction came true. The barometer dropped sharply, a biting north-west wind blew up, the sky became overcast with grey clouds, and it started to drizzle. Opposite Cape Terpeniya the *North Star* turned eastward and entered the open Sea of Okhotsk, sailing farther and farther away from Sakhalin Island. The ship began to roll heavily and the travellers had a restless night.

The weather was no better on the morrow. It rained and snowed intermittently all day. The white foaming crests of the dark waves rolled over the port side of the ship and washed the decks with spray. Everyone had to remain below, idling away the hours in conversation. Papochkin and Borovoi were both seasick and had not shown up for breakfast or for lunch. The captain stayed on the bridge most of the day, leaving his post for short periods of time. Luckily, the storm was not bad and even let up a bit during the night. Paramusir Island, the largest of the northern Kurils, loomed up before them in the morning. To the right were the smaller islands of Makanrusi and Onekotan, topped by the smoking Toorusyr Volcano. The wind subsided and the smoke rose straight upwards, spreading out into a hazy grey cloud. Avossi Cliff jutted sharply out of the water a few miles to the south; it was a gigantic pillar like a huge black finger menacing the ship. White breakers outlined its base against a sea that appeared olive-green in the grey light.

"How gloomy the islands are!" Papochkin exclaimed. "They're just black and red brush-covered cliffs."

"Plus constant fogs," Trukhanov added. "Rain in the summer and blizzards in the winter, but people live here, none the less."

"The Kuril Islands are all volcanic in origin," Kashtanov said. "There are twenty-three volcanoes here, and sixteen of them are active, erupting more or less regularly. This chain connects Kamchatka with Japan and stretches along the western edge of the Tuscarora Indenture on the sea floor which reaches twenty-eight and a half thousand feet at its deepest point. The lines of large breaks in the earth's crust is usually an area of volcanoes, and the frequent earthquakes there prove that there's still movement in the crust and the equilibrium has been violated."


# THE COUNTRY OF SMOKING VOLCANOES

In the afternoon all the sails were unfurled. A favourable wind doubled the *North Star*'s speed, carrying it towards the Kamchatka Peninsula, outlined on the distant horizon. Soon they were abreast of Cape Lopatka, where a long range of volcanic mountains stretched before them. Some rose in peaks, while others were blunt and linked by low even mountain ridges. The snow covering the majestic cones of the volcanoes and the ridges between them gleamed white against the dark sky. Bright moonlight made it possible to pass through the narrow gates of Avachi Bay in safety. The *North Star* took in its sails and slowly made its way between the high cliffs of the gates until it was in the wide bay. There was not a single light to be seen anywhere along the shore. It was past midnight, and the little town of Petropavlovsk was sound asleep. The quiet waters of the bay glistened in the silver moonlight, and far to the north the high cone of Mount Avachi seemed a white ghost in the night. There was a nip in the air, and it felt as if Kamchatka were still under the spell of its long winter's sleep.

An hour later the ship dropped anchor a hundred feet away from the sleeping town. The clanging of the anchor chains awoke all the dogs, and the stillness was broken by a general howling and barking, to which, however, none of the inhabitants paid the slightest attention; apparently, this sort of concert was a usual occurrence.

The travellers were awakened the next morning by the sound of running feet and by a general commotion on deck. The ship was taking on provisions, fresh water, and coal. Everyone hurried above. The sun was high over the mountain tops, and the town had come to life.

Anxious to feel solid ground under their feet after so many days aboard, the travellers had a quick breakfast and went ashore on a boat that was setting out for provisions. By that time the entire population of Petropavlovsk, from the smallest tots to the oldest inhabitant, had gathered on the beach to look at the ship and its passengers, to hear the latest news from their far-off homeland, and find out if the ship had brought them the supplies they needed.

The wretched little houses of the inhabitants were

strewn about the slope behind the crowd in artistic disarray. Standing out by comparison were such large substantial buildings as the school, the hospital, the new Provincial Council building, and several warehouses.

The travellers were stunned by the absence of anything that might have been called a street. The little houses looked as if they had been dumped haphazard: some looked out on the bay, and others away from it. Each house was surrounded by sheds, barns, and racks for drying fish. In many places the snow had not yet melted, and muddy rivulets ran out towards the sea from under the heaps and splotches of dirty snow. The pedestrians were forced to jump over the streams, as there were neither pavements nor bridges anywhere.

There were no fowl or small animals to be seen, because the work dogs, which are indispensable on the Kamchatka Peninsula, destroy all small living creatures, especially towards the end of the winter, when the supplies of *ukola* come to an end and the dogs are half-starved.

The yards surrounding the houses were alive with attractive shaggy dogs. Some lay warming themselves in the sun, some were burrowing in the garbage heaps, and others again were fighting or playing with each other. The travellers looked closely at the dogs, for it was dogs like these that would take part in the *North Star*'s expedition, hauling sledges over the ice and snow of the unknown continent. As the winter's work was over and the spring thaws were in full progress, the animals were having a well-deserved rest and an undeserved fast, a fact quite apparent from their hollow stomachs and the hungry look in their eyes.

Although they had to zigzag continuously between the houses and numerous out-buildings, it took no longer than half an hour for the travellers to see the whole town and reach the open country beyond it, where the botanist hoped to gather some specimens of spring flora. He was sorely disappointed, for the earth there was still covered by a deep layer of snow, and the only plants he  could find were some green anemone shoots on the steeper slope where the snow had already melted. Due to the great snow-fall and proximity to the cold Sea of Okhotsk, spring on Kamchatka arrives late, and the snow doesn't melt completely till the end of May. And as if to make up for this, there's a very late autumn, lasting until the middle or the end of November.

From the hill above the town there was a wonderful view of Avachi Bay amid a circle of mountains whose dark cliffs either plunged into the calm waters or sloped gently down, their sides furrowed by streams free of ice.

The circle of mountains receded inland in the west, revealing the low delta of the Avachi River and the small cottages nestling there. It was the village of Avachi, the only inhabited spot other than Petropavlovsk on the whole shore; the magnificent bay was nearly twenty miles across, with ample anchorage for every navy in the world, wonderfully protected from the sea and yet, by its utter barrenness, it astonished all who saw it for the first time. The surrounding wooded mountains were white beneath their winter blanket, but that whiteness was not repeated in a single sail upon the waters.

The travellers witnessed an amusing scene when they returned to the beach from their little excursion, where a group of sailors and a crowd of curious onlookers stood watching the thirty dogs that had been bought for the expedition. They were leashed together in pairs and were howling, snapping, and trying to escape. At the water's edge was a large unwieldy boat into which the sailors intended to dump the yelping mass. A heavy-set, bare-chested man who was evidently the *kaiur* (dog-sledge driver) grabbed a pair of squirming, barking animals by the scruff of their necks, carried them to the boat, and dropped them in. The moment he had turned his back and gone to fetch the next pair, the intelligent dogs, who didn't seem to relish the idea of a boat trip, scampered out on to the beach and got lost among the others. This procedure was repeated several times to the general enjoyment of the crowd. Neither cuffs nor curses would induce the dogs to leave their homeland. The *kaiur* was livid with rage and cursed the dogs in Russian and in Kamchadal, the crowd roared and had all manner of suggestions to offer him, the dogs howled, and the ensuing bedlam was unimaginable.

Finally, the *kaiur* thought of a way out, although not a very pleasant one for the shaggy passengers involved. He pushed the boat about five feet away from the beach and passed the line to one of the sailors. Then he started tossing the protesting dogs in pairs over the water and into the boat. They writhed in the air, flopped on the bottom of the boat, then scrambled up, put their front paws on the side of the boat and howled in misery, but didn't dare jump into the water. When the thirty nervous, yelping dogs had been transferred to the boat, it was pulled in towards the shore a bit. The sailors and the *kaiur* hopped in and shoved off. At the first stroke of the oars the whole mob quieted down and remained silent throughout the trip to the ship, but the moment the boat touched the *North Star*'s hull, the concert was renewed with twice as much vigour as before. The people on shore saw the dogs being hoisted up on to the deck in pairs in a basket, which was lowered down into the small boat on a rope. The *kaiur* then carried them to a specially built pen, where a generous portion of *ukola* helped to reconcile them to their fate.

The commotion on deck, the clanging of the anchor chain, and the barking of the frightened dogs wakened the travellers early the next morning. They were soon up and out to get a last glimpse of the town and its inhabitants, who had gathered on the beach to see the ship off. They were shouting *hurrah, bon voyage*, and waving their caps and handkerchiefs on shore, while the dogs never ceased barking on board, as the *North Star* swung round gracefully and headed across the bay towards the gates. The shore was quickly disappearing from sight; at the same time, the snow-capped Mount Avachi came into view from behind the mountains closest to the town. A thin, wispy trail of smoke rose from its summit.

"Our mountain is smoking!" said a voice behind the travellers, as they stood at the rail.

Everyone turned round. It was the same energetic man who had been tossing the dogs into the boat the day before. He was now wearing a *kukhlyanka*, a reindeer jacket with the fur on the outside. He was smiling and his narrow and somewhat slanted brown eyes and high cheekbones bespoke his Mongolian ancestry.

"Here's a new member of our expedition—Ilya Igolkin.

He's in charge of the thirty dogs and is the *kaiur* of the first dog sledge. He'll teach us to manage these restless creatures," Trukhanov said as he greeted the *kaiur*.

"Our dogs are very calm, sir," the latter objected. "See, they've quieted down already. No one ever feels like leaving his homeland, you know, and they're no exception."

When the *kaiur* had gone off to feed the dogs, Trukhanov told his friends about their new companion.

Igolkin was born on the Mongolian border in a small village beyond Lake Baikal. He had fought in the Russo-Japanese War and afterwards remained in Vladivostok. He had landed on Kamchatka with a scientific expedition and had taken a liking to the land of smoking volcanoes, with its wide open spaces, abundance of fish, and the bear-hunts. He had made his home there and had become famous in Petropavlovsk as a skilled *kaiur* and guide.

Trukhanov induced him to join the expedition by offering him high wages and paying him a year in advance, so that he could build himself a new house and buy some cattle and hunting equipment.

An hour after they had set sail, the *North Star* was entering the three-mile-long gates of Avachi Bay. On the right, opposite the sheer cliffs of Cape Babushkin, a black rock, flat-topped and over three hundred feet high, protruded from the water.

This was Babushkin Rock and hundreds of sea-gulls, noddies, and other feathered creatures, alarmed by the noise of the engines, rose up from their nests there and circled over the cliff, piercing the air with their shrill cries.

The *North Star* cleared Cape Dalny and turned sharply towards the north-east, heading along the eastern shore of Kamchatka, and then sailing farther and farther away from it.

For two days there was nothing in sight, save the rain, hail, and snow, brought on by a cold north-west wind. The warm cabins were much more attractive than the slippery decks and the troubled sea above.

When the wind died away a fog came down, and they were among ice-floes. The ship moved ahead slowly, so as not to run into an ice-field. When the sky cleared, the rocky shore of St. Lawrence Island appeared on the right and Cape Chukotsky on the left. There was a trading station on the shore of Provideniya Bay, west of the cape, where a chartered steamer had left a good supply of coal for the *North Star*. They dropped anchor and started loading the coal. After a week spent on board, everyone was eager to go ashore again, although the cliffs reached practically to the water's edge and were most forbidding, the slopes were still covered with snow, and only a small area around the trading station had been cleared.


## BERING STRAIT

On the third day the *North Star* cleared Cape Chukotsky and entered the Bering Strait, keeping close to the Asiatic continent, where low mountains dropped suddenly into the sea or sloped gently into wide valleys stretching far into the interior of the bleak land. Although it was the end of May, large areas were still buried under snow; only the steep southern and south-western slopes were free of it and covered with young grass or the small bright

leaves of creeping polar willow and birch bushes.

Fogs kept drifting across the strait, concealing the horizon. Low-lying heavy clouds regularly peppered the decks with rain or snow. At times the sun would break through the clouds, and although it brought no warmth, the uninviting shores of Asia's northeasternmost corner seemed less bleak in its bright rays.

When the fog cleared or was blown away by gusts of wind that capped the green waves with foam, the straight bluish shore-line of America would appear to the east. They were in an area of ice-floes, but as yet had not come across any solid ice-fields. The shapes of the frequent ice-packs they encountered were so fantastic as to delight the eyes of those who had never sailed the northern seas before.

An approaching large ice-field was usually preceded by the appearance of a strip of fog that gave the captains of ships in the vicinity ample opportunity to detour one way or the other and avoid running into the ice. It was not as dangerous here as in the North Atlantic, where ships would often meet treacherous icebergs. These mountains of ice drift southward and melt gradually until the submerged part loses its equilibrium and the whole mass will suddenly topple over without warning.

The shores seemed lifeless; there was neither a trace of smoke nor a single human being or animal to be seen. Therefore, the travellers were all the more amazed when they saw a man in a boat, rowing towards the *North Star* with all his might. He had appeared suddenly from a small lagoon concealed from those on deck by a rocky cape. When he noticed that the ship was overtaking him, he started yelling something and waving a scarf frantically.

The ship reduced speed and the captain, shouting through a megaphone, asked the man in the boat to row towards them. On closer inspection the little boat proved to be a native *kaiyak*. The captain thought that the man was a Chukcha who had stopped the ship to wrangle some tobacco or liquor out of them, and was about to say "Full speed ahead!" when the oarsman shouted from the waves below:

"Please take me aboard—I beg of you!"

The engines were stopped and a rope ladder let down. The stranger scrambled up and, once on deck, pulled off his large fur cap.

"Thank you, thank you—you've saved my life!" he cried fervently.

He was a tall, broad-shouldered man with blue eyes in a sunburned face, his light beard was dishevelled and the wind tore at his reddish hair, which had grown long. He wore native clothes and was holding a small and heavy-looking leather pouch in his left hand.

Trukhanov held out his hand and asked, "Were you shipwrecked?"

At the sound of Russian speech the stranger beamed. He glanced at the other members of the expedition, set down his pouch on the deck, and began to shake hands all around, keeping up a steady stream of conversation.

"I'm back among my fellow-countrymen! I'm Russian too—Yakov Maksheyev from Ekaterinburg. What luck—a ship with Russians aboard! I've discovered a gold-field on Chukotka, but my supplies gave out and I had to abandon it. I've been rowing for two days, trying to reach some village and I haven't had a thing to eat except clams. Can you give me some food?"

They all went below, and the new passenger was offered tea and cold meat, as dinner was not ready yet. While he was busy stuffing down the food, Maksheyev told them of his adventures.

"I'm a mining engineer... been working in the gold-fields of Siberia and the Far East for the past few years. I'm restless by nature... Love to travel and see new places. Last year I heard a rumor that there was gold on Chukotka... decided to go and find it. To tell you the truth... I was more attracted by the wilds of Chukotka than by the gold.

"Two natives went with me... We landed on Chukotka... no trouble at all... soon discovered a rich gold-field, and I panned quite a bit of gold there. We didn't take much food along... But I decided to stay on a while longer. So I sent the other two back to the nearest Chukcha settlement for food... They still haven't returned, although it's been more than a month since they left."

When Maksheyev had finished, Trukhanov explained that the *North Star* wasn't a cargo boat, and that as they were speeding northwards, they could not afford the time to take him to a port.

"All we can do is transfer you to a passing ship," he concluded.

"But if this isn't a cargo boat, what is it and where are you headed for?"

"We're members of a Russian polar expedition, and we're making for the Beaufort Sea."

"Well, I'm afraid I'll have to sail with you for a while, unless you care to drop me on some deserted island," Maksheyev laughed. "But as I said, I don't have a thing except what's on me: no linen, no decent clothes, nothing except this filthy gold, which, at least, will enable me to repay you in some way."

"We won't even hear of it," Trukhanov interrupted. "We're only too glad we were able to help a countryman in a fix. There are enough clothes on board and I'm sure you'll find something to fit."

Maksheyev was given a spare cabin where he had a chance to wash up, change, and put his gold away. That evening he looked a different man as he entertained the other travellers with stories of his adventures. The new passenger made a very good impression on them, and after he had retired later that evening, Trukhanov said:

"Do you think we should ask him to join us? He seems to be a man who's been around; he's strong, experienced, and very good company. A person like that is bound to be an asset."

"He's cultured too, in spite of his hard life in these wilds," Kashtanov added.

"And he speaks Eskimo. That will surely come in handy on the unknown continent, for if it *is* inhabited, then the inhabitants are Eskimos," Gromeko said.

"All right. I think I'll ask him to join the expedition— I take it I have your consent," Trukhanov concluded. "On second thought, I'll wait a few days until we get to know him better. He has no place to go anyway."

The next morning the *North Star* changed its course and headed into the wide St. Lawrence Bay and towards Maksheyev's gold-field that was located on the northern shore. He had asked them to side-track so that he could pick up his few belongings, and had also suggested that they dismantle his small hut and take it on board, as it would come in handy when the expedition camped out in winter on the unknown land. The hut and adjoining store-room were built of carefully fitted planks, so that they could be taken apart and loaded in a short time. The *North Star* dropped anchor near the shore, and the crew and members of the expedition all pitched in. By noon everything was aboard, and the ship continued on its way northward.

# SEEKING THE UNKNOWN LAND

Late that night, when the reddish sun was rolling towards the northern horizon, the *North Star* sailed out of the Bering Strait into the Arctic Ocean.

Far off to the west was Cape Dezhnev, the north-eastern tip of Asia, its steep slopes dappled with snow-fields, crimson in the glare of the never-setting sun. The travellers took a last look at the inhospitable and barren shore that was still a part of their native land.

Cape Prince of Wales could be seen through the mist, drifting away to the east. The sea ahead was almost free of ice, for southerly winds together with the warm current on the American side of the strait had driven most of the ice northwards. This was indeed favourable for their further journey.

When the travellers came on deck next morning no land was visible to the west. The shores of Alaska were still visible in the east: craggy Cape Lisburne and Point Hope, the northern boundaries of Kotzebue Sound.

The wind was with them and the ship, its sails unfurled, skimmed across the waves like a giant sea-gull. At times they encountered ice-packs and small icebergs that rocked slightly as they floated north-east.

As the shores of Alaska disappeared on the horizon, Maksheyev, who was standing at the rail with the others exclaimed:

"Farewell, one-time Russian land, a treasure and gift to the Americans."

"What do you mean?" Borovoi sounded really surprised. "As far as I recall our government *sold* this dreary land to the United States."

"Certainly. It was sold for seven million dollars. But do you know how much the Yankees have made on this 'dreary land' already?"

"Probably about that much, or, maybe, even twice that."

"How little you know about it! They've mined two hundred million dollars worth of gold alone in Alaska, and that's just scratching the surface. There's silver there, and copper, and lead, and they're just starting to mine the coal. Then there's the fur trade and there are great forests along the Yukon. They're building a railway and there's navigation on the Yukon."

"What does it matter?" Trukhanov said. "If we still owned Alaska it would be just as primitive a land as Chukotka—where there's also plenty of gold, coal, and furs, but a lot of good it does us."

"It may not always be like that," Kashtanov objected. "As things are now, the country can't possibly develop normally. But if the day ever comes that there's a change in the government we might be able to do things on a much bigger scale."

There was no land in sight the next morning. The *North Star* cut its speed and moved slowly through the thick fog, manoeuvring among the countless ice-floes. The sun broke through at noon and they were able to take their bearings: they were at latitude 70°3' North. And so, thanks to a fair wind and a clear sea, the *North Star* had covered one-third of the distance between the mouth of the Bering Strait and the shores of the unknown continent in thirty-six hours.

The same favourable conditions prevailed during the following two days and the ship reached latitude 73°39'. Towards evening of their fourth day on the Beaufort Sea the ice-packs began to melt and the ship was forced to proceed at low speed in the narrow strips of water left open between the now solid ice-fields.

Not once did they pass another ship; apparently, it was still too early in the season for whalers. When this became evident, Trukhanov told Maksheyev:

"I think you'll have to be my guest here, whether you like it or not. But perhaps you'd prefer to go ashore with the expedition—if we find the land we're looking for."

"Don't take it personally,' Maksheyev answered, "but I just can't see myself stuck on a ship among the ice-fields with nothing to do for the next six months or a year. I'll gladly join the expedition, and I'm sure I can be of some use. I can ski, drive a team of dogs, cook, survey, and help Professor Kashtanov in his geological observations."

"Well then, it's settled. I'm glad we've gained such an experienced and energetic member," Trukhanov said.

Maksheyev's place in the expedition was decided then and there. That evening he showed Kashtanov the colection of Alaska and Chukotka ores which he had brought along from his gold-field. The professor was much interested and impressed by Maksheyev's knowledge; he would certainly be a competent assistant in the work ahead.

The ship had stopped that night, as navigation was impossible. Next morning there was a northerly breeze and the fog began to drift and roll a little; the ship was preparing to resume its course when the breeze became a wind which lifted the fog and drove it southwards, moving the ice-fields too.

A fairly wide area of water opened up before them, and the *North Star* started out in a north-north-easterly direction at low speed to avoid colliding with the ice-packs and to be ready to stop or swing around at a moment's notice. They pushed onwards till midnight, proceeding by fits and starts. Then the sun, which had been playing hide-and-seek since noon, was suddenly lost in a blanket of fog which soon enveloped the *North Star* too. They spent a less peaceful night than the previous one. The rolling fog cut down visibility to zero. The ship was at a stand-still most of the time, and the captain was on the alert, lest they be caught between two ice-packs.

The north wind was stronger by morning. Although the fog had scattered, the ice was shifting and they were very tense all day. It took all the captain's experience to direct the ship slowly between the ice-fields, sometimes retreating or zigzagging. The sailors were lined up on either side along the rails and were armed with long boat-hooks to shove away the ice that crowded the ship. Luckily, the edges of the ice-fields were broken up, there were no icebergs at all, and it was only small ridges of ice, piled here and there on the ice-fields, which presented a somewhat more serious problem.

That night all the passengers took part in battling the ice, to give the sailors a chance to rest in shifts. Next morning they spotted a flock of birds flying northward and two bears walking on a large ice-field about a mile from the ship. These were the first signs of land.

At noon they were at latitude 75°12'5" North, which meant that the *North Star* had gone 1°33'5" northward in three days, in spite of the fog and ice.

When the captain had charted the ship's course, Trukhanov addressed the members of the expedition who had gathered round the map on the table:

"We've been very lucky so far! In 1879 the *Jeanette* followed the same course as the *North Star* out of the Bering Strait, but it was trapped among the ice-packs all summer and was not even able to reach latitude 73° North. It was finally crushed in the ice in the beginning of September, somewhere north-east of Wrangel Island. We, however, have passed latitude 75° without too much trouble."

"You can reach land on foot now if the ice blocks our way," the captain said. "I'd say there's not more than fifty or sixty miles left to go."


## FRIDTJOF NANSEN LAND

Late that evening the northern horizon was unusually clear and when the sun had dipped down to the very edge of the water a low mountain chain appeared in the distance against the crimson sky.

"No doubt about it—it's land!" the captain exclaimed as he trained his spyglass on the ridge.

"It's much nearer than we thought. It doesn't seem more than thirty or forty miles off," Maksheyev added.

Trukhanov was jubilant. "The polar continent exists! We haven't come on a fool's errand after all."

They were so excited by the discovery of land that no one went to bed till late that night. A clear sky made it possible for them to witness a rare sight: the midnight sun had rolled over the ridge of the far-off mountain chain like a ball of fire and was gradually rising again.

The *North Star* pushed on all through the night and the next morning, making its way through the ever-present ice-packs. At noon they took their bearings again; the ship had moved nearly half a degree northwards in twenty-four hours.

Towards evening the sky became overcast, the sun disappeared behind the clouds, and they were suddenly caught in a winter blizzard. The wind could cause no great disturbance on the surface of an ice-covered sea, but the ice-fields began to move; ice-packs up to twenty feet high began to rise along the edges of the ice-fields. The ship was in danger. They inched along, fighting off the ice, now moving forward, now retreating. Everyone had been alerted, and the ship was able to resist the tremendous pressure of the ice only because of its specially constructed hull.

Finally the *North Star* slipped through a large opening at the eastern edge of a huge ice-field and spent the rest of the night out of the danger zone.

The blizzard died down by noon. When the sun finally broke through the clouds they were in for an unpleasant surprise: the strong north wind had sent the ship southwards. At the same time, however, it had greatly broken up the ice-fields, so that in the calm, cloudy days which followed the *North Star* moved rapidly northward.

Judging by the fact that the sounding-lead, which till then had always reached a depth of from five to seven hundred fathoms in the Beaufort Sea, touched bottom at eighty fathoms, they were not far from land. Apparently, they had reached the shelf of the polar continent, but the bad weather completely hid the land from sight.

That evening, the 2nd of June, the depth reading was only twenty fathoms. The ship moved ahead slowly, so as not to run aground. Morning brought a brisk easterly wind which dispelled the fog. The *North Star* was close to an ice wall sixty feet high and stretching east and west as far as the eye could see.

"This is probably a barrier of continental ice that encircles the polar continent in exactly the same way it does the South Pole," Trukhanov told his comrades.

As the sledges could not be landed there, the ship turned eastwards in the hope of coming upon a bay or a break in the barrier that would make it possible to land. The depth reading was sixteen fathoms, which led them to believe that the ice barrier was resting on the sea bed.

They had to keep well clear of it, as great chunks of ice would often break off the cliffs and fall into the water with a muffled roar. There were even streams in some of the narrow canyon-like crevices.

They covered no more than forty miles that day. Towards evening they sighted a long jutting edge ahead. It seemed as if the ice barrier were protruding to the south, changing its direction, but as they drew closer they found that it was not part of the ice barrier but a rocky promontory of the land itself.

There was a lively discussion at supper as to a name for the newly discovered land, and it was decided that it would be known hereafter as Fridtjof Nansen Land, in honour of the great Norwegian explorer of polar seas and lands. In spite of Trukhanov's objections, the cape was named after him, as the organizer of the expedition.

At the edge of the cape the ice wall receded slightly to the north and formed a small bay, deep enough for the sledges to be landed.

Work was in full swing all night with everyone helping to unload the supplies. They had to hurry, for a south wind could move the ice towards the shore and block off the bay. While the members of the expedition were busy ashore, sorting the supplies and strapping everything on to the sledges, the sailors climbed to the top of Cape Trukhanov, built a high cairn around a pole, and hoisted the Russian flag. The *North Star*'s cannon boomed three times.

The cairn was to serve as a landmark both for the ship, which was to cruise along the coast, surveying and studying it, and for the men, who were to travel into the interior of the land and then return to the same spot on the cape where the ship would pick them up. A sealed zinc box was placed among the stones of the cairn. It contained a paper stating that the land was discovered on the 4th of June, 1914, by Trukhanov's expedition, sailing on the *North Star,* and had been named Fridtjof Nansen Land. The statement was signed by all the members of the expedition and sealed with the ship's seal.

The next evening they gathered in the mess for a farewell dinner, at which they decided upon the future course of the ship and discussed means of aiding the sledge party, should they be unable to return at the appointed time.

The *North Star* was to leave several months' supply of provisions, fuel, and clothing near the cairn, so that if for any reason the ship was not there waiting for them, they would be able to spend the winter on the cape.

The men were to go north for six or eight weeks and then return southwards, heading for Cape Trukhanov. In order to lighten their load and provide for the return trip, they were to leave a three days' supply of food every thirty miles or so, and information as to the direction they had taken, just in case a search party had to be sent out after them.

The next morning the *North Star* was decked in signal flags. As Trukhanov was bidding Kashtanov farewell, he handed him a sealed envelope and said:

"If, during your journey across Nansen Land, you find yourself in a desperate situation or if you are bewildered and puzzled by what you see, if you are unable to find an explanation and don't know what to do—then open this envelope. Perhaps its contents will help you to decide on further action. But don't open it unless it's absolutely imperative. If everything goes more or less according to plan, there will be no need for my instructions, which might then seem quite out of place."

After the last farewells and handshakes at the edge of the ice barrier, with all but a few of the *North Star*'s crew on hand to see them off, six men and three heavily laden sledges, each pulled by eight dogs, set out northwards. Six spare dogs ran alongside the sledges.

The *North Star* saluted them with its cannon.


## OVER THE RUSSIAN RIDGE

For the first two days the party's route to the interior of Nansen Land lay over a snowy waste which rose slightly to the north, but did not slow down their fast pace; there were very few cracks in the ice and these, for the most part, were packed with snow. The days were gloomy, and the south wind brought heavy clouds which obstructed the view and poured snow down on them at times. Both the men and the dogs were getting used to their work. Borovoi led the way, keeping an eye on his compass and testing the snow with his ski pole for cracks in the ice. Maksheyev, Papochkin, and Igolkin each kept close to his sledge and guided the dogs. Gromeko followed a little to the side, but close enough to help if any of the sledges stuck in the snow. Kashtanov brought up the rear. He too had a compass and was surveying the route; an odometer was attached to the last sled.

The members of the expedition were all dressed alike in Chukotsk *kukhlyanki*—long hooded fur shirts with the fur on the inside. There were extra fur shirts on the sledges to be worn fur side out over the ones they had on already, in case of extreme cold. As it was still summer, one shirt was quite sufficient; they had woollen jackets along in case of rain, fur pants—with the fur on the inside too, and soft fur boots. Each man had a change of woollen clothing, in case the weather became too warm for their fur suits.

They were all on skis. The plain was covered with mounds of snow and pock-marked by holes made on the surface of the ice by winter blizzards and just beginning to thaw out. The bumps and holes were more treacherous than the few cracks in the ice they had passed.

Maksheyev kept up a steady stream of conversation with his dogs. He had named them according to their characteristics, and the big black lead dog was called "General."

When they stopped that night they pitched a light-weight tent with a sturdy bamboo frame and placed their sleeping-bags in a circle round the inside wall of the tent. Then they set up an alcohol burner in the centre for a cook-stove and hung a lantern on the top cross-piece. The dogs were tied up to the sledges right outside.

By the end of the second day they had covered thirty-four miles and stopped to set up their first store of supplies for the return trip. The spot was marked by a pyramid of ice blocks, topped by a little red flag.

The rise was more noticeable on the third day; there were more cracks to slow them down, and they had to proceed more cautiously, testing the snow to avoid falling through a thin crust into a concealed canyon. Towards evening they noticed the first signs of a nearing change in the terrain.

The wind was tearing at the clouds in the north, and

a mysterious chain of high mountains that stretched along the horizon would suddenly appear and then vanish again among the ragged edges and masses of the clouds; rocky spurs formed a black pattern against the white background of the mountains.

It took them three days to climb the newly named Russian Ridge, for there were many ice cracks in the valley between the rocky spurs.

The glacier that covered the southern slope of the ridge and the valley was a mile wide and was hemmed in on both sides by steep rocky inclines that alternated with gently rising snow-covered slopes. The rocks were strewn with large and small basalt fragments; there were tiny patches of polar plants in sheltered spots. Kashtanov examined the rocks and Gromeko gathered plant specimens along the way. Papochkin didn't have much to show for the day, as he had found only a few half-dead insects on the snow and some live ones on the little patches.

Heavy clouds hung so low that they nearly touched the explorers' heads, and the men seemed to be moving along a low, wide corridor with a cracked white floor, black rocky walls, and a grey ceiling. At points where the descent grew steeper, the flat surface of the ice became an ice-fall that was either cracked in thousands of places, or was simply a mass of ice blocks over which they had to drag the sledges, or else unload them and carry the supplies themselves. Towards evening of the third day they reached a mountain pass nearly 4,500 feet above sea level. They moved on in a light mist which hid everything above a hundred yards away.

It was all very disappointing, as the crest of the ridge would have provided them with an excellent view on a clear day and they would have been able to chart most of Nansen Land.

They set up another supply store in the pass and also left the rock samples which Kashtanov had gathered on the spurs of the southern slope. Papochkin, the zoologist, had added to his small collection of insects the hide and skull of a musk ox from a small herd they had met near the pass.

## THE ENDLESS DESCENT

When they crossed the ridge, they saw that the northern slope was an endless, snow-covered expanse; the dogs had no difficulty in pulling the sledges downhill. Although it snowed frequently, the wind was behind them and the temperature never dropped below $14^0$, which was the only reason they could move ahead so easily. The many cracks were very narrow, but dangerous, because the wind would often pile a fresh layer of snow over them. The blizzard was so fierce by the end of that day that they could hardly put up the tent.

They were snowed in the next morning. Borovoi was the first one up, as he wanted to check his instruments. He pulled back the flap and stuck his head right into a snow-bank. They had no choice but to start tunnelling their way out of the tent. When they all crawled out, they saw that the dogs and sledges had disappeared. Obviously, they had all been snowed under, for there were large drifts everywhere. Everyone started digging at the snow-drifts.

When the dogs heard the men's voices they began to make their own way out, eager for their morning rations. It was amusing to see the snow bulge and buckle and a black, white, or spotted shaggy head poke through with a joyous yelp.

The snow was about two feet deep, but it was very soft, so that the dogs and sledges kept falling through. The skiers got on much better. They changed the sledges around regularly for the leading one made a trail for the others, and the dogs tired very quickly. They covered only fourteen miles that day, and when they stopped for the night, thirty-

four miles from the pass, they set up the third supply store.

A blizzard raged all night again, and they had to dig themselves out the next morning too, although this time the snow-banks were much smaller. The layer of fresh snow was now about three feet deep, and they were greatly handicapped as they plodded onward. After they had covered about ten miles, they were so tired that they decided to camp earlier than usual. Their surroundings and the day were as monotonously gloomy as ever.

The snow-storm died down towards evening; the sun, which hung low over the horizon, would occasionally break through the ever-present layer of clouds that seemed to cover the whole endless surface of the snow plain. The view was indeed fantastic: a snow-white plain, ever-changing puffs and shreds of low, fast-moving grey clouds; whirling columns of fine snow; and scattered in the grey-white moving haze, the bright-pink sunrays as the fiery ball broke through the clouds or disappeared behind the grey curtain. Fascinated, the men stood watching for a long time after supper, until fatigue at last sent them into the tent and into their sleeping-bags.

On the third day of their descent the barometer indicated that they had reached sea level, but the downward slope continued to the north.

When Borovoi noted the barometer reading and informed the others of it, Maksheyev exclaimed:

"How strange! We've slid down the Russian Ridge without coming across a single ice-fall or crevice!"

Kashtanov said, "Stranger still—the sea-shore must be somewhere around here and, therefore, the huge ice-field that covers the forty-mile northern slope of the ridge should also end here. We should have the same picture as at the edge of the Antarctic continent—a great precipice, an ice barrier a couple of hundred feet high, and at its base the open sea or a field of jagged ice blocks, open patches of water, and icebergs, for the glacier never stops moving and shoving the ice into the ocean!"

There was no change the next day, but they felt certain the descent would soon end; they hurried onwards, they peered into the distance, and spoke of the journey's end. But the hours slipped by, and they covered mile after mile until, finally, too exhausted to go on, they camped for the night.

As soon as the tent was up, they all crowded round Borovoi, who was setting up his mercury barometer. They all wanted to check his reading, as the arrows on their pocket aneroids had gone beyond the numbers on the dial-plates, and no longer registered the air pressure accurately.

The meteorologist was incredulous, "According to my rough estimate, we're twelve hundred feet below sea level now! That is, if there is not an area of an unheard-of anticyclone over Nansen Land at present. The barometer reads 800 millimetres."

"As far as I know," Kashtanov said, "there are no anticyclones of such pressure on earth. Besides, there's been no change in the weather since we landed on Nansen Land, and this is definitely not anticyclonic weather."

"What can it mean then?" Papochkin asked.

"Apparently, the land doesn't end here, and its northern edge is a deep hollow, or cavity, which goes hundreds of feet below sea level."

"Is such a thing possible?" Gromeko asked.

"Why not? There are such places on the earth—the Jordan Valley and the Dead Sea in Palestine, the Caspian Sea, Lukchun Hollow in Central Asia,—and the bottom of Lake Baikal in Siberia is over three thousand feet below sea level."

Maksheyev added, "The bottom of the Dead Sea is about twelve hundred feet below sea level."

"At any rate, the discovery of such a deep depression on a polar continent will be a very interesting and important outcome of our expedition," Borovoi concluded.

To everyone's amazement and surprise, the descent continued the following day.

"We're crawling into a bottomless pit," Maksheyev joked. "This isn't a hollow—it's more like a funnel. Do you think it might be the crater of a dead volcano?"

"There's never been such a volcano crater in the world before," Kashtanov said. "We've been going down into this funnel four days now, and the diameter of the crater seems to be almost two hundred miles across. The only known volcanoes as big as that are on the moon. It's too bad there's no cliff or even a piece of ore to show the origin of this hollow. The slopes of a crater should consist of lava and tuff."

"We saw basalt and basalt lava on the southern slope and on the crest of the Russian Ridge," Papochkin reminded him. "So we do have some evidence of the volcanic origin of the depression."

"And Alaska is full of dead volcano craters, filled to the brim with ice and snow," Maksheyev added.

That evening even the mercury barometer gave out completely—the mercury shot up to the top of the tube and stayed there. They had to get out the hypsometer and calculate the atmospheric pressure from the boiling point of water. It corresponded to a depth of 2,520 feet below sea level.

They all noticed that it was a little darker that evening. Apparently, the light of the midnight sun couldn't travel directly to so great a depth. They were further perplexed by the fact that their compasses went out of commission that day too. The needle spun around and trembled, but never stayed still for long enough to point to the north. They had to guide themselves by the unchanging direction of the wind and the general downward slope so that they could continue northwards as before. Kashtanov thought the mad spinning of the compass was caused by the volcanic origin of the depression, as great masses of basalt affect the magnetic needle.

But the very next day they met an unexpected barrier a few miles away from their last camping place. The snow-covered slope ended at the foot of a chain of ice cliffs extending as far as they could see on either side. In places the cliffs rose sheer thirty or forty feet, and elsewhere they were made up of large and small blocks of ice, piled chaotically on top of each other. It would be hard enough trying to scale the ice boulders without taking the heavily laden sledges, and so they stopped, and Maksheyev and Borovoi went to scout ahead. They scrambled up the highest pile of ice and were convinced that the cliffs stretched on ahead as far as the horizon.

"This isn't a belt of sea ice," Maksheyev told the others when he and Borovoi returned. "You never get such a solid wall of it for miles on end."

"I think we've reached the bottom of the depression," Kashtanov said, "and the chaos was caused by the tremendous pressure created by the glacier on the northern slope along which we've been descending."

"Therefore, the entire bottom should be covered by these masses of ice," Borovoi said, "and all the other slopes should likewise be covered by glaciers which are moving towards the bottom."

"The only reason the whole basin isn't full of ice like the craters of the Alaska volcanoes, is that it's so tremendous," Maksheyev added.

"We should try to cross the bottom if we possibly can, to determine the size of the depression and see what the opposite side looks like," Kashtanov proposed.

"The best thing to do would be to go along the edge of the ice blocks and circle round the bottom till we reach the opposite side," Gromeko suggested.

"But what if this depression isn't a crater, and turns out to be a valley between two ridges?" Papochkin said. "If it is, it might be a couple of hundred miles long and then we shouldn't have time to cross Nansen Land."

"Anyway, which direction should we take, left or right?" asked Borovoi.

"Let's try the left. We might come across a spot in the cliffs where it would be easier to cross the bottom," Kashtanov said.

It was decided to follow his suggestion. They started out to the left, which was westwards, judging by the wind, for the compass needle was still spinning crazily. The slightly inclined plain rose to the left of them, ice heaps and cliffs towered to the right, the sky was still overcast and low-lying clouds hung about the tops of the highest ice blocks. About noon they spotted what seemed to be a pass in the ice-field—the heaps of ice were lower and had spaces between them. They stopped to set up the fourth supply store, and Borovoi and Maksheyev set out once more to survey the interior of the ice-field. They returned towards evening with the news that the ice belt was about six miles wide. Although the crossing would be difficult, it *was* possible, and the belt ended where the opposite slope began.

It took two days of hard work to reach the other side; they often had to chop a path through the piles of ice blocks and drag the sledges through the narrow passages in single file, dogs and men working together. They did not pitch the tent that night, but found shelter from the wind behind a huge overhanging mass of ice, while the dogs crawled into cracks or holes between the blocks of ice. They all slept soundly, undisturbed by the weird howling of the wind tearing through the icy masses.

Finally, they reached the edge of the ice belt. When they camped for the night, Borovoi was sure that the hypsometer would register about 2,700 feet, that is, the same as it had before they crossed the ice belt. He lit the alcohol stove and placed the thermometer in the pipe of the boiling tank. The mercury rose to $220^0$ and kept moving upwards.

"This thing'll break in a minute," Borovoi shouted.

"What's the matter?" they all asked, rushing over.

"It's impossible! I've never seen anything like this before!" Borovoi said shakily. "Water boils at $248^0$ in this god-forsaken hole."

"What does that mean?"

"It means we dropped into an abyss when we crossed the ice belt. I can't even say offhand how many thousand feet below sea level this boiling point corresponds to. Wait a minute, I'll look it up."

He sat down on his sleeping-bag, pulled a book of tables of heights and depths from his pocket, and started going through it, jotting down numbers on the margin of one of the pages. Meanwhile, the others hovered over the thermometer, to take sure there had been no mistake. But there could be no doubt about it: the mercury had stopped at $248^0$.

The silence was broken only by the gurgling of the boiling water in the tank. Finally, Borovoi heaved a deep sigh and announced with great solemnity:

"Roughly speaking, a boiling point of 248⁰ equals a depth of 17,200 feet."

"Are you sure?"

"Impossible!"

"Here, check it yourselves. Here are the tables—but you won't find anything for a boiling point of 248⁰, for the simple reason that no one has ever seen anything like it outside a laboratory. You'll have to do it approximately."

Kashtanov checked the calculations and said, "He's right. While we were scrambling over the ice blocks these past two days, we descended 15,000 feet over a six- or seven-mile stretch."

"And we didn't notice it at all!"

"We were climbing down from the height of Mont Blanc and didn't know it! It's incredible!"

"And incomprehensible! The only answer seems to be that the chaos of ice is an ice-fall on the brink of a steep cliff, which leads right into the heart of this collosal volcano."

"And we'll have to climb up an identical ice-fall on the other side!"

"I still can't understand the heavy cloud-banks and the southerly wind that's been blowing constantly for so many days now," Borovoi said.

They were wrong in thinking there was a second ice belt. The next day they continued along a slightly rising slope. The going was harder because it was just a little above freezing point, the snow was turning into slush and sticking to the sledge runners, and the dogs could barely drag their feet along. In spite of the great effort involved in the uphill climb, by evening they had covered only fifteen miles. Borovoi set up the hypsometer and was certain it would show less than 248⁰.

It took a long time for the water to come to a boil;

4•

when it finally did, he stuck the thermometer into the tank. A moment later he shouted, "What's going on here?!"

"Has the thermometer burst?"

"What happened?"

"I'll be the one to burst or go mad in this hole!" he raged. "See who's crazy—me or the thermometer?"

They rushed over to where he was standing. The mercury had risen to $257^0$.

"We were climbing upwards today, weren't we?" Borovoi asked.

"We certainly were!"

"All day long!"

"No doubt about it!"

"But the water's boiling at $9^0$ higher than it was yesterday at the ice barrier. And that means that we *descended* —not ascended—approximately 4,300 feet today."

"Then we're about 21,500 feet below sea level," Maksheyev worked it out rapidly.

"This is crazy!" Papochkin laughed.

"We might have accepted the fact that we were going rapidly downhill when we were on the ice barrier," Kashtanov said, "but how can we ever believe we came down almost a mile, when we were obviously going uphill? It's just impossible."

"Unless we've all gone mad, I agree with you!" Borovoi answered glumly.

Gromeko and Igolkin had gone out to feed the dogs, and as they entered Gromeko said, "Another strange thing! It's much lighter today than it was yesterday at the barrier."

"And it was lighter yesterday than it had been before we crossed the ice," Maksheyev added.

"He's right!" Borovoi said. "The darkest night we had —like a Petersburg white night—was before the ice barrier. We thought we were on the very bottom of the depression, and the dim light was understandable then, for the rays of the polar sun couldn't penetrate so deep."

"But we've gone much deeper now, and the nights are getting lighter!"

They kept on discussing all these contradictory facts for a long time, and finally fell asleep without having found an answer to any of them. Borovoi was first up, as usual, the next morning, for he wanted to check on the weather.

The wind was from the south as it had been all along, and it drove the same low-lying clouds which hid everything above a hundred yards away.

It was $30^0$ and snowing.

"We should check whether we're going up or down today," Maksheyev suggested. "We have a level somewhere among the instruments."

The plain continued uninterrupted, but the snow was slightly frozen and travelling was easier. The slope was very slight, but undoubtedly upwards, and the several levellings they took in the course of the day confirmed what their eyes saw and what the dogs indicated by their pace.

They covered only fourteen miles that day, for the levellings had taken up a lot of time.

The moment the tent was set up Borovoi got out his instruments. The mercury rose to $262^0$.

He said a few choice words and spat.

"The only explanation I can think of is that the laws of science, which have been established for the rest of the earth's surface, do not apply to this lovely spot, and we'll have to find new ones," Kashtanov said.

"Easier said than done," Borovoi grumbled. "We can't do that at a moment's notice. Hundreds of scientists spent years and years discovering the laws we have, and now they're not worth a penny; it's as if we were on another planet. I just can't accept it, and I'm ready to resign!"

They all laughed at his threat, but he began to calculate again and announced that they had climbed—that is, descended—2,580 feet during the day and were now 27,000 feet below sea level.

"I've been looking through a physics handbook," Kashtanov said. "I find that water boils at 248⁰ under a pressure of two atmospheres, and at 273⁰ under a pressure of three atmospheres. That means we're approximately under a pressure of two and a half atmospheres now."

"I'm sure you feel as bad as I do and your head is spinning round from such pressure," Borovoi said.

At this, they all admitted to feeling pressure on their chests, their heads were heavy, their movements were unusually sluggish, and they had been sleeping fitfully ever since the night which they had spent among the ice blocks of the barrier.

"The dogs are feeling it too," Igolkin said. "They seem to have got weaker and have been pulling much worse, although the slope isn't steep. I thought they were just tired out, but now I know why they've been behaving like this."

"I'd like to feel your pulse, Ivan," Gromeko said. "What is it usually?"

"Seventy-two," Borovoi answered, as he turned back his sleeve.

"It's forty-four now! Quite a difference. Your heart beats more slowly under such pressure, and your whole system is affected."

"Will our hearts stop beating altogether if we keep on going down?" Maksheyev asked.

Gromeko laughed. "We aren't going as far as the middle of the earth, you know!"

"And why not? This monstrous crater may lead straight to the earth's centre. I'm ready to believe anything now, and I won't even be surprised if we come out at the other side and find ourselves among the ice-packs of the South Pole." Borovoi sounded none too cheerful.

"That's a lot of rot," declared Kashtanov. "There can't

be a hole right through the earth, nor a crater going down to its centre. It's against every law of geophysics and geology."

"Is that so? But you're willing to accept all the contradictions of every law of meteorology we've witnessed! Just wait—all your nice laws of geology will fly out of the window too."

Kashtanov laughed.

"Meteorology, my dear Ivan, is a frivolous science," he teased. "It deals with the ever-changing medium of the atmosphere, and with cyclones and anticyclones which scientists don't really understand yet. Geology, on the other hand, has a solid foundation—the hard crust of the earth."

"Solid!" Borovoi was indignant. "It's solid until it's shaken up by a good-sized earthquake, during which any geologist can lose his head—if not worse!"

There was general laughter.

"And then," he continued maliciously, "you only know about a few miles of the earth's crust, yet you go on to make statements about the earth's core! There are dozens of hypotheses about the nature of this core. Some say the core is solid, others that it's liquid, and others again that it's gaseous! See if you can puzzle it out!"

"We will in time. Each hypothesis, if it is well-founded, is but another step forward towards finding the ultimate truth. But you're wrong about the earth's crust. Nowadays seismology—the science of earthquakes—gives us new methods of discovering more about the earth's core."

"I wonder what tomorrow has in store for us," Kashtanov concluded. "Each new day now presents us with new facts whose meaning at first glance is not clear, but which, when we consider them carefully, add up to a single chain of causes and effects."

The incline of the snow plain was rather less the next day. Towards noon it had practically evened out, and by evening they began to go downwards. It was a little below freezing point and the going was easy. The dogs raced ahead, and the skiers were hard put to it to keep up with them. Suddenly Borovoi, who was leading the way, started waving his arms. "Stop!" he shouted. "I think we've gone off our course!"

They all gathered round him. He was studying his compass intently.

"What's wrong?" Kashtanov asked.

"We're heading south,—back to the ice barrier—not north. Look, the needle is pointing in the opposite direction to the one we're taking."

"When did you first notice it?"

"Just now. After my compass began playing tricks on me I stopped relying on it and guided myself by the wind, which has been coming from the south all the time. The opposite incline of the plain confused me, because we're certainly not out of the crater yet. When I took out my compass, I saw that it was back to normal again and indicated our course as being due-south."

"But the wind is still behind us!"

"It could have changed during the night."

"No, the wind didn't change," Maksheyev said. "We've been pitching the tent with the flap facing north, to keep the wind out. I definitely remember that the tent flap was still facing away from the wind this morning."

"That means it's been changing gradually during the day and we've made a half-circle and turned back."

"Or else the compass has become remagnetized in some way!"

"If only the sun would break through the clouds, or the stars would come out, we'd be able to check our course," sighed Borovoi.

"Let's stop here and retrace our way several miles, checking the compass all the while," Kashtanov said. "The tracks are still clear on the snow and we'll soon find out whether we were circling or not."

They camped for the night. Maksheyev and Gromeko started out quickly along the tracks; Borovoi set up the boiling tank, and the temperature was practically the same as it had been the night before. The slight rise in the slope that morning was offset by the decline of the afternoon.

In two hours the scouts returned, having retraced ten miles of the route with the wind in their faces and never once going off the straight. They decided that the wind was more reliable than the compass, and that the party would go ahead, keeping the wind behind them.

Once again it did not get dark that night; a dull light still came from behind the clouds.

The next day the downward slope was more noticeable. The mercury rose above freezing point and the snow began to get wet. By afternoon they were passing puddles and little streams which trickled among the mounds of snow and finally disappeared in the snow-packed crevices. They had to find a high place for the tent that night and dig a little trench around it, to drain off the melting snow.

When Borovoi set up his hypsometer he was sure it would show a higher boiling point than on the previous night, for they had been going downhill all day. But the mercury stopped at 259⁰, which seemed to indicate they were 1,700 feet higher than they had been the day before. The meteorologist was at a loss for any explanation and laughed nervously.

"Another impossible reading! This morning we decided we couldn't trust our compass any more. Now it's time to ask if the hypsometer is reliable!"

They all gathered round the unreliable instrument again. They checked and rechecked the readings; they boiled the water time and again with the same results. In spite of the obvious downward slope, which this time was proved by the melting snow trickling in the same direction as they were taking, the atmospheric pressure was decreasing instead of increasing—and on previous days the opposite had been the case.

It was clear that all the laws governing physical phenomena, which generations of scientists had discovered from observations of the earth's surface, either did not apply or had quite a different meaning here in the depression of the polar continent. The puzzling evidence kept growing. The travellers were excited and intrigued, but none of them could understand or explain what was happening. They could only hope that the near future held the answer to the riddle.

"What a desert of snow this is!" Papochkin exclaimed. "Gromeko and I both had hopes of coming across some interesting specimens on the way, but we've been travelling for twelve days now and we've covered over one hundred and twenty-five miles—and except for the musk oxen at the pass, we've seen nothing but ice and snow."

"Even Kashtanov, who's been luckier with his collection than the rest of us, has nothing to show for the last part of the journey," Gromeko added.

"Borovoi here is the only busy collector among us!" laughed Maksheyev.

"Me? What have I got so far?"

"A collection of incredible physical phenomena," Kashtanov answered, guessing what Maksheyev had wanted to say.

"It certainly is a strange collection, but at least it's lightweight and won't overload the sledges. Sorry I can't say the same for your rocks," Borovoi hit back.

The incline was even more noticeable the following day. The icy plain began to branch out into flat-topped mounds with streams running between them. The skis kept skidding on the wet snow and so the men got on to the sledges and used their ski poles to steer and balance them as the dogs pulled them downhill over the bumps.

They all noticed the change in the low clouds, which

were now tinted red, as if reflecting the light of an unseen setting sun.

The icy desert seemed reddish too. Borovoi now had another strange item to add to his collection: they couldn't understand how the bottom of the deep basin could be so bright, as the rays of the low polar sun could not possibly reach it.

That day they camped on top of a hill near a turbulent clear stream, which saved them the trouble of melting snow for tea and soup.

## THE STRANGE POSITION OF THE SUN

After supper Borovoi set up his boiling tank, never doubting for a moment that the mercury would rise to at least $226^0$, as they had been going steeply downhill all day, and should have reached a point about 30,000 feet below sea level, the lowest they had touched so far. He had even calculated the depths for boiling points from $266^0$ to $275^0$, to amaze the others. However, it was he who was startled, for the mercury stopped at $248^0$!

"Another gem for my collection," he solemnly announced. "Does anyone doubt that we were travelling downhill all day today?"

"No doubt about it."

"Water doesn't flow uphill."

"Well, then. The hypsometer here says we were going uphill and climbed over 5,000 feet today. Any comments?"

After they had all checked on the instrument and were convinced he wasn't joking, he went on:

"Apparently, if we continue to go downwards, we'll soon be out of this amazing hollow—perhaps we'll even land at the North Pole."

"But I think something's brewing," Gromeko said in a

mysterious voice. "The air is becoming rarefied and the pressure keeps falling, forecasting a hurricane, a cyclone, a typhoon, a waterspout, or something of the kind. Therefore, I suggest that the sanest way to await the coming holocaust is to crawl into our sleeping-bags!"

Even Borovoi laughed at the doctor's suggestion, but they all followed his advice. Before turning in, however, the meteorologist made sure that the tent was firmly secured to the ice. He was really worried about the possibility of some kind of atmospheric catastrophe and spent a restless night, waking and listening for any signs of an approaching hurricane. But everything was still; the wind was blowing steadily, as it had been all along; his companions were snoring peacefully, and the dogs were growling in their sleep. Then he would lie back on his pillow again, try to chase the alarming thoughts from his mind, and fall asleep.

He was first up next morning, and went out to check the instruments he had set out for the night. The others were still in their sleeping-bags.

In a moment he tumbled back inside, white as a ghost. His eyes were wild and he stammered:

"If I were alone, I'd no longer doubt I was raving mad."

"Well, what's the matter this time?"

"What's happened?"

Some sounded cynical, but the others were worried.

"The clouds or fog are nearly gone and the sun—the polar sun, mark you!—is high in the sky!" Borovoi shouted.

There was a general scramble to get out. The snow plain was covered by a slight haze, and the red disk of the sun was shining through. It was directly overhead, not low on the horizon, where a polar sun should have been at five a. m. in the beginning of June at latitude 80⁰ North.

They stood outside the tent in silence, watching the strange sun, which had lost its proper place in the sky.

"This Nansen Land certainly is a queer country," Maksheyev said.

"Could it be the moon?" Papochkin suggested. "Maybe it's the full moon?"

Borovoi leafed through his pocket guide.

"Yes, there should be a full moon now, but this red disk doesn't look like moon to me. It's much brighter, and it gives off heat."

"Maybe on Nansen Land . . ." Maksheyev began, but he was interrupted by Kashtanov:

"The moon is never overhead during the summer months in polar regions. It's either completely invisible, or very low on the horizon."

"What is it then, if it's neither the sun nor the moon?"

No one had an answer for this last question. They went on putting and rejecting each new supposition in turn all during breakfast. Then they were on their way once more. The sun was still directly overhead, never changing its position as they travelled on downhill along the bank of a large stream. The dogs were pulling well; the men would jump off the sledges from time to time to fix a harness or bridge a stream.

When they stopped for lunch they knew it was noon by their watches alone, for the sun was still high and showing no sign of changing its position.

Borovoi grumbled, "Even at latitude $80^0$ North the sun should move across the sky, and not stand still! The earth hasn't stopped spinning around, you know."

The sun still stood at $90^0$ when they stopped for a rest.

"You'd think we were in the tropics on Midsummer Day, or at the equator at an equinox!" Borovoi said noting its position. "What latitude should I write down? For the life of me, I can't tell you where we are, or what's going on all around us. My thoughts are all jumbled, and everything seems like a nightmare!"

As a matter of fact, they all shared this feeling, and

could find no explanation whatsoever for this new discovery, still more staggering than the others: the contradictory readings of the instruments, the constant wind from the south, the solid cloud-banks, the unexpected thaw, the reddish light, and the gigantic hollow, deeper than any other known depression on the earth.

All during lunch they kept guessing as to the possible catastrophe that might have befallen the Earth after they had set out on the *North Star*, then landed on Nansen Land and lost contact with the rest of the world.

## THE POLAR TUNDRA

By evening they were travelling over icy mounds. The sun remained overhead, as if it were mocking them.

It was nearly time to stop for the night, but they couldn't find a convenient camping place on the icy ridge. There was room enough, of course, but the water was far below, and it was impossible to go down the smooth, icy slope to fetch it. Therefore, they went on in the hope of coming upon a better place, and were encouraged by the fact that some sort of a dark plain was visible ahead through the mist.

About seven p. m. the ice mounds flattened out and the long white streaks of ice formed a scalloped edge around the dark plain, where the streams flowed between shallow swampy banks. The sledges stuck in the mud the moment they slid off the ice, and the panting dogs refused to budge. The men had covered the last mile in tense expectation of some new surprise which this strange land had in store for them in the shape of a snowless plain.

They bent down to touch and examine the long-awaited land after so many days of ice and snow. The earth was brownish-black, water-logged, and sticky, but not entirely barren. It was sparsely covered by short straight blades of yellowed grass and the crooked, trailing branches of small leafless bushes. Their feet sank into the soggy ground and yellow water squirted from under their boots.

"What do you think of it?" Kashtanov muttered. "At latitude 81⁰ North the snow's disappeared, it's as warm as early spring, and the sun is directly overhead."

"Must we pitch the tent in this swamp?" Papochkin's voice sounded tragic.

"It's not a swamp—it's a northern tundra," Maksheyev explained.

"That doesn't make it any drier," said Borovoi. "The dogs won't move, and the thought of spending the night in this mud doesn't appeal to me at all. I'd much rather get back on the ice!"

They began to look around, trying to find a dry spot somewhere.

"Look, over there!" cried Gromeko, pointing ahead to a flat hill about a mile away from the edge of the ice.

"How can we ever get there?"

"We'll manage if we help the dogs."

"Let's put on our skis, then we shan't sink so deep."

Indeed, it proved much easier to ski over the mud than to wade through it; the dogs dragged the lightened sledges slowly, the men helped by pushing the sledges from behind with their ski poles. It took about half an hour to reach the hill, which rose nearly twenty-five feet above the plain and was a dry, convenient place to spend the night. Bright-green blades of grass were poking up through the yellowed grass of the year before, and the low bushes were budding.

They put up the tent at the top of the hill and tied the dogs to the sledges farther down the slope. Behind them the ice-field was a stark white crest stretching across the horizon, while the brown-black plain ahead was turning a delicate green.

A quiet wide stream flowed between marshy banks fifty feet from the hill. The reddish sun broke through the fog at times—and it was still directly overhead, although the time was now 8 : 30 p. m. They had covered over thirty miles that day.

While Borovoi was busy boiling the water, the others tried to guess what the boiling point would be after such a long and obvious descent.

Some said it would be $257^0$, and others $239^0$. Maksheyev even had a bet on it with Papochkin.

"You're all wrong!" Borovoi said after the mercury had stopped rising. "The temperature is only $230^0$."

"I was nearest to it," Maksheyev said, "my guess was $239^0$."

"Personally I think we'd be much better off if we got rid of all these worthless instruments." Borovoi sounded unhappy.

"You take all these atmospheric somersaults too much to heart, as if you were personally responsible for them," Kashtanov tried to soothe him.

"That's not the point. If an instrument becomes worthless, there's no use dragging it around."

"It might be worthless now for reasons unknown, but there's a good chance of it coming in handy again later on."

They discussed future plans after a late supper that night. If the snowless tundra continued farther north, then most of the supplies would be not only useless, but cumbersome; the skis and sledges, the dogs and stores of dried fish, the extra suits of heavy clothing, most of the alcohol, and even the hut would all slow down their pace. The light tent would be quite sufficient during the warm spell that had set in and they would be able to gather fuel in the tundra.

It was decided to spend the following day on the hill and send out two scouting parties in different directions. Then, once the way ahead had been surveyed and the best method of travel agreed upon, they could leave all the unnecessary supplies on the hill and pick them up later for their journey back across the ice.

# THE MOVING HILLS

The next day Igolkin remained on the hill to keep an eye on the dogs, and Borovoi stayed to note the readings of his instruments. The other four divided into two parties: Kashtanov and Papochkin went south-east, and Maksheyev and Gromeko south-west. They all started out on skis, which they could take off if the ground became dry enough.

Each of them had a rifle, because it was quite possible that there was game in the tundra. The dogs, who were as sorely in need of fresh meat as were the men, had been very restless all night and that seemed to indicate the presence of animals in the area.

Soon after they started out, Kashtanov and Papochkin passed a wide stream. Farther on the ground became dry enough for them to take off their skis which they stood on end, tying the tops together, so that the four skis formed a cone; this would be easily spotted on the way back.

The dry ground was covered with young grass and creeping bushes in bloom. A mist floated over the plain, hiding the sun, but it was warm and bright whenever it did break through the clouds.

About six miles from camp they suddenly noticed several steep dark hills ahead, vaguely outlined in the haze.

"As soon as the fog lifts we should be able to get a good view of this flat plain from the top of one of those hills," said Papochkin.

"I think the basic rock samples we'll find there will be even more interesting," Kashtanov said. "Up till now the geological side of this expedition has been in a sad state indeed."

"What about the zoological side?"

"I'm sure the tundra will reward us now. Judging by

*65*

the colour and shape of those hills, I'd say they were basalt domes or some other volcanic rock."

They started out at a fast trot, heading towards the hills which kept disappearing and reappearing again in the fog.

They had been running steadily for about fifteen minutes, but the dark hills seemed as far away as ever.

"This fog makes it impossible to judge distances," Papochkin said, stopping to catch his breath. "I was certain we were near those hills, but we've been running and running and I don't think we're much nearer than when we started. I'm all in."

"Let's stop for a minute then," Kashtanov agreed. "The hills won't run off and desert us."

They stood leaning on their rifles. Papochkin, who had been looking straight at the hills, suddenly shouted:

"Maybe there's something wrong with my eyes, but I could swear the hills moved just now!"

"The fog's moving, and that's confusing you," Kashtanov said calmly, lighting his pipe.

"No! Now I'm sure they're moving! Look—hurry! Look!"

Not far away from them four dark masses were moving slowly across the tundra.

"I always thought basalt and other volcanic hills were stationary," Papochkin said sarcastically. "On second thought, perhaps in this crazy country even the hills wander from one place to another! What a pity Borovoi isn't here now!"

Meanwhile, Kashtanov had taken out his binoculars and trained them on the moving mounds.

In a voice that shook with excitement he said:

"Do you know, Semyon, these mounds are more in your line than mine, because they're large animals like elephants; I can see a long trunk quite clearly."

They began to run again and didn't stop until the mist

had cleared once more. The dark mounds were much nearer.

"Let's lie down," Papochkin suggested, "otherwise they might notice us and run away."

They dropped to the ground. Papochkin took up the binoculars and waited for the mist to lift. Finally he had a clear view of four elephant-like animals about a hundred yards away. They were pulling small branches off the creeping bushes and carrying them to their mouths with graceful curving movements of their trunks. One of the animals was smaller than the other three.

"They have huge curved tusks," Papochkin said. "Their bodies are covered with reddish-brown hair, they have small tails and they're swishing them around playfully. If I didn't know that mammoths have long since disappeared from the face of the earth, I'd say these were mammoths, and not elephants."

"Perhaps even mammoths have survived in this extra-ordinary land!"

Meanwhile, Kashtanov had loaded his long-range rifle with a dumdum bullet and aimed at the nearest animal.

There was a deafening roar as the gun went off. The animal threw back its trunk and fell on its forelegs; then it jumped up, ran a few feet, and collapsed in a heap.

The other animals shied away; then they raised their trunks and let out sounds like the drawn-out bellowing of a bull as they galloped off heavily across the tundra and disappeared in the fog.

The two men were burning with curiosity as they dashed towards their quarry. The animal was lying on its right side, with its feet wide apart and its great tusked head thrown back. There was a gaping wound under its left shoulder-blade and a river of blood was gushing out of it; the round belly heaved convulsively and the trunk was jerking.

"Careful," Kashtanov warned. "It might move its trunk or foot in its last agony with sufficient force to crush us both."

They stopped about ten feet away from the animal and examined it with understandable excitement and curiosity.

"I think it's a mammoth all right," Kashtanov said. "Look, it's about twenty feet long, its tusks are sharply curved up and in, and it has long reddish hair—exactly what we imagine mammoths were like. Then again, elephants never inhabited polar regions, but there were mammoths in the Siberian tundra."

"If I didn't see all this with my own eyes, I'd never believe it! What a discovery!" Papochkin was breathless.

"Well, it's no more of a discovery than this whole deep basin and a blossoming tundra at latitude 81⁰ North. Mammoths seem to have survived to the present day on this mild polar continent, completely isolated from the rest of the world by an ice barrier. These animals are living fossils."

"Or else they're the 'fossilized' animals of Nansen Land that have become adapted to new living conditions. I'd say that this land wasn't always isolated from the rest of the world by snow and ice, and that it had a fauna and flora identical with that of the northern regions of America and Asia. And then, perhaps ever since the Ice Age, the mammoths have found their last refuge here."

"And now we've discovered them! But what shall we do with this monster? It would take a goods train to get it back to camp!"

"If the mammoth can't go to the camp, the camp can certainly go to the mammoth!" Papochkin quipped.

"A wonderful idea! But hasn't it occurred to you that if there are mammoths in this tundra, there might also be bears, wolves, polar foxes, and other beasts of prey? And that by the time we migrate to this spot they might very well spoil our prize!"

"You're right! Let's measure and photograph the mammoth now. Then we can take a tooth, and some pieces of skin, brain, and flesh preserved in alcohol back to the *North Star.*"

"I think we should take the trunk too, to show it to the others. I can just see their faces! And then—we'll eat it! It'll certainly be a dish no naturalist ever dreamed of. They say that elephant's trunk is delicious! But we'll have to save the tip of the trunk, because they've never yet found one when they discovered the remains of mammoths, and no one knows what it looks like."*

When the animal had stopped quivering, the hunters walked over to it and began to measure and examine it carefully.

Papochkin took the measurements and Kashtanov jotted them down; then Kashtanov photographed the carcass from every angle while Papochkin, talking all the while. stood proudly alongside or climbed on top of the animal to indicate its size.

"It's really extraordinary: in the expedition's report

---

* At the end of. the nineteen-forties a mammoth's trunk was discovered on the Chukotka Peninsula, and its tip was sent to the U.S.S.R. Academy of Sciences.

there'll be a picture of a scientist named Papochkin standing on a mammoth's carcass—and not a fossil, but one that's still warm!"

They cut off the animal's tail, its trunk, and a tuft of long hair. Then they slung their rifles over their shoulders, gathered up their booty, and were ready to go back to the camp, when Papochkin looked about in confusion and said:

"Which way do we go? There's flat tundra all round, the fog is rolling in, and we can't see very far. We're lost! I've no idea which way to go."

For a moment Kashtanov was taken aback, but then he smiled and said:

"If a man has a compass in his pocket, he'll never get lost—even in a fog, if he knows the direction he came from. When we left the camp, we went south-east—therefore, we have to go north-west now to get back."

"But we didn't follow the compass when we spotted the mammoths and started chasing after them!"

"You're wrong. From force of habit I noted our direction before I put my compass away. Don't worry, I'll get you back in one piece!"

They continued along the flat ground for about two hours. The fog was still low over the land, but there were breaks in it at times. Suddenly, Kashtanov saw a strange object rising above the flat land a little way ahead and to the right of them. He pointed it out to his companion.

"What do you think it is?" Papochkin asked. "It looks like the frame of an Eskimo tent. Do you think there are people here too?"

"I think they're our skis. I expect you forgot about them?"

"Then we're on the right track!"

After they reached the skis they had no further use for the compass, as their tracks were clearly visible on the damp ground. Soon they sighted the hill and the tent in the distance.

# THE UNINVITED GUEST

When they were near enough to make out the shapes of men and dogs on the hill, Kashtanov said:

"Something's happened. The dogs are howling and everyone's running about."

They stopped for a moment to listen. The furious barking of the dogs was followed by a shot, then another, and another.

"Perhaps they've been attacked by mammoths or some other beasts?" Papochkin said.

"Let's run, they might need us!"

They ran as fast as their heavy loads and their fatigue would permit. Leaving their skis and the trunk at the foot of the hill they bounded up to the top in a flash.

The dogs were howling and straining at the leashes, and the tent was empty. Then they saw Borovoi and Igolkin on the opposite slope. They had guns and were standing beside something huge and dark.

The two runners didn't stop till they reached them.

"What happened?"

"Take a look," Borovoi sounded very excited. "This strange animal attacked the dogs—or else the dogs attacked it. We were inside the tent and didn't see how it started. Anyway, by the time we snatched up our guns and ran out, it had trampled two dogs! We spoiled the game by firing a couple of shots at it, which made it suddenly expire."

Igolkin led the dogs away from the dead animal, and the three men bent to examine it more closely. As they looked at its head Papochkin and Kashtanov cried in unison:

"Why, it's a rhinoceros!"

"A rhinoceros here, on a polar continent?" Borovoi was incredulous. "Certainly, it looks very much like those I've seen in pictures. But do you really think an animal that belongs to the tropics can exist here, in the tundra? It's impossible!"

"Well then, try to imagine that we've just been out hunting mammoths," Kashtanov interrupted. "Do you understand? Mammoths that until today were thought to exist only as fossils, as creatures that inhabited the earth tens of thousands of years ago!"

"Stop!" Borovoi shouted. "That's not fair. I'm sure I'll lose my sanity here. Everything we've seen during the past few days is so unusual and unnatural! Either it's all a dream, or I'm going mad."

"Don't take it so hard," Kashtanov said catching his arm. "We're all just as stunned and confused as you are. Everything we've seen here so far is strange and as yet unexplainable, but there is never anything unnatural in nature. Don't forget we're on an isolated polar continent, far below sea level, and separated from dry land by a wide barrier of ice. The physical conditions here are unique, and mammoths that have long since become extinct in the rest of the world are still alive here. Why couldn't the mammoth's contemporary—the rhinoceros—have survived here too?"

"An African or Indian rhinoceros in the polar tundra?"

"A Siberian one, not an African one. The long-haired rhino that used to inhabit the Siberian tundra in the age of the mammoths."

"Well! I never knew such a creature existed. But why do you think it isn't an African one?"

"Look at it! It has long, brownish hair, while the tropical rhinoceros has nothing but its thick skin to protect it. This one's much bigger than any of the species that exist today. Its front horn is a tremendous thing flattened at the sides."

When Borovoi saw that both Kashtanov and Papochkin were taking the amazing news quite calmly, he calmed down a bit himself and asked:

"Where's the mammoth you were hunting?"

"Surely you didn't expect us to lug it here on our backs, did you?" Papochkin laughed. "We shot it far away from here, in the tundra. There were four of them there, and our geologist friend decided they were steep basalt hills! And then, to our horror, the said volcanic hills went ambling across the tundra. By the way, where's the trunk? That's all we brought, just the trunk and the tail. I hope the dogs haven't found it!"

"Let's go and get it!"

The next three hours were spent in photographing, measuring, and noting descriptions of the rhinoceros, and only after they had finished, did they decide it was time they took a break. Then they finally remembered the missing scouts and began to worry about their long absence.

"You lose all conception of time with this sun that's always overhead," Borovoi grumbled. "It's noon in the morning and noon at night too! The day never seems to end."

"It actually is endless, if the sun is always in the same spot," Kashtanov agreed.

"Last night it wasn't as bright as it is now," Borovoi said. "You thought it was due to a denser fog, but I went outside about midnight and noticed that the fog was no denser than it had been during the day, but that this strange sun was much fainter and its surface seemed to be covered by large dark spots."

"That's very interesting!" Kashtanov exclaimed. "But why didn't you mention such an odd thing?"

"There are enough odd things going on here to fill a book! And I wanted to check on it. About noon today I looked again and convinced myself that there were no dark spots on the sun. That's why I decided I must have been mistaken last night."

"I think some great catastrophe has befallen the sun

while we've been travelling through the fogs of Nansen Land," Papochkin said. "That's why it suddenly appeared overhead at latitude 81⁰ North and keeps shining around the clock."

"Perhaps the earth has turned so that its northern polar region is now directly opposite the sun?"

"I can't understand it," said Borovoi. "How could the earth's axis incline so sharply, in such a short period of time, without any noticeable after-effects?"

"We might not have noticed anything unusual because of the fog and ice. I can't find any other explanation," Kashtanov insisted.

"Why are you so sure that the luminary we see above us now is the same one we last saw over the Russian Ridge?" Borovoi asked.

"What else could it be?" Papochkin sounded really surprised.

"Perhaps the moon has begun to burn again or a new self-luminous body has accidently entered our solar system and carried off the earth as its satellite," Borovoi suggested with a mysterious smile.

"Why bother with such fantastic explanations?" Kashtanov exclaimed. "There are theories based on geological evidence that the axis of the earth has shifted its position in the past. That would explain the glaciers which covered India, Africa, Australia, and China during several geological periods, and the traces of subtropical flora on Franz Josef Land, Greenland, and other places."

"I won't argue—that's your subject; but I measured the angular radius of this luminary today and it was twenty minutes. As you both know without my telling you, the angular radius of the sun is nearly sixteen minutes."*

"That's very interesting!" Kashtanov was amazed.

---

* The radius of the sun, the moon, the planets, and stars is measured by telescopes and other instruments according to the angle at which the earth stands in relation to these bodies.

"And then what about the reddish light, instead of the usual yellow?"

"Maybe that's due to the fog," Papochkin suggested.

"That's what I thought at first. But I saw the luminary quite clearly today, when the fog lifted completely for a while. It was definitely a reddish colour, the colour of the sun when it's almost setting or shining through a dust-storm."

"That's very strange too."

"And what about the dark spots which tone down the light at a certain time of the night? I'll try to check on it again tonight. If the spots reappear, I'll be firmly convinced it's something other than the sun, that's up there."

"Then where's the sun? What could have happened to it?" Papochkin's voice was full of anxiety.

"How do I know! It's just another link in the long chain of inexplicable things we've come across in the past few days."

"Yes, a whole long chain!" Kashtanov sounded thoughtful. "An immense depression on the continent, the strange behaviour of the magnetic needle, the weird changes in the atmospheric pressure, warm weather at latitude 81° North—and not a fluke either, judging by the edge of the ice-fields and the green tundra around us—mammoths and rhinoceroses out for their constitutionals, and a sun that isn't a sun, directly overhead day and night.

"I'm sure that this is only the beginning ... Here come the others at last! They're carrying something, and I'm willing to bet that it's another strange fact."

They all jumped up and looked off into the distance, where their two comrades could be seen carrying some dark object slung on a pole between them. Papochkin put the kettle on the alcohol stove and began to make *shashlik* from rhinoceros meat. The others ran to meet the returning men.

"What a day!" Maksheyev said. "We saw cows and bulls,

and shot at them, but all we hit was this calf that we've been dragging along for the past three hours."

"And we found some interesting specimens of tundra flora," Gromeko added, pointing to a bag on his shoulder. "It's quite unique, and I would even say it was fossil flora if I hadn't gathered it myself."

While they were eating and sipping their tea, Maksheyev and Gromeko told the others of their adventures during the day.

"The first six miles the tundra was the same as it is here, except that it wasn't so damp, there was more vegetation, and it was more varied. We came across bushes, and even small trees."

"Polar birch and polar willow of some species I've never run across, and then a scrawny larch-tree," Gromeko added. "There were flowering plants too. Some I've never seen or heard of before, and others I've read about in the descriptions of the fossilized flora of Canada.

"Then we came to a very deep, narrow stream which we couldn't cross, so we set off downstream. The trees there were over six feet high, and the underbrush turned into a real thicket. It was there that we suddenly came upon a herd of bulls that had come down to their watering-place."

"What kind of bulls?" Papochkin asked with interest.

"They were really more like wild yaks," Gromeko explained. "They were long-haired black animals with great thick horns and a hump on their backs."

"The cows were smaller and had thinner, smaller horns," Maksheyev continued. "Then there were a few calves too. I hadn't expected to find anything more than swamp fowl and small animals, and I had nothing but my fowling-piece."

"And I didn't take a gun at all!"

"So, you see, I could only try for one of the calves with some buck-shot I found in my bandolier. The herd vanished into the thicket, but the calf fell into the stream.

We pulled it out and finished it off with a knife."

"It weighed at least 125 pounds and we were about seven miles from camp, so we disembowelled it to make our load lighter, even though we knew Semyon would be mad."

"Don't worry about Papochkin," Kashtanov laughed. "He feels quite smug today. Do you know what the *shashlik* you've just eaten was made from?"

"Oh, probably from some polar hare, if there is such a species."

"Not from a hare, but from a rhinoceros, and a fossil at that!"

"Ugh! You mean you found a rhinoceros carcass in the frozen ground and decided to see what meat that was thousands of years old tasted like?" Gromeko asked. "If I'd known what it was, I'd never have eaten it. In fact, I feel sick already."

"You can't deny the *shashlik* was tasty, even if it was a bit tough," Maksheyev said.

"No wonder! It's been lying around long enough!"

"Do you know what's on the menu for supper?" Papochkin sounded very innocent. "Sauteed mammoth trunk!"

"No, that's just too much!" Gromeko said indignantly. "What do you want to do—poison us? Are you experimenting to see the effect of all kinds of geological carrion on the digestive tract of modern man?!"

Maksheyev, who had forgotten how to be squeamish during his years of wandering over Alaska and Chukotka Peninsula, said:

"I read somewhere that elephant trunk is a delicacy, but mammoth trunk must be the height of perfection."

"None for me, thanks," Gromeko said weakly. "I'd rather fry some calf's liver, at least I know it's fresh."

After a while the others relented and told of the day's adventures; Gromeko regained his normal, healthy colour, and even took an active part in deciding the serious matter of how best to prepare the famous trunk.

"This will help the flavour," he said, producing some wild garlic from his pocket, "I'm sorry I didn't see any more."

During supper they decided to camp on the hill for one more day in order to go the next morning to where the dead mammoth was and bring back a supply of fresh meat, as well as the parts which they intended to preserve for scientific purposes.

"I think we should discuss our future plans in some detail now," Kashtanov proposed after they had finished eating. "Where and how are we to proceed? Our scouting expeditions have furnished some data for discussion, and as we talk, we can help Papochkin clean the calf and rhinoceros skulls. By the way, Semyon, what species would you say the calf belonged to?"

"If I hadn't seen a live mammoth and a Siberian rhinoceros with my own eyes," he answered, "I would have said that the bulls you saw were closely related to the modern Tibetan yak. But now I'm inclined to think these were primitive bulls which disappeared from the face of the earth at the same time the mammoth and rhinoceros did."

## TRUKHANOV'S LETTER

While discussing their plans, they all agreed that Nansen Land had already offered the expedition many new, as well as completely inexplicable, facts, and that the strange surprises were multiplying with each passing day.

The two scouting parties had discovered that a forest belt began a short distance ahead of them, at the edge of the tundra, and that it would be completely insane to try to take the dogs and sledges along; therefore, it was decided that the dogs, sledges, skis, and some of the supplies should be left behind, while the men went on foot, carrying the bare essentials in their knapsacks.

On the other hand, they had no idea as to the width of the forest belt or what lay on the other side of it, but it seemed likely that the warm climate, the plants, and the animal life were peculiar to the bottom of the deep basin, and that the opposite side was covered with ice and snow; therefore, they would need the dogs, the sledges, and the skis again.

Since such a possibility existed, an alternative plan was that they should travel by sledges along the icy edge of the tundra in order to explore the circumference of the depression, and make sorties on foot into the depths of it as they went along. That, however, might mean that its centre, perhaps the most interesting area as regards animal and plant life and geological discoveries, would remain unexplored. As there were many streams flowing towards the centre, there was probably at least one large lake there.

Both plans had their good and bad points. Which was the better plan? Borovoi, Igolkin, and Maksheyev were in favour of keeping to the icy edge of the basin; but the naturalists preferred to make for the centre, where they expected to find many interesting specimens for their collections.

Of course, they could split into two parties, the first taking the heavy supplies and moving along the edge of the ice, while the other went on foot straight across the bottom, so that both parties would meet on the opposite side. But who could tell how far the depression stretched to the east and west, and whether they'd be able to skirt it? Supposing one or both of the parties got into difficulties? Such a division of forces might lead to the loss of the whole expedition.

It was hard to make such a decision.

"Don't forget," Kashtanov interrupted a heated discussion, "that we have the sealed envelope Trukhanov gave us, in case we found ourselves in a quandary. We were to open it if we didn't know where we were, or what to do. I think the moment has arrived. We've seen many strange, inexplicable things lately, but now we don't even know which way to go!"

They had forgotten all about the mysterious envelope, and met Kashtanov's suggestion with unanimous approval. They took the letter from the crate in which the more valuable instruments and money were kept; Kashtanov broke the seal and read aloud:

> June 14, 1914
> *Aboard the "North Star"*

*Dear Friends,*

*Perhaps, when you read these lines, you'll be feeling very depressed. I hope that my advice and suggestions will not disappoint you.*

*First of all, I must confess that I drew you into a venture so dangerous and unusual, that you would have thought me insane and would have refused to join in the expedition, had you had any idea at all of your destination. I had an occasion to test this possibility when I discussed my ideas with a scientist whom I knew well and invited him to organize an expedition which I would have financed. He refused categorically and called me an irresponsible dreamer.*

*Therefore, to be able to organize an expedition to verify my theories, I realized that I would have to conceal its real destination and its purpose from those who were to take part in it. The expedition was, supposedly, to explore* an unknown area of the Arctic Circle. It was quite possible that my theories were incorrect, and that the expedition would merely discover some island or an ice-covered continent, and would return safely, after exploring the newly discovered land. If such were the case, I would not consider the expedition a failure, as my hypothesis would be refuted once and for all, and, at the same time, the last large blank spot on the map of the Arctic would be filled in.

To come to the point: I have reached the conclusion that the earth's core is not at all what modern geologists and geophysicists believe it to be. This statement is based on data provided by the observatories on Mont Blanc and Munku-Sardyk, on scientific papers I have studied, on the many readings supplied by seismographic stations, and research in the field of the distribution and irregularities of the force of gravity. I am convinced that there is a fairly large cavity inside the earth, a space which probably has its own small central luminary—altough perhaps that may be extinguished by now. The cavity may communicate with the earth's surface by means of one or two large or small openings, which make it possible to reach the inner surface of this hollow globe.

The only way of testing my theory was to send a special expedition to look for one of these openings, which, of course, could only be located in the unexplored wastes of one of the polar regions. I chose the Arctic, as being more accessible to a Russian expedition.

If you have found an opening, try to go down it. Perhaps, you have already gone into it, thinking all the while that you were descending into a deep continental depression. If that is the case, and if you still have enough strength and supplies to continue your journey, try to go farther and explore this inner surface as thoroughly as you can, without risking your lives unnecessarily.

If, for any reason, you are unable to explore the region,

*then return, for even the fact that you have found such
an opening will be a great discovery, and a new expedition,
equipped on the basis of your experience, can then set off
to explore the inner surface. Knowing you for the true
scientists you are, I am certain that the great and wonderful discoveries that await you will inspire you to go on.
But I beg you to weigh up the situation carefully, and
choose the wisest course, to avoid the risk of losing what
you have already achieved.*

*Perhaps you will split into two groups, one of which
will proceed into the interior of the inner surface, while
the other remains at the entrance, ready, if necessary, to
go to the rescue of the first group, or else to bring the
news of your wonderful discovery to the scientific
world.*

*I am most unhappy to be deprived of the chance to
share in your work, your hardships, and your discoveries,
to which I can contribute no more than this letter. If it
has not made things clearer, disregard it. In any case, I
wish you the best of luck with all my heart.*

*Sincerely yours,
N. Trukhanov*

## THE LAND OF PERPETUAL LIGHT

Their interest and amazement grew as they listened to
the letter and there was a moment of silence after
Kashtanov had finished reading.

Each one was thinking of what he had just heard, trying
to connect it with all the strange facts and things he had
been witness to during the past few days.

"Everything is much clearer now," Borovoi said,
heaving a sigh of relief. "Now I understand why the sun
is overhead, why there are mammoths and rhinoceroses
here, and why the compass has been playing tricks on us.

The only thing that remains a mystery is the strange behaviour of the barometer."

"Yes, so many things are clear now!" Kashtanov agreed. "I think that we began going down into the opening in the earth's surface when we crossed the Russian Ridge. The icy ridge is probably the edge of the inner surface and once we were inside we were going south instead of north—the compass *was* right—although we never changed our direction. Then we climbed and crossed a flattened ridge of ice, came down on the other side, and found ourselves in the tundra. The mammoth, rhinoceros, and primitive bull have survived here because of a moderate climate and because man, the great killer, has been missing from the scene."

"That's right. We've only just dropped in and already we've killed three local inhabitants," Gromeko said.

"Apparently this sun above us is a small nucleus of the earth which is still burning hot and which lights and heats the inner surface of a thick and completely hardened crust, the outside of which we know so well. Now we'll have a chance to explore some of the inner surface, which, undoubtedly, has very many more interesting surprises in store for us."

"We should find a name for this new land, otherwise we'll just go on calling it the 'inner surface' for ever. This isn't Nansen Land any more, you know!" Maksheyev said.

"It's always day-time here. The central luminary burning deep inside the earth seems to correspond to the conception the ancients had of an underworld god of fire. I suggest we name the luminary 'Pluto' in his honour, and the country 'Plutonia,'" Kashtanov said.

Several other names were suggested, but after a heated discussion, it was agreed that "Plutonia" was the most appropriate.

"We have an important decision to make," Kashtanov continued. "Are we going to be satisfied with discovering the opening, going down it and even exploring a small part of Plutonia? Should we now return to the *North Star* and tell Trukhanov how completely his theory has been corroborated? Or should we try to reach farther into the land of light?"

"We should go on, of course!"

"At least as long as we can!"

"We still have a lot of time at our disposal!"

"I agree with you. But how shall we go about organizing the rest of our journey?" Kashtanov asked.

"I would say that the farther from the ice and snow, and the deeper into the land we go, the higher will be the temperature," Borovoi said. "The dogs, sledges, and skis will only hamper us—they should all be left behind.

"We can't leave the dogs here by themselves. I think we should follow Trukhanov's suggestion that at least two men should stay behind, for I take it that no one would care to stay here alone for any length of time. We can set up the hut and the two who remain with the dogs and extra supplies can explore the surrounding tundra and the edge of the ice-field. If the others haven't come back by a certain date, the two men should take one of the sledges and start back to the *North Star* to report our discoveries and guide a new expedition back to search for the lost men and carry on with exploring Plutonia."

"What happens if the lost men show up a few days late? How will they ever be able to cross the ice-fields?" Maksheyev asked.

"Two sledges, the skis, and a supply of food can be left here just in case such a thing happens. The late-comers will have to get back without dogs and drag the sledges themselves, but this shouldn't be too difficult, for the stores of food we left along the whole route will make the load on the sledges much lighter."

They all agreed that this was by far the best plan, but no one wanted to stay behind in the tundra, on the very threshold of the mysterious country. They now had to decide who would be of most value on the expedition to the interior of Plutonia. It was obvious that the zoologist, botanist, and geologist must go; in any case there would be little for any of them to do in the tundra. Therefore, Papochkin, Gromeko, and Kashtanov were to go. Igolkin, on the other hand, as the only non-scientist among them, was obviously condemned to sit it out in the tundra. There remained, then, Borovoi and Maksheyev, one of whom would go.

As each of the two generously insisted that the other should join the expedition, it was decided that the two would draw lots. Borovoi pulled out a slip of paper with "sit it out" on it, and Maksheyev pulled the one that said "go".

A long time was spent in discussing the plans of the expedition. First they had to choose a means of travel and, on the basis of that decision, agree on what they would take with them. They were against taking tinned foods, as they counted on supplying their needs by hunting; but even then, each man would have quite a load to carry and they could not expect to find macadam roads there.

"Suppose we take some of the dogs along and load the supplies on them, although they haven't been trained for that and will probably suffer from the heat," Gromeko said.

"It doesn't seem a good plan to me, as we might lose the animals we'll need for the journey back across the ice," Maksheyev said. "I suggest we make use of a much stronger and more reliable force to carry us as well as our baggage."

"What do you mean?"

"Water. The deep stream we saw and couldn't cross today flows southwards, which is where we're going. We have the two small canvas boats we took along, for crossing the open patches of water in the ice-fields. I guess we all forgot about them, and no wonder, we haven't used them once since we started out, but there's room for two men in each boat, so we'll just climb in and float away! If the boats are overloaded, we can build a raft when we reach the forest regions and float downstream as far as the river will carry us."

"A wonderful plan!" Kashtanov exclaimed.

"It's so easy and convenient! We'll just sit there looking about us and noting what we see as we float along," Papochkin enthused.

"You seem to forget that the banks of the river will probably be thick with foliage, and we'll be sailing down this green corridor without seeing a thing," Gromeko objected.

"What's to stop us from going ashore and making trips into the interior whenever we come to an interesting spot? And we'll sleep ashore too," Maksheyev said.

"I'm glad we shan't have any heavy knapsacks on our backs on these side trips," Papochkin added.

"And then we needn't worry about adding to our collections if we have the boats and a raft. It would be really hard if we had to drag the collections around, and kept adding to them every day," Kashtanov said.

"Travelling by boat we'll be better protected from all the animals and snakes in the forests and swamps. After all, we still don't know the surprises that are in store for us in this mysterious country," Gromeko said.

"You've given us a wonderful idea, Yakov, and we're all greatly indebted to you," declared Kashtanov. "Therefore, I propose that we name the river after you—the Maksheyev River. And now, let's get into our sleeping-bags—or rather on top of them, as it's so warm—and visit the mammoth tomorrow. We can bring back the hide, tusks, and a supply of meat on the sledges."

"But we wanted to move the camp site to where the mammoth is, remember?" Papochkin reminded him.

"There's no sense doing that now, because the river

flows in the opposite direction, and we'd be moving away from it. This hill has a lot of good points: it's dry, it's a good landmark, it's far enough from the edge of the woods and the wild beasts, it's close to the ice, it's a windy place —a very important point as far as the dogs are concerned, especially when it starts getting warmer. You can see a long way from here and any approaching enemy would be easily spotted."

"We can set up a real meteorological station here, and I hope my barometers will begin to react to changes in atmospheric pressure," Borovoi added.

## THE UNINVITED GRAVE-DIGGERS

The hands of their watches were pointing to ten by the time they finally decided to lie down and call it a day.

Next morning at breakfast they discussed the question of who was to go and fetch the mammoth meat, and whether it was worth bothering with at all, or perhaps it would be better if they simply started preparing for the journey ahead.

"If we knew we'd come across other mammoths, then there'd be no need to return to this one; it's been photographed and described already. But since a forest region begins a short way from here, there's a good chance we'll never see any others—especially if they live only in the tundra along the edge of the ice-fields," Kashtanov said.

They decided to go to the mammoth, and four men and three dog sledges set off soon afterwards.

Gromeko and Kashtanov stayed behind. Gromeko wanted to add to his collection some specimens of spring flora that was growing around the hill, and Kashtanov had decided to dig into the slope of the hill, to find out its structure. He was puzzled by the existence of a single hill in the middle of the flat tundra.

Papochkin led the others to the place where the mammoth had been brought down. On the way they shot several swamp fowl that were wandering near the river, and then a peculiar-looking hare that seemed more like a huge jerboa than anything else. Papochkin was overjoyed.

From a distance the mammoth's carcass resembled a hillock on the tundra. As they approached, Igolkin, who had a keener eye than the others, said he saw some grey animals scurrying about it.

They left the sledges at a distance and began to move cautiously towards the mammoth. Suddenly, they stopped in amazement: the grey animals that had been darting back and forth had disappeared, as if the earth had swallowed them up.

"O-ho!" cried Papochkin when they finally reached the mammoth. "Someone's been monkeying about here!"

It seemed as if huge moles had taken over the site: the roots of bushes were sticking out of mounds of earth that were piled three feet high around the carcass, and the hind-quarters lay in a hole, barely showing above the surface of the tundra.

"Who could have done all this?" The men were at a loss.

"They were experienced grave-diggers! I think they were planning to bury the whole carcass, either to conceal it from wolves, or to use it as a future supply of food," Maksheyev said.

Igolkin led one of the dogs over to a mound of earth. The dog sniffed it and suddenly dashed under the mammoth's belly. In a second it was dragging a strange-looking animal out by the leg. The little creature was jerking its short paws madly and squealing like a piglet. They took it away from the dog, slit its throat, and examined it carefully. In colouring and shape it resembled a badger.

On further examination, they found several other such animals crouching underneath the carcass which they had intended to bury and consume bit by bit later on.

The uninvited grave-diggers had made it impossible for the hide to be removed in one piece; therefore, the men removed it from the left side of the body. They examined the insides, cut off a front and hind foot, hacked out one of the tusks, removed an eye, half of the brain, the tongue, and two teeth. They gave the dogs as much meat as they could eat, and cut several large pieces from the thigh, which they loaded on the sledges. Then they started on the slow trip back to camp. Papochkin was completely satisfied with the day's haul: a grave-digger, a hare, and the swamp fowls.

"The grave-diggers can go on burying the rest," Borovoi joked. "When we run out of meat for the dogs, Igolkin and I will drop over again to pick up some supplies. Perhaps we'll even make the trip sooner, before the meat begins to rot."

"Will you take the skull back with you if you go?" Papochkin asked. "I think the grave-diggers will have picked it clean by then."

When the hunters approached the hill, they saw Kashtanov and Gromeko busy at a strange task. They were dragging chunks of some kind of white stone from a hole dug in the hillside and stacking them in a pile.

"This hill is really a find as far as we're concerned," Kashtanov called out to them. "I dug a hole to examine the structure of the hill and hit solid ice at five feet; when I dug another hole a bit farther off I found ice again. Then I thought of digging a cave deep in the side of the hill. It will be an excellent ice-box for storing our food and the hides. Mammoths and rhinoceroses won't always be dropping in just in time for supper, you know!"

"Do you think the whole hill is solid ice, covered by a layer of earth?" Borovoi asked.

"Yes. Fossilized glaciers like this have been found in the north of Siberia. It's either a large winter snow-bank which has for some reason survived the warm weather, or else it's part of a retreating mass of ice. It gradually became covered with the sand and slime of the streams that drained off the glacier, and that's why it's been preserved."

Kashtanov's discovery proved invaluable to the two men who were to remain on the hill, and who would now have a wonderful store-room for their provisions right under their hut.

"We'll broaden and deepen the cave and make a proper door on the outside," Borovoi said.

"Then we can dig another ice cave on the other side of the hill and keep the dogs there when it gets too hot," Igolkin added.

As soon as they had unloaded the sledges, they set up the hut and then helped Kashtanov and Gromeko make the cave large enough to hold all the parts of the mammoth which they had brought, as well as the remains of the rhinoceros' carcass. When the store-room was ready and filled up, they stacked blocks of ice at the entrance and made a fence of sledges and skis around it, to keep the dogs from getting at the meat.

They started preparing for the journey the next morning. First, they sorted out everything they had. Then they put the tinned food, the alcohol, and the dried *ukola* into the ice-house and loaded the boats and supplies they would need on the journey on to the sledges. After they had had their last meal together the whole party made for the Maksheyev River, except Borovoi, who was left behind to guard the tent and the storehouse. Igolkin was to return with the sledges by evening. They decided to take General along as a watchdog, and they cropped him to make him feel cooler. The once-shaggy dog looked so silly that they all burst out laughing, for Maksheyev, the barber, had left a tuft of hair on the dog's head, a fringe on his haunches, and a tassle at the end of his tail, saying that these decorations would frighten off any wild beast they came across.

They reached the river which was about twenty feet wide and about five or six feet deep. The men got in, two to a boat: one at the oars and the other at the helm. General took his place in the bow of the leading boat, with Maksheyev and Gromeko. His odd-looking muzzle with its large pointed ears and the fuzzy tuft between them peeped over the side.

Igolkin waited on the bank until both swiftly moving boats had disappeared. On the horizon a white flag flew over the barely visible hut. The expedition had split up. Until then the six men had shared all the work as a team. but now four of them were off into the interior of the strange country. It was impossible to tell when they would return or whether they would all return safely.


## DOWN THE MAKSHEYEV RIVER

Both boats were swept swiftly downstream. The fresh green leaves on the polar willows hung low over the dark water, and the flat tundra with its creeping bushes lay on either side of the river; the wind was still behind them, but now they knew it was a north wind, coming from the ice-fields of the cold opening in the earth's crust and rushing towards the warm inner surface. The fog was still thick, but occasionally it lifted and they could see the reddish luminary, still motionless overhead. The temperature rose to $53^0$, and it drizzled on and off.

The boats sped on at about five miles an hour; the men at the helm mapped out every turn and bend of the river. They stopped for the night after covering about fifteen miles.

During their short excursion along the bank they noticed that the tundra bushes grew higher there, and that there were dwarfish larch-trees, willows, and birches growing close to the bushes, forming small dense thickets here and there. There were well-beaten narrow animal paths leading through the bushes to the watering-places along the river-bank.

They spent the night in the light summer tent and slept without sleeping-bags for the first time since they had set out.

"The perpetual light here plays havoc with all our ideas of time," Maksheyev said settling down. "You say morning, noon, or night only after you've looked at your watch, because the sun is always directly overhead, as if it were laughing at you."

The night, or period of rest, slipped by quietly.

They rowed about thirty miles the next day and stopped for the night early, as they wanted to explore the bank more thoroughly and go farther inland than they had the previous day. Each bank was covered by a wall of high bushes and trees that blocked the view completely.

After dinner Gromeko remained near the tent to collect plants, Maksheyev took General and made for the west, while Kashtanov and Papochkin went eastwards, following the animal trails that wound through the dense bushes. At times there were plainly visible tracks along the paths, and

Papochkin could pick out those of a solid-hoofed animal and the prints of soft-pawed beasts of prey of various sizes. One such set of prints sent chills down their spines. Each footmark was about eight inches long, and the claws had sunk two inches into the ground. Papochkin said the prints had been made by an enormous bear.

"It's probably a cave bear, a contemporary of the mammoth," Kashtanov said.

"I wonder if it hunts cave men?" Papochkin mused.

"Well, there have been cases of the bones of these bears having been found in the caves of primitive men," Kashtanov answered, "but I haven't heard of any skeletons of primitive men being found in the bears' caves!"

"We'll keep a safe distance away!"

"What! Our ancestors fought them with clubs and stone axes, and you want us to run when we have rifles and bullets! Are you that scared?"

Before long they came upon a large flower-decked meadow where various mammals were grazing singly or in herds. The men stopped among the bushes. It wasn't difficult to see that all these animals had long since disappeared from the face of the earth: there were primitive black bulls with huge horns and humps, giant deer with antlers to match, small shaggy wild horses with short manes and sparse tails. Two rhinoceroses had their heads in a clump of bushes, and several mammoths stood in a group, waving their heads and trunks about to shake off the clouds of annoying mosquitoes, horse-flies, and midges.

After having a good look at the pastoral scene of "living fossils," the men decided to move closer, in order to photograph some of the animals. They crept along the edge of the clearing until they reached the bulls and got a few shots of them; then they made for the two rhinos and snapped them just as they locked their giant horns playfully and jumped clumsily at each other, trampling the grass and digging up clods of earth.

The mammoths were almost in the centre, and before the men had a chance to get close enough to them, there was a commotion at the opposite end of the meadow, where the deer were grazing. The deer raised their heads suddenly, stood poised for a second, and took flight, frightened away by some unseen, but apparently vicious enemy. They flashed past the mammoths, which also became alarmed and made off at a heavy gallop, their trunks held high. Both the deer and the mammoths were making straight for the two crouching men.

"When the deer are within a hundred feet, shoot the one in front," Kashtanov said hurriedly. "I'll photograph them when they stop for a split second, and then you fire again, otherwise, we might be trampled."

Papochkin had his rifle ready. When the giant lead buck, his neck straining forward and his nostrils quivering, was almost on top of them, he fired point-blank, hitting the animal full in the chest; its forelegs buckled and it fell. The others jostled each other as they came to a halt in a tight knot.

Kashtanov's shutter clicked and Papochkin took another shot at the herd. One deer leaped forward and fell, dead; the others turned sharply and raced along the edge of the clearing.

By then the mammoths had reached the two victims and stopped. Papochkin loaded the guns while Kashtanov took a photograph.

"Do we shoot?" Papochkin asked in a voice that was shaking with excitement.

"What for? We've enough meat already and we've dissected a mammoth before. We don't want to shoot unless they attack us."

The six mammoths stood close together, waving their trunks, as if deciding what to do. Two were still youngsters with short tusks and short hair; they soon calmed down and began playing with each other, jumping round

their elders, who trumpeted anxiously from time to time. Finally, an old bull turned right and the rest followed him along the edge of the clearing. The two rhinoceroses were the only ones left.

"I wonder what could have scared them," Kashtanov mused. "Perhaps a cave bear?"

"Or an even fiercer living fossil from your palaeontological zoo!"

"Who knows! I suggest we stay on this side of the clearing, because whatever it is it can attack us unexpectedly from the thicket before we have time to fire a shot!"

"Well, let's start on the deer then. We have to measure them, skin them, and drag them back to the boats."

They skinned both animals, cut off the hind legs of the

smaller one, and, thus laden, started slowly back to the river. They decided to return for more meat if the others had bagged nothing—provided the unknown beast that was roaming near the clearing left them some.

## HUNTING THE HUNTER

When they returned to camp they found Gromeko anxiously awaiting them. He had explored the immediate vicinity, collected all sorts of plants, and was roasting a goose they had shot that morning. Suddenly General came bounding up. He was alone, but a note was tied to his collar. Maksheyev had written:

*I shot a huge beast which I can't possibly drag back to camp. I want Semyon to have a look at it. General knows the way, but I've sketched my route in any case.*

There was a pencil drawing on the other side with the distances marked off in feet.

After a short rest, Papochkin and Gromeko set out to find Maksheyev. General led them well, except that he got confused when there was a fork in the path; then they were glad of the sketch. The two men had been walking quickly for about half an hour, and were quite near to where they expected to find Maksheyev when two shots rang out. General dashed on ahead, barking furiously, and the two men, worried lest their friend be in danger, followed close behind.

They soon reached a large clearing. There was a cluster of trees and bushes in the centre, and they could see Maksheyev's head above a yellowish mass. Circling round him were well over a dozen rust-coloured animals: they were wolves.

General stopped short, hesitating to attack with the forces so unequal.

When the wolves saw the men coming they began to move off, and Maksheyev shouted:

"Let them have a couple of rounds of buck-shot if you've got a shot-gun, because I don't want to waste my bullets."

Gromeko quickly loaded his shot-gun and fired into the midst of the pack. The wolves ran for the bushes, pursued by General, who finished off one of the wounded animals on the way. Maksheyev told the others what had happened:

"When I came to this clearing, I stopped at the edge of the woods, because General began to growl and quiver. I saw deer grazing in the clearing beyond this grove and decided to shoot some, as they were the first we had come across. I made my way through the bushes along the edge of the woods, but when I reached the grove I noticed a large yellow animal that had its eye on the deer too and was creeping towards them from behind the grove. I decided the yellow animal was more interesting than the deer, and I began to follow it, keeping about a hundred paces between us. The yellow beast was too preoccupied with its prey to notice me, or else it paid no attention to a two-legged creature it had never set eyes upon before. When it had reached the little grove it stood up to its full height with its vicious eyes picking out a victim. Only the bushes were between it and the deer, who were grazing peacefully, quite unaware of its presence. Then I saw several dark stripes on the beast's sides and realized he was a large tiger.

"He looked very majestic standing there, and I took the chance and let him have a broadside. The bullet laid him out on the spot.

"The deer were frightened by the shot and they flashed past the grove, but when they saw the tiger's carcass still jerking they turned sharply and made straight for me. I had barely time to jump aside. They were really magnificent—an old buck with huge antlers and several does and fawns.

"At first I thought I'd skin the tiger myself, but when I had a good look at it, I was convinced that it belonged to some species long since extinct in the outside world. I wanted to fetch Semyon myself, but I was afraid some other beast would find the carcass and damage the skin, so I relied on General. I'm glad I stayed on, for I soon heard a wolf howling. It was joined by a second, then a third, and, finally, there were about a dozen of them prowling around the clearing. When they saw me standing by the dead tiger they didn't dare to come up, but then they got so bold I had to waste a couple of shots on them."

The animal he had shot was dull-yellow, with a dark-brown stripe running down its back and several smaller stripes on its sides. The stripes made it seem like a tiger, but the shape of its head and body, its scrawny tail and the way its paws were placed, made Papochkin exclaim, "It's not a tiger—it's some kind of a bear!"

Maksheyev was obviously disappointed, but after a careful examination of the beast, he had to admit that the only similarity between it and that most terrible member of the cat family were its stripes; everything else about it resembled a bear.

"I think it's a cave bear. So far it has been known to man only by fragments of its skeleton," Papochkin explained. "This is much better than an ordinary tiger."

After they had measured the animal, they skinned it and took the skin, the skull, and a hind leg back to camp.

Supper that night was really a feast: wild-onion soup with goose, venison *shashlik*, and bear steaks. However, the bear steaks were none too popular, as they had a very strong odour.

The fog was less dense that day, with Pluto shining through a thin mist and rarely disappearing completely; the mercury was steady at $55^0$, and the wind had died down somewhat.

Gromeko said, "I think the fog will disappear in another day or two, and at last we'll know the colour of Plutonia's sky."

The only sound that interrupted their rest was the far-off howling of the wolves, who were probably gorging themselves on the carcasses of the deer, the bear, and their fellow wolves; but even General ignored them, as he lay near the tent flap, where the smoke from the fire discouraged the persistent insects.

Then they continued on down the river, which was growing wider and deeper all the time, so that the heavily laden boats no longer risked bumping into the banks at every sharp bend or turn.

On the banks the thick green bushes were about twelve feet high. There were several varieties of willow, bird-cherry, hawthorn, and sweetbriar all closely intertwined; here and there white birches and larch-trees looked down on the tall underbrush. The temperature was $57^0$; the fog rarely obscured the sky now, and was more like a mass of shapeless, torn clouds high in the air; Pluto's red ball shone powerfully through the haze.

"I'm sure the fog will soon disappear," Maksheyev said, "but will these green walls never end? We can't see a thing from the boats except bushes and trees."

"If we were trudging through the dense forests with heavy packs on our backs we shouldn't see much more, and our speed couldn't compare with this!" said Gromeko. The botanist was the only one who was really interested in the green walls.

They stopped for lunch at a little clearing on the riverbank. Kashtanov and Gromeko went to explore the surrounding forest, Papochkin decided to try his luck at fishing, and Maksheyev climbed the highest tree he could find. When he came down, he told Papochkin:

"The terrain will soon change. I saw some flat hills and large meadows in the distance, and our river flows straight towards them."

"What about our immediate surroundings?"

"There's nothing but forest in every direction, a whole sea of trees, with not a single open space."

"The others will be back soon then, if there's nothing but trees all around."

The two men returned in about an hour, practically empty-handed. They had followed a narrow path between the high green walls and had gathered a few plants. They had seen a lot of small birds, heard all kinds of rustling noises in the thicket, but had not come across any clearings. Papochkin war more successful. He had caught several large fish that resembled a Siberian *moksun,* and an enormous green frog, nearly a foot long.

They rested a while and then sailed on. About two hours later they saw a fairly large hill on the right bank; soon a second and then a third hill appeared. Their slopes were wooded, the trees being those of a temperate zone: linden, maple, beech, elm, oak, and ash. In the valleys between the hills were firs and spruce-trees whose low-hanging branches were entwined with ivy and other vines. Birds sang and chirped in the green thicket, and they saw squirrels and chipmunks jumping on the branches.

"We'll see something new today when we go on our evening excursion," Gromeko said. "The vegetation has changed and seems to indicate a warmer climate in these parts."

"Undoubtedly!" Papochkin agreed. "Yesterday I still felt that we were in northern Siberia, but now everything reminds me of my own district—the south of Russia."

"We might even see some real tigers," Maksheyev said hopefully.

"I don't think we should split up into two groups today," Kashtanov said. "It'll be easier to fight off any attackers if we all stay together."

The hills were becoming gradually higher, and could actually be classified as low mountains. The northern slopes were densely wooded, but the southern sides were green and smooth with clumps of bushes or single trees growing here and there; they thought they could see cliffs jutting up in the distance, and this excited Kashtanov greatly.

"Well, perhaps geology will finally benefit from our excursion today," Maksheyev teased him.

"It's about time! My hammer's getting rusty on this trip. The only decent hill in the whole tundra turned out to be an ice-box," Kashtanov answered.

"I suggest we stop here for the night. We've made over sixty miles today," Gromeko said.


## ADVENTURES ON THE HILL

They stopped near the foot of a high hill that was separated from the right bank of the river by a strip of tall trees. They had something to eat and set out together towards the hill, leaving General tied to a tree near the tent.

There was a path through the forest, and the underbrush was so thick on either side of it, that it would have been impossible for them to step off it unless they hacked their way through with axes. Above them the bushes and vines were interwoven in a solid green mass, and only a few pale rays of the red sun were able to penetrate the green dome.

They proceeded silently in single file. Their guns were cocked, and they kept a wary eye on the path ahead and the branches above them, in case interesting or dangerous animals might suddenly appear. However, they saw nothing but small birds and squirrels.

They soon reached the foot of the hill and began to climb. The grass was knee-high, and Gromeko fell behind the others, for he was engrossed in collecting the various new plants he came across.

While Papochkin was examining and making notes about a large snake he had killed, Kashtanov was having great difficulty in chipping off a piece of rock. It was a strange and very tenacious sort of yellowish-green rock, speckled with a silver-white metal. Kashtanov examined it carefully through a magnifying glass and exclaimed:

"Do you know what these cliffs are? They have the same composition as the aerolites of the mesosiderite group: half-iron, with an olivine main mass containing nickeliferous iron."

"What does all that mean?" Papochkin asked.

"It means that the geologist's hypotheses concerning the composition of the lower layers of the earth's crust have been corroborated. Apparently, we're now in the olivine belt,* an area of heavy rock, rich in iron ore, and similar in content to the stone meteorites that fall on to the earth

* Geophysicists surmise that an olivine area, or so-called olivine belt, lies far beneath the thick layer of light rock that forms the earth's crust; it consists of heavy minerals (with a high proportion of a mineral called olivine) and separates the light upper strata from the metallic core of the earth.

and are really chips of small planets. I think we might even come across hills of solid ore."

After waiting for Gromeko with his armful of plants, they began their climb again. They walked cautiously through the tall grass to avoid stepping on poisonous reptiles. At times they actually heard a rustling as if something moved rapidly away from them, but they had no desire at all to pursue the sound.

There was a rocky ridge at the top of the hill where a number of large lizards were sunning themselves. They were yellowish-green with dark spots and looked so much like the rocks in colour, that Kashtanov took hold of one by mistake—and paid for it with a bitten finger. After that he tapped all protruding rocks with his hammer, so as not to make the same mistake twice.

The northern slope of the hill faced the damp winds and was covered by a forest so dense, that it was impossible to explore its depths without a hatchet; they had already explored the meadows on the southern slope. From the top of the hill there was a wonderful view of the countryside. To the south, east, and west were similar or larger hills right up to the horizon, but to the north the hills became smaller and more scattered, and they could see a solid forest region in the distance, crossed in places by the silver threads of rivers.

As they sat on the crest of the hill and looked about them, a herd of wild pigs came out of the forest a few yards away on the northern slope. The leading boar stopped and raised his head. There were long bristles along his spine and he had huge white tusks. His little eyes glittered menacingly, and his snout moved up and down, sniffing the air. The sows and sucking-pigs crowded behind him. These animals were much larger than any wild pigs Papochkin had ever seen.

"Here's our dinner!" Maksheyev said. "I'm sure a wild sucking-pig roasted on a spit must be delicious."

"It isn't actually necessary, we still have some venison left," said Gromeko, who was in charge of provisions.

"No harm in having an extra supply of meat—after all, we aren't always lucky in our hunting expeditions."

"I hope you realize it's no joke to shoot a few of those pigs, because a raging boar is a terrible opponent," Papochkin warned.

"Let's climb to the top of the rocks, then they won't be able to reach us, and we can shoot a couple of sucklings from up there," Kashtanov suggested.

They climbed up. Maksheyev loaded his rifle with buckshot and fired. The herd scattered in all directions, but three sucking-pigs remained wounded on the grass. Then the boar and the sows rushed back to the rocky cliff and started circling round the foot of it. They tried in vain to scale the smooth crags and this enraged them further. The siege gave the men a good chance to examine the animals at close range. When Papochkin's professional curiosity had been satisfied, they were faced with the problem of what to do next.

"We could spend the day here easily! They have their food right under their snouts, and we have nothing. Besides, this rock is no easy chair," Kashtanov said. "We'll have to fire a couple of shots to chase them away."

Suddenly, Maksheyev, who had been watching the edge of the forest, exclaimed:

"There's a large animal creeping towards us or the pigs. All I can see from here is its yellow back."

"Where?"

"It just disappeared behind that bush, the one that sticks out into the clearing. Keep watching to the right of it."

They all peered at the bush, just in time to see a dark-yellow mass with dark horizontal stripes across its body moving slowly towards them.

"Do you think it's another bear?" Maksheyev asked.

"Maybe it's a tiger this time," Papochkin said.

"It's slinking along like a cat."

"I think it's time to fire a couple of shots," Kashtanov said.

"What at? The beast or the boar?"

"The boar. If the pigs run towards the forest they'll be right in the animal's path, and he'll take over from there. On the other hand, if they turn and run the other way, the animal will turn too, and we'll get a better view of it, or even shoot it. All we can see now is its back, and that's a hard target to hit."

"Let's fire one shot at the boar, and keep the other three rifles on the beast."

Papochkin was perched on a jutting rock and from there he took aim at the boar, just as it was pawing the rock, trying to reach Maksheyev's boot with its tusks. The point-blank shot killed the boar instantly; the rest of the herd made a mad dash for the forest. Just as they were nearing the edge of it, the dark-yellow beast sprang out at them from the left. It sailed about eight feet through the air and blocked their path as it landed in front of them. One of the pigs was caught in the monster's paws, the others raced on squealing towards the forest.

"That's no bear—it's a tiger!" Papochkin shouted.

"It certainly is," Kashtanov agreed. "And it's probably a sabre tiger, judging by the huge fangs in its upper jaw. It was a widely spread species in the Tertiary period, but seems to have disappeared towards the end of it."

"It's a shame, but I think this one will get away. Look, he's dragging his prey towards the forest; he's probably decided that we're dangerous neighbours," Maksheyev exclaimed.

"Who cares? We've quite enough for one day," Papochkin said, as he began measuring the dead boar. "Shall we drag this monstrosity to the boats too, or just the sucking-pig?"

"If he's fat, we might as well take some lard," Gromeko
suggested. "Then we could cook our meat in a frying-pan
Anyway, hurry up with your measuring. I'll look for some
more plants in the meantime."

## HOW TO FLY

Kashtanov went back to studying rock formations, Maksheyev and Papochkin were fussing with the pigs, and
Gromeko started down the southern slope of the hill, completely engrossed in collecting the many new specimens of
plants growing there. Suddenly, a huge shadow crossed
the hill. It startled Maksheyev and Papochkin, and they
looked up to see an enormous black bird that resembled
an eagle circling over the meadow. It dived unexpectedly,

snatched Gromeko by the back—he had been bending over, looking into the grass—and flew off with him.

However, the load proved to be more than even such a feathered giant could carry: the bird flew along heavily, unable to rise above twelve feet, but it would not part with the prey that hung limply in its claws.

Papochkin and Maksheyev grabbed their guns; however, Papochkin put his down immediately, saying:

"Mine's loaded with buck-shot, I'm afraid I'll wound him if I shoot."

Maksheyev aimed at the bird and fired as it passed overhead. The bullet that had been intended for the tiger found its mark; the bird dipped, dropped Gromeko, and collapsed on the rocks after flying a few more feet.

The two men ran to their friend, who was lying unconscious, face downwards. His heavy knitted jacket was torn to shreds, but it was loose-fitting, and the bird's claws had sunk into its folds and done no more than scratch his back severely. They revived him and dressed his injuries, and as soon as he felt better, Papochkin and Maksheyev climbed the rocky ridge to get the bird. It was a vulture, bigger than any they had ever heard of. It had a wing-spread of nearly fifteen feet and its over-all length was about five feet; its plumage was dark-brown on top and light-brown with dark stripes underneath. Round its almost bare neck was a large collar of dirty-white feathers, and there was a big yellow lump at the base of its huge beak.

Such a bird could easily carry off a sheep, a goat, or a small pig, but a man weighing a hundred and seventy-five pounds was just too much for it. The bird had apparently mistaken the botanist for some sort of four-legged creature grazing on the slope of the hill.

They measured the vulture and then photographed it with its wings spread out on the cliff; Gromeko had climbed the ridge too, in order to get a close look at his kidnapper. He told his friends that when he suddenly felt the bird's claws on his jacket, and the hard thud of its great body against his back, he thought he had been attacked by a tiger and fainted.

"How about starting back to camp?" Papochkin said. "I think we've had enough adventures for a day. We were attacked by wild pigs, and then by a vulture, and we saw a tiger at close range. Let's not tempt fate any more."

Weary from walking and excitement, they started back to the river, laden with the sucking-pig, fat and hams from the boar, rock samples, and many plants.

As they were nearing the tent they heard General barking savagely, and rushed to his aid.

The dog had stretched his long rope as far as it would go and was barking from behind the tent. A huge hippopotamus was standing half in the water, half on the bank. It had probably wanted to graze on the bank or roll in the grass, but it was confused by the noise the dog was making. The hippo's beady eyes were staring blankly at the strange nervous creature on the bank. It kept opening its hideous mouth, baring its few long teeth and huge pink tongue. Whenever General saw the gaping jaws he would begin to howl and squeal with fright.

When the monster saw the men running, it turned clumsily, sank heavily into the water, and swam off downstream, with only its broad, fat, wart-covered back showing above the surface.

"It's a good thing we came back," Gromeko said untying General. "That monster could have made a mess of the place; it might have torn up the tent, trampled everything we had, and sunk or broken the boats."

"Are the boats all right?" Maksheyev said. He rushed down to the river and a second later he shouted:

"One's here, but the other's gone! Maybe that devil broke the moorings?"

"We'll have to chase after it, before it floats too far away!" Kashtanov said running up to him.

The two men grabbed their guns, got into the remaining boat, and pushed off. They soon caught sight of the lost boat, but instead of floating slowly downstream with the current, it kept spinning round in the middle of the river. They were gaining on it quickly and Kashtanov was ready to grab it with a boat-hook, when suddenly the boat jumped aside as if it were alive and sped on downstream—much faster than the current. They had to give chase again. Maksheyev was rowing for dear life, and Kashtanov stood in the prow with the boat-hook poised in his hand.

"Something's pulling it," he cried, as the boat bobbed along jerkily.

"Maybe the hippo got tangled in the line?"

"He certainly did," Kashtanov answered, catching sight of the animal's broad back and head as it came up for air. "If we take a couple of shots at that piece of floating blubber it'll either put on more speed or drag the boat down."

"We'll have to catch up with it and cut the line, there's no other way to get the boat back."

Maksheyev began to row with desperate energy. Kashtanov was soon able to grapple the boat and pull them alongside it, so that the hippo was towing them along. Maksheyev slashed the taut line, and the end immediately disappeared beneath the surface.

"I couldn't keep that pace up for ever," Maksheyev said as he sat breathing heavily at the oars. "If we didn't have to count our bullets, I'd have shot him for his tricks."

"We're quite a bit from the tent," Kashtanov said, "and we'll have to row back upstream. Let me row while you get your breath back."

They changed places and took the second boat in tow.

"The river's a lot deeper here," Maksheyev said. He was trying to punt, using the boat-hook for a pole, but he could not reach bottom, as the river was about six feet deep. "No wonder there are such big animals in it here. To be on the safe side, we'll have to drag the boats up on the shore at night, or when we go inland."

They were moving slowly upstream between the solid green walls of trees and bushes that towered over the dark waters. There were lovely butterflies and bees on the large crimson flowers of a strange vine hanging far out over the river.

The water gurgled under the two bows, the oars rose and dipped rhythmically, and the chirping and singing of birds could be heard from the thicket.

Maksheyev sat bent over the side, peering into the water and following the darting fishes with his eyes.

"How wonderful nature is here, if you see it from the boat," he said. "But if you go ashore, you get trapped in the dense forest and can't take a step without falling over a poisonous or predatory animal. It's hard to believe that we're floating down a river that flows on the inner surface of the earth, especially after so many days of fighting the ice-fields, fogs, and blizzards. Everything here is so near those ice-fields, and yet, so very much like the virgin forests of Africa or South America. I wonder which part of North America we're under now?"

"That's not hard to work out, if we chart our course on a map, starting from the ice barrier. I don't think we've gone beyond the Beaufort Sea, or, at best, as far as the tundra of Northern Alaska. It's miserably cold there, with nothing but ice and polar bears in every direction, but here we are in a land of exotic flowers, tigers, hippopotamuses, and snakes."

At that moment Maksheyev saw a clear reflection of the sun in the water and looked up quickly.

"Well, here's the sun at last! See!"

They were used to seeing Pluto through a mist or fog, and had had no idea of the colour of the sky and the actual appearance of Pluto. Now the film of fog was parting and forming cumulous clouds; they could see the clear sky in the spaces between the clouds, but it wasn't the light-blue they knew so well—it was dark-blue.

Pluto was overhead, and its diameter appeared slightly greater than the visible diameter of the sun.

This underground, or "interground" luminary was like the sun before sunset, or shortly after sunrise, if seen through a thick layer of the atmosphere. Many dark spots of various sizes were clearly visible on its disk.

"This central luminary, or actual core of the earth, is in its last stage of burning. It's a dying red star. A little more time and it will be snuffed out! The inner surface will be plunged into darkness and cold, and all this flourishing wild life will gradually become extinct," Kashtanov said.

"It's lucky we were able to get here and explore it," Maksheyev exclaimed. "If we'd come later we'd have had to go back, for we'd have seen nothing but black night ahead."

"When I said 'a little more time' I meant time in terms of geology, which might mean thousands of years. So you see, our descendants will have plenty of opportunities to study the inner surface and even colonize it."

"How nice! You're suggesting settling in a country that's doomed to disappear into the blackness of eternal night!"

## A TROPICAL STORM

The time slipped by in animated conversation, and they scarcely noticed the distance back to camp, where Papochkin and Gromeko were waiting to begin supper. The sucking-pig, stewed with wild-onion sauce, was excellent. They decided to gather more edible fruit, roots, and plants in future, to make their diet more appetizing. They had left all their tinned vegetables and starches in the ice-house and had only taken tea, sugar, coffee, salt, pepper, extracts, and some biscuits with them. Hunting and fishing were to supply the main part of their food, but fresh greens would add a necessary variety to it.

All through the night they kept a camp-fire going near the tent and took turns standing watch, as their encounter with the tiger had made them cautious. Each sentry heard suspicious sounds, branches cracking, and the startled cries of frightened birds in the nearby woods, and General was alert and growling many times during the night.

For the first few hours of sailing the next day there were no visible changes in the terrain: there were more hills, with wooded northern slopes and grassland on the southern slopes, and the solid forest walls still towered on both sides of the river. They camped on the left bank that day, and Kashtanov and Gromeko went off to explore it after dinner.

There were many new plants there, including evergreens like myrtle and laurel; the nut-trees were tremendous—as tall as oaks; they came across beech-trees, cypresses, and yews. Great magnolias were covered with large, fragrant white blossoms. Bamboo and various lianas grew in the thicket along the river-bank. Gromeko was in seventh heaven.

The temperature was 77⁰ in the shade that day, as the north wind had finally died down. The damp air was heavy with forest vapours. The explorers climbed the hill with difficulty, sweating profusely, although the sun was shining only dimly through the clouds.

All nature seemed to have sunk into a torpor from the heat, the birds and animals were hiding in the shade.

Kashtanov and Gromeko reached the crest of the hill and sat down. They turned northwards to look at the countryside and discovered the reason for the unbearable heat: an enormous, fantastic, purple-black cloud with ragged edges was advancing from the far-off horizon. A reddish-blue billow of fast-moving clouds preceded the storm-cloud, and blinding flashes of lightning struck out from below it.

"We'll have to make a dash for it to reach the boats!" Gromeko said excitedly. "It looks like a tropical storm!"

They ran down the hill, slipping on the steep slopes and getting caught in the tall grass. It took them about ten minutes to reach camp, and they found Maksheyev and Papochkin waiting anxiously and wondering what to do next. It was quite possible that the tent would be unable to withstand the torrents of rain or hail. It was also quite possible that the river would flood its banks and drag the uprooted trees downstream; therefore, it was risky to weather it on the river. It seemed that the best thing to do would be to pull the boats up on the bank, unload everything, and try to shelter in the tall bushes.

As they were discussing this plan, Papochkin remembered that he had seen an overhanging cliff downstream a bit, at the edge of the hill, when he had gone off after a large water snake. The cliff would protect them, but they had to hurry—the storm was almost on them!

They jumped into the boats, pushed off, and soon reached the cliff. It took only a few minutes to drag everything under the jutting edge. The stone roof was large enough for the men, the dog, the supplies, and even the boats, which they used as a shield against the wind.

They chased out a few small snakes that had taken over the cracks in the stones and could calmly watch the magnificent spectacle of an atmospheric catastrophe.

The reddish-blue cloud mass had covered half the sky and obscured the sun; from below it seemed pitch black, slashed by jagged flashes of lightning and accompanied by such deafening claps of thunder as they had never heard before. The explosions followed close on one another; something cracked, as if a huge piece of fabric had been ripped, and then there was a roar like hundreds of cannons booming in unison.

The trees were swaying in the first gusts of wind. From the north came a terrible rattling noise that drowned out even the thunder. It seemed as if a giant train was racing along a track, sweeping everything before it.

The men felt really frightened and utterly helpless in their little cave.

The whirlwind was upon them. It was a spinning mass of flowers, leaves, twigs, branches, bushes torn up by the roots, and birds that had not had time to hide in the depths of the forest. It grew darker and darker. Everything whistled, hissed, and cracked between the crashes of thunder. Huge raindrops and hailstones slapped on the earth and churned the water into a white foam. The darkness was complete now but for blinding flashes of lightning which revealed a terrible sight: the entire forest seemed to have been swept up into the air and to be racing along with the torrents of rain and hail. They could not make themselves heard even by shouting in each other's ear.

The chaos lasted about five minutes and then it began to get much lighter, the gusts of wind died down greatly, the clatter and thunder moved off to the south, and the torrents of rain turned to a drizzle. The river was swollen; it was reddish-brown and muddy, with a foamy film on the surface of the water and leaves, branches, and small trees being carried away by the current. Tattered grey shreds of clouds were fleeing across the sky, but Pluto was already glinting through, shining down on the ruin wrought by the storm.

The men crawled out and looked around. Leaves and branches mixed with walnut-sized hailstones were piled beyond the boats, whose canvas sides had been pierced in places by the sharp edges of broken branches hurled against them. The men at once got out some needles, heavy thread, and patches of tarred canvas and started repairs.

They were busy mending the boats for nearly an hour.

The river had by then returned to normal, the wreckage had disappeared, and they could continue downstream. The black cloud had vanished behind the hills far to the south, and for the first time they saw the cloudless, dark-blue sky above them.

"Just think," Papochkin said, when they were in the boats once more, "that directly over this blue sky, about six thousand miles above us, there's another world, just like this one, with its forests, its rivers, and its animal life. I wish we could see it overhead!"

"It's too far away," Kashtanov noted. "A thick layer of air like that, full of vapours and dust particles, would never be transparent enough, and land covered with vegetation is not bright enough—it reflects too little light."

"When we were at the top of that small hill yesterday, did you notice that visibility is much better here than on earth?" Maksheyev said. "We could see a wooded area over sixty miles around because the surface we are on is concave, it was as if we were standing on the bottom of a flat bowl.

"Theoretically, our horizon should be unlimited—we should be able to see the country around us five hundred or a thousand miles away, rising higher and higher to the sky. But the lower layers of the atmosphere are much less transparent at a great distance, and outlines become hazy and blend together. In fact, there's actually no horizon here at all—what we see is a gradual transition of earth into sky. The only reason we didn't discover this until now was because of the low-lying cloud-banks."

By evening they noticed that the river was getting wider; the current was slower, and they had to row vigorously to make any headway at all. There were breaks in the green walls, narrow branches along which the water flowed out of or into the main channel, and they came upon quite a few small islands surrounded by tall rushes.

As they were rounding one such island, they saw a break

in the thick rushes and a path leading from the water's edge into the green thicket. Maksheyev steered his boat towards the path, intending to go ashore and see what the island was like. As the boat touched the bank, a sabre tiger's head poked through the thicket. Two shining white fangs about a foot long protruded from its upper jaw, just like a sea lion's. The beast was not hungry, as it showed no signs of attacking them. The great jaws opened wide, as if in a yawn, and then the head vanished among the reeds. They quickly changed their minds about landing.

The river narrowed again the next day, and the current became faster. They felt more and more that they were now in a subtropical zone: the oaks, maples, and beech-trees had given place to magnolias, laurels, rubber-trees, and many other varieties which the botanist knew only by name, or from pale hot-house specimens. The yucca, fan and sago palms were easily identified from the boats.

The hills were getting lower, broader, and less frequent. Their slopes were overgrown with luxuriant waist-high grasses and dotted with trees, growing singly or in groups, that reminded them of the gallery forests of Central Africa.

They stopped for lunch near a hill so that they could study the plants growing there. Maksheyev agreed to stay behind to keep an eye on the boats, and the other three men set off for the hill after lunch.


## THE MOVING HILLOCK

They had to hack their way through the first ten feet of intertwined lianas and underbrush, but then, in the semi-darkness beneath the huge eucalyptus, myrtle, laurel, and other trees, the bushes thinned out considerably. The ground between the tree trunks and the clumps of large ferns was covered with various mosses and magnificent orchids. From high above came a steady hum of insects, but there was stillness below. At times a snake or a lizard would slither across the ground.

Near the foot of the hill the woods were less dense, letting through Pluto's reddish rays; there was more life there, more grass, flowers, and bushes. They came upon a winding path and followed it, in the hope of its leading them out of the forest. Kashtanov led the way with Papochkin close behind. Both men had their rifles ready and kept a sharp look-out all round them. Gromeko brought up the rear, dropping behind frequently to gather plant specimens.

Kashtanov stopped suddenly and raised his arm to draw their attention. They could hear a low growling and loud cracking noises ahead. Then a big strange-looking creature appeared on the path. It was like a bear, but it had a long fluffy tail and a long, thin head.

"It's an ant-eater," Papochkin whispered. "The South American ones are very tame, in spite of their ferocious appearance and huge claws. But they're much smaller than this thing—it's over six feet high!"

The ant-eater noticed the people that were blocking its way and stopped indecisively.

"Let's get off the path, so that it can pass us and we'll get a better look at it," Papochkin whispered again.

They stepped off the path and hid behind a clump of bushes. For a few minutes the ant-eater stood still, peering into the woods distrustfully, and then it advanced slowly, stopping every five or six steps, and looking round. Papochkin took a photograph of the animal during one of these pauses, but when it heard the click of the shutter, it made off, lumbering down the path on its large paws, its tail straight out behind it. From the tip of its nose to the tip of its tail it was at least twelve feet long.

When they came out of the forest, they found themselves at the foot of a gently sloping hill. Kashtanov looked at the monotonous slope with disappointment, as it promised nothing of interest to him, but the botanist was delighted by the profusion of strange bright flowers among the tall grass and began to gather them. Suddenly Kashtanov noticed a fair-sized, cupola-shaped hillock at the bottom of the hill. Its bare sides had a metallic glitter.

"Something for me, at last!" he shouted pulling out his little hammer and running off towards the hillock.

Meanwhile, Papochkin was trying to catch a lizard that had fled from him by climbing a small tree.

When Kashtanov reached the hillock, he stopped in amazement. It was completely bare, there wasn't even a blade of grass growing on it, and the entire surface was made up of six-sided brown plates, each with a dark border.

He tried to chip off a piece of rock, but his hammer bounced off the surface. He then tried to climb to the top, as he thought there would be more cracks there; although the hillock was only about ten feet high, its slopes were absolutely smooth, and he had a hard time scrambling to the top. He found that the rock there was just as invulnerable, and so he pulled a large chisel out of his belt, stuck it in a crack between two of the plates, and began pounding away. The sharp edge of the chisel finally began to sink into the hard rock.

A sharp jolt caught him unawares. He had been kneeling, and had the presence of mind to grab the chisel, thus saving himself from rolling off. The jolts continued, and Kashtanov looked round, bewildered. The ground seemed to be rocking under him and all the trees were swaying.

"An earthquake!" he shouted. His friends were about forty feet away, and he shouted again, "Can you feel the tremors?"

Gromeko and Papochkin looked up in surprise, for they had felt nothing, but when they turned towards Kashtanov, they were thunderstruck: the hillock with the geologist on top was slowly moving down the hillside.

In another minute they were running to intercept the strange moving mound, whose base was hidden in the tall grass. As they came closer, Papochkin burst out laughing:

"It's a giant turtle! Pyotr, you're riding on turtle-back!"

Just then the hillock turned towards the pursuers and they saw a rather long neck ending in an ugly head about the size of a bull's and covered with small scales; there were sharp, flat teeth sticking out of the open jaws.

Kashtanov finally realized what had happened. He left his chisel sticking in the turtle's shell, slid down its side, and quickly jumped out of its way. Only then did he notice a huge fast-moving tail like a big log, which could easily have broken his legs at a single blow.

The animal, feeling itself free, ran off down the slope. As soon as its head and tail were swallowed up by the grass, it was again exactly like a bare moving hillock.

After they had laughed over the incident Kashtanov said:

"I think it wasn't really a turtle, but a glyptodont, a member of the armadillo family that inhabited the earth in the Pliocene period, when the great ant-eaters, giant sloths, mastodons, and the large rhinoceroses were still alive. The remains of these monsters have been found by the hundred in South America."

"We did meet a huge ant-eater in the forest," Papochkin added.

"That's what made me think of it. If, in a northern area, close to the edge of the ice-fields, we came across the mammoth and other living fossils which inhabited the earth in post-tertiary times, then there's every reason to think that moving southwards where it's so much warmer we've been bound to come upon animals that lived in a still more ancient period, namely, during the Pliocen."

"According to your theory," Papochkin said with apparent disbelief, "the farther south we go, the more ancient the fauna we'll come across. Is that what you're getting at?"

"It doesn't surprise me a bit," Gromeko said. "From the moment we discovered this inter-earth world, I stopped being surprised at anything at all, and I'm ready to welcome every iguanodon, plesiosaur, pterodactyl, trilobite, or other palaeontological wonder that comes our way."

"If that's the case, then I'm sorry we didn't shoot the ant-eater and the glyptodont. How can we ever prove their existence? I didn't even get a picture of the glyptodont."

"Maybe we'll see some others later."

"By the way, it's time to replenish our supply of meat," Gromeko said. "Otherwise, we'll have nothing but fat pork tomorrow."

They had been slowly climbing the hill as they talked, and they finally reached the top. There was a narrow strip of dense bushes across the ridge, and Kashtanov was elated to find rocks in the ground there. He was chipping away, when Papochkin, who had crawled through to the other side of the bushes, hissed at him:

"Shh! Be quiet, over there! There's a whole zoo of herbivorous animals on the other slope."

Kashtanov stopped tapping, stuck the sliver of rock he had chipped off into his pocket, and crawled through the bushes with Gromeko close on his heels. They saw various animals grazing peacefully on the southern slope. There was a family of rhinoceroses, very different both from the Indian and African varieties, and from the long-haired type they had seen previously. These were fat, stocky, short-legged creatures, more like hippopotamuses, but the shape of the male's head and his short, thick horn betrayed the rhinoceros. The female had a great lump instead of a horn on her head. The calf looked like a huge sausage as it clumped round its mother playfully; it would lie on the ground in order to reach its source of food and squeeze itself sideways under its mother's belly, but mamma would

move on and smother baby, which made him squeal in protest.

Farther down the slope was a herd of enormous elephants. Kashtanov took a look at them through his binoculars and said they were probably mastodons. They differed from the mammoths and had long, straight tusks, retreating foreheads, and longer bodies.

Several enormous antelopes were grazing near the mastodons. They were dark-yellow with black spots like leopards, and had long, sabre-like antlers. They bounded about, their hind legs being much longer than their front ones. Gromeko actually thought at first that they were some kind of enormous hares.

At the very edge of the forest were even stranger-looking animals—half-giraffes, half-camels. They had very long necks and two small horns on their heads; at the same time, they were dirty-yellow and each had a hump on its back. Kashtanov classified them as the ancestors of both the camel and the giraffe. A pair of these animals nibbled at the leaves and branches as high as twelve feet off the ground.

They split up, each man making for a group of animals. Kashtanov circled round to the camel-giraffes, Papochkin headed towards the antelopes, and Gromeko was to photograph the rhinoceroses and mastodons.

The tasty-looking little rhinoceros tempted Gromeko, and he decided to take a shot at it. When its parents saw it lying dead in the grass, they sniffed the carcass and ran towards the botanist with loud grunting noises. As he had expected them to flee in the opposite direction, he had not taken the precaution of hiding, and now he had to jump into the bushes to get out of their way. A few seconds later there was a furious cracking and smashing, and both animals appeared on the crest of the hill, trampling the bushes and flinging them aside with their snouts. They kept on running, until they suddenly noticed that their enemy had disappeared; then they turned and dashed towards the waving bushes that betrayed him.

Just then Papochkin fired a shot at the antelopes, and the herd tore up the slope; the mastodons followed, trumpeting through their raised trunks. Gromeko's situation was becoming desperate: on the one hand, he had to dodge the raging rhinoceroses by running back and forth among the bushes; on the other hand, the antelopes and mastodons were closing in on him. Then he had a wonderful idea. He saw that, although the antelopes and mastodons were running up the slope from different directions, they seemed to be making for the same spot on the ridge. Instead of running about, trying to escape the rhinoceroses, he ran down the slope, in the space between the two herds, hoping that one or the other would head off his pursuers. His plan was realized when one of the rhinoceroses crashed through the bushes and bumped into the mastodons, while the other found itself among the antelopes. There was a general confusion in which the first rhinoceros was knocked over and trampled, and the second frightened the antelopes and made off after them. Gromeko had won the battle.

When at last he got his breath back, he climbed up again to the bushes on the ridge, found the gun he had dropped as he ran, and began to look for the rhinoceros calf that had caused him so much trouble. The barrel-shaped carcass was easy to find among the trampled grass.

Then he joined the others, and the three of them started out towards camp, heavily laden with skins, skulls, and meat.

Maksheyev was beginning to worry about their long absence. He had also shot something. As he was guarding the boats, an animal had crept up to the tent, apparently with the intention of devouring General, but it had stopped a bullet instead. It looked like a wolf, althought its head was unusually large, its body was that of a cat, and it had a long mane. Kashtanov said it was probably a Pliocene ancestor of the modern wolf.


## PLUTO GETS DIMMER

While the antelope meat was boiling in the pot and the rhinoceros calf was turning on a spit, the explorers sorted the many specimens they had gathered in the course of the day.

They soon noticed that the light was growing dimmer and redder than usual; also, the air was cooler. They looked up and saw a cloudless sky, with Pluto shining dully. Half its surface was covered by large dark spots.

The drop in temperature was a welcome relief, but the dimness caused them some concern.

"Suppose Pluto goes out completely?" Gromeko said, for they had noted a further increase in the number of dark spots on its disc and a decrease in light during supper.

"We'll suddenly be lost in complete darkness, which will then be followed by a polar cold," Papochkin added.

"All our warm clothes are at the main camp," Maksheyev groaned.

"I think this dimness is only temporary," Kashtanov said. "Judging by the red light and abundant dark spots, Pluto has actually reached its last stage of burning, but this stage can last hundreds and thousands of years. Stars like Pluto in outer space have been known to fade and practically go out, but then they blaze up again. They still have great reserves of heat, and although cooling crusts form on their surfaces and cause these dark spots, the heat keeps breaking open and melting the crusts again and again. A star never fades all at once."

"But Pluto may stop burning from lack of oxygen. After all, it gets the oxygen it needs from the atmosphere that surrounds the earth and draws it in through the polar opening."

"If that were the case, then Pluto should have used up all the oxygen in the atmosphere in the many millions of years it has been burning, and the earth's inhabitants would have suffocated in nitrogen. We know very little of the stars' burning processes which may be quite different from burning as we understand it on earth. Maybe oxygen is formed as a product of the dissociation of other chemical elements. The discoveries of the past few years concerning the transformations of radium have changed our conception of the constancy of these elements, a fact we considered indisputable before."

"In other words, 'There are more things in heaven and earth, Horatio, than are dreamt of in your philosophy'— and Hamlet ought to have paid a visit to Plutonia!" Gromeko said, and then suggested that they all go to bed and take advantage of the coolness and the dark.

The forest creatures were uneasy too. The birds were silent, and in place of their usual songs and chirping the shrill cries of various animals could be heard. General howled mournfully at times as he lifted his head to the sky.

The men paid no attention to these noises and slept much longer than usual, their small camp-fire burning in front of the tent.

It was still dark when they woke. Everything was drowned in the red twilight; there were so many dark spots on Pluto that the light had diminished by nine-tenths. The grass, the leaves, and even the sky, seemed black in the strange light. Everything was still, except for an occasional gust of wind tearing through the leaves. There was something menacing in the stillness.

They talked things over and decided it was too dangerous to sail down an unknown river in the dark through a dense forest full of wild beasts that might attack without warning. There was also the risk of running aground on a sandbank, or ripping their canvas boats on a snag.

"Suppose this twilight lasts for weeks, or even months?" Gromeko asked. "Do we just sit here? After all, our supplies won't last more than three or four days."

"Give it time before you jump to the worst conclusions," Kashtanov said. "We'll wait here for a day or two and then see whether to go on downstream or turn back."

"We can mend the leaks in the boats, maybe build a raft, and tidy things up while we're waiting," Maksheyev suggested.

They all agreed, and sat down to work by the light of the camp-fire. They patched the boats and sawed down a few large bamboos growing near the camp. The sawing took a long time, as they had only a small hand saw. They trimmed the trunks and sawed them into poles as long as the boats. Then they bound the poles together into a raft five feet wide, which was to be fastened between the two boats. They decided to put the bulky things on it and cover them with animal skins. The two boats with the raft

125

between them looked like a small, light, firm, and manoeuvrable ferry.

They were busy at their tasks all day; there was no change in the size or number of dark spots on Pluto. They turned in early, leaving a small fire burning outside the tent. General was lying in the doorway, and they counted on spending a quiet night, with one or the other of them getting up occasionally to throw some wood on the fire.

But as soon as everything was quiet inside the tent, they began to hear rustling noises in the thicket all round them. General pricked up his ears and growled. The rustling ceased and the dog dozed off again. Then the noises began once more, as if some beast were prowling in the bushes around the little clearing, but not daring to spring out. There was no sense in all of them being on the alert, and so they decided to keep watch in turn. Papochkin was first to sit by the fire with his rifle on his arm. The rustling kept coming closer and then moving off, until he became so used to it that he fell sound asleep. Gradually, the fire died down, till it was just a little heap of glowing embers.

Suddenly, the dog began barking furiously. Papochkin jumped up and saw a large animal at the edge of the clearing. It looked like a lion, but had a shorter mane and long fangs like the sabre tiger's. The beast stood hesitating, its jaws half-open, while General, his tail between his legs, retreated, barking furiously, behind the fire and closer to the protection of the tent.

Papochkin fired and hit the animal in the chest at twenty feet range. It had strength enough to spring—and it landed on the hot embers, burning its belly. Then it rolled over and swung at the tent with its hind leg, ripping the canvas in two and hitting Maksheyev's boots standing near his head. Its front paw was clutching at the air convulsively and narrowly missed Kashtanov's face, as it smashed his pocket watch, which lay in his hat on the ground; the hat was torn to shreds. General, crouching at the entrance, was caught by a third paw and sent flying to the far corner of the tent, where he fell, scratched and shivering, right on top of Gromeko.

The chaos was fantastic. Something enormous was howling and thrashing about in the twilight outside the tent. The thin canvas ripped and flew apart under its blows. Gromeko was struggling with General in his bed, for the dog was trying to crawl in beside him and hide, and he thought it was some terrible beast attacking him. Kashtanov was groping around in the dark for some matches that he had left beside his watch in his hat, but he couldn't even find his hat. Papochkin was shouting from outside:

"Hurry! Get out the back way! It's a lion, and I'm afraid I'll hit someone if I take another shot at it!"

The animal shuddered a last time and was still; Maksheyev found the box of matches and lit a candle; Gromeko let General go, and the three men, scared and half-dressed, crawled out through the rear flap in the tent and looked about. Papochkin confessed that he had fallen asleep and let the fire go out, the only reason why the animal had become bold enough to attack.

The dead beast was a sabre lion, although in body structure it resembled a bear, and only its head and the shape of its paws indicated its relationship to the cat family. Its mane was short and nearly black, its coat was dark-yellow, and its tail had no tassel at the end. The claws on its tremendous paws were as big as the horrible fangs of its upper jaw. Both the tent and Maksheyev's boots were badly in need of repairs. It took them a long time to find the remains of Kashtanov's hat and watch in the jumble inside the tent.

They pulled General out of Gromeko's bed and washed the shivering dog's wounds. Then they dragged the dead lion away from the tent and went back to get a few more hours of sleep. Maksheyev took over the watch, and the rest of the night passed quietly. In the morning it was not so dark, and the spots on Pluto seemed smaller and fewer. They decided to wait a while longer and began mending the tent and measuring and skinning the lion. Towards noon it became much lighter; a little later Pluto seemed to have gathered strength to melt most of the dark spots and burst forth in all its glory. Its light seemed all the brighter after the forty-hour twilight.

They loaded the boats and raft and set off once more, but their pace was much slower now, for the vessel was less manoeuvrable than they had expected, and they had to row hard. Towards evening the countryside began to change, the hills along the banks became smaller and smaller till they finally disappeared altogether, and the dense forest and underbrush gave way to flat plains, whose monotony was broken by small groves of trees and giant baobabs. Along each bank was a narrow strip of lush vegetation made up of palm-trees, bamboos, and lianas full of birds and monkeys of many varieties. Everywhere there were herds of animals of the kinds they had recently come across.

## MONSTROUS LIZARDS AND TOOTHED BIRDS

They spent the night on a large island that was a continuation of the plains around them; only at the water's edge were there clumps of bushes and rushes. They set up the tent on the northern tip of the island, where they had a good view of the river as it branched out into two streams, each of which was at least a hundred *feet* wide.

After supper the quiet was suddenly broken by a noise like the shouting of a large crowd of people coming from the opposite bank. The noise was drowned at times by a loud barking and howling.

A small herd of reddish, white-spotted animals tore through the thicket, trampling the reeds and pulling apart the bushes. They began to swim towards the island, and a pack of howling, barking beasts jumped into the water after them and also swam towards the island. They were trying  to overtake and head off one of the animals, which had dropped behind the rest and was apparently exhausted.

A few minutes later the herd clambered ashore and raced past the tent. The creatures resembled horses, although they had almost no manes.

The animal that had dropped behind the rest reached the island ahead of its pursuers, but had great difficulty in climbing the steep bank. The pack was close on its heels, and the howling beasts surrounded it in a tight circle. It struck out with its hoofs and bit them, but the battle was unequal. The beasts dodged its blows and kept the circle tight, waiting for their victim to drop from exhaustion.

The men took a hand and fired three shots into the pack, killing two of the beasts and making the rest flee in panic. The weakened victim could not take advantage of its unexpected deliverance and died as the men drew near. There was a large ragged wound on its neck, that had probably been inflicted by one of the beasts when the pack had first attacked the herd; the animal had been weak because it was bleeding to death.

The two dead beasts proved to be primitive mammals. They were about the size of Siberian wolves, but their bodies and long, thin tails were feline. The hair on their

backs and sides was dark-brown with yellow vertical
stripes, and their bellies were yellow. Their fang-like teeth
were almost all the same size.

Their victim could be called a horse only by a long
stretch of the imagination. It was no bigger than a donkey,
but more graceful, with thin legs, each having four hoofs
instead of a single one like the horse's. The middle hoof
alone was fully developed; the other three were rudimentary.

As Kashtanov and Papochkin studied the strange animal they came to the conclusion that it was a primitive
horse, the ancestor of the modern horse, and very like the
South American llama.

The plains stretched on the next day too. These were
savannas and prairie lands, covered with high grass and
thickets, but there were separate clumps of bushes and
trees along the banks of the river and on the many islands.
They noticed a herd of titanotheriums on one of the large
islands, animals that seemed a cross between a hippopotamus and a rhinoceros.

They wanted to tie the boats up a little farther downstream behind some bushes and then creep up and shoot
one of the titanotheriums, but they came across a more
interesting animal on the way. It was one of the most ancient pachyderms, a four-horned rhinoceros, that had come
down to the river to quench its thirst and was standing
there with its forelegs in the water. When the raft drifted
into its line of vision it lifted its ugly head and opened
its mouth wide, as if it wanted to swallow up or spit at

the intruders. There were two long yellow fangs in its upper jaw, two small horns on the bridge of its nose between two small beady eyes, and two blunt horns that looked like stumps on the top of its head.

While they were tying up the raft and then creeping cautiously through the bushes to get a close-up of the strange animal, it climbed out of the water and trotted off clumsily. Kashtanov and Papochkin ran after it in the hope that it would soon come to a halt. As they ran they noticed a gigantic animal standing beside a tall tree and nibbling the leaves fifteen feet off the ground. The shape of its body and the colour of its skin were those of an enormous elephant whose back was twelve feet high; but its head and long neck had nothing in common with the elephant: in proportion to the rest of its body the head was very small, like a tapir's, with an elongated upper lip, which the animal used as a scoop to shovel whole bunches of leaves into its mouth.

"What a monster!" Papochkin whispered. "It has the body of an elephant, the neck of a horse, the head of a tapir, and the habits of a giraffe!"

"I think it's a rare specimen of the subfamily of hornless rhinoceroses," Kashtanov said. "The remains of one of them were found in Baluchistan recently, and that's why this largest member of the land-mammal family was named Baluchitherium."

"It's really colossal! I'm sure I could walk right under its belly if I bent my head," Papochkin said.

"If we put a full grown Indian rhinoceros next to it, its back would just touch the monster's belly, and it would look like its baby.

"Too bad we can't get up close to it, to have an idea of scale in the photograph," he continued as he took several snaps. "It seems harmless enough, but I'd never go near it. It could break every bone in your body if it moved its foot casually to one side."

"Get the tree in the picture. We can measure it later."

They waited until the animal had lumbered on and then they took the height of the tree by means of a dipping compass. They also measured the footprints, which turned out to be surprisingly small in comparison to the animal's height.

That same evening they spotted a pair of coryphodons on the edge of a large island. They were large pachyderms that resembled the titanotherium.

When the male noticed the raft, it raised its head and opened its mouth, showing two long, sharp fangs in each jaw.

They couldn't land on the island to hunt, as they saw a large beast devouring its prey a little way along the bank. It stood up and bared its teeth menacingly when it noticed the raft coming towards it.

This animal had short thin legs, its head was elongated like that of a borzoi dog, but the animal was the size of a large tiger, and they lost all desire to land.

Thus, the day went by without their being able to kill a single one of these strange new animals.

As they floated downstream the next day they spotted horses, titanotheriums, four-horned rhinoceroses, antelopes, carnivorous creodonts, and other animals along the river-banks and on the islands. Kashtanov said the general appearance of the fauna suggested the beginning of the Tertiary period.

They went ashore after lunch to see what the prairie was like farther away from the river.

As they approached a small lake, their attention was attracted by an animal which, to their relief, was grazing peacefully. They had been making their way through the bushes to the edge of the lake and had grabbed their guns when they suddenly came upon the animal. Even General, who by then had become quite used to the many different, weird-looking creatures, and who could instantly distinguish the carnivorous from the herbivorous, showed signs of terror and, growling, pressed close to Maksheyev's legs.

"It's a giant rhinoceros," Maksheyev whispered as they came to a halt in the bushes, fearful lest they frighten off the monster or enrage it. The only shred of evidence that the animal was a variety of rhinoceros was the small horn at the bridge of its nose. High on its forehead it had two large forward-growing horns that made it seem like a type of bull; but it had nothing else in common with either bulls or rhinoceroses. Its head was nearly seven feet long and out of all proportion to the rest of its body; the back of its skull broadened out into a wide, flat comb which might have been taken for huge floppy ears, but was in fact either a protective or a decorative flap around the upper neck; it was covered by fine scales and ended in a sharp ridge. The collar obviously added to the weight of the all-too-heavy skull and prevented the monster from raising its head.

Its forelegs were much shorter than the hind legs, and thus the animal's rump was higher than its head when it moved. With its head and legs hidden in the tall grass, it was like a mound fifteen feet high. Its massive body was covered with armour made up of round plates, larger on its back and sides and smaller on its rump, feet, and belly. Its short, thick tail served as a support for the hindquarters. It had a sharp beak and from the tip of its head to the bottom of its tail the animal was about twenty-five feet long.

"What a monster! What a monster!" Gromeko kept whispering as he watched the unusual creature move slowly along the edge of the lake, devouring the grass and bushes in its path.

"What is it?" Papochkin asked.

"It's probably a triceratops, one of the dinosaurs which included various giant lizards," Kashtanov answered.

"Then it's a reptile! I didn't know there were horned reptiles," Maksheyev exclaimed.

"There certainly were! Dinosaurs consisted of a wide variety of lizards, large and small."

"That means we're in the Cretaceous period now!" Papochkin exclaimed. "And the farther downstream we go, the more of these monsters we'll probably meet."

"I don't mind at all, so long as they're as harmless as this one," Gromeko said. "But suppose we bump into a carnivorous one as big as this fellow? We'll be gobbled up before we even have a chance to fire."

"Large animals are usually very clumsy," Kashtanov objected. "I think a sabre tiger is much more dangerous than these giants."

"I wish we could make it lift its head," Papochkin said, "or else lure it out into the open. I've taken two photographs, but the feet and the front of its head are hidden in the grass."

"Should I take a shot at it?" Maksheyev asked.

"No. It'll either get scared and run away, or else it'll attack us. A bullet wouldn't kill such a mountain."

"Let's see what General can do!"

It took a lot of coaxing and prodding to make the dog attack the monster. Finally he rushed towards it, barking loudly, but stopped a safe distance away. The result was quite unexpected. The monster plunged into the lake, churning up a wall of water, and disappeared in the muddy depths.

They all laughed at this undignified retreat, and General ran to the water's edge and barked victoriously at the muddy circles on the surface. A few minutes later the monster put its head out of the water in the middle of the lake to get some air. Papochkin had his camera set, but he had to be satisfied with a shot of its head, for the lizard gulped some air and disappeared again, as soon as it saw its strange pursuers on the shore.

When they came to another lake General flushed a whole flock of odd-looking birds from the rushes. They were as big as very large swans, but their bodies were longer, their necks shorter, and they had long, pointed beaks full of small, sharp teeth. The birds were excellent swimmers and fed on the fish they dived for. Maksheyev shot one and when Kashtanov examined it more thoroughly, he decided it must be an hesperornis, a wingless toothed bird of the Cretaceous period, resembling the modern penguin in bodily structure. It had rudimentary wings, concealed beneath the soft, hairlike plumage.

# THE SWAMP AND LAKE DISTRICT

After sailing down the river through a region of arid plains for three more days, the explorers reached its southernmost end, where there was an entirely different flora. The banks were covered with pines, sago palms, and ferns of many varieties; for the most part these were unfamiliar types, at least six feet tall. There were thickets of tall plants like rushes along the banks; the flat sandbanks were covered with horsetails five feet high and over an inch around. A constant buzzing came from the thicket, and strange insects circled over the water. They looked like dragon-flies, but their wing-spread was over a foot; their bodies had a metallic glint and were about ten inches long; some were golden-yellow, some were steel-grey, some were emerald-green, others were deep-blue, and others again were fiery-red. They flitted about in the sunshine, chasing each other with a tuneful clicking that made you think of castanets.

Spellbound by the beauty of the scene, the rowers put down their oars to enjoy it more fully. The raft floated slowly downstream, while the four men sat silently in the boats. Papochkin pulled out his butterfly net and with great difficulty caught a dragon-fly which he at once let go, for it bit him painfully as he was disentangling it from the net.

The solid green walls along the river-banks made it impossible to land, and the tired explorers looked in vain for a small clearing where they could spend the night.

They were getting very hungry, but the green walls of horsetail got denser.

"We should have stopped at the edge of the prairie," Gromeko said.

"We'll know better next time," Maksheyev laughed.

The green walls went on for mile upon mile. Then, at last, they saw a long, narrow sandbank on the left. It was covered with horsetail, but for want of anything better they decided to stop there and clear a few feet for the tent. They tied up the boats in a little inlet between the bank and the sand and attacked the horsetail with their hunting knives. It was not as easy as they had thought, for the thick stems were tough, containing large quantities of silica which dulled the knives. Where they had been able to hack away the horsetail the remaining stubble was so sharp that they could neither sit nor lie on it.

"Let's try to pull them out," Gromeko suggested. "The roots should come easily from this bog."

It proved to be a good idea, and in about half an hour they had cleared a place for the tent and a camp-fire. But there was nothing to start a fire with, as the green horsetail would not burn. They could not even boil a kettle for tea, let alone cook supper. To make matters worse, swarms of angry mosquitoes an inch long flew up from among the green stalks, and only the smoke from a camp-fire could save them from the insects.

"Wait a minute!" Maksheyev said. "I noticed a dry log sticking out from the thicket somewhere near here. Come on, Mikhail, let's get it!"

The two men took their hatchets and a length of rope, untied one of the boats from the raft, and went upstream to a spot about a hundred feet along the bank, where a large dead tree was sticking out from the solid green wall. However, the tree was so high above the water that they could not reach it with their axes.

"Let's try to lasso one of the branches, it might snap off," Maksheyev suggested.

Gromeko grabbed a couple of horsetail stems and steadied the boat, while Maksheyev tossed one end of the rope over a branch, caught it on the other side, and began to pull The branch didn't break off, but the whole trees started to crack.

"Let go and help me pull!" he shouted.

They were both standing up in the frail boat and pulling with all their might. The tree came crashing down, hitting the front of the boat and making it settle in the water under the great weight. Gromeko had just caught the horsetail on the bank in time to pull the stern in a bit, when the prow disappeared beneath the water.

"This is lovely. What shall we do now?" Maksheyev exclaimed.

They were both sitting in the stern with their feet in the water, each man holding on to the stalks with one hand and the rope with the other to keep the tree from floating off downstream.

"We can't get ashore, and we've nothing to bail out the water with, so we might as well yell for help," Gromeko said.

They hallooed in unison several times, and finally heard Kashtanov shouting, "What's the matter?"

"Get a pail and row back here—our boat capsized!"

"I'll be there in a minute!"

At that moment, a huge head came up out of the water beside the sunken prow. It was muddy-green, with a wide, short snout and small eyes beneath a flat skull. The animal looked at the petrified men for a few seconds, and then bared several rows of sharp teeth and began to clamber up the prow, making it sink deeper under the added weight. A short thick neck emerged from the water, followed by a pair of large front feet with claws that sank deep into the side of the boat.

The men had not taken their guns when they went to look for firewood so close to the camp, and now they found themselves unarmed and face to face with an unknown reptile—undoubtedly powerful and carnivorous. Their axes were under water in the prow, beneath the creature's feet.

"Tie your knife to the handle of your oar!" Maksheyev shouted. "I'll try to keep him off with mine."

He pulled out his knife and stuck it between his teeth, and then grabbed the other oar and shoved it down the monster's half-open mouth. The reptile clamped its jaws and there was a crunching sound, as its sharp teeth splintered the wood and dug into the metal rim of the blade. Maksheyev kept shoving the oar farther down its throat, but the jaws crushed the oar and spat out bloody chips and splinters.

Meanwhile, Gromeko had been feverishly trying to tie his big hunting knife to the handle of the oar with his boot thongs. He then stood up behind Maksheyev and thrust the makeshift spear right into the monster's eye. The creature lurched sideways, tearing the oar out of Maksheyev's hand, and disappeared under the water. They had a glimpse of its wide back with two rows of scales along the spine, and its short, heavy tail that hit the water with such force that they were soaked from head to foot. The boat had been jerked away from the bank when the monster fell off, and now it settled on the bottom completely.

By this time Kashtanov had almost reached the scene of the disaster. As he rounded the bend he saw a column of water rising from the surface, but he had no idea what had caused it. The dry log went bobbing downstream past him, and he thought it was a crocodile. He was getting ready to swing at it with his boat-hook, when Gromeko shouted:

"Catch the log—it's our firewood!" He did not want to lose a prize so dearly won.

Kashtanov hooked the tree and towed it towards his two friends, standing waist-deep in the water.

It took them some time to lift the boat and bail out the water. Then they set off with the big log in tow and found Papochkin waging a fierce and losing battle against the mosquitoes, while General had found an easy way out by sitting in the water up to his ears.

They pulled the log up on the bank, chopped it into firewood, and soon had the flames crackling. Then they dumped some green horsetail stalks on the fire and a cloud of acrid smoke arose, chasing every last mosquito from the clearing. Maksheyev and Gromeko, who were drying themselves at the fire, found tears running down their cheeks from the smoke.

They described the monster and Maksheyev asked:

"Do you think it could have been an ichthyosaur?"

"Not from your description of it. Ichthyosaurs were much larger, their heads were shaped differently, and they belonged to a much earlier period. Your friend seems to have been a small Cretaceous crocodile," Kashtanov said.

"You'd never have got rid of an ichthyosaur so easily," Papochkin added, "a plesiosaur's neck would have been much longer than your oar, and it would have plucked you right out of the boat instead of trying to climb into it."

"We can expect to come across these giant lizards too," Kashtanov said, "for we've been finding more and more ancient species as we go downstream. We're now in the middle, or perhaps the beginning, of the Cretaceous period."

"Yes. Everything keeps getting less and less like what we see on the earth," Gromeko said. "The change is so gradual that we don't notice it, but many foliage trees, flowers, and plants have disappeared completely and have been replaced by palm-trees, sedges, and ferns."

"This underground world still has plenty of surprises for us. We should be more careful and never move a step out of camp without loaded rifles!"

"I don't think we should stay on here after supper, because we shan't have enough wood to make a big fire and keep the wild animals away," Papochkin said.

They pulled the damaged boat up on the bank to dry. After mending it they sat down to supper, slept near the fire for a few hours, and set out again, having lashed the rest of the wood to the raft. The dense thicket continued for about two more hours. In the still water close to the bank fishes swam or jumped out of the water to escape their pursuers. Sometimes a lizard's ugly head would emerge for a second, its mouth agape, trying to catch a fish. Then a whirlpool and circles on the surface would indicate where a heavy body had sunk rapidly to the slimy bottom. At times, the carefree dragon-flies would scatter and disappear among the reeds and leaves. They were hiding from a large light-blue bird with a huge beak that would swoop down with a swooshing noise and swallow a careless insect in flight.

Presently, the green walls began to thin out, the current became slower, and the river began to widen: it became a lake with some islands on it. One especially attracted their attention. Half the island was overgrown with tall trees, while the other half was grassy, with several dried-up trees. They rowed over and tied up the raft.

The clear half of the island was covered with short, stubby grass that turned out to be a new variety of clubmoss. The wind was blowing downstream and away from them, for they were on the top of the island; they had a lot of firewood and decided to start a few smoke fires along the edge of the thicket to force out the animals hiding there.

When the flames began to shoot up and clouds of smoke poured into the thicket, all kinds of small birds and insects flew out; some fell and were immediately added to Papochkin's collection. Suddenly, a fearful thing dashed towards them. It was very much like a porcupine, but about the size of a large bull—its needles were nearly a yard long.

It bristled and became a huge prickly ball as it ran past the dumbfounded men and disappeared among the rushes.

Next came something that looked like a carnivorous

beast. It moved along in short, high jumps. Its coat was dark-yellow and it had a feline head, a rather long, thick tail, short legs, a blunt nose, and sharp teeth. On the whole it resembled a large river otter, but its ears were bigger, its mane shorter, and it was about six feet long. Kashtanov was so intrigued, that he took a shot at it, although it showed no signs of wanting to attack them and was making straight for the river.

The prize was really unusual. It had neither the flat incisors nor the sharp molars associated with carnivorous animals of later periods. All its teeth were more or less sharp and conic like a reptile's. The front teeth which served as incisors were slightly smaller than the rest, and fangs stuck out of its mouth.

"Here's an interesting specimen of a primitive mammal which still has the teeth of a lizard and the origins of peculiarities which developed in later periods," Kashtanov said.

Nothing else came out of the thicket, and so the explorers were finally able to go to sleep, although they took turns to keep watch and replenish the smoke fires which kept the insects away. They had a very quiet night.

They set out again the next morning. The river was now unmistakably a lake, thickly dotted with small islands; there was hardly any current and they had to row steadily. Brilliant dragon-flies and huge horned beetles buzzed over the woods and the water. There were lovely butterflies, whose wings were each as large as a man's palm. At times they saw strange-looking large and small grey-blue birds rather like herons. They had short feet, long tails, and short beaks studded with tiny teeth.

They shot one of the birds in the air, and Kashtanov told them the odd creature represented a transitional form from lizards to birds. It was as big as a crane and covered with grey-blue feathers; its long tail, having vertebrae as well as feathers, suggested both a reptile and a bird. It had three long fingers on each wing and each finger ended in a claw, as did its toes, which enabled the bird to climb trees and scale cliffs by using all four of its extremities. Kashtanov said he thought the bird was an archaeopteryx, but it was much larger than the specimens found in the Upper Jura in Europe.

Late that day the bank became very low and in many places it was swampy and full of ferns, horsetail, and clumps of strange trees which grew right out of the water, towering above the thickets. All kinds of stinging insects attacked the men viciously each time they tried to land and gather specimens. The insects even pursued them over the water. There were mosquitoes an inch long, flies as big as bumble-bees, horse-flies and gad-flies two inches long, all of which took part in the winged attacks on the four men who were forced to flee in disgrace and were beginning to worry at the thought of having to spend the night among the hordes of tormentors.

They rowed for several hours, trying to get clear of the swampland, which seemed to be inhabited solely by insects and primitive birds and by fishes and lizards whose presence in the deep water was indicated by splashes and whirlpools.

"Can you think of a single land animal that could survive these blood-thirsty bugs?" Gromeko asked.

Soon, they all felt a fresh southerly breeze and from time to time heard a steady noise coming from that direction.

"There's a large open lake with barren shores or a sea ahead," Maksheyev said, for he was the first to hear the noise.

"A sea?" Papochkin sounded surprised. "Do you mean there's even a sea in Plutonia?"

"Well, where you have rivers they eventually empty themselves into a static piece of water. They can't flow on endlessly."

"Can't rivers just disperse in swampy lakes like the one we're on now, or get lost in desert sands?"

"Of course they can! But where there's so much water, it's more likely there's a large body of water, and the overgrown lake we're on now is the beginning of it."

## THE SEA OF LIZARDS

They were all wondering how big the reservoir was and whether it would mark the end of their travels into the interior of Plutonia, for it would be out of the question to make a long sea voyage in canvas boats.

In another hour they saw a blue strip ahead, beyond the wide river-lake. They pulled hard on their oars and in half an hour they were at the mouth of the river.

The vegetation growing so abundantly along the river-banks was now separated from the water by a wide bare strip of sand, for the breakers kept plants from taking root there.

They camped on the sandy beach, cooled by a sea breeze and free of buzzing insects.

As soon as they had put up the tent and got a fire going, they all rushed to the water's edge. They wanted to find out if this was an ocean of salt water or merely a large lake, fed by a current; also they were eager for a swim which they had not been able to have in a river that was full of large lizards.

They undressed quickly on the sandy beach and waded into the shallow water. Sixty feet from shore it was still only waist-deep. It was salty, but not so much as were the oceans on the earth's surface; it was rather like the water of the Baltic Sea.

Refreshed by the swim, they began to discuss their future plans. They could see the southern shore of the sea quite clearly. Kashtanov's binoculars disclosed a green wall of vegetation, with groups of trees above it, and dark, purplish patches that were probably cliffs and precipices. Because of the concave surface, he could see hazily in the distance a solid mass of the same purple colour and scattered groups of higher mountains. The terrain of the southern shore intrigued them, and they decided to explore it, which was not impossible, as it was only about twenty-five or thirty miles away, and on a calm day, with a light breeze behind them, they could make the trip without any risk.

Since they had not been able to hunt in the marshes or on the lake during the past few days, there was no meat left, and so they set a pot of gruel to cook. Maksheyev and Papochkin decided to try their luck at fishing, for they had noticed a large fish when they were swimming. They took their rods and set off along the river-bank, to a place where it was clear of reeds and the water was deeper.

Their floats bobbed quietly on the surface for a long time, but just as they were about to try another place, they both felt a bite.

Maksheyev hooked a large fish and pulled it out on to the bank, but Papochkin's catch was so heavy that it threatened to snap his line. He began reeling it in slowly, meaning to catch it with his net, but the water churned up unexpectedly, there was a sharp tug on the line, and something dark carried off both fish and hook. All he saw was a scaly back and a short tail.

Maksheyev was busy taking his fish off the hook, and when he heard the loud splash, he shouted:

"That's quite a fish you have there! It must weigh about twenty pounds!"

"Twenty? You mean two thousand!!" the zoologist said irritably. "It snapped the line and vanished!"

Maksheyev came over with his fish. It was a queer-looking thing, wide and flat like a flounder, and covered with rough scales; it had a single-blade tail, two eyes on the same side of its body, and long spikes along its spine.

"Can we eat a thing like that?" he asked doubtfully.

"Of course. It looks quite like a flounder, but it's probably a ray. You can eat any fresh fish, because only some fishes have poisonous roe, or black stomach linings. Provided you clean it thoroughly, you can even eat one you've never seen before. The only risk is that it'll turn out to be full of bones or too smelly."

"Then let's try again. What was the one that got away like?"

"I don't think it was a fish. A big lizard swallowed my fish and part of my line."

"That means the water here is full of those monsters too! We were certainly splashing around light-heartedly a while ago."

"We should be more careful. There were giant ichthyosaurs, plesiosaurs, and other carnivorous lizards in the seas during the Jurassic period. They'd think nothing of biting a man in two."

"Weren't there any sharks then?"

"Yes, and they were enormous. Some shark teeth have been discovered that were over two feet long! Can you imagine a mouth that size?!"

Within a short time they caught a few large fish that resembled sterlets. They cleaned them and started a kettle of chowder. While it was cooking they went back and caught about a dozen more fish.

After supper they all sat around smoking and discussing the coming voyage. The sea was calm, and the waves lapped the shore at their feet. The beach was strewn with sea-shells that Kashtanov found of great interest. While his friends had been busy fishing, he had collected them by the handful and had classified them as ammonites.

Gromeko suddenly shouted:

"Look at the huge sea serpents!"

About a hundred yards off shore a head on a long neck

broke through the surface of the water and was soon joined by another. The heads were as flat as snakes', and the
necks swayed and curved gracefully. It seemed as if two
great black swans, whose bodies were hidden beneath the
waves, were swimming towards them.

"They're not serpents," Kashtanov said as he followed
them with his binoculars. "I imagine they're plesiosaurs."

"What monstrosities!" Papochkin exclaimed as he too
caught sight of them in his binoculars. "Their necks are
at least two yards long."

"Are they coming to visit us?" Gromeko asked, for he
still had a vivid recollection of his recent encounter with
the lizard.

"Perhaps. But I think they're very clumsy on land, and
we'll be able to outrun them. Anyway, let's fetch our
rifles—just in case."

The sea monsters, however, had no intention of getting
out of the water. They began diving for fish; they would
swim along the shore slowly, peering into the water ahead
of them, then suddenly duck for a second, and come up
with a fish. Their heads and necks darted at lightning
speed; when one had the fish in its mouth, it would toss
the fish in the air and catch it head-first to avoid swallowing it against the scales and fins. Sometimes the fish would
slip away, and then the huge animal would all but jump
out of the water, cleaving the waves with a great splash,
and stretching its long neck after its prey.

The men were absorbed in watching the fishing, till it
ended in a fight. Both plesiosaurs grabbed the same fish
at the same time. As it was a fairly large one, each tried
to pull it out of the other's mouth.

One succeeded in getting hold of it and raced off with
the other directly behind. The second one caught up,
wound its neck around the other's and tried to make it
drop the fish. The intertwined necks waved back and forth,
the dark bodies pressed against each other, and the short

tails and fin-like flippers beat the water savagely, raising fountains of spray. Finally, one plesiosaur became so enraged that it let the fish go, sank its teeth into its rival's neck, and dragged it down to the bottom. For a long time afterwards the water boiled and churned over the place where the monsters had disappeared.

About an hour later Gromeko and Kashtanov went out to gather drift-wood for a night fire and saw a dark mass floating on the waves. It was being carried towards them along the shore-line and suddenly it stopped, having probably gone aground on a shoal.

By the time they returned with the wood, the other two were asleep, and so they untied one of the boats and rowed towards the dark object which proved to be one of the plesiosaurs. Large birds sat on the carcass, pecking at it, and quite a few smaller birds were circling overhead, probably waiting till the larger ones had finished. The circling birds made sounds like the croaking of huge bullfrogs, and their flying reminded you of bats.

The men had to fire several shots into the flock of birds before they could row up to the carcass. The head and upper part of the neck were dangling by a few shreds of skin. The dead creature was floating belly-up, its huge fin-like flippers showing above the water. The belly was covered with bare dark-green skin.

It was impossible to drag the monster out of the water, as its body alone was over seven feet long, its tail slightly shorter, and its neck longer still; its caudal fins were nearly five feet long.

The birds they had shot were flying lizards of two genera: the larger ones were pterodactyls and were bigger than eagles and the smaller ones were about the size of large ducks.

Both varieties had huge heads and toothed bills, featherless bodies and wings and feet webbed together like bats'. The smaller birds had also long tails.


## CROSSING THE SEA

Next day there was good sailing weather. The sky was cloudless, and there was a light northerly breeze that would fill out their sail, without stirring up any big waves. Having thoroughly examined the boats and the raft, they stretched the tent between two upright boat-hooks that served as masts. Maksheyev built a pile of drift-wood on the shore and they stuck a pole with a white flag in it, to serve as a landmark for their return. Then they dug a hole in the sand, at the very edge of the thicket, where there was little chance of the breakers reaching it, and hid all the collections in it. There were rock samples, plants, skulls, bones, and animal skins, which might have got wet during the voyage and in any case would have made extra weight on the raft. They filled in the hole and built another pile of drift-wood over it, to protect it from animals which might be attracted by the smell of the skins. They attached a little sealed bottle to the pyramid containing a short account of their journey from the edge of the ice-belt to the sea-shore.

Then they got into the boats and pushed off towards the thin line of the opposite shore, barely visible on the horizon. A little way out a brisk wind filled the sail and carried them swiftly along.

From the sea they had a wider view of the shore they had just left. East and west of the mouth of the Maksheyev River the shore was lined by the same tall green wall, broken in several places by the mouths of other rivers. The flag and landmark were prominent against the green background. There were neither mountains nor even hills beyond the green belt, and the terrain seemed to be flat woodland and swamps for many miles around.

After rowing for about two hours, they rested and let the raft drift with the wind. The sea was calm. A light breeze rippled the surface of the water which was very deep; when they dropped a weighted cord a hundred yards long over the side it had not touched bottom, and they had no other way of measuring the depth. They rested a while, took up their oars once more, and continued rowing for another hour.

By then they had gone half-way, because both shores now looked equally far away. The breeze grew stronger, and the raft gathered speed. They could now make out the high black, purple, and reddish cliffs that rose in ledges away on the southern shore. The cliffs stretched along the shore-line and gave way to a green forest wall to the right; still farther to the right were high reddish hills which sometimes reached the water's edge and sometimes receded behind a green strip of foliage.

As they neared the opposite shore, the sea came alive. Transparent jelly-like medusae a yard in diameter floated on the waves. When they lifted their oars out of the water, they saw schools of large and small fishes. At times they glimpsed sails and red feelers above the pearl-white shells of nautiluses.

When they were within two miles off land, the number

of sea creatures increased still more. In some places the seaweed formed floating islands, and the oars would get stuck in the tangled masses of soft green stuff full of small shells, fishes, and insects.

They cast their makeshift lead again: the water was seventy-five feet deep. The white line of the surf at the foot of the cliffs could be seen very clearly from where they were.

Till then their voyage had been quite a pleasure trip, but they had some uneasy moments towards the end. When they were about a mile off shore, a plesiosaur's head popped out of water not more than thirty yards away, its long neck swaying gracefully as it advanced slowly towards them. Evidently, it took the raft and the men in the boats for some large, unknown animal.

They had their rifles ready and two shots rang out as soon as the creature came a little closer. Both bullets hit their mark; the graceful neck snapped, and a stream of blood spurted from its mouth, as its head dangled helplessly over the waves. They had begun to row towards the shore and away from the sinking animal when something dark sped past, setting off two rows of waves like a submarine. They could see a dark-green back and a great, long head like a crocodile's. The monster was making for the dead plesiosaur and counting on an easy prize.

"It looks like an ichthyosaur!" Kashtanov exclaimed as he followed the fierce lizard with his eyes.

"It's more ferocious than the plesiosaur," Maksheyev said.

"And much harder to spot and shoot in the water," Gromeko added.

They were now close to the shore, and had a good chance to watch the young ichthyosaur with its pike's mouth.

They kept clear of the pounding surf at the foot of the bare cliffs and steered for a flat sandy clearing with a strip of green behind it: an ideal camp site. The water was so shallow near the shore, that they had to wade in and drag the boats and raft up on the beach. The voyage across the sea had taken about six hours;

it was almost noon, and they would have time to do some exploring after lunch and a short rest. They had set up the tent and begun to cook, when they realized there was hardly any drinking water left.

"We were very foolish not to have taken a few days' supply of fresh water with us," Papochkin said. "How do we know if there's any fresh water on this shore or not?"

"If we don't find any water, we'll have to go back without having seen very much of this side of the sea," Gromeko added.

"I think you're wrong," Kashtanov said. "If this shore had been completely barren, we'd have seen that and brought a supply of fresh water."

"I'm sure we'll find a brook or a spring near by," Maksheyev said. "All these trees could never survive on salt water."

In the afternoon they split up, Gromeko and Papochkin going off into the forest to look for water, while Kashtanov and Maksheyev went eastwards to survey the cliffs along the beach to the east of their camp.

They loaded their rifles with dumdums for safety. General was left tied up near the tent, and a big bonfire was lit on the beach to scare off unwanted visitors.

# MAKSHEYEV'S BILLIONS

The nearest cliffs, charcoal black with red and yellow spots and veins on the surface, turned out to be solid magnetic iron ore. Kashtanov kept chipping off pieces of rock from different parts of the cliff, and each chip was iron ore. In only a few places dark rock appeared through the ore.

"What treasures lie neglected here!" cried Maksheyev after several of the cliffs had proved to be each a mountain of ore, slightly weathered and oxidized on the surface.

"We could have a mine here rich enough to supply the whole world with iron ore," Kashtanov said. "Of course, we'd have to build a railway across Plutonia and Nansen Land first, and have giant ice-breakers in the Beaufort Sea."

"That'a a project for the future, and I'd even say the not-too-distant future! When the supplies of iron ore on the earth diminish, a project like this will not be fantastic but most necessary."

They walked about a mile along the beach, exploring the rocks, but had to stop when they came to a place where surf broke at the foot of the sheer cliffs. There wasn't even a small strip of dry sand they could walk on.

"We'll have to continue by boat on a calm day," Maksheyev said.

"What about scaling the cliffs? We've passed quite a few canyons already," Kashtanov suggested.

They went back to the nearest opening. The mouth of the canyon was piled high with huge ore boulders, which they had difficulty in climbing over.

Suddenly Maksheyev stopped in amazement.

"Look!" he shouted excitedly, pointing to a shining bright-yellow streak, about three inches wide, running through a boulder. "I'll bet you anything in the world it's pure gold!"

"You're right! It looks like 24-carat gold too!"

"And here it is, lying out in the open. You know, I've prospected in California and in Alaska, but I've never seen such a streak, and I've never heard of the likes of it."

"I've never read of anything like it either," Kashtanov said. "But look, it only runs through the boulder and there's nothing in the cliff. There can't be much more than a hundredweight here."

"If there's a streak in the boulder, why can't there be one in the cliff it cracked off from?"

"It sounds logical enough. We can look for it, but if it's in the middle of a sheer cliff, we'll be like the fox looking at the grapes in Aesop's fable."

"There's no such thing as an inaccessible cliff!" Maksheyev said fervently. "All we have to do is find it, and dynamite will do the rest."

"Wait a minute. Even if we do find the main vein, we shan't be able to take back much in our little canvas tubs."

"Well, we'll take as much as we can, and then send a special expedition into the depths of the earth for the rest."

They followed the line of cliffs that towered above the pile of boulders in the mouth of the canyon, and were convinced there was no gold to be found there. They went farther into the widening canyon whose bottom was covered with chips and gravel. The cliffs themselves seemed to be of solid iron ore, but Kashtanov noticed that the gravel was of a different consistency.

"Here's some more gold!" Maksheyev said, as he picked up a chip of brightly speckled ore.

About two hundred feet into the canyon the bottom began to rise noticeably and then turned into a series of ledges. They climbed the first few and came to a sheer rock wall, about twelve feet high.

Maksheyev banged his little hammer against the wall and said in disgust:

"Good-bye, gold. Here's where we turn back."

"We'd better look for another canyon."

"Here, what's this?" Maksheyev sounded angry. "Instead of giving us some gold, the cliff wants to snatch my only hammer from me."

In fact, the hammer seemed to be stuck to the cliff, and he tugged at it in vain.

Kashtanov, meantime, was examining a rock near the ledge and had turned his back towards the wall. His rifle was slung over his shoulder and he suddenly felt a tremendous force pulling him towards the cliff. The rifle clattered against it, and he was pinned to the wall.

"The magnetic attraction here is terrific!" he said when he realized what had happened. "The iron ore has drawn your hammer and my gun to it."

"How can we pull them off? We can't leave them here as souvenirs of our unsuccessful excursion."

Kashtanov squirmed out of the strap, and the rifle remained plastered to the wall. Maksheyev got a firm grip on his hammer, yanked it with all his might, and tore it away from the cliff. Then they both pulled on the rifle until they were able to detach it too.

"We might as well start back," Kashtanov said, "because we'll have nothing but trouble with all the iron things we're carrying."

"Wait! I've got a wonderful idea! We'll leave our guns here below, because I don't think there are any wild animals in this bleak place."

"What then?"

"Then? Just look!"

Maksheyev gathered an armful of large rocks from the bottom of the canyon and began to set them, one by one, smooth side on the wall. They stuck to it as if they had been nailed on and he placed them in such a way that they formed a ladder, which they could risk climbing to the top of the cliff.

"You amaze me at times," Kashtanov said. "You're a real prospector—you can get out of any difficulty."

"Thanks, but the credit belongs to my hammer for it was while I was tugging at the handle, trying to pull it off the wall, that I suddenly thought what a firm step it would make."

They left their rifles, bandoliers, and bag of rock samples at the bottom of the canyon and started up the wall. Maksheyev went first, adding the rocks which his friend passed up to him, until they both reached the top.

On both sides were sheer cliffs, still more or less solid iron ore. They advanced another hundred feet and came across a bright-yellow rock the size of a big pumpkin. It was pure gold.

"Well, my dear prospector, I'd like to see you carry this titbit back to camp!" Kashtanov laughed.

"Yes, it's not bad," Maksheyev said as he kicked the rock. It did not move. "It must weigh about two hundred pounds, and it's worth a fortune! We're close to the vein now, I'm certain!"

They looked up at the cliffs and there, to the right, about twenty feet above them, was a jagged yellow vein of gold, bright against the dark iron ore. In places the vein was two feet wide, and there were many smaller offshoots.

"There are millions here!" said Maksheyev gazing at the visible part of the vein. "Tons of gold right out in the open!"

"You're too excited about the gold," Kashtanov said. "Even if the vein is worth millions, it's only a vein. Look around—it's surrounded by a mountain of precious iron ore. There are billions of tons of it, worth billions!"

"But maybe there are other veins in the mountain. Maybe a large part of the mountain is pure gold too, and then the gold will be worth billions too!"

"You're forgetting something. If we mined tons and tons of gold, its market value would drop rapidly. The only reason gold is so expensive is that there's so little of it. Then again, gold is much less important to people than iron, for industry cannot get along without iron. If gold coins and trinkets went out of use, I'm sure there'd be almost no demand for gold."

"You're too impressed by the value of iron," Maksheyev argued. "If there was a lot of gold, it could be used as a substitute for many metals, especially in copper, lead, and zinc alloys. Industry needs durable, non-rusting metals and alloys. Cheap gold could be used for making bronze, for wires, and in many other ways that copper and its alloys are now used, for want of anything better."

"You'll still agree that there are tremendous stores of iron and doubtful ones of gold here."

"All right then. You can have the iron—just leave the gold to me when we come back to mine them," laughed Maksheyev.

"With pleasure. You can have the billions and billions worth of iron, too," Kashtanov answered.

They retraced their steps and came out on to the seashore again. They explored a few more canyons which they found were also of solid iron ore with streaks and pockets of gold running through them. But nowhere did they come across a vein as big as the first one they had discovered, and Maksheyev had to agree that the iron ore was worth much more than the gold. They took as many samples of ore and pieces of gold as they could carry, and made for the camp, where they astounded the others with an account of their fantastic experience.

# A FOREST OF HORSETAIL

The pebbly beach was bordered by dense foliage: huge horsetails grew thirty feet high and branched out almost from the base of their stems, so that the only way to enter the thicket was on all fours, or bent nearly double. Many different kinds of tree-ferns grew among the horsetails, and altogether the thicket was all but impenetrable.

Papochkin and Gromeko began to look for a path or a break in the thicket, and along the foot of a cliff they found a narrow, dry river-bed which branched out near the sea: the left branch led between the cliffs and the forest, and the right one was lost in the thicket. Vegetation changed, and sago and other palms towered above the horsetail and ferns. The ground in the forest was covered with short, bristly grass. There were other plants growing along the river-bed at the edge of the forest, and Gromeko kept calling out their names and getting more and more excited.

"Do you know what geological age we're in now?" he finally asked.

"Maybe it's the Carboniferous period," growled Papochkin, who was feeling irritable. He hadn't found a single item of interest, and had somehow managed to cut his hands on the prickly grass.

"That's going too far! We've been around a geologist long enough to know there weren't any ichthyosaurs or plesiosaurs in the Carboniferous period. No, my friend, this is the Jura now. Look, here's a typical fern of the period—here's a slim gingko—and this prickly grass was first discovered among the Jurassic deposits near Irkutsk by a geologist named Chekanovsky. It's even been named in his honour."

"What an honour! It's even worse than nettles, and I think the only creature that could swallow it would be some kind of lizard with a cast-iron stomach."

"Talk of the devil!" Gromeko interrupted his grouchy companion. "Look at this little footprint here, it seems to be in your line."

He had stopped in the middle of the dry river-bed and was pointing to the ground where there were huge deep, three-toed prints in the fine sand. Each toe ended in a blunt claw, and each print was over a foot long.

Papochkin's voice shook slightly as he said, "What a monster passed by here! I'm positive it was a lizard—but what kind? Herbivorous or carnivorous? There's quite a difference, you know."

He bent over and examined the prints carefully; they were clear on the sand and disappeared where the sand turned into gravel.

"Isn't it strange, all the prints are of the same size," Gromeko said. "As far as I know, the front paws are usually smaller than the hind ones. I wonder what this line between the right and left feet can be? It looks as if the lizard were dragging a log behind it."

Papochkin laughed.

"It's the track of its tail. I'd say the animal was walking on its hind legs alone—as the prints are equal in size—and that it used its tail as a support."

"Have you ever heard of two-legged lizards?"

"Yes, and they existed only in the Jura. There was one called an iguanodon, for instance. It looked like a giant kangaroo and had powerful hind legs and small front ones."

"What did it live on?"

"Judging from the shape of its teeth, it fed on plants, and if these prints are really those of an iguanodon, then we needn't be afraid, even though some of the creatures were thirty feet long."

"That's fine!" Gromeko heaved a sigh of relief. "I can't seem to forget that horrible thing that was choosing between Maksheyev and me for supper that day on the river."

When they reached the fork in the river-bed, they decided to follow the right branch along the foot of the cliffs, where they thought there would be more chance of finding a spring, as that, after all, was the object of their excursion. They were lucky, for they soon noticed that the soil was more moist and the small plants along the banks were becoming denser and more varied.

Soon they saw a silver streak of water among the stalks in the river-bed.

"Hooray!" shouted Papochkin. "There's a spring just beside our camp!"

"Maybe it's salt water?" Gromeko teased.

"Taste it. It looks like fresh water."

"How can you tell by the look of water whether it's salty or not? Tell me the secret."

"You're supposed to be a botanist, and you don't even know what kind of plants grow near salt water!"

"We're in the Jura now, and we've no idea what the

salt-water plants were like then. Anyway, you said you could tell whether water was salty or not by the way it looked, and not by the surrounding plant life."

"What I meant was that I could tell by the appearance of the river-bed. If there were salt in the water, the whole river-bed would have been covered by a white crust."

They had been walking quickly as they talked and soon they reached a point where the river-bed became a narrow pass between the high cliffs. Here there was a little fresh-water stream that gradually disappeared from view, and the ground beside it was covered with large and small prints of the lizards that used it as a watering-place.

"There are so many of them here that we might easily bump into one of the monsters," said Gromeko.

They both drank the cool water and went on up along the narrow gorge, close to the water's edge. The stream widened and flowed through a hollow, bordered by sheer dark-red cliffs that provided a striking background for the fresh green of the trees and bushes growing along the bottom. In the middle of a green clearing at the bottom of the hollow was a little lake where several springs came straight out of the ground. A wide, well-beaten path led across the meadow to the lake, whose bottom was faintly visible through the clear water.

Having filled the tins they brought with them they decided to hide among the bushes and see if some animal might come for a drink. The minutes passed slowly, but there was still nothing in sight. There were a few dragon-flies, still larger than the ones they had seen on the Maksheyev River, flitting over the water. Papochkin, watching them, suddenly grabbed his gun.

"Are you going to shoot a dragon-fly?" Gromeko laughed.

"Shh! Look, over there—on the cliff!" Papochkin whispered as he pointed to the cliffs at the entrance to the hollow.

A fair-sized kangaroo-like lizard was standing near a

ledge on its hind legs and supporting its body on its long, thick tail. It was dark-green with muddy spots; its head resembled a tapir's and it had an overhanging trunk-like upper lip.

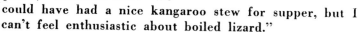

"It must be an iguanodon!" Papochkin whispered.

"Too bad it's not a kangaroo," Gromeko said. "We could have had a nice kangaroo stew for supper, but I can't feel enthusiastic about boiled lizard."

"Don't forget we're in the Jura and there won't be any birds or mammals hanging around, waiting to be shot for supper. If we don't want to die of starvation, we'll have to switch to lizards. In spite of all your botanical delight in the new plants we've come across here, you still haven't found a single edible root, grass, or fruit. Unless you suggest we chew horsetail or prickly grass for a change of diet!"

"How about fish? There must be fish in the sea."

"That's strange. You don't mind eating some unknown fish, but you're afraid to taste the meat of a grass-eating lizard. These are all prejudices you'll have to forget down here."

A shot echoed through the hollow. The animal jumped sideways and plunged down on to the grass. They came out of their hiding-place and ran over to the dead beast.

The young lizard was about seven feet long. Its clumsy body ended in a thick tail that tapered to a point. On the small thin front legs were fine sharp-clawed fingers; the large, thick hind legs had three large, dull-clawed toes. There were small beady eyes in the large ugly head. Its body was completely bare, like a frog's, and it was just as cold and clammy to the touch.

"It's funny, but I don't feel in the least hungry," said Gromeko, prodding the lizard's thigh with the toe of his boot. "It's just like a huge frog!"

"If Frenchmen find frog's legs such a delicacy, why shouldn't Russian explorers enjoy fresh iguanodon steak? Let's measure it first and quarter it later."

They measured the lizard, photographed it, and noted their impressions of it. Then they severed the meaty hind legs, each of which weighed about forty pounds, and went back to camp, laden with the water-tins and fresh meat.

They fried small cubes of lizard meat in a pan and it was so tender and tasty, that even the squeamish Gromeko had a hearty meal and enjoyed it.

At supper they discussed further plans. They could not go on by boats, which had proved such a boon up till then, unless, of course, they found a river on this side.

And so, they decided first to explore the shore, looking for a river. If there was none, they would have to proceed on foot, which would greatly limit the journey.

## CARNIVOROUS AND HERBIVOROUS LIZARDS

There was a strong wind the next day. The sea was choppy, and the spray even reached the tent. There was no sense setting out in their flimsy boats, and they decided to explore the interior of the unknown shore together, following the dry river-bed into the forest.

There seemed little chance of sea lizards attacking an empty tent, and so they left General to guard it alone, but did not tie him up, so that he could hide in the thicket in case of real danger.

At the fork in the river-bed they turned left. The

walls of horsetail and ferns continued along the left branch. At times they saw narrow winding paths, beaten out in the thicket by small animals. The air was full of enormous dragon-flies and other giant insects and their pursuers, the pterodactyls. Apart from this the forest seemed devoid of life: there were no birds chirping nor leaves rustling underfoot, as there had been along the banks of the Maksheyev River.

Once Gromeko, who was leading the way, noticed a dark, dog-sized animal on the path ahead, but it disappeared so quickly that he had no chance to shoot. They had to be satisfied with insects. Papochkin caught a moth with a fifteen-inch wing-spread that had alighted on a palm blossom and several beetles that bit and scratched horribly and were as big as his fist.

The forest thinned out, and they came to a wide clearing, overgrown with the same prickly grass. In places where the ground was moist it was covered with various mosses and small bushes of creeping ferns. The meadow was over a mile long and about two hundred yards wide, ending at the foot of steep, bare, dark-red mountains, cut in two by a deep gorge, which was apparently the source of water that flowed on to the meadow and made it swampy. In rainy seasons it probably coursed down the river-bed to the sea.

The two geologists were interested in the mountain gorge, and so they all went towards it. They had been walking for a few minutes when they noticed a small group of lizards grazing at the northern tip of the meadow, near the edge of the forest.

Some stood on their hind legs and nibbled at the palm leaves and tender young fern and horsetail shoots. The young animals were eating the grass, standing on all fours, with their hind-quarters high above their heads and their tails thumping up and down for balance. At times they played and chased each other, either on their hind legs or on all fours, jumping about comically.

They couldn't miss such an opportunity to photograph the grazing, frolicking iguanodons, and the men went quickly back to the edge of the forest and began to creep towards the herd. But just as they had taken one picture, the animals suddenly became alarmed: the adults stopped eating, looked round, and whistled sharply. When the young animals heard the whistles they stood up on their hind legs and hobbled clumsily over to their parents, who, facing inwards, formed a tight circle round their young.

The second and third photographs recorded the animals' alarm—for which they had plenty of cause. A monster that the hunters at first mistook for another iguanodon came bounding out of the forest from the other side of the meadow.

It was about the same size as the adult lizards and it too used only its hind legs as it advanced by ten-foot leaps. When it came closer they saw that its body was thinner and its movements quicker than the others'; it

hopped over to the circle of iguanodons and hissed loudly. It was answered by a chorus of whining whistles. Then it began to circle round the ring of lizards in small, jerky jumps, but everywhere - it came up against the raised hind-quarters and heavy thumping tails of its enemies. Apparently, a blow inflicted by the massive hind legs or heavy tails was enough to disable the creature.

When the monster saw that it would be impossible to break the circle and snatch one of the young animals, it took a sudden flying jump over the heads of the defenders and landed among the shivering young iguanodons. The cowardly creatures scattered in all directions in their haste to escape but their enemy grabbed one of the young animals and bit right through its neck.

The men took several photographs of the attack and flight; then two shots rang out, and the killer fell dead beside its victim.

The large reptile's long hind legs and the thick tail supporting its body were very much like those of the iguanodons. Its short front legs ended in four sharp-clawed toes. It had a short neck and small head, slit by a huge mouth full of sharp teeth. On the bridge of its nose was a short, flat horn which seemed more like an ornament than a weapon.

Two smaller horns grew above its eyes, and there was a row of small sharp spikes all along its spine. The bare, wrinkled skin was greyish-green; the animal was sixteen feet long and there could be no doubt of its strength; its recent attack on the herd had shown its agility and courage.

Kashtanov classified the dead lizard as a ceratosaur, belonging to the same order of dinosaurs as the iguanodon and other land lizards of the Mesozoic era.

"I hope we needn't eat this monstrosity!" Gromeko said when they had finished measuring it.

"Why not? If we had nothing better, we'd have to be content with this," Maksheyev said. "But we've got the iguanodon, it's all in one piece, except for a slit throat."

"Let's hide it before the pterodactyls tear it to bits. Look, here they come, hot on the trail of fresh blood!"

High above the flying lizards were croaking hoarsely as they circled the meadow. The hunters cut off the young iguanodon's hind legs and hid them in the thicket by tying them up to some branches. Then they went towards the gorge across the meadow, now empty after the battle and the rifle shots.

## THE PTERODACTYL GORGE

The mouth of the gorge was very wide, and a little stream banked by clumps of ferns twisted along its bottom. Kashtanov and Maksheyev made for the bare rocky sides which were reddish, black, or yellow in colour. Gromeko decided to look for new types of plants along the banks

of the stream, and Papochkin went after the giant butterflies.

The first cliff the geologists reached was dark-red.
Kashtanov was sure they would find iron ore again, but
after he had chipped off a piece of rock and examined it
through his magnifying glass, he murmured, "I wonder
what it can be?"

He chipped off a few more pieces from different places
and they all proved to be exactly the same. The cliffs
were so smooth and hard that it was impossible to chip
off a larger piece, and so the two men attacked a red
boulder lying near the foot of the cliff. Together they
pounded at it until finally it cracked and split in two.
There were shining streaks and pockets in the centre.

Kashtanov bent down to get a better look and exclaimed:
"It's pure silver in solid red silver ore!"

"Another treasure worth millions!" Maksheyev jeered.
Since his learned friend had doubted the value of the
solid vein of gold, Maksheyev had been rather contemp-
tuous of the fabulous gifts of the enchanted land.

They went on along the foot of the cliff and soon
reached a place where the dark-red gave way to the black,
streaked and spotted with yellow and red. It turned out
to be solid magnetite again. The bright-yellow and greenish-
yellow cliffs farther ahead were pock-marked and ragged-
looking. Kashtanov said they were lead ochres and oxidized lead ores and thought there might even be a massive
lead glance far below the surface.

Soon they came to a dark-green cliff that seemed, from
afar, to be covered with moss or fungi. Their hammers
bounced ringingly off the rock, and with greatest difficulty they managed to chip off a few small pieces. Kashtanov was even more amazed than before.

"Do you know what this is? It's a solid mass of pure
copper, slightly oxidized on the surface," he said.

"What a country!" Maksheyev said. "You can have your

pick of whatever kind of ore you like. All we need now
is an all-round metallurgical plant."

"Yes, when we've used all the ore upstairs I expect
we'll have to come down here for it," Kashtanov agreed.

"Why not drill a hole right through the earth's crust?
After all, a straight line is the shortest way," Maksheyev
joked.

Suddenly, a large shadow passed over them and they
heard Gromeko shout:

"Watch out! It's a flying lizard!"

They grabbed their guns and looked up to see a huge
dark creature soaring about sixty feet over them. They
recognized it as a flying lizard similar to the pterodactyls,
although it was much larger than those they had seen
at the sea-shore—its wing-spread alone seemed to be
about twenty feet. The lizard was looking down at them
and trying to choose between these strange two-legged
creatures.

They could not wait for it to make up its mind, for
it could easily kill or maim the one it dived on. Maksheyev aimed and fired. The lizard dipped, flapping its
wings heavily as it flew to one side, and landed on a
ledge; it began to jerk its head about and kept opening
and closing its toothy beak.

"I must have grazed it," Maksheyev said, but he did
not want to waste another bullet on the creature, because
it was too far away.

Just then a loud cry and then a shot rang out from
the meadow where the other two men were.

A second pterodactyl flew out of the grove of ferns
and horsetail that separated the river-bed from the foot
of the cliffs. It was carrying off a large dark object.
Kashtanov decided that the bird had one of his friends in
its talons and fired at it in his excitement. The robber
flapped its wings, dropped its load, and tumbled down
behind the trees.

The two geologists rushed towards the spot where their companion had dropped from such a height, but as they pushed through the clumps of ferns they all but fell over Gromeko and Papochkin, who were both running towards them.

"You! Then who just fell out of the sky!"

The other two burst out laughing.

"The lizard pinched my raincoat. I had wrapped all my plants in it and left it on the grass. I suppose it thought it was some sort of carrion," Gromeko explained.

"I tried to get it, but I must have missed," Papochkin added.

The four men made for the place where the wounded lizard lay flapping its wings. When it saw them coming, it jumped up and rushed at them, dragging one of its wings along the ground.

It wobbled from side to side like a duck and croaked viciously, with its neck stretched forward and its mouth agape. The fleshy bump on top of its beak grew red and bloodshot. As the lizard was a good six feet tall and would be a dangerous enemy despite its wounded wing, they were forced to take another shot at it.

While Kashtanov and Papochkin were studying the dead lizard, Maksheyev and Gromeko went to look for the stolen raincoat. They covered the whole clearing up to the edge of the cliffs and looked all through the underbrush, but found nothing.

"I'm tired of playing hide-and-seek," Gromeko grumbled as he wiped the sweat from his face. "Where in the world can it be? The lizard certainly didn't swallow it."

"I saw the lizard drop it after the shot," Maksheyev said.

Suddenly the pterodactyl that had been sitting on the ledge glided down over the tops of the horsetail. It scooped up a dark object from the top of one of the plants and took off again.

"What the devil! There goes my raincoat again!"
Gromeko shouted. "It was up there on top of the tree all
the time."

Maksheyev was trying to get the lizard in his sights,
but all of a sudden the raincoat unrolled and a pile of
green plants rained down on them. The startled creature
let go of the coat, and Maksheyev lowered his rifle.

"I don't think these birds are very bright—they carry
off such indigestible items," Gromeko said trotting off
towards his coat.

"Maybe they're brighter than you think. Maybe they
wanted to line their nest with your coat and your straw,"
Maksheyev teased.

"Straw? Have you no respect at all for my labours?
Why don't you try to prove that the lizards were taking
my coat home to dress their naked children in it!"

"Well, that's going a bit too far," laughed Maksheyev.
"But why did you gather so many of the same plants?" he
asked as he watched his friend pick up some reed-like
stalks that had scattered about when they dropped out of
the raincoat.

"Guess what it is?" Gromeko handed him a stalk.

"Some kind of thick, prickly reed, just the thing for
an iguanodon."

"You're right. The iguanodons find them delicious, and
I think we'll be just as pleased with them."

"Why, are they good for soup?"

"No, not for soup—but they're just the thing for tea.
Here, crack one of the stalks."

Maksheyev broke a stalk in two and a colourless liquid
dripped out of the broken ends.

"Taste the juice of the lowly reed," Gromeko said.

It turned out to be sweet and sticky.

"Do you mean it's sugar-cane?"

"Well, it's not exactly the sugar-cane we're used to,
but at least it's a sugar-bearing plant."

"How did you find out it was sweet?"

"I found a stalk in the dead young iguanodon's mouth, back on the meadow, and it felt sticky. I began to look for more of it and found the whole river-bank covered with it. Of course, I tasted it, and it's a good thing I did, for our sugar supplies are getting low and now we can use this juice instead. We can even cook the sugar out of the stalks. So you see, my straw will come in handy after all!"

When Gromeko showed the other two his find, which had been the cause of the whole adventure, they decided to cut as many sugar reeds as they could on the way back.

They followed the bank of the little stream and soon the gorge became a real crevice, its bottom completely under water. It was gloomy, dark, and damp. The men advanced in single file, Maksheyev in the lead with his gun cocked and Kashtanov last, tapping the rocks with his hammer.

Soon everything grew brighter, and they had a glimpse of green vegetation ahead. The crevice broadened into a rather large basin, surrounded by cliffs that were steep at the bottom and had receding ledges farther up, like an amphitheatre. The bottom of the basin was covered with thick green grass, and in the middle was a lake, the source of the little stream.

"What a stench!" cried Gromeko as they reached the edge of the lake.

"Yes, it smells like carrion," Maksheyev agreed.

"Maybe it's a mineral lake with sulphur springs?" Papochkin mused as he bent to smell the water.

They began looking around and heard a strange hissing and screeching, coming from far up on the bare cliffs.

Just then something large and black hurtled above them and landed on one of the ledges; the hissing and screeching increased the moment it landed.

"It's a pterodactyl!" Maksheyev exclaimed.

"This must be their nesting ground," Papochkin said.

"Well then, that's where the stench comes from. They're disgustingly messy."

The lizard on the ledge took off a few moments later and noticed the men below. It circled over them, croaking loudly. The hissing and screeching on the ledges stopped instantly.

"See how they listen to their pa!"

"It would be interesting to get a few eggs and young chicks from the nests," Papochkin said.

"Try to climb the smooth cliffs and pick a fight with their parents if you care to. They'll show you a thing or two!"

"Hey, there's quite a lot of them here!" Kashtanov said pointing to a pterodactyl that was peering out from one of the ledges while two more soared high above them.

"Well, shall we open fire?" Maksheyev asked, anxious to make up for his recent miss.

"Why? We've killed and studied one already, and we shouldn't waste our bullets," Kashtanov warned him.

"Let's retreat before it's too late and all the nests are alarmed. About face! Forward, march!" Gromeko said, for the horrible stench was beginning to make him feel sick.

Several lizards were flying and croaking above them, and the hunters thought it best to follow Gromeko's advice. As they neared the crevice they noticed heaps of bones of all sizes mixed with droppings at the foot of the cliffs.

"On your right—the city dump!" Maksheyev announced. "They have a real fortress here."

"Probably because other lizards hunt their eggs and their young," Papochkin explained. "Even though they're reptiles, they behave like birds in many ways."

"I'm still sorry we weren't able to see what their nests and eggs, and their young, look like—and especially what their hatched eggs are like," Papochkin said.

"I don't think they hatch their eggs as birds do, but leave them for the sun to warm like all the other reptiles," Kashtanov disagreed.

"Don't worry, we're sure to come across some iguanodon or plesiosaur eggs sooner or later," said Gromeko consolingly.

"If they're fresh, let's make a giant fried egg—one should be quite enough for all of us!" Maksheyev suggested.

They went back through the canyon and came out on to the clearing at the foot of the cliffs. They had gathered enough sugar reeds on the way and they made for the place where they had killed the lizard.

A great commotion was going on. Flying lizards of all sizes were perched all over the carcasses of the iguanodon and the ceratosaur, and the sky above was black with them. They were tearing chunks of meat from the bodies, some swallowing them at once, while others carried off pieces towards their nests in the ledges. The air was filled with croaking, hissing, and screeching.

The whole flock became alarmed.

when they saw the men coming towards them. Some took to the air and began circling over the clearing; others wobbled along on their short legs, dragging their partly spread wings as they tried to run away. They had apparently gorged to such an extent that they could not raise themselves from the ground. Papochkin was able to take two snapshots of the scene.

The bloated lizards did not attack the intruders, but expressed their anger by piercing shrieks.

Having picked up the iguanodon meat, hidden in the thicket, they went back along the river-bed. As they were nearing the mouth, Gromeko, who was in the lead, stopped suddenly and pointed out huge footprints sunk deep into the damp sand.

"That's not an iguanodon," Papochkin said. "The creature was walking on all fours. Look, here are the hind feet with three toes, and the front ones with five each!"

"The prints are differently shaped from an iguanodon's and much larger," Kashtanov added.

"Can you tell whether it's fierce or tame from the prints?" Maksheyev asked.

"I think it's a grass eater. The toes end in some sort of a hoof that it can't grab with as it could have done if it had claws."

"Here's the mark of its tail—it's much shorter and thinner than the iguanodon's," Papochkin said pointing to a zigzagging line between the footprints.

"At any rate, it's a very large animal, and it must still be somewhere near the lake, because there are no tracks leading back," Gromeko said.

"Have your guns ready. And be careful!" Maksheyev warned.

They went slowly up the river-bed, keeping a sharp look-out, but they saw nothing except the dragon-flies and beetles, buzzing and darting over the ferns and horsetail. At the foot of the cliffs they halted, uncertain what to do next.

Maksheyev whispered that he would go and see if the animal was anywhere about. He disappeared in the canyon and they soon heard his low whistle. They joined him and hid behind some trees at the entrance to the hollow. They had an excellent view of a monster grazing on the clearing. It exceeded anything they had seen so far in that land of extinct giants.

It was about twenty-five feet long and twelve feet high. Its front legs were much shorter than its hind legs and the great body was bent forward; the head was amazingly small and it resembled a lizard's. There were two rows of armoured plates sticking out like little wings along

its spine. Four pairs of the largest plates protruded from its body, three pairs of small ones from its thick neck, and two from its tail which had also three pairs of long spikes beyond the plates. The bare, wrinkled skin was dotted with wart-like growths, smaller and more numerous on its head and neck, larger and farther apart on its body and tail. The dark-brown spots and splotches on the muddy-green skin added to the general repulsive effect.

The creature was grazing peacefully at the edge of the lake, tearing up tufts of sugar reeds and young horsetail with its oversized mouth. The plates along its back rustled at every movement of its body.

"Just like Cupid's wings!" Maksheyev whispered.

"This Jurassic Cupid isn't bad at all!" Gromeko laughed. "I never dreamed such hideous things existed."

"You know, its menacing appearance, the plates and spikes, the warts and splotches are only to scare off its enemies, for it's a peaceful and probably very harmless thing," said Papochkin taking a few photographs. "What's Cupid's real name?" he asked Kashtanov.

"It's a stegosaur, the most extraordinary of the same order of dinosaurs as the iguanodon, ceratosaur, and triceratops belong to. The remains of these monsters have been found in North America."

When they had watched for a while longer, they fired a shot into the air which resounded through the canyon. Then they began to yell at the top of their voices.

The frightened monster made off at top speed, joggling along with the large plates on its back slapping against each other and clacking loudly.

When it disappeared, they came out of their hiding-place, replenished their supply of water from the lake, and made their leisurely way back to camp, looking forward to a dinner of fried young iguanodon and a rest on the quiet beach.

# ROBBED

They came out of the forest and stopped dead in their tracks. The tent had disappeared.

"We must have come out at the wrong part of the beach," Kashtanov said.

"No, that's impossible!" Maksheyev answered. "We've just climbed over the fence we put up in the mouth of the river-bed near camp."

"Of course. Where's the tent then?"

"And where's everything else?"

"Where's General?"

They ran to the spot where the tent had been. There was nothing—neither tent, nor supplies, nor even a crumb left. The camp-fire had gone out, and the only things to be seen were the holes made by the tent poles in the sand.

"What could it have been?" Gromeko said as they stood round the cold fire they had intended to fry the meat on.

"It's beyond me." Papochkin sounded very depressed.

"Well, we've been robbed—that's certain!" cried Maksheyev.

"But who did it? Who?" Kashtanov kept repeating. "This looks like the work of intelligent creatures, but we haven't seen any at all since the day we left the *North Star*."

"The iguanodons couldn't have done it!"

"Or the stegosaurs!"

"Or the plesiosaurs!"

"Maybe those cursed pterodactyls carried everything off to their nests?" Gromeko said thinking of his raincoat.

"It's fantastic! The tent, the dishes, the bedrolls, and everything else! I can't believe the birds are so clever," Kashtanov answered.

"What about the boats?" Maksheyev said. They rushed towards the edge of the wood where they had concealed the boats and oars before starting out on their excursion. They found them just as they had left them.

"We left the raft on the beach near the tent, and it's gone too," Gromeko announced.

"What shall we do?" Papochkin expressed their bewilderment. "We'll die here without our tent and supplies!"

"Let's try to be calm about it," Kashtanov said. "First of all, I think we should rest and eat, because fatigue and a hungry stomach are bad advisers. We might as well start another fire and roast the meat."

"And we can wash it down with sugar water!" Gromeko said.

They built another fire, cut the meat into cubes, and roasted it on sticks. They sat around the fire, sucking sugar reeds and drinking water, as they discussed the mysterious disappearance of their possessions.

"We're just like Robinson Crusoe on a desert island," laughed Maksheyev.

"Except that there are four of us, and we're armed," Kashtanov added.

"We should count our bullets and use them sparingly."

"I've about two glasses of cognac in my flask," said Gromeko who, as a doctor, carried it with him for emergency purposes.

"And I've a small tea-pot, a collapsible mug, and some tea," Papochkin said, rummaging through his shoulder case.

"Not bad! At least we can treat ourselves to tea occasionally," Maksheyev said. "All I have is my pipe, some tobacco, a compass, and a notebook."

"I've got the same. Plus our two hammers."

"Dinner's ready!" Gromeko said taking the sticks off the fire.

They each took a stick and began to eat the cubes of meat which, being unsalted, were not very tasty.

"We'll have to look for salt on the beach, or at least dip the meat in salt water," Maksheyev said.

When the water in Papochkin's tea-pot boiled they each had a small mug of tea sweetened with sugar-reed juice.

After dinner they continued to discuss further action. It was agreed that the first thing to do was to find the thieves' trail and follow them.

"We'll examine every inch of beach round the camp," Maksheyev suggested. "They might have come and gone by air as Gromeko suggested—but I don't think that's the case—or by land, or gone off to sea on our raft. But then, they would have had to cross the sand to reach the water. In other words, if they didn't fly away, they must have left tracks on the beach going either towards the water or the woods."

"Pity we didn't think of that at once. We've been running about so much that we've probably trampled all the prints there were."

"They couldn't have gone far to the east along the foot of the cliffs—we found that out for ourselves yesterday," Maksheyev continued. "I don't think they followed the river-bed, because we blocked the mouth of it. Besides, we saw no one and no suspicious tracks. Therefore, we should look for prints either here, on the beach, or else along the beach to the west."

"You're right again!" Kashtanov said. "These are probably the only two ways they could have gone."

"Let's get started then. And as I'm an old trapper, I want you all to sit here while I study the ground round about."

Maksheyev knelt down and began to examine the ground where the tent had been; he moved to the water's edge, where they had left the raft; and then he turned and walked westward along the beach. When he was about a hundred feet away, they saw him stick a dry branch into the sand and begin to walk back.

"Our stuff hasn't been stolen by people or even by lizards. Judging by the tracks everywhere in the sand, it was carted off by some kind of large insects—there were several dozen of them. At first I thought everything had been hauled down to the raft and taken away by water, but then I saw that the tracks didn't go right down to the water and there was no indication that the raft had been dragged there either. Its disappearance is a complete mystery. Some of the supplies were carried off and some, including the tent, were dragged along the beach to the west. The thieves have six legs each and their bodies are about three feet long, judging by the tracks on the sand."

"Nice little insects!" Gromeko exclaimed.

"What could have happened to General?" Kashtanov wondered. "Was he killed or dragged off to be eaten later, or did he run off and escape the thieves?"

"There are a lot of his tracks round the tent, but they're all covered over by insect tracks—that means the insects came later. There's no blood on the sand, and no pieces of insects the dog might have chewed up. I think General must have run away because he was outnumbered, and he's probably hiding somewhere in the thicket. We should have a look at the ground at the edge of the woods too."

Maksheyev crossed the sand to the edge of the forest. When he reached it he walked to and fro several times, stopped, and beckoned to the others.

"Here's where General went into the woods, but there was something wrong with him, because he was dragging his hind legs."

He took out his hunting knife and hacked away the lowest branches of horsetail. Then he got down and crawled into the thicket, whistling softly for the dog and stopping to listen for an answer. Finally, he heard a faint whine. A few moments later General crawled towards him from the underbrush—but how terrible he looked! His whole body was bloated and he dragged his stiff legs along the ground.

"What's the matter, boy?" Maksheyev asked, gently stroking the dog's head. General only licked his hand and crawled behind him out of the dark woods.

"Maybe they broke his spine?" Papochkin said.

"I don't think so," said Gromeko as he examined the dog. "No, they seem to have wounded him with poisoned arrows—there are several small fresh wounds on his back— but his spine isn't injured at all."

"What do you mean 'poisoned arrows'?" Maksheyev asked. "The thieves were insects, remember?"

"I forgot! In that case, the wounds are poisonous stings or bites."

"Can we do anything? Can we save him?"

"I'm sure we can. If the poison were lethal, he'd have been dead long ago. It's a pity our first-aid kit was stolen with the other things. We'll have to try cold compresses."

Maksheyev picked up the whining dog and carried him towards the water, which Gromeko began to pour over him in handfuls. Squealing, the dog tried to break free, but the soothing effect of the cold water quieted him in a few moments. Then they made him sit in the water up to his neck.

While the two men were looking after General, the others had pulled the two boats and the oars out of the thicket, lowered them into the water, and put in all their remaining supplies. Then Kashtanov and Maksheyev went off to the lake in the canyon to fill the tins with fresh water. Meanwhile, the other two roasted the remains of the iguanodon meat, so that they need not stop for food on the way.

It took an hour to get everything ready and during that time the swelling all over General's body went down considerably. He even tried to stand up. They decided to take him in one of the boats. Two of them were to row the boats along the shore, while the other two were to follow the tracks for as long as they were visible on the beach. In this way, the men in the boats could help those on the beach in case of danger or could take them into the boats, and those on the beach could stop the others as soon as the tracks led into the woods.

## TRACKING THE THIEVES

Maksheyev and Gromeko walked along the beach; Kashtanov and Papochkin each rowed one of the boats, keeping abreast of the other two. Luckily, it was a very calm day; the waves lapped the shore rhythmically. Maksheyev led the way, following the tracks on the sand and stopping now and then to exchange a few words with his companion. At one place, where the sand was moist, there were clear impressions of many of the stolen supplies which the thieves had stacked in a pile, apparently during a short halt; in another place there was a clear impression of the raft, and when Maksheyev saw it he exclaimed:

"Well, that's one mystery cleared up! They're carrying the raft!"

"Why in the world do they want it?" Gromeko asked.

"Why do they want everything else? They even took the samples of gold and iron ore that Kashtanov and I brought back yesterday!"

"I can't understand what sort of creatures these are! You'd think they were really intelligent. I shan't be surprised to find they've pitched our tent, slept in our beds, and eaten from our dishes."

"Anything can happen here. Why couldn't some Jurassic insects have a highly developed brain and rule the animal world?"

"Well, even now there are intelligent insects that live in well-governed colonies—bees and ants, for example."

"Wait a minute! That gives me an idea! Maybe the thieves were ants!"

"Why not bees or wasps?"

"Ants are more likely. You know that modern ants will drag anything into their ant-hill—even junk they've no earthly use for—and their strength is phenomenal as compared with their size."

"Yes. Bees are much weaker, and you never find anything but beeswax and honey in a beehive. And wasps will take only food to their nests. Anyway, these fellows don't seem to have wings."

"It seems logical, although winged insects could drag anything they couldn't fly off with along the ground."

"I think we're on the right track. There are three possibilities: ants, bees, and wasps."

"All three have poisonous stings. They must have stung General when he tried to defend the tent."

"Right! These stings produce a painful swelling and, considering the size of the insects, the poison could easily cause temporary paralysis."

After two hours' walking over soft sand the two men felt very tired.

"I'm all in!" Gromeko said stopping to wipe his damp forehead with the back of his arm. "It's so clammy today, and there's not even the slightest breeze."

"But at least the sea is calm, and the boats can keep up with us."

"Why not change places for a while? Our legs are tired and their arms must be tired too."

"Do you think they'll be able to follow the tracks? Well, let's give it a try."

Maksheyev hailed the others, who made for the shore. He showed them the tracks and walked a little way along the beach with them. Then he and Gromeko got into the boats and pushed off.

There was no change in the terrain. The sandy-pebbly

beach along the coast was about a hundred feet wide, and it bore the marks of flooding in heavy storms. The green wall of horsetail and ferns was sometimes broken by a narrow, dry river-bed like the one they had explored the previous day. Iguanodons sunning themselves on the beach would disappear into the forest when they caught sight of the men. Plesiosaurs cut through the waves gracefully from time to time and flying lizards, looking for prey, appeared above the tops of the trees.

About two hours later they saw some reddish hills ahead, coming down to the water's edge. They crossed a large, dry river-bed leading far inland and separating the edge of the forest from the hills, which turned out to be red sand dunes. The insect tracks led up along the river-bed and the men on the beach shouted to those in the boats to come ashore.

After they had all examined the tracks, they discussed what to do. They would have to leave the boats behind and continue the chase on foot.

They were beginning to feel the effects of the day's excitement, worry, and walking, and General was still very weak. Therefore they decided to rest for a few hours on the beach, as it was slightly cooler near the water than it would be when they went farther inland on that scorching, stifling day.

They pulled the boats up on the sand and lit a fire to warm up the meat and make tea. Then they made General sit in the water again.

After dinner three of them went to sleep in the shade of the boats and the fourth stayed awake in case of attack by lizards or the mysterious insects.

Three hours passed quietly. Kashtanov, who was on watch, lay on the sand at the water's edge, thinking about their possible fate if they could not get their things back. He dozed off with the intense heat and awoke with a start from a nightmare: he had been dreaming that a giant lizard had rolled over on top of him and was licking his face with its huge sticky tongue.

He moaned in terror and opened his eyes. General's face was a few inches away from his and the whimpering dog had put one of its paws on his chest.

He had not awoken him in vain. As Kashtanov looked around he saw that the north horizon was menacingly black. A tropical storm of the kind they had already experienced on the Maksheyev River was advancing from the north. There was a constant far-off rumbling and the black mass of clouds was streaked with bright flashes of lightning.

There was no time to lose, they would have to get as far away from the beach as possible, for it would be very dangerous there at the height of the storm.

Kashtanov woke his friends. They decided to make for the dunes, because the forest would be just as dangerous as the beach. They dragged the boats with them, fearing that the waves would wash them away.

They saw a deep valley from the crest of the first ridge. It was parallel to the shore-line and was as barren as the two slopes of the ridge. For as far as they could see, the reddish sand burned under Pluto's rays which were not yet obscured by the storm-cloud.

They descended into the valley, turned the boats upside-down, and got under them. It was the only way they could escape the downpour.

The storm was not long in coming. Dark-blue clouds covered half the sky, Pluto was lost behind them, and it was getting darker every minute. The first gusts of wind ripped across the valley, whisking sand off the tops of the dunes, so that they seemed to be smoking. The air, filled with hot sand, was more stifling than ever. Suddenly, the hurricane was upon them. Kashtanov took a quick look around from under the boat, and it seemed as if the entire first ridge of dunes had been lifted into the air and then plunged into the valley. The sand poured down steadily on the boats. The forest of horsetail in the wide mouth of the valley trembled as if it had been a grove of cat's-tail. The tall trees were bent to the ground, the branches were strands of green hair in the wind, and the air was full of broken stalks, branches, and tops being swept away by the storm. Lightning came in blinding flashes, after which everything seemed twice as dark. The thunder rolled on.

Then the first large drops hit the overturned boats, and the rain came in a torrent. The air was instantly cleared of sand and dust, for the roaring wind could not lift the wet sand. Sheets of rain fell, to be absorbed at once by the parched sand.

The storm passed quickly, and soon Pluto broke through the clouds again. As soon as it stopped raining the men tried to get out from under the boats, where it was really suffocating, but the boats were buried under mounds of heavy wet sand that strained the canvas bottoms.

"We're stuck here!" Papochkin shouted. "Give us a hand."

"We're stuck ourselves!" Maksheyev shouted back. He, Kashtanov, and General were pinned under the other boat.

"Any suggestions about how to get out?"

"We're going to tunnel our way under the side of the boat."

"Fine! We'll do the same."

All was quiet for a while, the only sounds being the grunts and puffing of the men burrowing like moles through the loose sand.

A dishevelled and sandy Maksheyev crawled out on his belly from under the bow of the first boat; he was followed by a sandy Kashtanov and a sandy General. A few moments later the other two appeared from under the second boat.

They scraped the sand off the boats and dragged them down the valley towards the dry river-bed. When they reached it they were amazed to see the turbulent yellow-red waters of a fair-sized river which they could neither cross nor sail on.

"We'll have to wait till the water runs off," Gromeko said.

"That's the least of our worries," Maksheyev answered. "The heavy rain and the water in the river-bed have wiped out the thieves' tracks, and we don't know which way they went."

"Why did we stop for lunch!" Papochkin said angrily. "We could easily have covered six miles before the storm. We might even have reached their hide-out."

"No use talking about it now. But I don't think we'll have far to go—they couldn't have dragged all our stuff for miles and miles on end," Kashtanov reasoned.

The water-level in the river-bed fell rapidly, and in another half-hour there were only muddy puddles left.

"We're off!" said Maksheyev.

"What shall we do with the boats? We can't very well drag them over land endlessly," Kashtanov said.

"Let's leave them near the water, but we'll have to find a way to hide them from our friends, the robbers."

"We can bury them on the beach," Gromeko suggested.

"Good idea! We'll have to dig the pits with our hands, but the sand is loose, and anyway there's nothing else we can do."


## THE RULERS OF THE JURASSIC WORLD

They buried the boats and went up the damp river-bed. At times they had to climb up the banks when the puddles were too large or the clay underfoot was too sticky. They walked carefully, their guns ready in case they came upon the thieves unexpectedly. Along the left bank was a solid green forest of horsetail, ferns, and palm-trees, and along the right was a chain of reddish dunes. The thieves' den might be either in the forest or among the dunes.

A little later they came upon something black lying half-buried in the sand and silt of the river-bed. They cleared the slime away and saw that it was a huge black ant with a body about three feet long, a head slightly smaller than a man's, and sharp-clawed legs bent rigidly in death.

"So here's the king of them all!" cried Kashtanov.

"If their colonies or ant-hills are as densely populated as those on earth, we'll be faced by thousands of enemies," Papochkin said.

"Enemies that are vicious, clever, and merciless," added Gromeko.

Then General came up. He had been dragging along behind and stopping to rest on the way. When he saw the dead ant he pounced on it with an agry growl.

"Oho! I see our friend has recognized his tormentor!" Maksheyev said holding the dog back.

A little farther upstream they came upon the body of another ant, and then a third one. Apparently, the storm had overtaken them and they had been carried downstream by the current.

"These devils must have got all our things soaked and ruined!" Gromeko wailed.

"I doubt if they had enough brains to pitch the tent and hide themselves and all their treasures under it," Papochkin said ironically.

"I think they reached their ant-hill before the storm," Maksheyev said. "Don't forget that they had a good start on us, and twice we stopped to rest for a couple of hours."

They trudged on in silence for two more miles. The forest began to thin out and they caught glimpses of the many paths that crossed it. The sand ridges, and especially the valleys between them, began to come alive with clumps of grass, bushes, and small horsetail.

Suddenly, Maksheyev stopped and drew their attention to the nearest valley between two sand ridges. Two dark shapes were crossing the sand, dragging and rolling a large white ball.

"Are they ants?"

"I think so. What are they dragging? We had nothing round and white like that."

"They must have found it somewhere else."

"Should we get it away from them?"

"No. Let's hide and follow them to the ant-hill."

"Hold on to General or he'll go after them."

They turned, walked back to the edge of the forest, and hid among the trees. Soon the two ants appeared from behind the bushes at the mouth of the valley. They were rolling a large white, egg-shaped object.

"Are their eggs as big as that?" Maksheyev asked.

"No, it's probably some flying lizard's egg they stole and are taking back to the ant-hill," Papochkin answered.

"Do you think lizards' eggs are edible?"

"Why not? If turtle eggs are, these must be also."

"We should bear that in mind," Gromeko said. "An omelette would be a pleasant change, and it would help to save bullets."

"Where can we get a pan to match the size of the egg?"

"Don't worry! We can use a small one. We'll make a hole in the shell and mix the white and yolk with a stick, then we can pour out as much egg as we need at a time."

"That's a good idea—except that we don't own a pan any more, the ants stole it."

"It slipped my mind completely. Perhaps we can make a frying-pan from the shell, by slicing off the top of it and using it for a pan?"

"Then we've no grease."

"We have iguanodon fat."

As they discussed this, the ants had rolled the egg to the river-bank and now they stopped, apparently worried about the steepness of the banks. It would have been easy enough to roll the egg down, as it would not have cracked on the soft sand below, but the problem of getting it up on to the opposite side stumped them.

They scurried back and forth along the bank and round the egg, waving their feelers and touching each other with them, as if discussing what to do.

Finally, one went down into the river-bed and stopped in front of the opposite bank, trying to make up its mind. Then it ran along the bank, stopping frequently to look at the steep incline.

About fifty feet from where it had gone down, it came to a place where the bank was not quite so steep and where it apparently thought the egg could be rolled up. It began to prepare the ground, working with feet and jaws, tearing up clods of earth and dragging them to the side.

The ant that had stayed behind to guard the egg soon got tired of this and scurried down the bank along the river-bed, following the tracks of its partner who was out of its sight beyond a curve in the river-bed.

"Let's get the egg!" Gromeko suggested.

At first they agreed, but then they began to have doubts.

"First, they might notice us, which means giving ourselves away prematurely. Secondly, when they find the egg's gone, they'll start looking for it, so we'll have to hide in the bushes and lose valuable time instead of following them to the ant-hill," Kashtanov said.

Just then Papochkin noticed another pair of ants rolling another egg from the same direction as the first pair had come.

"I think that disposes of all your good reasons for not touching the first egg," he said.

"Well then, let's get to it!"

Maksheyev and Gromeko ran across the river-bed, lifted the heavy egg between them, and carried it back to their hiding-place.

Maksheyev broke off a few ferns, ran down the slope and brushed away their footprints in the sand—just in case the ants were clever enough to notice them and realize what had happened to the egg.

A few minutes later the two ants ran back up the river-bed to the place where they had left the egg. They climbed up the slope and couldn't find it; then they began to run about and up to each other, waving their feelers and evidently at a loss.

The second pair of ants appeared on the scene, rolling the other egg before them. When the first pair saw it, they charged down on the other two, who, they were convinced, had stolen their egg.

It was a free-for-all. The ants rose on their four hind legs, waving their front two and trying to grab their opponents' necks and snap them off with their jaws. In the heat of battle one pair of fighting ants got too near the edge of the bank and tumbled down the slope. When they reached the bottom, one was on top of the other; it saw its chance and nearly severed its enemy's head.

It left it dying and ran to help its comrade. Together they made short work of the other ant and rolled the egg towards the river-bed.

The four men were absorbed in watching the battle but they could not tell which pair had won, as the four insects were identical.

The victors stopped at the edge of the bank to consult; then they rolled the egg down the slope and started rolling it farther upstream.

Every time they saw a slight dip in the opposite bank

they stopped and tried to roll the egg up the slope, but it kept slipping in their claws and rolling back.

When they came to the place where the little path had been dug up the slope they stopped to examine it. Then they tried to drag up the egg by supporting it with their bodies from below.

They finally succeeded and went on along a path that disappeared in the forest. Obviously, the second pair had been victorious.

Now the men had only to follow the ants into ·the forest, but they didn't know how long the journey would be, and so they had to do something about the egg. It was too heavy to carry, and it would be very difficult to roll along the path in the woods. They made a hole in the sand, started a fire in it, and baked the egg whole; then they cut the cooked egg into sections and used the shell for plates.

Afterwards they went into the woods by the too-narrow, well-beaten path. The branches of horsetail were a tangled mass about three feet off the ground and the men were forced to crawl or double over, for the ants seemed to be the only ones who used the path.

In another half-hour the trees began to thin out, the path forked frequently and was intersected by other paths. Maksheyev had to keep his eyes on the ground to follow the track of the egg, while Kashtanov was busy noting the route to make a map of the enemy's territory.

"Don't you think it strange that we haven't seen a single ant in the forest?" Kashtanov asked.

"They probably have regular hours for resting and sleeping, and the other animals don't dare approach the ant-hill."

Then ˳they saw a wide light area ahead, which seemed to indicate the edge of the forest. As it was quite possible that the ant-hill was there, they had to be doubly cautious.

Papochkin, Gromeko, and General stayed behind, while the other two went on to scout.

At the edge of the forest they stopped behind the last few trees and looked around. In front of them was a large piece of waste-land, on which there were only bits of chewed-off stalks sticking up from the ground here and there. A huge flattened cone of a hill stood about a hundred yards away from them. About forty feet high and over one hundred yards in diameter, it was made of tree trunks heaped on top of each other.

Kashtanov focused his binoculars on it and then handed them to Maksheyev. The trunks were not heaped anyhow on top of each other, but formed a definite pattern that was quite complicated, although crudely done. In many places there were dark entrance holes at different levels, but there was not an ant in sight, they must have been sleeping.

The wasteland was completely surrounded by woods, hills, and dunes, and the ants were masters there. There seemed to be a stream in the west, along the foot of the dunes, for a strip of light-green grass and bushes stood out against the reddish sand there.

## COULD THEY ENTER THE ANT-HILL?

The two men went back to the others and sat down to talk things over.

"It won't be difficult to attack the sleeping ant-hill," Kashtanov said, "but do you think that's the right thing to do? After all, we've no idea where our things are in that huge place, and we'd soon get lost in the labyrinth."

"It's probably dark inside and we don't have any candles or flash-lights," Papochkin added.

"We can make torches from the sap of the trees in the forest," Gromeko said.

"Oh, fine! If we go marching along with burning torches we'll have the whole ant-hill on top of us in no time! And I don't think there's any doubt who'll win," Maksheyev said.

"You're right. There are hundreds and thousands of them and, no matter how many we shoot or knife, there'll be enough left to tear us apart or sting us to death."

"What shall we do?" Kashtanov muttered. "We can't just abandon our things, we need them for the journey back."

"Suppose we set fire to the ant-hill from one side? Then the ants will start pulling all their stores and treasures out, including our things too."

"First they'll save their larvae and chrysalises and our things can burn to ashes in the meantime. And then, even if they do drag our stuff out, we'll still have to fight them to get it back."

"Perhaps we should try smoking them out, and then go in for the things when they have left the ant-hill empty?"

"That's a better plan, but we ourselves won't be able to go into the smoke-filled passages, and when they begin to clear of smoke, the ants might come back."

"It doesn't look as if there's much we can do!"

"I've an idea," Maksheyev said. "I'll lie on the ground near the ant-hill and pretend to be dead. The ants will drag me inside and I may have a chance to find out where our things are. Then I'll be able to get them out tomorrow night."

"That's too dangerous," Kashtanov objected. "The ants might not drag you in as you are, but in pieces. Anyway, suppose they do get you inside, in one piece and alive, how in the world will you find your way out later, if you're in complete darkness and pretending to be dead?"

"I'll take a reel of thread and let it out as I go, so that I can retrace my steps, as Theseus did."

"That's all very well, but what if the ants notice the thread and pick it up as you let it out? By the way, have you got a reel of thread?"

Nobody had one, and so the dangerous plan was scrapped. They sat dejectedly, thinking up new plans which, one by one, they had to reject too, as being impossible.

"I've thought of something," Kashtanov said finally. "We'll have to make the ants unconscious with poison gases long enough to let us look for our things. I know of three suitable gases: chlorine, bromine, and sulphur gas. Therefore, we must first find something that we can prepare enough gas from. We can get chlorine from the salt in the sea and we could probably get bromine from the ashes of the seaweed there, but it would be even more difficult to extract than chlorine. The easiest of all would be sulphur gas, if only we could find sulphur, pyrites, or some other sulphur ore. We saw lead glance in Pterodactyl Gorge, and maybe we'll find some here too, in the cliffs round about."

"But think of the time it'll take!" Maksheyev said.

"We've no choice. We've enough bullets to last a few days for hunting, and it's better to have a plan that's least likely to fail. We can always fall back on the more dangerous ones if we have to."

"That means we have to get out of here without touching the thieves!"

"Let's leave before they spot us and get alarmed by our hasty preparations. If they're on the alert, they'll be more cautious and they'll post sentries at the entrances. They'll scout round the forest too and make our plan more difficult to carry out. After all, we don't even know the mental capacity of these rulers of the Jurassic world."

They all agreed with Kashtanov, although they were disappointed at not being able to wipe out the enemy there and then. They decided to go back to the sand dunes and follow the river-bed to the hills in search of sulphur ore or pyrites.

As they went along the edge of the woods towards the river-bed they could see no trace of any animals or even insects; apparently, the ants hunted down every living creature in the vicinity quite methodically. Now and then they noticed a flying lizard passing swiftly above them. The river-bed followed the edge of the waste-land and cut into the sand hills, forming a rather deep valley a little farther upstream. Small bushes and horsetail, sugar reeds, and ferns grew along the banks. They walked a few miles and then decided to stop for a much-needed rest after the excitement of the chase, which had now lasted for a day and a night. There was a lot of water in the river-bed, and the shade of the palm-trees and horsetail was very tempting. They brewed some tea, finished the last of the egg yolk, and had a good night's sleep.

Next morning they saw some ants in the distance. They had a hurried breakfast and set out before their enemies had a chance to spot them.

A few miles upstream the sandy slopes of the valley became rocky, as the river-bed began to cut into a plateau. Maksheyev walked slowly along the right slope, and Kashtanov along the left. They examined every inch of rock for sulphur ores while Papochkin and Gromeko remained near the water to ward off any attacking lizards or ants. They met none, for the country was becoming more barren; even the trees and bushes along the river were thinning out considerably; there remained a narrow strip of sugar reeds and grass along the banks. They were glad of the sugar reed, their only source of food in this barren land.

The only creatures they saw were the giant dragon-flies that darted over the water and several pterodactyls chasing them. The air was very still; Pluto's rays beat down unmercifully on the narrow valley, making the bare slopes hotter than an oven; the closeness of the water made it possible for them to quench their thirst and wet their hair continuously, otherwise they could not have kept going in the heat.

There was no trace of sulphur ores anywhere.

They stopped for lunch on the river-bank, made some tea, sucked the sweet reeds, and divided their last biscuit.

"We'll have to try dragon-flies for supper, or else shoot a pterodactyl!" said Papochkin sadly as he munched his last few crumbs.


## INTO THE BLACK DESERT

Rested, they went farther up the valley. On both sides were the same gloomy black cliffs split and cracked into great clumsy cubes or tall graceful columns. The vegetation along the river-banks consisted solely of grass and sugar reeds.

They stopped for the night at the last dead tree and used it for firewood. They made tea and tried to satisfy their hunger by drinking great quantities of it with the sweet syrup of the sugar reed.

Afterwards Maksheyev and Kashtanov climbed to the top of the cliff. All round them was a flat plain stretching to the horizon, except where it was broken by a group of flat-coned hills about twenty miles to the south.

When they walked away from the edge of the cliff, so that the river valley disappeared from sight, they felt the depressing majesty of the desert before them.

The bare black cliff they stood on was covered with large and small rocks that had cracked off it as a result of the constant heat and was the same as the desert below. There wasn't a blade of grass nor a bush in sight. The earth was black to the edge of the sky, and fiery Pluto blazed overhead. It was an impassable desert that meant certain death from hunger and thirst for anyone foolhardy enough to try to cross its boundless wastes.

It was as hot as a furnace on the black rock, where there was not an inch of shade, and the scorching rays beat down unmercifully. Only the hills to the south broke the black monotony, for they were full of white, red, and yellow spots and streaks.

"I think we're near the end of our journey into this mysterious country," said Kashtanov. "The valley probably ends near those hills over there, and I'm afraid the same bleak desert goes on beyond them. We'd never survive a trip across it without special equipment and large quantities of water, food, and fuel."

"Do you think all the rest of Plutonia is like this burning desert?"

"It probably is, at least as far as the opening at the South Pole, if there is such an opening. Remember, the inner surface gets all its life-giving moisture through these openings, and the sea we crossed is evidently the last reservoir of water."

"But we've already seen that the northern winds are strong enough to carry the moisture farther inland."

"We haven't had much wind recently, except the two hurricanes. Clouds from the north probably rain themselves out over the sea and a small area to the south, and only patches of cloud get as far as the desert. You can see that the air here is never saturated with moisture and it never rains."

"That means we'll have to turn back when we reach those mountains to the south."

"Yes, we'll go as far as that and see if my theory is correct."

"What'll we do if we don't find any sulphur ores on the way?"

"From the shape and colour of those mountains, I'd say they were dead volcanoes, and there's always some sulphur on the slopes of dead volcanoes. I'm nearly sure we'll find what we're looking for there."

"And then we'll go back?"

"We've come so far away from the sea that we might as well go a little farther south, to make sure the desert is *really* impassable and that we did everything humanly possible to explore the land beyond it—only then will our consciences be clear."

"Maybe the sea goes farther southwards at some other point."

"If we get our things back from the ants, we can sail up and down along the coast and find out for ourselves."

After they had been standing on the cliff for some time, looking out at the desert below them, they turned back to have a last look at the far-off sea to the north and the green shore along the water's edge. Then they came down the slope on their way back to camp. As they slid over the loose stones and jumped from rock to rock, they suddenly heard two shots in close succession.

"Do you think the ants have found them?" Kashtanov asked.

"Hurry! There's no time to lose!" Maksheyev shouted. They reached the bottom in a few minutes and ran towards the camp site, but there were no ants in sight.

"What's the matter?" Papochkin asked as the two came panting up.

"That's what we'd like to know," Maksheyev answered.

"You mean the shots? Oh, we were just sitting here when we noticed a black shadow crossing the ground. It was a large pterodactyl circling over the valley which was probably attracted by the sun's reflection in the water-tin. Anyway, we grabbed our guns and fired at it as it circled lower. One of the bullets hit it, and there it is," he said, pointing to a large mass lying a little way off and partly behind the tree.

They had a hearty meal of lizard steaks and slept well,

taking turns to guard the remaining meat which had been laid out on the rocks to dry, as they were afraid some flying lizards might come after it.

The next day they continued up the valley. They were laden with chunks of dried meat, sugar reeds, and firewood, as they doubted that they would find these things farther on. And in fact the valley was becoming more and more desolate, there were hardly any plants at all along the river-banks. They saw no traces of sulphur ores, and Kashtanov was pinning all his hopes on the volçanic hills to the south, which now seemed so close after their long trek over the hot sand. When they were about a mile away from the hills, the valley narrowed into a gorge which led them to a wide basin at the very foot of the great cones.

They were astonished to see a fairly large lake at the bottom of the basin, its rocky banks spotted with green. There were low horsetails, ferns, and sugar reeds growing in clumps on the slopes between the low jagged rocks. The shore was a good place for a camp site where they could leave their extra things when they went into the hills in search of sulphur.

They sat down in the shade of the ferns and suddenly decided to go for a swim in the dark calm waters of the lake. It was like a large smooth mirror in a black wooden frame studded with emeralds. Papochkin was undressed first and dived in bravely, but bolted right out.

"The water's boiling hot!" he shouted as he scrambled up on the bank.

The others dipped their hands or toes in and agreed.

Gromeko pulled out his pocket thermometer—the sole surviving instrument they had, for it was always clipped on to his pocket. He put it in the water: the mercury rose to $104^0$

"That's not too bad," he said. "It's just the temperature of a really hot bath."

A hot bath on a hot day did not sound very refreshing, and they limited their bathing to a good scrubbing, using the fine white silt on the bottom of the lake instead of soap. The silt was even hotter than the water and really burned their feet when they stood on the thick white mat on the bottom, but it was as foamy as soap and a splendid substitute.

"Here's another treasure going to waste in this land of wonders!" Maksheyev said rubbing himself vigorously with a handful of silt.

"A smart man could make a fortune from it. Just think of the advertisements: 'Hurry! Hurry! Nature's own miracle soap! Guaranteed to cure the common cold, asthma, fallen arches, rheumatism, and all the diseases of mankind!'" laughed Gromeko who liked to tease the enterprising businessman in Maksheyev.

"If you really want to make money, we should form a company to export all these living fossils. After all, gold, copper, and iron are nothing new, but every museum and zoo in the world would swamp us with orders for live plesiosaurs, mammoths, or pterodactyls," Papochkin commented from his perch on a rock, where he was getting dry after his bath.

"This hot lake intrigues me," Gromeko said. "I noticed the water in the river was lukewarm, but I thought it was because of the hot rays beating down on the black banks. It's quite clear now that the lake is the source of warm water."

"We're at the foot of these old volcanoes," Kashtanov explained, "and the lake is fed by the springs that come from their hot depths."

"Let's explore the whole lake to see where the springs are," Papochkin suggested.

"You and Gromeko start out while supper's cooking, and we two can have a look at the volcanoes," Kashtanov answered as they finished dressing.

He and Maksheyev walked towards the western part of the lake, where the warm stream flowed from between the black boulders, and began to climb the bare hills that rose at the foot of the volcano. When they had crossed over they found themselves at the first large mountain whose steep slope was covered with lava that had poured from the crater at different times and had hardened on the surface as scallops and chaotic heaps of boulders.

The older lava streams were spotted with yellow, red, and white, and Kashtanov said there was ochre, sulphur, and ammonium chloride there.

"Here's the sulphur we've been looking for, but there's so little of it that it would be very hard to collect. I hope there's more in the crater."

They clambered among the boulders for nearly an hour before they finally reached the top. It was flat, except for a black chasm in the centre.

"What a huge crater!"

"Pity the sides are so steep and smooth."

"Let's walk round the rim. We may come across a break in the wall."

From the top of the mountain they could see for many miles. To the north was the lake in its black-and-emerald frame. It was nearly a perfect circle and might have been the crater of a more ancient volcano. Huge lava streams covered the east and west slopes and disappeared among the ridges and black cliffs on the surface of the desert. To the south was another, larger mountain which seemed to be the main cone of the volcano. It blocked out the entire horizon to the south.

They circled the crater and saw that it would be impossible to try to go down into it, and so they crossed a narrow rocky saddle which led to the other mountain. Its crater was just as large, but there was a huge cavity on the south-eastern edge, where a river of hardened lava—probably from the last eruption—covered the whole side of the volcano.

The cavity in the swell of the crater made it possible to reach the very bottom at no great risk.

From the top they had an unobstructed view to the south. Near the main volcano, there were several smaller ones with caved-in craters, and beyond them the same black sand covered the land to the very horizon.

"There's no sense in going any farther this way!" cried Maksheyev, peering into the distance. "There's nothing but black rock for a hundred miles around."

"And there's no use going sightseeing in this direction," Kashtanov added. "We'll explore the volcanoes and get as much sulphur as we need; then back to the ant-hill to claim our possessions."

The view was indeed depressing.

There was a chain of black hills, broken by deep gorges with yellow, red, and white splotches, as if some giant painter had splattered them with a careless brush; beyond the hills was the flat desert waste. The whole was reddened by Pluto's rays and had a truly menacing look.

"This kingdom of death is more frightening than the ice-fields!" Kashtanov exclaimed.

"Yes, and if there were such a thing as an evil spirit, it could find no better home than this," Maksheyev agreed.

"You've given me a good idea. Let's call this place Black Desert."

"And the volcanoes Satan's Throne. Just imagine that the time has come when Pluto is about to go out, and Plutonia is plunged into a red twilight. The evil spirit in the shape of a giant pterodactyl rises from this crater and soars above the mountains and desert, its screeching and shrieking rend the air. Then it swoops down into the hot waves of the lake and flies up the tall black cliffs to rest and survey its domain . . ."

They walked round the cavity till they found the best place to go down into the crater; then they headed back to the lake, taking a short cut to camp, to guide them in returning for sulphur the next day.

## INTO SATAN'S CRATER

The next day the four men set out for the main volcano. They took a rifle, some fried meat, and sugar reeds in case of emergency, and left General below to guard everything else, as it was very unlikely that anything would happen to the things in the lifeless desert.

They made their way over the low black hills and lava ridges, and then up the slope of the bigger volcano, along the massive lava stream that originated at the cavity in the crater. It took them another half-hour to reach the cavity, and then they began to climb down a huge stairway of hard lava boulders.

At last they were at the bottom, which was like a flat landing, covered with caked, cracked, black dirt which had, apparently, at one time been covered by the water of a little lake. The opposite side rose steeply and had a thick crust of white, yellow, and red streaks and splotches. The yellow parts were large and small crystals of pure sulphur, either wedged in air pockets in the lava or covering its surface with a thin film.

With their hunting knives they began to scrape off the film and pry the larger crystals loose. Only when they had filled their knapsacks with sulphur did they first realize that they each had about forty pounds to carry.

"We can get over 2,500 gallons of sulphur gas from forty pounds of sulphur," Kashtanov said. "That means two hundred pounds will give us nearly ten thousand gallons. It should be enough for the ant-hill."

"We couldn't take any more if we wanted to," Papochkin said. "We still have our guns and some supplies down there, and we'll have to lug everything for nearly two days."

"General can help," Maksheyev said. "He's quite better now, and he's been resting all day today. I think he should be able to carry about seventy-five pounds."

"We can carry his load down to the lake, and I really think we should get some more to be on the safe side."

They had a light lunch and then scraped and chipped off another seventy-five pounds, which Maksheyev tied into his shirt. They even scraped off a handful of salt from one of the cracks in the wall.

As they were resting after lunch Kashtanov stretched out and leaned his head against the side of the crater. Suddenly, he felt several sharp jolts coming from the depths of the mountain.

He wondered if the volcano could still be active.

He said nothing to the others, but a little later he put his ear to the wall again. The rumbling was louder and he could feel the rock trembling slightly.

"I may be wrong," he cried jumping up, "but I don't think we should stay here any longer. There's something going on down there—it may be getting ready to erupt! Listen!"

They all leaned towards the wall and heard the far-off rumbling.

"Perhaps nothing will happen at all. Or there may be an eruption in a week or a month, but I can't guarantee it won't take place today!" Kashtanov said.

"Right! There's no sense in sitting here, especially as we have a hard climb up to the edge of the crater ahead of us," Gromeko added.

They hoisted the heavy packs on to their backs and started climbing the giant stairway. Clambering up with heavy loads took them twice as long as scrambling down with empty knapsacks, and it was an hour before they reached the top of the mountain. They looked down and saw that they had been right to hurry: a thin wisp of yellow smoke was rising from the depths of the crater and the air began to smell of sulphur and chlorine.

The sides of the crater shook noticeably. They wasted no time in getting down, for the lava cork might fly out of the crater at any minute. Two hours later they were back in camp. General was feeling quite lonely by then and barked joyfully when he saw them coming.

The volcano was taking its time. A thin straight pillar of dark smoke rose high above the mountain top and vanished in the distant air. No underground noises could be heard near the lake and everything was calm and quiet.

As they stacked their knapsacks on the ground next to the rest of their things, Papochkin suddenly realized that he had left his gun either in the crater, or at the top of the mountain where they stopped to rest. He said he was going to fetch it.

"We have three other guns, and there's a spare one in the ant-hill, so we can manage without that one. It's senseless to run such a risk when we've just escaped from there," Kashtanov said.

"The mountain's only smoking," Papochkin insisted. He was fond of his old shot-gun and bothered by his own absent-mindedness. "I'll have time to get there and back while you're resting."

"You probably left it on the floor of the crater, but you can't go down there because the poisonous gas would kill you." Kashtanov tried to talk him out of it.

"You're wrong. I'm nearly positive I left it at the edge of the crater *before* we climbed down, to save having to carry it down and then up again for nothing. It's not as dangerous as you think. I'll be there and back in no time," Papochkin said.

"The whole mountain could blow up any minute. I

don't know if it's wise even to stay here overnight. Perhaps we should start walking away now."

But they were all exhausted from their day of climbing. The volcano didn't seem very menacing, and the lake was about a mile and a half from it. They decided to spend the night on the bank in the hope of witnessing at least the beginning of a volcanic eruption.

The quiet lasted four brief hours. Then they were jolted out of their dreams by a terrific crash and the earth moving under them. They felt as if they had been tossed up into the air and were falling into the lake.

They jumped up and looked round fearfully. The earth was trembling, and the trees at the edge of the lake were swaying in all directions.

The top of the mountain was enveloped in a thick cloud of black smoke; white-hot stones shot out of the crater and pierced the black cloud as streaks of lightning.

This was the beginning.

"Where's Papochkin?" Maksheyev shouted, noticing there were only three of them.

"Maybe the jolt landed him in the water—he was nearest the edge," Gromeko said.

The surface of the water was rippled by the trembling earth but there were no circles indicating that something heavy had been thrown into the water.

"Do you think he might have gone back to get his gun?" Kashtanov asked.

That seemed most probable, for he was very stubborn and might have waited till the others had fallen asleep and then set out for the mountain.

After hallooing and searching without result, they decided he must have gone to get his gun.

"I hope he wasn't at the top of the mountain when the eruption began, for he would certainly be killed," Kashtanov said.

"What shall we do?" Maksheyev exclaimed. "I think we should try to get to him!"

"Let's wait," Gromeko said. "It takes three or four hours from here to the floor of the crater and back. If he left as soon as we fell asleep, then he should be back in an hour, or less."

"And meanwhile we can judge from the course of the eruption whether we can reach the crater without getting killed on the way."

"But don't you understand—we'll be sitting here twiddling our thumbs when we could be on our way to him!"

"We *do* understand, but we can save him only if he didn't reach the crater. If he was at the top of the mountain or in the crater at the time it erupted, then he's been killed, if not by flying rocks, then by poisonous gases. If we try to climb the mountain now, we won't save him anyway and we'll risk the whole expedition being killed. Look!"

A huge white cloud of steam shot upwards from the crater.


## THE ROARING VOLCANO

A few seconds later there was a deafening roar. It seemed as if the whole mountain had blown up or shot up into the sky. The cloud rushed downhill, mushrooming out and turning into a purple-black mass that billowed, fumed, and swirled, and was slashed by blinding flashes of lightning. The black mass was coming down at the speed of an express train. In a few minutes it had reached the foot of the mountain, while great bursts kept rising high over the peak.

"It's like what I've heard of the terrible eruption of Mont Pelé on Martinique in 1902. The entire population of St. Pierre was wiped out within a few minutes," Kashtanov said. "It's a so-called burning or scorching cloud composed of tremendously compressed and overheated steam and gases, along with hot ashes, pebbles, and even huge rocks and boulders," he explained.

"We're lucky the cloud is heading out towards the desert and not towards the lake," Gromeko said.

"What happens now?" Maksheyev asked.

"These scorching clouds usually follow each other within a certain time—so many hours or days—and then comes the lava."

"Is there any chance that the other clouds will blow towards us?"

"If the rim of the crater hasn't changed after the first great explosion, the other clouds should take the same direction as the first. Otherwise they'll change their course."

"Towards us?"

"Yes. But meantime let's hope for the best. Actually, we're relatively safe here; at least for the moment."

The cloud had spread, covering a large part of the eastern slope; then it began to get higher. The three men stood in silence, watching the terrible, yet magnificent scene.

Suddenly, Papochkin came over the top of the hill nearest to the foot of the mountain. He was running as fast as he could, jumping over rocks. They ran towards him, showering him with questions which he had no breath to answer.

Only after he had rested in the shade by the lake and drunk two glasses of cold tea, could he tell them what had happened to him.

"I decided to go after my gun, because I didn't think the volcano was ready to blow up for a long time yet. I hoped the gun was at one of the two places where we stopped to rest when we first climbed the mountain, or at least at the top. So I waited till you'd all fallen asleep and started out about ten o'clock. I couldn't find the gun at the first camp site, so I climbed higher. But it wasn't at the second site either. By then I was only about half a mile from the top and the accursed crater was still smoking faintly. I hated to turn back.

"I was near the cavity in the crater and I was sure I could see my gun propped against a boulder about a hundred feet away. Then there was a terrific roar, and a column of smoke shot straight up from the crater. I stopped, not knowing what to do. It was too dangerous to go farther and yet it seemed a shame to leave my gun there, just ahead of me. Little stones and clods of dirt, raining down on me, brought me to my senses, for one stone hit me right on the shoulder. I can hardly move my arm. I felt that the second explosion would not be long after the first, and it would bring the big, red-hot stones. So I started down the bumpy slope at top speed and heard the second explosion when I had run about half a mile. The top of the mountain was covered by smoke. The stones came raining down about me again, and I kept on running downhill. The last terrible explosion caught me near the foot of the mountain and knocked me down with such force that I nearly dislocated both arms. As I scrambled to my feet, I saw the cloud coming towards me and I gathered my last strength to escape from its gases."

"You don't know how lucky you were to get away in time!" Kashtanov said as Papochkin finished.

"Let's just be thankful he's back, and try to think what to do next," Maksheyev said.

"We should get as far away as possible from this choking mountain!" cried Papochkin.

"You're in no state to go anywhere now, after yesterday's exertions, plus your sprint just now. Get some sleep, we can certainly wait another two hours."

"Shouldn't we move back a few miles first?" Maksheyev

suggested. "We're at the very foot of the mountain here and its nearness is getting dangerous."

Gromeko was of the same opinion, and they decided to go back to the Black Desert, near the edge of the gorge, at the junction of the lake and the river valley. From there they would have a good view of the erupting volcano. They filled their water-tin, strapped on their heavy knapsacks, tied two sacks of sulphur together, and slung them over General's back. At first he protested and tried to squirm out from under the heavy load, but then he accepted his fate and trailed along slowly with the men instead of dashing about, looking for something to eat.

They climbed the low ledges from the lake basin to the Black Desert and walked about two miles over the sand to the place where the gorge widened out into the river valley. The eruption seemed to have stopped for the moment; the first scorching cloud was lifting, the peak was clear of smoke, and a thin black column rose from the crater.

They made themselves comfortable on the sand and dozed off. They had been sleeping for about three hours when another terrible explosion woke them up and drew their eyes to the crater. A sinister cloud had risen from the depth of the mountain and was spreading rapidly down the slope, but this time it was heading straight for the lake. Kashtanov timed its speed. The cloud was mushrooming as the first one had done and became a wall of purple-grey. Four minutes after the explosion it reached the lake and engulfed it.

"The cloud is travelling at the rate of forty miles an hour! That's the speed of an express train!" Kashtanov exclaimed. "It's about $80^0$ off the other one's course, probably because of a change in the rim of the crater. Good thing we got out of there, otherwise we would have been burned and choked to death in the overheated steam and ashes that form the main part of the cloud, or else we'd have been killed by the hot stones. The cloud can lift boulders up to about twenty cubic feet and carry them several miles. It destroys everything in its wake, leaving behind it a bleak strip of hot ashes, stones, charred trees, and dead bodies."

"What's happened to the lake?"

"It's full of hot ashes and stones, and the river flowing out of it has turned into a dirty hot stream—at least for the present."

Just then the cloud passed over the lake basin and headed towards the Black Desert, about two miles from the men. A strong, scorching blast of wind made them drop to the ground and cover their faces. They lay sweating profusely for about half an hour, waiting for a drop in temperature.

They looked up and saw a long, high wall of billowing white and grey steam extending for about six miles beyond them and rising five thousand feet into the sky. The air was still hot and stifling.

"Let's get away from this terrible mountain!" Gromeko said. "The next cloud might come rolling this way."

"If this is what it's like two miles from the edge of the cloud, you can imagine what it's like in the middle!"

They gathered up their belongings and crossed the sand, heading north towards the river valley, as they intended to go down into it at the first convenient place. But they found that the clear, calm little stream was now a turbulent dirty-white torrent which had overflowed its banks and was rushing down the valley, destroying all the plants on either bank.

"Is there any point in going down there?" Kashtanov asked the others. "I think it would be easier to walk across the even desert than along the sandy bottom of the valley, and we can't drink that filthy water anyway."

It was agreed to continue along the edge of the desert and go down when they reached the end of the valley, for there were deep ravines in the slopes there. They walked over to the edge of the cliff occasionally to look down. About an hour after the second explosion the swift torrent began to diminish and it soon disappeared completely. They saw nothing but the bare river-bed, the uprooted trees and bushes along the banks, and grass that was plastered to the ground and full of dirty-white silt.

"The volcano got even with us for pinching its sulphur," Maksheyev said. "It did away with the stream to make us die of thirst."

"Yes, we'll be hard up for water now," Gromeko said. "We'll have to ration what we have till we find another stream somewhere near the ant-hill."

"That may delay our siege."

In spite of their heavy packs and the unbearable heat of the Black Desert, the little band plodded doggedly on. They didn't stop for the night until they were at the bottom of the valley, not far from where it opened on to the plateau and the ant-hill.

Kashtanov and Maksheyev went ahead to study the enemy's fortress at close range. They climbed up from the valley and walked east along the black sand and the edge of the cliffs, from where they had a good view of the ant-hill.

At close range it was a huge hill, divided into different levels by the intricate arrangement of dry tree trunks and branches. The main entrances were on the ground floor—one at each of the four sides of the hill. They were not high, but they were wide enough for four or five ants abreast to pass through them. There was a constant stream of ants going in and out. Long columns left the ant-hill and dispersed in different directions in their search for food; others returned singly and in pairs, dragging tree trunks and branches, live and dead insects, larvae and chrysalises, and sugar reeds into the catacombs of their fortress.

There were many dark openings in the upper floors too, but they seemed to be for ventilation or for use as emergency exits in case of a sudden attack. They were lower and narrower than the main entrances, and the ants could pass through them only in single file. Every now and then ants would come out of these holes and run up and down the ledges, as if they were checking to see that everything was in order.

"I hope all these openings won't spoil our plans," Maksheyev said. "If there are too many draughts in the ant-hill, the sulphur gas will blow right through it before it has a chance to do its job."

"No, you're wrong. This gas is heavier than air, and it displaces it very gradually," Kashtanov said. "Besides, the strategic points in the ant-hill are the chambers with the larvae, chrysalises, eggs, and food stores, and these are probably at the bottom, maybe in underground chambers. The gas will go down into these chambers first and from there it will begin to rise and fill the upper floors. If the worst comes to the worst, we can block off some of the exits to lessen the draught."

"Why not burn some of the sulphur at the openings on the top floors?"

"We'd burn down the whole ant-hill for we've no insulating mats, or even frying-pans, and we'd have to put the sulphur on the dry wood."

"What about the iguanodon's egg-shell that we've been using for plates and a pan these past few days?"

"We've only five pieces of shell, and there are far more exits than that."

"Why not try to find a few more eggs today? Even if we find only two, we'll be able to make ten bowls for burning the sulphur in."

"That's a good idea! It's a long time till evening and we can go back to the desert to see where the ants get the eggs."

They turned round and went back to camp, where they discussed their new plan.

It was decided that the other two would set out for lizard eggs the next morning, while Maksheyev and Kashtanov would be busy pounding the sulphur into powder.

## THE END OF THE ANT-HILL

When the last ants had returned home the next evening and everything grew quiet inside the ant-hill, the men were ready to go into action. It had taken almost all day to pound the sulphur into powder. They filled their knapsacks, took the egg-shell bowls, and set out for the ant-hill. Each man was to place a certain amount of powder at one of the four main entrances, arranging it in a strip across the passage, so that the gas would go deep into the ant-hill. Once they had set the sulphur on fire, they would block the opening with tree trunks taken from the surrounding walls; then they were to climb along the trunks to the nearest openings, where they would put the bowls with the remaining sulphur, to poison all the air in the lower part of the ant-hill and prevent the ants from escaping upwards. To keep the sulphur in the bowls from burning too quickly and setting fire to the dry logs of the ant-hill, they damped the powder slightly with water.

Everything went according to plan. Maksheyev and Gromeko came upon sentry-ants in their entrances, but luckily, the insects were half-asleep, and had no time to send out an alarm before the two men stabbed them.

When they had set fire to all the sulphur, they retreated, their rifles ready in case any of the ants tried to escape. About fifteen minutes later they noticed ants in several of the exits on the very top floors, where they had left no sulphur. The ants were dragging large white bundles, probably chrysalises; they scurried about, picking their way down the outside scaffolding, but kept dropping before they reached the ground, because they had been affected by the sulphur fumes rising from the main entrances. A few ants which succeeded in reaching the ground began feverishly dragging away the logs that blocked one of the main entrances, trying to save their choking comrades inside. The unexpected rescuers were finished off by a few shots; no more ants appeared after that: the rest of the population of the ant-hill had been trapped as they slept.

When the sulphur had burned away and wisps of blue smoke drifted from every opening in the ant-hill as proof that the whole structure was full of gas, Papochkin asked a very logical question that none of them had thought of before:

"How are we going to get inside now? The gas is just as poisonous to us as it is to them!"

"We'll have to pull the logs away from the main entrances to increase the draught and then wait a couple of days for the gas to clear," Kashtanov answered.

"It's going to be dull sitting here with nothing to do for so long," Maksheyev said. "Can't we do something to blow out the gas?"

"What with? We can't use fire or we'll burn the whole place down, and we've nothing else at our disposal."

"If we shot an iguanodon or a large pterodactyl," Maksheyev said, "I could make a bellows from the hide."

"That sounds good! But what can we use for pipes to blow the air deep into the passage-ways?"

"Can't we use horsetail?" suggested Gromeko. "The stems are hollow, all we have to do is to pierce through the partitions between the separate nodes and we'll have fine long pipes. Then we can connect them."

"Necessity is the mother of invention!" Papochkin cried.

"We're sure to find a way out of any predicament—just like Robinson Crusoe."

"In fact, better than old Crusoe," Kashtanov said. "We'd have cause to be ashamed of ourselves if we couldn't find a way out of any difficulty by putting our heads together."

"Well, let's get down to business!" Maksheyev said. "Two of us will take General and go after a lizard, and the other two will stay here and make the pipes; there's plenty of material, for most of the ant-hill is made of dry horsetail stalks."

Papochkin and Gromeko went back to the camp site, untied General, and brought their things nearer to the ant-hill; then they went east, along the edge of the forest.

Maksheyev and Kashtanov walked to within twenty feet of the ant-hill, but could get no closer, for there was a strong smell of sulphur gas which set them coughing.

"We'll have to wait a while longer."

"We can get a supply of putty for the pipes in the meantime," Maksheyev suggested. "There was a lot of sticky white stuff left in the river-bed after the torrent ran off, and we can bring some here before it hardens."

They took their empty knapsacks to the river-bed, and after a few trips had a huge pile of soft mud that was as good as putty. They covered the pile with their knapsacks and extra clothes to protect it from Pluto's hot rays.

Then they began to split the horsetail stalks lengthwise, using their knives, wedges, and a large stone for a hammer; they cut out the partitions between the nodes and joined the two halves with putty, tying the new pipe in several places with flexible twigs.

Within a few hours they had made a dozen pipes each about twenty feet long. As the stalks were much thinner at the top, it was easy to link them by putting the narrow end of one pipe, generously smeared with putty, into the wide end of another.

Soon the other two men returned with an iguanodon hide.

Maksheyev used thin stalks of horsetail to make a frame for the bellows which they set up near one of the main entrances. Then they began to move the pipes into the passage-way, thin end first, pushing them in a little way at a time and adding new sections to the wide end. Soon all twelve pipes had disappeared in the dark gallery. As the entrance was still full of gas, they kept running off to a side every few minutes to fill their lungs with fresh air. At last they stuck the wide end of the last pipe into the bellows and secured it firmly: the home-made ventilator was complete.

After supper they took turns to work the bellows, so that three rested or slept while one kept a steady stream of fresh air blowing through the ant-hill. Soon the gas was pouring out of every crack.

By morning they were ready to enter the fortress. They lit the torches which Gromeko had prepared from the dry trunk of a pine-tree rich in sap. The gallery where they had laid the pipeline ran through the ant-hill and sloped down gently. It was over six feet wide but less than five feet high, and so they had to bend as they walked. They came upon the first bodies of the dead ants right near the entrance, and the farther they went the more bodies there were, so that by the time they reached the end of the ventilator pipe, they had to push the bodies aside before they could go on.

The gallery ended in a large central chamber to which the other three main entrances also led. The chamber was about twelve feet below ground, and the ceiling was made of stalks of horsetail, laid out in an intricate radial pattern like the rafters of a circus tent. There were four other passages off the chamber between the four main entrances, but they led down and outwards from the centre and were completely underground, dug in the hard-packed ocean sand and the layers of gravel running through it. The chamber was jammed with the bodies of ants and the larvae and chrysalises that they had been trying to save, and the men had to climb over the heaps.

They picked a lower passage-way at random. It was as low-ceilinged as the upper passages, and to be able to move at all, they had to stack the bodies in two rows along the walls, clearing a path in the middle. The passage kept going down, and about seventy feet from the central chamber it led into a transverse gallery which was about six feet high, so that they could at last straighten out. The gallery ran under the entire circumference of the ground floor of the ant-hill and was its main thoroughfare. To left and right of it were chambers of different sizes, intended for different purposes: in one they saw row upon row of white chrysalises; in another dead larvae—thick white worms—lay scattered and in heaps; in a third were ant-eggs that looked like large loaves of yellowish bread. All these chambers were on the inner side of the circular gallery, and the chambers along the outer side were food store-rooms: there were piles of sugar reeds, young bushes and grasses, and all kinds of insects—dragonflies, beetles, worms, and caterpillars— either whole or torn apart. The stench was so strong that even the remaining fumes of sulphur gas could not kill it.

They searched the chambers on both sides of the circular gallery till finally they came upon their belongings. Everything had been put in a row in one of the outer chambers. The tent, the raft, the boxes with instruments and supplies, the canvas bags with their clothes, the axe, the gun, the dishes, and even the iron and gold samples they had brought back from their first trip into the canyon and had not packed away with the rest of the collection—everything was there.

To take the things out, the first had to take them up to the central chamber, and then out of the ant-hill into the air that seemed so refreshing after the hour they had spent underground in the stench of rotting insects and the fumes of sulphur gas.

They had a rest and went through their possessions, and were delighted to find their tins of tobacco, as they had had none for a week. They decided to explore the upper floors of the ant-hill to get a better idea of how it was constructed.

The structure above ground was mainly a means of protecting the underground one from rain and possible enemies. The passage-ways there were also built on a radial system and were narrow and low; they converged in a small central chamber on each floor. There were short, steep passages connecting the floors.


## SAILING WEST

After their long journey through the Black Desert and the arid region around the ant-hill, where the only water they had was dirty, as they collected it with great difficulty from a hole dug in the bottom of the river-bed, they were overjoyed to see the beach once more, and had a long swim in the Sea of Lizards. They unearthed their boats and sailed farther on.

Their climb up the volcano had given Kashtanov a fair idea of the surrounding country, and he had little hope of their being able to go farther south. He felt certain there was bleak, waterless desert for many thousands of miles into the interior, south of the Sea of Lizards, and the present expedition had not the means to explore the desert.

On the other hand, they ought to see as much as they could of the land along the western part of the sea.

They sailed close to the shore for twenty-five miles; it was a solid chain of huge sand dunes. Then the dunes finally disappeared; the sea grew very shallow, and there were many large reddish shoals that forced them away from the coastline. There were no plesiosaurs or ichthyosaurs near the shore, as they preferred the deep water, but between the shoals were whole schools of small fishes hiding from the big fishes and lizards. In some places the sea bed was completely covered by exotic seaweed of every description that both Papochkin and Gromeko hastened to add to their collections, for there were starfish, sea urchins, and fantastic molluscs in great numbers among the seaweed.

Along the beach was a narrow forest strip of horsetail, ferns, and palm-trees. They stopped for lunch and then resumed their journey. The number of shoals was increasing steadily, and low islands overgrown with reeds and small horsetail slipped by the boats. The reddish peaks of the dunes were barely visible beyond the tree-tops, there were more and more islands, and the sea was changing into a large, calm river with many branches. There was hardly any salt in the water.

"There's probably a large river flowing into the sea from the west, and this must be its delta," Kashtanov said.

"Too bad there's no surf and no beach. It was so easy to pitch the tent on the sand," Maksheyev sighed.

"We'll have to spend the night in the woods and be eaten alive by swarms of insects," Papochkin complained.

They were already surrounded by insects: there were many-coloured dragon-flies in the air, the droning of giant mosquitoes could be heard from the thicket, and enormous red, black, and bronze beetles kept crawling up the stalks, sometimes falling into the water, and thrashing about there, trying to catch hold of the overhanging leaves.

They sailed up the river for a few hours, between the low southern bank, overgrown by a dense forest, and the labyrinth of islands, none of which offered a clear space for camping.

They had no choice but to tie up the boats at the shore,

rest in them, and have a dry meal, as there was no fuel left. They were depressed to think of the long battle against the mosquitoes that was ahead of them.

However, a small incident did much to raise their spirits. They were sailing very close to a large island, looking for a dry tree among the endless green of horsetail and small ferns.

"Hooray!" shouted Gromeko suddenly, as the boats turned a bend, and they could see a new stretch of shore. "Look at that log! It might have been left there just for us!"

They saw sticking way out of the thicket a thick greygreen log that looked like the trunk of a horsetail which had been knocked over during a storm. They rowed faster and brought the boats up to the edge of the thicket.

Maksheyev stood up in the prow, ready to catch the log with his boat-hook; Gromeko had a long rope with a weight on the end which he was going to throw round the log to pull it into the boat. He tossed it swiftly, and the weighted end wrapped itself several times round the log. Then, the log bent over gracefully and disappeared in the thicket, carrying off the rope, which Gromeko had let go in astonishment. The ferns and horsetail cracked and swayed as if some huge creature were trampling them.

"A wonderful log, eh?" Maksheyev got out with difficulty through his laugther, for he had seen a small head on the end of the "log." "Mikhail decided to lasso a lizard! Why did you let go? You should have pulled him into the boat!"

"He must have had his eyes closed when he decided the lizard's neck was a log! Ha-ha-ha!" Papochkin and Kashtanov were wiping away tears of laughter.

"It was standing absolutely still with its body hidden behind the trees." The flustered botanist tried to justify himself.

"Ha-ha-ha!" the others roared.

"There's nothing to laugh at!" Gromeko said angrily.

"I'd like to remind you of the time someone took a couple of mammoths for some basalt hills, and the time someone went riding on a glyptodont that he was hammering away at, because he thought it was a boulder!"

This only added to the general merriment, and he finally began to laugh himself.

They forgot their fatigue, the mosquitoes, and the lack of fuel as they tried to see who could remember the funniest incident from their underground travels.

When the laughter had died down a bit, Maksheyev said:

"I can hear the surf somewhere ahead. It must be the open sea."

The rowers lifted their oars from the water and listened: yes, a faint noise was coming from the west.

"Come on then! Where there's surf there's driftwood, and a good place to pitch a tent."

"Let's fill our water-tins here where the water's fresh," Gromeko suggested. "Otherwise we'll have to go looking for another stream."

They filled every available vessel with water and then rowed swiftly on. Half an hour later they sailed out of the labyrinth of islands. The banks widened, revealing the open sea as far as the horizon in the west. The southern shore had turned into a wide sandy beach where they camped for the night.

The second sea was linked with the first by a long, narrow strait, abounding in islands and shoals, and was actually a continuation of the Sea of Lizards.

The northern shore was a green mass of trees, and on the southern shore they could see dark cliffs beyond the forest strip. The air was full of dragon-flies; flying lizards circled over them, croaking and whistling shrilly; from time to time plesiosaurs raised their heads and necks from the water.

"Do you think we could have got mixed up among the

islands and gone back to the Sea of Lizards?" Papochkin said as they commented on the similarity of the two seas.

"They do seem very much alike. But you've forgotten the sand dunes on the southern shore there. Suppose we have our directions mixed—after all, we can't use Pluto as a guide when it's shining directly overhead for twenty-four hours a day—suppose, then, we're sailing east instead of west, we should have come in sight of the sand dunes long ago," Kashtanov said.

"There's no river flowing from the south, which means we can't go any farther that way," Gromeko despaired.

"Cheer up! It's not as bad as all that!"

They had a difficult time trying *not* to despair, for next morning they sailed several hours without noticing any change in the southern bank; it had the same wall of trees at the water's edge, and the same cliffs beyond, for miles on end. They were getting bored and restless. The plesiosaurs, flying lizards, and dragon-flies were no longer curiosities, as there were so many of them, and the men paid no more attention than if they had been ducks, crows, or beetles on some river on earth. Several times ichthyosaurs broke the monotony by appearing suddenly out of the water close to the boats, and they reached for their guns at the sight of the wide dark-green backs, or ugly heads of the terrible creatures.

## SUPERMONSTERS

Half the day went by, and the tired oarsmen were scanning the shore for driftwood and a place to stop for lunch. They had caught a lot of fish during the morning and wanted to fry it.

"Look, there are piles of logs over there," Maksheyev said at last.

They headed towards the shore and could all but taste the fried fish already.

When they were a few hundred feet away from the logs, Kashtanov took a good look at them and said:

"Those aren't piles of logs at all. They're some kind of gigantic dead or sleeping animals."

"Let's get away from the shore!" Maksheyev shouted, for he noticed that the heap was stirring.

They stopped the boats about two hundred feet away and watched in terrified fascination. Four monsters lay beside each other on the sand like four long, high hills. There was a flat narrow ridge along their spines; it had no spikes or plates like the stegosaurs', but was very smooth and, apparently, quite bare. Their sides were sandy-yellow with long, narrow stripes running lengthwise along their bodies, and it was this that made the creatures look like piled-up logs from a distance.

Even from so close up it was hard to believe that these were not four piles of logs, but fifty feet long monsters. The piles heaved up and down at every breath; sometimes they shuddered, and their tails moved in the water, rippling the clear surface.

"I wonder how we can get them to stand up," Papochkin said. "We should get a good look at them and a few pictures too."

"It would be easy to send a few bullets into those heaps," Maksheyev said, "but I think there's a real chance we'd be the losers this time. If those fellows got mad they could swallow us, boats and all, at one gulp."

"Are they carnivorous or herbivorous?" Gromeko wondered. "It's quite clear that they're enormous lizards."

"I don't think they're carnivorous," Kashtanov said. "They were never so big, because they would have needed too much fresh meat to keep going, and Nature has always been very economical in that respect. After all, none of the modern monsters—the elephants, rhinoceroses, hippopotamuses, or whales—are meat-eaters."

"Let's shoot one! Think of all that meat! It's enough for a regiment," said Gromeko reaching for his rifle.

"Wait a while," Kashtanov warned him. "Even if they're not meat-eaters, they can still rush towards us in their rage and sink our boats."

"Well then, let's fire a shot into the air, or try some buck-shot, to wake them up," Gromeko kept insisting. "Buck-shot will only tickle them."

"All right. But let's get opposite them and at least a hundred feet off shore. If they *are* land animals, they won't come in so far after us."

When the boats had come abreast of the monsters, Gromeko let them have a double dose of buck-shot. It was either that or the loud report of the gun that made the creatures jump up.

They waved their long necks about awkwardly and then made off along the shore, joggling from side to side as they ran. Their legs seemed short and weak compared with their massive bodies, and the tiny heads looked silly as they bobbed up and down.

"They must be brontosaurs," Kashtanov said. "They were the largest herbivorous lizards of the Upper Jura, but they died out quickly, because they were so clumsy and had no means of defending themselves."

"Who'd ever dare to attack these giants? They're at least fifty feet long and about fifteen feet high," Maksheyev said.

"A ceratosaur wouldn't think twice about chewing up one of those monsters, to say nothing of devouring its eggs and young ones."

"There don't seem to be many of them about, and this is the first time we've actually come across any," Papochkin noted. "Since they're so cowardly, I suggest that we move closer in to get a better picture."

The lizards ran off down the beach in the same direction as the men were sailing. They stopped about half a mile away, and soon the boats were abreast of them once more. Papochkin took two photographs and was about to snap a third, when he asked Gromeko to startle the lizards with some buck-shot to make them run.

Gromeko fired straight at them from close range. The men were not at all prepared for what followed. Instead of running away along the beach as they had done before, the monsters rushed into the water, jostling each other and churning up huge waves and fountains of spray that soaked the men in the boats. Gromeko, who was standing in the prow, was hit fair and square by a wave; he lost balance and tumbled into the water, still holding on to his gun. Papochkin barely had time to shove the camera under his jacket as he met the wave head-on. Kashtanov and Maksheyev had been rowing, and both had had the presence of mind to hang on to their oars. With all their strength they steadied the boats against the onrushing waves and kept them from capsizing.

If the monsters had headed straight towards the men it would have meant certain death, for the boats would have been crushed and sunk by the gigantic bodies. But the lizards were running at an angle, as if they hadn't even noticed their attackers, and they didn't stop until the water covered their bodies and most of their necks.

Four ugly heads stuck out of the foaming water and kept twisting and turning, trying to get a good look at their strange enemies and understand what had happened.

Gromeko had surfaced by then and was swimming towards the boats, which had been carried off by the waves. He had not dropped his rifle and was holding it above his head as he waited for Maksheyev to help him into the boat.

He was dripping wet and so was everything he had on him: his notebook, watch, first-aid kit, and tobacco pouch. He had lost his pipe in the course of his ducking.

"We'll have to go ashore," he said after he had stopped fuming. "If we don't dry the instruments immediately they'll rust, and all my notes will vanish if I don't dry my notebook at a fire."

"What about the brontosaurs?" Papochkin said in alarm. "We'll make ourselves at home on the shore and then they'll crawl out of the water and decide to get better acquainted."

"Well, that'll be your golden opportunity to get a close-up shot of them."

"Thanks! If they feel like romping about near our camp site, we'll have to make a dash for the nearest trees in the forest."

"I don't think they're very bright," Kashtanov said, "and I don't think they'll present any real danger if we're more careful in future. Let's land and have something to eat while we're watching them."

They went ashore, gathered some dry firewood at the edge of the forest, and started preparing their lunch, while keeping a wary eye on the monsters which were still up to their necks in the water and were reluctant to come out.

"I don't think they can swim," Papochkin said. "They seem to have taken refuge in the water and they'll probably stay there till we leave."

While the fish was frying, Gromeko spread out his clothes to dry on the sand, and began to clean his instruments and dry his notebook. They breakfasted and rested, watching the motionless lizards.

When Gromeko had dressed, they went back to the boats and set off westward again. Soon they noticed that the southern bank was beginning to retreat quite noticeably southwards, but the long wooded cape that lay before them blocked their view. When they had rounded it, they saw that their hopes that the sea would extend far to the south, making it possible for them to continue by boat into the interior, were unfounded. There was a large bay there, and they could see the opposite shore a few miles away.

On the chance that there might be a large river flowing into the bay from the south, they decided to go on. An hour later they reached the southern shore, where they found a smaller river than they had hoped for. They decided that two of them would take one of the boats and explore the river and the countryside beyond the wall of trees along the water's edge. They camped on a clearing at the mouth of the river, and Gromeko and Maksheyev stayed behind, as painful experience had taught them that it was not safe to leave General on guard alone. There might be other ants in that part of the bay, as it was quite far away from the poisoned ant-hill.

## KASHTANOV'S FIRE-SHIP

Kashtanov and Papochkin took a change of clothes, several days' supply of food, and ammunition in one of the boats and started out upstream. The river was shallow, but its current was rather swift, and so instead of rowing they punted with poles. The narrow river flowed between palms, ferns, and horsetail that often formed a closed canopy above the water, shutting out the sun and daylight.

It was cool and dark; the boat slid along noiselessly, and the only sounds were the creaking of the poles as they scraped the pebbly bottom and the swish of the prow cutting through the water.

There were darting dragon-flies and buzzing beetles in the open stretches of water where the green canopy lifted and the wind rustled through the palms and ferns along the shore.

A few miles upstream the green corridor ended abruptly, and the river passed through a large open space where several kinds of short, stubby grass grew sparsely.

"Do you think the river has its source near the volcanoes we've already explored?" Papochkin asked.

"Perhaps. In that case we're wasting our time," Kashtanov said. "On the other hand, there seems to be quite a lot of water in this river. Maybe its upper reaches are beyond the volcanoes, farther into the Black Desert."

They went upstream through the open space for about two more miles. Then they suddenly noticed a big log lying across the river at a place where it narrowed considerably. It was too low for them to sail under it.

"I'm quite ready to believe that someone built a bridge across the water," laughed Papochkin. "At any rate, we'll have to get out and pull the log away."

"It really does look like a bridge!" Kashtanov exclaimed when they had gone ashore and found that the barrier consisted of three logs, laid carefully side by side.

"It seems very unlikely that the river did it all by itself," Papochkin agreed. "But if it is a bridge, who built it? Do you think there are people here? That would be really interesting!"

"There were no superior mammals in the Jura, you know that! Even the so-called 'birds' were still lizards."

"Well, no lizard ever built a bridge like that!"

"You're forgetting the ants. If they can build such a complicated and well-planned structure as an ant-hill, they're surely capable of throwing a bridge across a river, for they can't swim and they're afraid of water."

"You're right! There's another ant-hill!" cried Papochkin pointing westwards.

Towering over the meadow was a giant ant-hill, exactly like the one they had poisoned.

They tossed the light, dry horsetail logs into the water and went back to the boat. To their astonishment an ant was in it, inspecting their belongings, while another stood guard on the bank.

"Look at that—our guns are in the boat!"

"Get your knife out, we'll rush the one on the bank first. I'll distract its attention while you get it from behind."

They both ran towards the ant, which backed towards a little bush and took up a defensive position. As it watched Kashtanov advance with his knife bared, Papochkin leaned over the bush and slashed the ant in two.

He didn't notice the ant in the boat dashing out and running towards them till it clamped its jaws into his calf from behind. He yelled with pain and fright.

Kashtanov ran up and killed the ant but he had to hack the ant's head into pieces before he could unlock its jaws and free his friend.

The wound was small, as Papochkin had been wearing thick woollen socks, but the poison was spreading rapidly, and his leg began to burn and stiffen.

"Sit down here till I get some ammonia and bandages from the first-aid kit," Kashtanov said.

"There's no time for that—look behind you!"

About twenty ants were hurrying towards them from the ant-hill. There was not a moment to lose. Kashtanov half-carried his lame companion to the boat, jumped in after him, and pushed off a split-second before their pursuers reached the edge of the bank.

There could be no thought of continuing their trip: one oarsman was lying helpless on the bottom of the boat and the angry ants could easily pursue the slow-moving craft upstream and keep them from landing. Therefore, Kashtanov turned the boat and began to row back downstream, trying to keep to the middle of the river and out of reach of the ants. With great difficulty Papochkin pulled off his boot and sock and found the ammonia and bandages. By then his leg had become so inflamed and swollen that every movement was painful.

Half an hour later the boat was at the edge of the forest between the sea and the northern part of the open space. The ants had vanished, and Kashtanov decided to stop to make Papochkin more comfortable in the bottom of the boat. He spread their raincoats under him; then he dipped a spare shirt in the water and wrapped it round the wounded leg. The cool compress eased the pain considerably, and Papochkin dozed off. Kashtanov rested for a while and then went on.

Rounding a small bend before the green corridor began, Kashtanov stopped suddenly, shuddering. He made straight for the bank and grabbed some bushes to pull the boat in and out of sight of the ants.

They were very close. On the left bank at the edge of the corridor several dozen of them were gnawing through the stalks of horsetail and pushing them into the river, building up a dam which the boat could never cross. Obviously, their intention was to cut off the escape of their two-legged enemies to the sea. The situation was becoming desperate, for Kashtanov alone would stand no chance against the army of insects, and one poisonous bite would make him as helpless as Papochkin.

Should he turn and go back upstream again? But they were just as likely to be attacked by ants there sooner or later. Since the river was their only means of escape, they had to get through the dam somehow. Perhaps he could frighten off the ants with buck-shot? But they might not be so easily scared. He could never kill them all and they would probably hide in the forest, ready to attack him in swarms as soon as he got out to pull the barrier apart.

Meantime, the ants were still piling up stalks in the river.

Suddenly, he had an idea which promised a way out, if only it were carried out immediately. The busy ants had not noticed the boat clinging to the bank among the bushes. He began to punt stealthily, pulling the boat under the overhanging bushes until he was back round the bend once more and out of sight of the ants. The edge of the forest came down to the river-bank there, and the ground was covered with dry horsetail stalks and twigs. He tied up the boat, and while Papochkin slept on, he dragged several thick stalks into the water, tied them together hastily with flexible twigs, and then heaped on top of them stalks, trunks, and twigs, interspersed with green horsetail and sugar reed.

When he had piled up as many branches and stalks as his makeshift raft would hold, he got back into the boat and moved off downstream, pushing the raft ahead, so that the boat was completely hidden by the floating green mound. Round the bend the current bore them straight towards the spot, about a hundred yards away, where their enemies were still busy on the dam. Kashtanov pulled the raft closer, set the dry wood on fire, and pushed the raft ahead as before. The fire blazed up quickly, and the layers of green stalks gave off a thick black cloud of smoke.

When they were about a hundred feet away from the dam, Kashtanov let go the stalk he had been using as a rope, and the raft floated off with the current; meanwhile, he stuck his pole deep into the mud on the bottom to anchor the boat in the middle of the river. The huge bonfire reached the barrier and stopped, smothering the busy ants in acrid smoke and scorching them with flames. Some of the stunned, charred insects fell into the water; the others ran to the bank and huddled there, shocked by the strange sight. Then Kashtanov loaded his gun with buck-shot and fired into the crowd of ants as he floated up to them. The terrible crackling flames, the clouds of black smoke, the deafening bangs which brought a hail of buck-shot into their midst sent every able-bodied ant streaking off upstream. The burning raft set fire to the dam which contained a large number of dry stalks as well as green ones, so that the whole middle part was blazing by the time the ants fled.

When he had made sure they were gone for good, Kashtanov tied up the boat at the bank, beside the flaming barrier. He finished off the wounded ants with his knife and then began to pull the burning and smouldering stalks apart and toss them into the water. He worked steadily for about fifteen minutes and cleared away the dam; the still-flaming raft floated on downstream and the boat followed it.

The current was swift in the green corridor, and it was not long before Kashtanov caught a glimpse of the bright blue sea ahead.

As the boat neared the river mouth he heard several shots ring out; General was barking, and the two men were yelling. He rowed as fast as he could to the shore, where he jumped out and ran towards the camp.

## BATTLE WITH THE ANTS

After their friends had gone off upstream, Maksheyev and Gromeko decided to try fishing in the river mouth. They were very lucky and within an hour Gromeko was busy cleaning a mound of fish which he hung up on strings to dry in the sun for future use.

While Maksheyev went on fishing, Gromeko set off to explore the edge of the forest and gather some new plants there. He came upon a sago palm quite unexpectedly and decided to use it for food. He called to Maksheyev and together they chopped it down. They split it, scooped out the edible core, and left the pulp to dry on their blankets.

Then they put some chowder on to boil and made plans for the afternoon.

"We can't go too far away," Gromeko said, "especially as we can't trust General with the fish."

"That's true," Maksheyev agreed. "He's faithful enough, but I don't think he could resist stuffing himself on dried fish and recalling the days of his puppyhood."

"Well, let's just go on fishing. We'll put away a big stock for General and ourselves, because I doubt if we'll ever find another place like this. You know, I never felt happy about that lizard meat, although every time we sat down to it I kept telling myself it was sturgeon or salmon and not a near relative of a frog or a salamander."

The chowder came to the boil, and Gromeko got up to get some of the drying sago to put into it.

"Oh, no! Hurry, look over there!" he yelled.

Maksheyev was behind the tent near the camp-fire, and at the sound of Gromeko's voice he ran towards the water.

Several monsters were coming along the beach, their striped sides identifying them as brontosaurs. They were moving slowly, nibbling the young palm fonds and ferns and stopping from time to time at an especially tasty tree.

"What shall we do?" asked Gromeko. "They're cowardly and won't attack us first, but they'll trample the fish and the tent if we let them come this way."

"We'll have to fire buck-shot at them, and bullets if the buck-shot doesn't work," Maksheyev said.

They raised their guns, and four shots rang out over the sea.

The sudden roar and the rain of shot scared the monsters to death, but instead of turning round, the clumsy beasts splashed into the water and raced along the surf past the camp, churning up huge waves and showers of spray.

The two men were drenched in a moment, and it was all they could do to keep their boat from being whisked out to sea on the crest of a wave. The stick supporting the string of drying fish was washed away and the fish fell on the sand: the blankets and the drying sago were soaked.

"Damn those lizards!" Maksheyev said wringing the water out of his shirt. "They managed to mess things up after all!"

"Well, at least we have something to do now," Gromeko consoled him. "We didn't know what to do after lunch, but they took care of that. Now we have to clean the sandy fish all over again and wash the sago in the river and lay it out to dry again."

"And dry ourselves first! The chowder must have boiled over long ago."

The brontosaurs clambered out on to the beach not far from the camp and hurried on eastwards.

"Look at them go! Their faces are probably full of buck-shot!" Maksheyev gloated as he took his wet things off near the tent while Gromeko was salvaging what he could of the chowder.

They hung up their clothes to dry, replaced the stick with the string of fish, and sat down to have some lunch. General, who had had as many fish heads and entrails as he could eat that morning, was dozing on the sand, so that neither he nor the two men noticed six ants appear not far from the tent at the edge of the wood. The insects stopped, looked round, and disappeared in the thicket as silently as they had come.

The men finished eating, got dressed, and lay down for

a rest and a smoke in the tent before cleaning the fish again.

Suddenly General growled, jumped up, and began to bark viciously. They ran out of the tent and saw that the camp was surrounded by ants. One column had cut them off from the mouth of the river and another was advancing from the opposite direction, towards the string of fish and the blankets with the drying sago.

"Our guns are empty!" Gromeko wailed reaching for his bandolier.

"Let's use buck-shot!" Maksheyev shouted as he loaded his shot-gun. "You take the right column, and I'll take the left!"

The right column had reached the fish and began to pull it off the string, and the left one was still about twenty feet away from the tent when the guns barked. The loud noise, the smoke, and the fact that the front ants had fallen, confused those behind and they stopped, but the ones behind them kept pressing forward, attracted by the smell of the fish, and the column advanced again. The two men were standing outside the tent, where General was hiding—although bristling and barking as loudly as he could—and were getting ready to fire another round before taking up their knives and using their gun butts as clubs in hand-to-hand combat. The battle seemed hopeless, because they were so greatly outnumbered.

Suddenly two shots rang out in quick succession from behind the bushes at the mouth of the river. Then Kashtanov was running into the very midst of the enemy army, waving a flaming bunch of dry branches which made the insects scatter in all directions.

The two men dashed towards the camp-fire and began tossing the charred logs at the other ants. Their new weapons were most effective, as the first column scattered and beat a hasty retreat into the thicket, leaving its dead, wounded, and burned on the battle-field.

When they had demolished the last remnants of the column, the three men, aided by a now fearless General, attacked the ants that were devouring the fish with knives and flaming torches. Some ants paid for their gluttony with their lives, and others were able to flee, carrying off whole fishes or pieces of sticky, wet sago in their jaws. Two ants tried to drag away one of the blankets, but they were overtaken and killed. General finished off the wounded ants by biting their heads off.

When the last fugitives had vanished in the forest, the men paused to take stock. There were forty-five dead and dying ants on the beach. Only fifteen fishes were left of the fifty they had strung up—plus a few near the edge of the woods, that the ants had probably dropped as they ran. More than half of the sago had been eaten or trampled in the sand. Gromeko had a slight scratch on his hand and Kashtanov had been nipped in his leg, but the ant's jaws hadn't been able to pierce his heavy leather boot.

"You were just in time," Maksheyev said when at last they sat down near the tent. "If it hadn't been for your support and your bright idea of using fire, we'd have stood no chance against that horde. They would have bitten us to death."

"Where's Semyon?" Gromeko suddenly asked.

"In the heat of battle I quite forgot I'd left him lying in the boat!"

"Lying?"

"Why? What happened?"

"Is he alive?" his friends asked, as they realized Kashtanov had returned too soon.

"Yes, he's alive! We had our own skirmish with the ants, and he was so severely bitten in the leg that he's helpless. Come, help me carry him to the tent."

On the way they told Kashtanov about their shower-bath and the ants' sudden attack on the camp. Papochkin, left in the boat which Kashtanov had tied up before he had run off to help the others, had been sound asleep throughout the whole battle. He wakened only when he felt himself being lifted out of the boat and carried towards the tent.

They made him comfortable, hung up the remaining fish, and dropped the dead ants into the sea. Not until they had finished that unpleasant task did Kashtanov sit down to a plateful of chowder and tell his friends of his experiences during the short journey upstream.

As they had every reason to believe that the ants, having been twice defeated, would return in swarms for their revenge, they had to decide what to do. Papochkin and Gromeko both suggested leaving immediately and rowing as far away from the ant-hill as possible. But Kashtanov was all for continuing upstream to explore the interior of the strange Black Desert, and Maksheyev seconded his plan. Before they could carry it out they would have to dispose of the cunning insects in one way or another, as their very existence would be a constant threat to the expedition. Therefore, it was decided to wait till evening, then row upstream towards the ant-hill, and set fire to it while the inhabitants were sleeping. If the plan succeeded, all four of them would then be able to sail up the river, taking both boats and leaving the raft and extra supplies hidden in the thicket near the beach.

## THE END OF THE SECOND ANT-HILL

After resting for several hours, Kashtanov and Maksheyev took their rifles, an axe, and some bundles of dry twigs, and set off in one of the boats. Papochkin was still quite lame, and Gromeko's hand was beginning to hurt from the slight scratch; therefore, the two invalids remained behind to guard the tent.

The other two men moved quickly upstream; they passed the smoking remnants of the dam with the charred bodies of the ants around it. When they reached the meadow they surveyed the ant-hill from behind some bushes to make sure there were no ants about. But apparently the insects were all asleep inside. They moved up to the place where the ants had laid a new log bridge across the river and saw that there was a well-trodden path leading from the bridge to the ant-hill.

They tied the boat up near the bridge, loaded their guns with buck-shot, slung the faggots over their shoulders, and headed towards the ant-hill. When they were about fifty yards away they hid behind some bushes again to make certain there would be no interference with their plan.

Everything was silent; they could begin. They placed a faggot in each of the main entrances and heaped the driest and thinnest stalks, pulled out of the structure itself, on top of the dry twigs.

First they set fire to the western entrance which was farthest away; then each raced towards one of the other entrances, which they set on fire. They were to meet at the eastern entrance, nearest to the river and the boat.

Kashtanov noticed an ant in the gallery behind the northern entrance as he was setting fire to it. He crouched down behind the fire, hoping the insect would run out; then he could kill the guard and prevent it from waking the others. But the ant ran off down the tunnel for help after it had tried, unsuccessfully, to pull the burning twigs away. The whole colony would soon be up in arms! Kashtanov ran towards the last entrance.

Maksheyev was there before him, and was hastily setting the faggot on fire.

"Hurry! We must get back to the boat!" he said as Kashtanov ran up to him.

They both dashed down the road leading to the bridge, but stopped to look back. Huge flames were leaping out of the eastern exit; the northern side was burning in several places, and clouds of thick smoke were pouring out of the upper exits; but Maksheyev had been too hasty in setting fire to the southern entrance which had not caught on well, so that the whole south side of the ant-hill was covered with black forms scurrying back and forth. Some were dragging out larvae or chrysalises and stacking them on the ground away from the flaming structure; others were bustling about senselessly, running up to the flames or the smoking exits and falling back burned and dazed.

"We've made a mess of it!" Kashtanov said. "Too many ants have escaped. They'll wander about the countryside and they're sure to find us. We'll have to pack up and move tomorrow."

"I think we'd better move at once!" Maksheyev shouted, pointing to a column of ants hurrying down the road towards the bridge.

"Maybe they're off to get some water to put out the fire?" Kashtanov said as he galloped down the path after his companion.

There was no doubt that the ants had spotted the fire-raisers and were chasing them. The insects were steadily gaining on the men.

"I can't keep up with you! My lungs are bursting!" Kashtanov gasped. He was older than Maksheyev and had not run like that for a long time.

"Let's stop and fire a volley at them," Maksheyev said.

By the time they got their breath back the ants were fifty feet away. Then they fired. The front row fell over, and the others came to a halt. There were over a dozen ants in the first column, and a second one was hurrying towards it from the ant-hill.

With a final burst of energy the two men ran on towards

the bridge and got there just as the reserves reached the scene of the battle.

"Where's out boat?" Maksheyev yelled.

"Is it gone?"

"It's vanished!"

"Are you sure we left it here?"

"Yes ... Look, here's the rope, hanging on a bush!"

"Who could have untied it?"

"Maybe it just got loose and floated downstream?"

"Perhaps the ants carted it off."

"What shall we do?"

"Let's get across to the other side and then pull the bridge apart," Kashtanov suggested. "At least we'll have the river between us then."

They sprinted across the swaying bridge. The ants were not more than a hundred feet away.

"Pull the logs up towards us, or the ants will fish them out of the water again," Maksheyev said.

In another minute the first ants were at the opposite bank, but they were too late: the logs were on the other side already. Twenty insects stopped in confusion at the edge of the deep water, but others were rushing up from behind. And beyond them all the ant-hill was a blazing inferno. Flames shot up into the air and clouds of smoke rose in a black column.

"You'd think it was a volcanic eruption," Maksheyev said. "We've paid them out for their dirty tricks."

"But we haven't carried out our plan and got rid of them. Now we'll have to retreat in disgrace."

"How will we ever reach the sea?"

"We can't possibly follow the river through the woods."

"We'd never get through the thicket, and by then the ants would have a chance to race ahead and attack the camp again."

"I've got an idea! If we can't walk, let's float. We can

make a little raft from these two logs and let the current take care of the rest."

"That's a brain wave! But let's scare off the ants so that we can launch the raft."

They loaded their guns and fired four shots into the milling crowd of ants on the opposite bank, killing about a dozen; some fell into the water and the rest scattered. A few minutes later the two logs had been hastily bound together with green twigs. The men boarded their raft; they were caught up with the current and raced downstream, using their guns to push the raft away from the bank when necessary. Some of the ants kept up the chase along the shore, but the current was too swift for them, and soon they dropped behind and out of sight.

When they reached the bend in the river where Kashtanov had so recently built his floating bonfire, they caught sight of their boat, stuck in the bushes near the bank.

The current pulled the raft along in the same direction so that they were able to catch hold of it, get in, and row to the beach.


## INTO THE INTERIOR ONCE MORE

They got ready to leave at once, for they were likely to meet ants anywhere in the interior and they would have to use their remaining ammunition, plus all their energy, in a senseless battle with the enraged and homeless insects. There was every reason to believe that their camp would be attacked again with less fortunate results.

In the course of an early breakfast they debated hotly whether they should sail on westward along the southern shore of the Sea of Lizards or turn and sail eastwards. Finally, they decided to continue westwards.

As before, they kept close to the shore and had soon

left the bay behind. The southern shore ahead was monotonously dull. They had spent two weeks among the plants and animals of the Jura and were beginning to wish for a change of surroundings. They hoped that farther south they might discover a still more ancient flora and fauna which would provide new experiences and adventures.

The Black Desert barred their way to the south; the east and west promised nothing but the world of the Jura. They were beginning to think of turning back altogether and heading north.

They spotted ants in several places along the shore and came to the conclusion that the genus was widespread on the southern shore of the Sea of Lizards and that the ants were the real rulers of the Jurassic world.

"Thank goodness, at least they spend some of their time sleeping!" Papochkin said. "Otherwise we'd have been done for long ago."

"They're worse than sabre tigers and carnivorous lizards put together," Maksheyev added.

They spent the night on the beach and decided to sail westwards for one more day; if there was no chance of penetrating south, they would turn back.

The next day brought what they were seeking. The coastline began to recede sharply to the south without changing its character. After a few hours they noticed that the green wall of trees was ending and there were cliffs ahead.

"The same plateau, and the same Black Desert!" Kashtanov exclaimed dejectedly looking through his binoculars.

Passing the edge of the forest, they found themselves in a large bay lying between it and the plateau. Beyond the bay was a green valley, and a group of tall, dark, pointed mountains loomed in the background.

"Volcanoes again! But look how close to the sea they are!" Gromeko said.

They steered towards the southern tip of the bay, to a flat sandy patch of beach where the valley began.

There was a large stream flowing through the valley, bordered by trees, bushes, and open spaces. They pitched the tent on the beach and saw beetles, dragon-flies, and flies in the clearings and the tracks of iguanodons and flying lizards on the sand, but there were no ants in sight.

They set out towards the volcanoes after lunch, but as a precautionary measure hid the boats, the tent, and the extra supplies in the forest, and even slung some of the things in the trees. This time General went with them.

Their way lay through the valley, close to the bank of the stream. The groves there were no longer impassable thickets and were broken by iguanodon paths. Kashtanov noted that the cliffs were olivine with veins of nickeliferous iron, the same as they had seen much farther north, along the Maksheyev River. The difference was that these veins often turned into large sockets of solid metal, up to a yard in diameter.

"Steel could be made from this metal very easily!" Maksheyev exclaimed standing before a sheer cliff, where many large and small sockets of metal glinted in the sunshine.

"You're just like a little boy gazing at a huge cinnamon bun, full of plump raisins," laughed Kashtanov.

"What a site for a gigantic plant!" Maksheyev grieved.

"Despite the ants?" Kashtanov smiled.

"Despite everything! Do you think man would think twice about annihilating those pests if he stood to gain such treasures? It would take only a cannon and a few dozen grenades to blow every ant-hill and every ant to smithereens."

From time to time large pterodactyls flew over the valley looking for prey; they apparently had their nests not far away, in the sheer cliffs. They dared not attack the men, but whenever General ran ahead or lagged

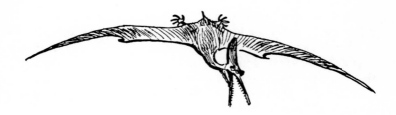

behind, a pterodactyl kept circling over him, ready to
swoop down at any moment. Gromeko took two shots at
the lizard and hit it the second time. It flapped its wings
heavily as it dived into a large fern.

They saw a herd of iguanodons resting in a clearing
at the foot of the cliffs, but decided to shoot one on the
way back, to save carrying the meat.

They had been walking steadily for about three hours
when they finally came to a place where the valley turned
sharply west. From there it went on past a group of volcanoes which formed its right slope. The going was rough-
er, for they had to clamber over black lava crusts and
boulders.

They stopped for the night at a little clearing, gathered
some dry horsetails for a fire, and piled all their belongings in a heap, so that they need not take their knapsacks
when they went exploring.

A small lake lay in a hollow between the ends of two
wide streams of hardened lava running down the side of
a volcano; clumps of small palms, horsetails, and a narrow
strip of sugar reeds grew around the lake. A brook flowed from the lake and down through the lower stream of
lava. The surface of the lake was mirror smooth, reflecting every detail of the green frame, the black streams of
lava, and the gloomy cliffs of the plateau.

"It would be a perfect place for someone who wanted
to get away from it all," Papochkin said. "He could build

a hut beside the black cliff and spend his days contemplating the clear sky, the eternal sun, and the majestic volcano from the shade of the palms on the bank of the peaceful lake."

"And one fine day he'd be killed by a shower of stones or a stream of hot lava thrown at him by the treacherous mountain," Kashtanov added.

"Or else he'd starve to death, because these palms don't seem to produce edible fruit, and the reeds aren't sweet at all," Gromeko said.

"There doesn't seem to be any game here either," Maksheyev added.

"What a bunch of miserable realists you are! You won't even let a fellow dream. A hermit could plough up some land, plant an orchard and a garden. There's enough water here, grape-vines flourish on old lava, and . . ."

Before he could finish there came a loud, thunderous roar from the nearest volcano. Its main peak was concealed by the most recent layers of hardened lava, but a few minutes later a cloud of small black pebbles rained down on them.

"See! His Highness has just informed us that he won't tolerate any hermit growing grapes on his favourite old lava stream," Maksheyev said.

"Let's have a look at the lake and go back to camp, it's dangerous here," Kashtanov suggested.

While they were going down towards the lake, there came another roar and another shower of pebbles.

"The volcano's angry at its uninvited visitors! It's afraid we'll steal the treasure from its crater, just as we took the sulphur from Satan, before he had a chance to wake up."

"Let's name the volcano Old Grouchy," Gromeko suggested.

They all liked the name, and Kashtanov wrote it down on the map he was drawing. They named the lake Hermit Lake and the stream that flowed out of it—the Papochkin River.

"Now we've immortalized your castles in the air!" laughed Maksheyev.

The lake water was cold, fresh, and slightly reminiscent of Vichy water.

Going round the lake they found a suitable place for a swim. The refreshing water was no more than ten feet deep, and contained neither fish, nor plants, nor insects.

As it was still too early to go back and settle down for the night, they decided to climb on to the plateau. This was not difficult, because the top stream of lava led to the edge of the plateau and the boulders seemed to form a giant stairway, so that by climbing from one boulder to another they soon reached the top.

Below them, to the east, the lake huddled in a deep hollow. The scarred, black slopes of Old Grouchy, crowned by a pointed peak, rose behind it. A straight dark column of smoke drifted miles up into the still air. The same Black Desert that had surrounded the other group of volcanoes stretched before them to the north, south, and west. Still farther north, the desert ended at the sea, but to the south and west it reached the horizon.

"Old Grouchy's much higher than Satan, and his slopes are steeper," Kashtanov noted.

"We can't climb him now that the eruption has begun," Maksheyev said.

"We'll see about that tomorrow. We don't need any more sulphur and we can turn back when we want to."

They went down to the lake, and then crossed the hardened streams of lava till, an hour later, they were back at the camp.

# OLD GROUCHY'S JOKES

Old Grouchy didn't let them rest that night. A few hours after they had fallen asleep, a terrible roar made them jump up in fright.

"Is this volcano putting out scorching clouds, too? Look what's going on there!" Gromeko shouted.

The mountain was covered by heavy black clouds which were rolling down the slope and spreading out in all directions. There was a strong smell of sulphur and chlorine. Flashes of lightning pierced the clouds, and loud thunderclaps were lost in the terrible roaring of the volcano.

"No," Kashtanov said, "we needn't worry about a scorching cloud. This is a different kind of eruption. The volcano is throwing up ashes and rocks now, and the lava will probably come later."

"I suppose that's the end of our mountain-climbing?"

"I'm not insane enough to climb an erupting volcano!"

"Well, what shall we do now?"

"Let's stay here for a while, or go to sleep again and then start back to the sea."

"Why not start out now?"

"And miss the chance to watch an eruption at close range?"

"The hot rocks might come down on us."

"I doubt it. We're at the very foot of the mountain and they won't get so far."

"But the lava might come this way."

"It doesn't flow very quickly, and we'll have time enough to get out of its way at a walking pace."

"In that case we might just as well stay here and watch Old Grouchy at work. In the meantime, I suggest breakfast."

They started a fire, put the kettle on to boil, and watched the volcano while they ate.

It was completely concealed behind the clouds, and even the sky overhead was covered by a grey film that made Pluto look like a red rayless disc shedding a dull, menacing light on the gloomy surroundings.

Soon black ashes poured about them, and they had to cover their cups to save getting mouthfuls of volcanic dust with their tea. The grass, the reeds, the palms, and the very water in the stream grew sooty black.

"I'm glad we filled the water-tin this morning," Maksheyev said. "Otherwise we'd have been left without water for the day. Listen! What's that noise?"

Because the volcano was not roaring quite so loudly, they heard between the thunderclaps a dull noise like pounding surf gradually coming nearer. They exchanged startled glances.

"We must get out of here!" Kashtanov shouted. "There's a wave or a stream of mud rolling down the river! I forgot that might happen! Hurry! Grab everything and let's get as high as we can!"

They emptied their cups, snatched their things, and rushed up the hardened lava, scrambling over the boulders, slipping in their haste and trying to rise above the river-bed.

They stopped for breath about a hundred and fifty feet above their camp site and looked back. A raging black torrent was racing down the slope of the volcano, tearing up chunks of hardened lava. A few minutes later the terrible ten-foot wave reached the spot where they had been so calmly sipping tea a short while before. In an instant the green bushes vanished beneath the murky water, the palm-trees shuddered and fell under the terrific impact, and the whole clearing disappeared as if it had never existed.

"Not bad!" cried Papochkin. "We got out just in time!"

They had climbed above the lava stream and had a good view of both peaks. The river of mud had come down past the right peak; they turned to see what was happening on the left one. A few minutes later a second stream of mud flowed through the narrow valley beside the left peak. It was moving slower, as the water was full of ashes and pebbles and the whole was like thin black gruel, with uprooted bushes and palms spinning round in it.

"They're coming from the lake," Papochkin said.

"That disposes of your lovely pastoral scene! The lake is just a big mud pie now," Kashtanov said.

"These volcanoes aren't very good neighbours," Gromeko added. "Satan blew a scorching cloud at us, and Old Grouchy spit out a torrent of mud."

"But we escaped both and had a chance to see the terrible wonders of nature," Kashtanov said.

"Look, we're cut off from the sea and our boats on both sides by the streams, and Old Grouchy's there behind us, probably thinking up some new surprise," said Papochkin despairingly.

"If lava comes pouring out now, we're between fire and water—at least we have a choice!" Gromeko said ironically.

"Old Grouchy still has something up his sleeve," Maksheyev added.

"Cheer up, things might be worse!" declared Kashtanov. "The mud streams will soon pass on and if the lava does come this way, we can still reach the sea before it catches up with us."

"Meantime, we'll be drenched, there's not a bush to hide under," Papochkin grumbled.

He was right. It had been drizzling for some time, but they had been so busy watching the streams of mud that they had paid no attention. It was raining harder now and they looked around for some sort of shelter. The weather had been good for so long that they had taken it for granted and had left the tent and their raincoats in the forest with the boats.

"I think we'd be drier up there near the huge boulders," Maksheyev said pointing farther up the slope.

"We'd also be closer to the volcano," Papochkin sighed.

"No one's forcing you, stay here if you like," Gromeko told him.

But he didn't want to stay behind alone, and they all began to climb the steep lava stream. Both the rocks and their boots were wet, and they kept slipping all the time. They came to a ridge of piled-up boulders marking the edge of a more recent stream that had flowed over the previous one. In some places there was enough space between the boulders to shelter one person, and the four men settled in four crevices; Maksheyev was not too happy when a very wet, dripping General chose him as a cave-mate.

Cold and wet, they crouched awkwardly on the uneven stones, and kept calling to each other to keep up their spirits whenever Old Grouchy quietened down a bit.

The rain was pouring by then, and soon trickles and streams of dirty ash-laden water were running down the hardened lava to add to the men's discomfort.

One got a cold spray on his side and another on his back. Papochkin, who had been lying on his stomach in a narrow trench, suddenly felt the hole fill with water. He crawled out and began darting back and forth among the boulders, looking for a new place.

Maksheyev laughed watching him, for he and General were quite protected in their little cave.

"That's no Grouchy!" Papochkin yelled as he scrambled over the wet boulders. "Goodness knows what it is: Rainy, Teary, or Wetty."

"Let's name it Aquarius!" Maksheyev shouted back.

Papochkin didn't hear him. He had found a crevice and was crawling in, head first, but the crevice was too small and his legs stuck out.

Suddenly there was a terrible explosion. They felt they

would be crushed beneath the boulders and scrambled out into the open.

"It's an earthquake!" Gromeko shouted.

"The volcano's exploded! It's coming down on us!" Papochkin yelled.

"I hope it's not a scorching cloud!" Kashtanov turned pale.

They could see nothing through the rain and the clouds, and after the first few frightening moments they calmed down. Then a rock the size of a big ball fell at their feet with a dull thud. It was covered with deep grooves and began to hiss, crack, and smoke in the rain. From all sides of them, above and below, left and right, they could hear the same thudding noises as other rocks showered down.

"Get back!" shouted Maksheyev. "Old Grouchy's firing big shells this time!"

They all hurried back to their burrows and crouched fearfully, watching the "bombs" fall and hiss all around. Some fell on boulders and splintered like grenades. The rain was stopping. A gust of hot wind swept down the slope, filling the air with sulphur fumes and the smell of burning. The clouds drifted higher or scattered. The shelling ceased, and Maksheyev ventured out of his cave.

"Look!" he shouted.

The others crawled out and looked up.

The volcano's peak appeared between the black clouds. A short, fiery-red tongue of lava hung suspended over the slope, as if teasing the men who had dared to infringe upon the eternal stillness of the mountain.

"I suppose this is the end," Maksheyev said solemnly to Papochkin.

"You'd be off like a shot if it were," he snapped back.

"There's no rush. We can always walk away from the lava stream," Kashtanov repeated.

But there was nowhere to go. Muddy torrents were still rushing down both river-beds which were impossible to cross. The red tongue grew longer every minute; clouds of white steam rose from its surface.

"Old Grouchy soaked us, and now he'll dry us. When the lava gets closer, we'll dry our clothes and then..."

"And then we'll get soaked again when we try to cross the mud, if we don't drown in it," Papochkin finished.

The sky was clearing, and Pluto suddenly broke through the scattering clouds and ashes, drying the slopes of the volcano. The black mounds of hardened lava steamed as if a hidden fire were burning under them.

The men took off their dripping clothes, wrung them out, and spread them on the rocks to dry.

"Once the stream of lava appears, it's usually a sign that the explosions and showers of stones are over," Kashtanov said.

"But if we have to run from the lava, we shan't have a chance to get dressed," Maksheyev said.

Just then a white cloud of steam shot out of the crater, a fiery wave appeared over the edge and began to move rapidly down the slope.

"The first stream went into the lake, but this one might easily reach us," Kashtanov said.

"When?" they all wanted to know.

"Maybe in an hour, maybe later. It all depends on the type of lava. If it's heavy and melts easily, it flows quickly, but, if not, it flows slowly. Judging by the old lava streams, only the heavy type has been pouring out from the volcano, and this is probably the same."

"Which means we'd better get out of here fast."

"Right. I hope the mud streams will dry up before the lava reaches us, so we'll be able to cross one of the river-beds."

Pluto and the hot wind blowing from the volcano soon dried their clothes. They dressed and continued to watch the volcano as they waited for a chance to leave the place.

The tip of the long tongue of lava had disappeared

behind the ridge of the mountain, and seemed to be moving towards the hollow at the foot of the western slope where a lake had once been. New waves of lava were rising from the crater and pouring out, partly along the same path, and partly to the north, where a new stream was evidently flowing down the north or north-west slope, in which case it would be heading towards the men, who could not see it for the masses of hardened lava.

Both rivers had diminished greatly: the one on the left especially was no longer a rushing torrent, but a small muddy stream which they could risk wading across.

## TRAPPED

Half an hour passed. The eruption was proceeding slowly and methodically; the faint explosions in the crater were few and far between. But from higher up on the slope which the men were on, came a dull noise and rustling like the sound of ice breaking on a large river. The noise came from behind the huge boulders along the edge of an old lava stream.

"We'd better go now, the lava's getting closer," said Kashtanov rising.

They set off down the slope, towards the place where they had spent the previous night, but kept turning to look in the direction from which the ever-increasing noise was coming. They could see the edge of the new lava stream over the ridge of the old one. Kashtanov was the only one of the group who had seen molten lava before, and it was not the fiery wall which the other three had imagined, but rather a black wave of boulders, moved by an unseen but monstrous force.

The boulders were moving on slowly, piling up and cracking against each other; as the top ones rolled off the ridge, new ones took their place, while others rolled far down the slope. Clouds and jets of steam shot out and blue flames flickered here and there; sometimes fiery spots appeared, like the last burning embers among the ashes of a dying fire. But the fire came on: a great crawling monster, belching forth poisonous fumes and hot flames as it crept downhill beneath its quivering black armour.

To escape the rolling boulders the men ran towards the right branch of the river, a little above the place where they had camped the night before; the surface was now bumpy with muddy rivulets running off it.

They began to cross, but had taken only a few steps before they were stuck knee-deep in the mud.

"Oh!"

"I can't pull my feet out!"

"It's like dough!"

Gromeko, who had been behind the others, was not so deeply embedded as they were. He managed to pull his feet out of his boots, which he left in the mire; then he got on to a large boulder on the bank and had quite a time fishing his boots out of the mud. The other three were as helpless as flies on a fly-paper.

Meanwhile, the lava stream was moving on relentlessly and was only about two hundred yards away from them. Their situation was becoming desperate. There was not a log or a board, or even a stick which Gromeko could lay across the mud to help his friends to get out.

Suddenly, he had an idea. He laid a bridge of stepping-stones, made of flat chunks of lava, towards Papochkin, who was the lightest. Then he put down his rifle, tore off his knapsack and shirt, and rolled his pants up above his knees. He walked across the stones gingerly until he reached Papochkin, took off *his* knapsack and gun, grabbed him under the arms and hauled him out. Luckily, Papochkin had lacing boots which did not come off. Together they laid a second path to Maksheyev and pulled him out, but without his boots. Kashtanov was the tallest and heaviest of all, and the three of them pulled him out, also without his boots.

By then the lava stream was much closer, and they could feel the burning heat. They had no time to dry to retrieve the lost boots, they had to flee from the creeping death-wave.

They grabbed up their things and ran along the bank, looking for a good place to cross.

But the treacherous grey mud was everywhere, and they dared not step into it.

Their futile search led them to the place where they had spent the night, and there they found a small lake. There was very little water in it, but the bottom was covered with a layer of the same grey mud; they could not tell how thick it was.

Behind them the stream of lava came closer.

The rustling and cracking noises of the rolling boulders and the hissing of steam never ceased for a second; it grew hotter every minute.

They ran across the edge of the old lava stream near the lake, where the two branches of the river merged, but when they came to the river-bed near the left peak, they saw that it too was full of mud. Their only chance was to continue up the left branch, as they had done the day before, as far as Hermit Lake, where they would escape the second stream of lava, but would risk running into the first one. The river-bed narrowed between the sheer cliffs of the plateau and the slope of the volcano, and they hoped to find a narrow place where they could pave the mud with flat boulders or even jump from one bank to the other. They did find such a place, but the opposite side was a smooth wall of cliffs ten feet high. There was no chance at all of scaling them or even of going a bit farther up or down along the edge of the cliffs, as it too was covered with mud.

They were completely exhausted by running and excitement, and in despair they sat down on some boulders near the mud. They had no choice but wait for death in one form or another: if they tried to ford the river, they would be sucked down by the mud; if they remained on the bank they would roast and burn when the stream of lava reached them.

After they had been sitting for a few minutes, Kashtanov noticed that the lava was not flowing as quickly as it had been. He jumped up and shouted:

"Come on! If we hurry up this side of the river, we'll be able to pass in front of the lava—it's nearly stopped!"

"But then we'll run into the other stream that flooded Hermit Lake and must have turned down the river-bed!" Papochkin said hopelessly.

"It's our only chance!" Kashtanov insisted. "We might find a shallow ford across the river where the cliffs on the other side are not so steep. And there's still the possibility that the two lava streams don't merge, which means that . . ."

"That there's a clear space between them!" Maksheyev shouted.

"Yes, and we can sit there and wait till the mud forms a crust thick enough to hold our weight."

"Hooray!" Papochkin and Gromeko both yelled.

They all scrambled to their feet and headed south with high hopes, climbing over the old lava streams and following the path they had taken the previous day. The scorching ridge of molten lava was a few hundred feet to the left of them, but it was advancing more slowly now, and they kept increasing the distance between themselves and the fatal black mass. Soon they noticed that the ridge was turning as it crept up the slope of the volcano. They were out of danger at last.

They passed several points where the river-bed was narrow enough to cross, but in each case there was a sheer wall of rock at the other side. They had to keep going; soon they were climbing up the highest of the old lava streams on the western slope of the volcano. Hermit Lake lay beyond it. As they climbed they saw that their chances of escaping were much better.

The old stream rose in a flat hump dividing the new lava into two streams. They sat at the top and had a good view of the hollow below, where the day before there had been a placid, mirror-clear lake. Now the lake, palms, and grass had disappeared and there was nothing but a field of mud, with puddles of black water. The second lava stream was moving towards it, and the hot mass of boulders at the front edge was exploding and letting off bursts of steam as it came in contact with the wet mud.

They were about five hundred feet away from the hot stream, but everything around them was hot. To add to their discomfort, Pluto was blazing down from a cloudless sky.

Apart from the heat, they were hungry and tired; they had not slept much the night before and had been on the move ever since.

"I'd give anything for a cup of tea!" Papochkin sighed.

"In all this heat we've no firewood! Should I run over and put our kettle on the hot lava? It would boil in a second there!" Maksheyev teased.

"Have we any water left?"

"Yes, there's quite a lot here," Gromeko said, looking into the tin.

"We might as well have something to eat, even if we can't have tea."

They sat round and really enjoyed their meal of dried fish, biscuits, and warm water.

"We're paying for our foolish mistake of this morning," Kasthanov said.

"What do you mean?"

"When we heard the mud stream rushing towards us, we should have crossed the river right away, instead of climbing the mountain. We'd have been on the beach by now, instead of trying to keep clear of the mud and lava."

"You're right. It would have been easy to reach the sea from the other bank."

"Not as easy as all that! There were two mud rivers flowing into the valley and it's probably flooded too."

"And we'd have been trapped in the valley!"

"But we could have climbed up to the Black Desert and gone on to the sea."

"What's the use of thinking about it? Who could have known then how it would all end? At the time we felt we had to climb as high as we could, to get out of the way of the mud."

"If we'd had a couple of volcano experts with us, they'd have known which way to run!"

"I think we made our biggest mistake yesterday when we decided to spend the night at the foot of the volcano, in spite of all the indications that it was ready to blow."

"But that's why we stayed—to watch the eruption!"

"We saw it all right! I'll be only too happy never to see another volcano for the rest of my life! I made a present of my gun to Satan, and old Grouchy . . ."

"And we donated our boots to the Old Grouchy Fund. Believe me, our donation cost us more than yours. You have your boots and you're grumbling, but Yakov and I will have to walk to the sea in our bare feet over the broiling stones of the Black Desert."

"You're right. I won't say another word."

"What shall we do now?"

"It would be sensible to try to get some sleep, that is, if we *can* sleep on these bumpy rocks."

"We can try. I think we should take turns to watch. Better keep an eye on Old Grouchy for you never can tell what'll happen."

"How long should we sleep?"

"As long as we can."

"Or until the mud in the river-bed is dry enough to cross it."

Three of them curled up on the hard rocks and actually fell asleep, while the fourth stayed awake to watch the volcano and the mud which dried very slowly, despite the heat from the lava and Pluto combined, so that it was a good six hours before they dared set foot on the caked mud.

They gathered up their belongings and crossed safely. one at a time. Then they climbed up a cleft, scrambling up on rocks and ledges and boosting each other until, half an hour later, they were on the desert and out of danger.

Papochkin turned to face the volcano, took off his hat, bowed solemnly, and said:

"Farewell, Old Grouchy! I thank you for all your trouble and attention."

They all chuckled. Kashtanov said:

"Ah, if only I had my boots, I wouldn't leave this place!"

"What would you do here?"

"I'd keep on south over the desert to see what's behind the volcano."

"You can see from here that there's nothing but desert there."

"Besides having no boots, we haven't much food left either," Maksheyev said.

"And hardly any water now," added Gromeko shaking the tin.

"You're right, we'd better hurry back to the sea. But these blac stones are scorching, and my woollen socks are a thing of the past after all that running we did. I feel as if I'm standing on a hot stove."

"We'll have to wrap our shirts round our feet," Maksheyev suggested. "We can't go any farther like this."

As they talked, he and Kashtanov had been hopping up and down, trying to cool their feet. They took off their shirts which they wrapped round their feet, securing them with rifle straps, and after taking one last look at the smoking volcano, they set off northwards over the desert. The going was easy across an ancient mass of greenish-black lava smoothed by the wind. There was no more sign of vegetation than there had been in the desert near Satan's Volcano. The black plain stretched to the horizon. There was a clear sky above and Pluto's reddish rays were reflected in a million green sparks from the flat surface. The men blinked and closed their eyes against the brightness.

They headed north-east, to come out at the lower reaches of the river, where they might find a good place to climb down from the plateau. Three hours later they reached the edge of the cliff and began looking for a cleft. Only yesterday the valley below had been a green oasis: now it lay ravaged under a thick layer of mud. The trees and bushes had been uprooted, and the grass had disappeared completely. A few tufts of green near the foot of the cliff had somehow managed to escape the flood. At the sight of this depressing scene the men remembered that they had planned to shoot an iguanodon in the valley on their way back.

"They must have escaped to the sea."

"Or else drowned in the mud."

They found this was what had happened. A little farther down they saw a flock of pterodactyls circling over the valley. As they came closer they saw there was a feast going on. The carcasses of several iguanodons rose from the mud like large hills, and dozens of flying lizards were perched on them. They were tearing at the flesh and entrails with their toothed beaks, squabbling and fighting, chasing each other, flying up and settling down again. The screeching and croaking never stopped for a second.

"Well, there goes our game!" Gromeko said as they watched the repulsive scene. "What shall we do?"

"We can shoot a pterodactyl," Maksheyev suggested.

"After they've been stuffing themselves on carrion? No thank you!"

"But we've eaten them before."

"We didn't know then that they fed on carrion. And the only reason we ate a pterodactyl was because there was nothing else to be had after the ants robbed us."

"We've no meat now, either."

"There's still some dried fish in the boats and we can catch more at the mouth of the river."

"You're forgetting there's *no* river now!" Kashtanov said. "And the whole bay is probably full of mud, so that the fish must either have died or fled to the open sea."

"I'm afraid we shan't be able to get fresh water," Gromeko said.

"Of course, since there's no river now."

"And I'm afraid everything we left in the forest will be gone," cried Maksheyev. "It was near the river and not too high above the water. If the mud river was as swift at the mouth as it was farther up, it could have swept everything out to sea or, at best, drowned the things in mud."

This made them forget about the pterodactyl and they hurried on. Papochkin, as a true scientist, had managed to take some photographs of the lizards' feast.

A steep narrow ravine led down into the valley not far from its mouth. They all wanted to run, to get to the sea as quickly as possible, but they had to drag their feet through the sticky mud, for although there was only a thin layer of it, it was quite wet. When they were still a fair distance from the mouth of the river, they could see that the muddy torrent had done its damage there too. Where the river had flowed along a narrow corridor between walls of horsetail and ferns, there was now a wide road, and the piled-up trees were covered with mud. The main rush of water had been along the river-bed, but it had left its mark on the rest of the forest, which was flooded with muddy water.

Trudging slowly through the mud, they finally reached the bay and gasped at what they saw. Instead of clear blue water, the bay was filled with floating refuse made up of leaves, branches, bushes, and tree trunks.

Maksheyev and Gromeko ran towards the place where they had hidden the boats; they were sure they would find nothing, for mud covered even the beach near the mouth of the river.

"Hey! Come on! Give us a hand, everything's here!" they shouted jubilantly.

They had been lucky, because they had put everything into the boats, covered them with the tent, and put the raft on top of that, securing the whole to the surrounding tree trunks. They all sighed with relief and began to dig out the boats and drag them and the other things to a spot farther away from the river that hadn't been caught in the torrent of mud. As the river had run dry, they were forced to move on. Going farther west would be too risky, because the shore was a sheer wall of cliffs at the edge of the Black Desert, and they were very unlikely to find any fresh water there.

"We know where there's a spring to the east, the one where we stopped for the night," Gromeko said conclusively.


## SAILING BACK


An hour later they were crossing the immense dirty puddle that had once been a bay. They rounded the cape, turned east and continued along the low monotonous shore-line and the green wall of trees. They were rowing hard to get to the source of fresh water as quickly as possible and have a much-needed rest after the ordeal of the past two days, but they stopped to hunt some iguanodons which they spotted on the beach.

They kept up the same speed the next day, so that by evening they had reached the mouth of the river where the ant-hill had been burned. The beach there was sandy, and they could fill their tins with fresh water, something they would not be able to do farther east.

They spent an uneventful night on the beach.

Next day they sailed on eastwards between the islands that separated the East Sea from the West Sea.

This time they steered closer to the northern shore, to examine the mouth of a river that was much larger than the Maksheyev River, but seemed very much like it. On its low banks were solid walls of trees growing at the water's edge, and as there was not an inch of space for a camp site, they had a dry lunch in the boats.

While they were resting afterwards, Papochkin suddenly said:

"This is the northern shore, isn't it?"

"Of course."

"Then let's follow it right to the mouth of the Maksheyev River and avoid a dangerous crossing."

"But we wanted to explore the southern shore to the east of our first landing place," Gromeko reminded him.

"I think it's time we began to think of getting back to the ice-fields," Papochkin declared.

"Why so soon?"

"Because it'll take us three or four times as long to row upstream against the current as it did to sail downstream."

"Even so, we still have plenty of time."

"Not so much as you think. This is the end of August, and, while there's probably eternal summer here, I'm sure there's winter as well farther north, nearer to the ice-fields. If we start back too late, we'll find ourselves tramping along the snow-covered banks of a frozen river, instead of rowing. upstream as we planned."

"And we've no skis or warm clothes!" Maksheyev added.

"That's a very important point and we can't dismiss it lightly," Kashtanov said. "But I don't think it will make much difference if we spend an extra week exploring the southern shore."

"There's another point," Papochkin insisted. "Every excursion along the southern shore was made dangerous and difficult because of the ants. There are sure to be some of them along the eastern part of the coast as well. We can't waste ammunition fighting them, because we'll need every bullet we have for hunting or keeping off wild beasts on the way back."

"And last, but not least," Gromeko said, "I doubt very much that we'd discover anything of interest in the three or four days we'd have at our disposal. We know that the sheer cliffs of the plateau stretch for miles along the coast, and when we looked east from Satan's peak we saw nothing but the Black Desert."

"At best we might discover another river with another group of temperamental volcanoes in its upper reaches," Papochkin added with some feeling, as he recalled his recent experiences. "We escaped death miraculously twice. Do you think we should tempt fate again?"

"Well, that makes it three to one," Kashtanov said with some disappointment. "I'd better bow to your superior arguments."

"Then we continue along the northern shore?" Gromeko asked.

"It's been decided, hasn't it?"

"We'd better fill the water-tins now, because we'll never get to the Maksheyev River this evening, and we don't know if there's another river on the way."

They filled both tins at the mouth of a small river which they named the Gromeko River, and sailed on among the islands and shoals of its delta, trying to keep to their course.

The islands became fewer in number until, finally, they disappeared altogether. The shore-line receded sharply northwards. This was where the sand dunes began on the opposite shore. The sky there was full of the black smoke that was still pouring out of Satan's crater.

Insects flitted over the water, small flying lizards hunted them, and plesiosaurs' heads appeared off shore from time to time. The water was very shallow near the shore, and the oars scraped the bottom several times. They saw many animal paths leading to the sea through green corridors of reeds and trees.

Late the next morning they reached the landmark they had built on the bank of the Maksheyev River. They spent the next twenty-four hours there, fishing and drying the fish they caught, and overhauling the boats and the raft for the long journey ahead.

The journey upstream was slow and difficult. They had to row constantly, leaving a minimum of time for rest, sleep, and meals, but could still do only twenty to twenty-five miles a day, depending on the swiftness of the current.

There were no noticeable changes in their surroundings during the first few weeks of sailing, but farther on, when they reached the zone of foliage forest, they found that the trees had turned yellow and lost their leaves, and the farther north they went, the more bare trees there were.

The weather changed for the worse, too. Pluto was often hidden behind dense clouds, and the cool north wind brought rain. It grew hot again as soon as the clouds disappeared, but the average temperature fell steadily.

The cold wind blowing in their faces and the frequent rainy days slowed them down considerably, as they had to stop to get warm in the tent or at a small fire. They had spent several months in a dry, warm climate and were now feeling the cold and dampness all the more keenly.

When they reached the belt inhabited by mammoths, they found that winter had set in. The temperature settled at freezing point and although it rose slightly on clear days the sky was usually completely concealed behind a mass of grey clouds; there was a strong north wind, with intermittent snow. At the same time, the water level in the river dropped noticeably. There was a layer of ice near the banks and a thin layer of snow on the fields and forests along the river. The fast current kept the middle of the river free from ice, but they expected it to freeze over any day. They had abandoned the raft when the channel became too narrow, and so the heavily laden boats crept slowly upstream against the swift current, covering ten to thirteen miles a day.

They were still over sixty miles from their base.

# THE MYSTERIOUS TRACKS

One evening after supper Gromeko and Maksheyev went to fish from a sandy patch that was bright-yellow against the frost-bitten, shrivelled grass along the bank. Maksheyev tossed in his line and stood watching the float. He looked down suddenly and saw the clear print of a bare human foot beside his own on the sand.

He bent over and examined the print. It was a left flat-footed print, bigger than the print of his own large boot next to it, and its owner was obviously used to going barefoot. All five toes were extremely long, and the big toe was set at an angle to the other four. In fact, it seemed more like the print of a huge hand with a very long palm.

The right foot-mark was two feet away, but most of it was under water and had been washed away. The creature seemed to have waded across the river, as there were no prints leading out of the water and back up the shore.

"Come here! Hurry!" Maksheyev shouted.

"What's the matter? Wait a minute, I think I've got a bite!" Gromeko answered.

"Oh, leave your rod! Come and see what I've found!"

"Well, what is it, a crab or a turtle?"

"A human footprint on the sand."

"What?"

Gromeko dropped his rod and ran over. When he too had examined the print, he agreed that the shape of the foot was very unusual.

"Maybe it was an ape?" he suggested.

"Here, in a subpolar region, among the larch-trees and birches?"

"If mammoths and rhinoceroses here live in the tundra and northern forests, while their relatives on earth inhabit the tropics, why shouldn't monkeys and apes have got used to the cold here as well?"

"True. Let's call our zoologist and geologist to settle the problem."

"You keep an eye on the rods and I'll fetch them."

Gromeko rowed to the camp and brought the other two.

"I think it's a huge ape," Kashtanov said.

"I don't agree," Papochkin said. "I think it's an ape-like-human. See, it walked upright and didn't use its hands at all. An ape going down such a steep bank would certainly have leaned on its knuckles, but there are no hand-prints at all here."

When they had had a better look at the banks, they saw a path leading down to the water on both sides and a shallow ford across the river-bed. The prints were not too clear on the path, but, judging by the distance between them, the creature must have been about six feet tall.

"Well, what do you make of it?" Maksheyev asked when the others came back to where he sat fishing.

"Most likely it was an ape-like human, following a familiar path to a shallow crossing in the river," Kashtanov said.

"That means people have got here before us?"

"And what people! They walk barefoot on the snow and calmly wade across icy rivers!" cried Gromeko.

"They're probably savages, no wonder their feet are so much like apes'!"

"I'd prefer not to meet them, they must be cannibals."

"We've survived all the other inhabitants of Plutonia, I'm sure we could make friends with the savages."

They had to be more cautious now than ever before, in case of a sudden attack. They took turns to keep watch when they halted and their eyes searched the banks as they rowed upstream.

After another day they were caught in a snow-storm; the river froze over and had six inches of snow on it.

To avoid leaving the boats and carrying everything on their backs, they decided to make runners for the heavy boats which they hauled along the river-bed. It was hard going, and they never covered more than seven or ten miles a day across the soft snow. Pluto no longer broke through the dense clouds, and the temperature dropped to $23^0$ and even $14^0$. As they were all very cold in their light clothing, and the canvas tent offered little protection, they took turns to keep the fire going whenever they stopped. They were so preoccupied with pushing ahead and keeping warm, that they forgot about the primitive people. But then, they found no more footprints. Every living creature seemed to have migrated to the south and the sparse forests were silent in their white shrouds.

On the eighth day of dragging the boats up the frozen river they came to the end of the forest, and far to the north they saw the white edges of the ice-field. There was a dark spot against the white snow: it was their hut on the hill!

They had another six hard miles to go, and then—reunion with their friends and a long rest in the warm hut after their journey. Three hours later they were within a mile of the camp and expected to hear the dogs barking and see the men running out of the hut and rushing to meet them with the sledges and skis. But they heard and saw nothing, and the half-buried hut looked desolate and abandoned on the white hill.

They began to worry.

"Are they asleep at this time of day?"

"Where are the dogs?"

"Maybe something's happened?"

Urged on by their fears, they quickened their pace and stumbled, knee-deep in snow, towards the hut.

As they reached the bottom of the hill, everything was still quiet. They stopped and shouted in unison:

"Hey! Halloo! Ivan! Ilya! We've come back!"

They called a few more times, but the only response from the hut on the hill was deadly silence.

"If they aren't dead, all I can think of is that they've

taken the sledges and dogs and gone to hunt some large animal," Maksheyev said.

"But we've seen nothing to hunt for over a week," Papochkin objected.

"They've probably gone farther south."

"Maybe they've gone to meet us, since we were away so long," Gromeko suggested. "After it got cold and began to snow they may have remembered that we left in our summer clothes and without our skis."

"That doesn't seem probable, because they knew we'd gone down the river, and they couldn't have missed us if they followed it," Kashtanov said.

"I think we'll find the answer in the hut, but I suggest we go round the hill first to see if there are any tracks and make sure we don't trample them accidentally," Maksheyev said.

They left the sledges and walked round the bottom of the hill, scrutinizing the snow all the way. But there were no tracks, fresh or old, and it was quite plain that no one had gone up or down the hill since the last snow-fall.


## IN THE ABANDONED HUT

The heavy felt door of the hut was tightly shut and fastened on the outside: that meant there was no one inside. They opened the door and went in. The crates with instruments, collections, and their more valuable possessions were stacked along the back wall. The men's rifles, bandoliers, and clothes hung on the walls, and their sleeping-bags were rolled up in a corner. There were ashes in the fire-place in the middle of the floor, and a tea-pot was hanging on a tripod over it. There was a bundle of firewood at the fire-place. Everything looked as if the two men had gone out for a short time.

When they saw this, they grew still more worried. Their

friends had not gone hunting or on a trip, for both their rifles and their sleeping-bags were in the hut. Some enemies—either wild beasts or savages—must have ambushed them near the hut, and the dogs, left to themselves, must have starved to death or fled into the forest. But if they *had*  been attacked by some horde, why was the hut untouched?

On closer examination they saw there was dust on everything, and when Maksheyev looked into the tea-pot, he saw thick green mould on the tea leaves; that meant the two men had left the hut many weeks before.

"What's this?" said Kashtanov pointing to a strange wooden object on one of the crates.

They crowded round and saw that it was a crude figure of a mammoth, carved out of wood. It was quite repulsive, being covered with dark smears and a coat of grease.

"Maybe Ilya decided to become a sculptor?" Papochkin suggested.

"No! That's an idol," Maksheyev said. "It was smeared with the blood and fat of killed animals as a sacrifice. I expect our friends found it somewhere."

"If we consider the strange prints we saw on the sand that day and this idol, there can be no doubt that there *are* primitive people here," Kashtanov said.

"They've murdered them or taken them prisoner!" cried Gromeko.

"But why did they take nothing from the hut?"

When Maksheyev picked the idol up to get a better look at it, they were amazed to see two carefully folded slips of paper under it. Kashtanov smoothed them out quickly and read them aloud.

The first was dated September 25, and read:

*We are prisoners of a tribe of savages that appeared suddenly in the tundra two weeks ago. We were unarmed when they trapped us in the ice-house, where we had gone to check the supplies, and they led us off into the forest. They didn't touch the hut or the ice-house, but they didn't let us take anything with us. The dogs followed us. They treat us well, feed us, and are even very respectful towards us, as they seem to think we are medicine-men or gods. They watch our every step and we are guarded closely. They've taken our boots and almost all our clothes. They wear skins and live in tents made of skins stretched on poles. They have no fire, and eat raw meat. Their weapons are of bone and wood: spears, arrows, and knives. There are over a hundred people in the tribe, but there are more women than men. Both men and women hunt. The men are all weak and puny, and the women are tall and strong. Their bodies are covered with thick, short hair, and they resemble large tailless apes, but they have a spoken language which we have learned to understand. That's how we found out that they regard our hut as a sacred place and go there to worship. We've taken advantage of that to send this note as a sacrifice to our god. They promised to leave it in the hut. They took us about thirty or forty miles to the south-east, down the river we crossed when we went to fetch the dead mammoth. We think you can free us peacefully if you appear suddenly as gods. Bring us some warm clothes, some matches, and tobacco. We had a good summer and stocked up the ice-house.*

*Ivan, Ilya*

The other note was dated November 2nd.

*It has got much colder and has been snowing on and off. The savages are getting ready to go south. We keep a fire going to roast the meat and warm ourselves, but the savages are terrified by it and worship us more than ever. The women are our principal captors; they've taken a liking to us as we're stronger and better-looking than their own men. The men will be only too happy to help us escape. This is the last note, as they won't go to the hut any more. We'll probably travel down the same river, and we'll leave notes at every camp, or else we'll stick them on bushes on the way to leave a trail. If we can't escape with the help of the men, then fire a few shots to let us know you've come. Advance openly, firing into the air, to dazzle and cow the savages. If that fails, wound a few of the women. We're in good spirits and aren't afraid, but we're terribly cold and are tired of the monotonous meat diet. Why haven't you come back yet? Is everything all right?*

*Ivan, Ilya*

"They're alive!" Papochkin exclaimed.

"We'll have to hurry, they've been captives for nearly three months ... Today's the 5th of December," Gromeko said looking at his diary.

"They say the savages didn't touch anything here," Maksheyev said. "That means the sledges and skis should be in the ice-house with the food. Let's dig through to it and start getting ready."

"Everything seems to be in order here," Papochkin said. "The ice-house should be all right too, if only they didn't leave the door open so that the dogs could get at it."

After the hardships of the long journey over the snow, nights spent in a light canvas tent, and a steady diet of meat and biscuits, the warm hut and tinned food were a very welcome change. They decided to rest a few days, while preparing for a new journey that might take several weeks, depending on how far south the tribe had migrated.

There were a few feet of snow on the hill, and they found everything safe inside the ice-house. The first thing they did was to pull out the skis and sledges, to see if they were in need of repair. The main store-room was shut off by a solid door that had prevented wild animals from reaching the unguarded food. Their busy friends had put in a large supply of smoked meat that came in very handy, as it saved spending time on hunting.

Borovoi had built a little meteorological cabin near the hut. The instruments inside were in good condition, and they found his log, which gave them an idea of the climate in the tundra during the latter part of the summer and early autumn.

They decided to take the hut with them, store all the extra things in the ice-house, put a strong padlock on the door, and heap snow over the entrance to conceal it from unwanted visitors.

They took two sledges, six pairs of skis, a month's supply of food, warm clothing, and their sleeping-bags. They also made a package of some sweets, sugar, knives, and needles and thread to take along as gifts in case the savages were willing to give up their prisoners peaceably.

## FOLLOWING THE TRAIL

Having rested for three days they set out, first to the south-east, until they reached the river which Kashtanov and Papochkin had crossed when they first went mammoth-hunting, and then down the river.

On the second day they came upon a clearing on the left bank where the savages had camped. About twenty tent frames stuck up from the snow; they were cone-shaped, like Eskimo and Indian tepees.

A note was attached to one of the poles:

*We've been living here some time, but the tribe is moving farther south today. We'll try to esca . . .*

The rest had been torn off.

They decided to keep following the river, looking carefully for notes every ten or twelve miles, as that seemed to be the slow daily pace of the tribe, burdened by household possessions.

That evening at the edge of a large clearing they found a note tied to a bush with a piece of thread. The contents were as follows:

*We're doing about twelve miles a day, either walking along forest paths near the river, or else wading along the river-bed. The water is icy cold and often above our knees, but they don't seem to mind it at all. They've returned some of our clothes, but they take them away at night and give us animal skins to keep us warm. They don't set up their tents for the night, but sleep under the bushes. The only reason we're still alive is that we light a fire every time we stop.*

*Ivan*

The next day they covered twenty-five miles without seeing any notes: the wind might have blown them away. After lunch the following day they found a note:

*When the savages see our notes on the bushes they take them off and keep them as amulets, because they think we're leaving them as a sacrifice to the evil spirit that causes the cold and snow of winter. It's only by chance that we can leave you a message. We'll try to put scraps of paper on the bushes near the water, so you'll know we've passed that way. When you reach a point where the snow ends and the river isn't frozen over, be very cautious. We think the tribe will stop there for some time.*

*Ivan*

They kept on for six more days, sometimes finding short notes, but more often just little scraps of paper, stuck on bushes near the bank. On the tenth day there were only about five inches of snow left on the ground, and the ice on the river would crack underfoot occasionally. The temperature was steady at one or two degrees below freezing point. The next day they went on along the bank, as the ice was getting very thin and there were large patches of open water on the river. They found a path in the forest near the bank and followed it. By evening the middle of the river was clear of ice, and there were no more than two inches of snow on the ground.

Finally, on the twelfth day of their journey, there were only small snow-drifts under the bushes and in the forest, so that they had to drag the sledges over the layer of dry leaves on the path. They found another note before lunch saying that within a day they would come to a large clearing where the tribe planned to spend the rest of the winter, unless it was forced farther south by the snow.

They went more cautiously than ever before, because they ran the risk of bumping into some of the savages who might be out hunting near the camp. They took turns to walk ahead of the sledges with General, in order to give warning of any danger.

They stopped for the night at a small clearing near the river, and Kashtanov and Maksheyev went out to scout. About two miles farther downstream they heard a lot of noise and shouting. They crept stealthily to the edge of a large clearing and saw the primitive nomads' camp at the other end.

It consisted of twelve cone-shaped tents forming a circle around a smaller, thirteenth, tent. Each tent was made of animal skins spread out on a frame of poles, and the tent flaps were all at the centre of the circle. A fire burned in front of the small central tent, and they were certain that was where their friends were.

The space in the centre of the circle was full of children. Most of them were running about on all fours and resembled tailless black apes. They were playing, jumpiug, fighting and squabbling, and they kept screeching all the time. An ape-like man squatted near the entrance of one of the tents. Watching him through binoculars they could see that his body was entirely covered by dark hair. The bone structure of his face was like an Australian aborigine's, but his jaws were more prominent and his forehead more receding. His face was a dull brown with a small beard below his chin.

Presently a second figure appeared from within the tent and pushed the first one in the back, to make him move aside. The squatting man lurched forward and jumped to his feet, so that the two stood beside each other. The newcomer was taller, more broad-shouldered, and had larger hips than the other who looked like a frail youth by comparison. The second person's face was more comely and the matted hair on its head hung down to its shoulders, but on the whole the body was less covered with hair. This was a primitive woman.

She crossed the circle towards the small tent. She had a slightly stooped and rolling gait and her loosely hanging arms nearly reached her knees; the muscles of her arms and legs were very well developed.

When she came up to the captives' tent she fell on her knees before the fire with her arms outstretched, and then crawled into the tent.

"She's dropped in to visit them!" Kashtanov said.

"There don't seem to be many of the savages about. I think we should let our friends know we're here," Maksheyev said.

"How? We can't get any closer without being spotted."

"We can fire a few shots from the forest; that's just what they suggested."

"It might alarm the savages."

"They won't know what's happening."

"Suppose they come to look for us?"

"I doubt if they will. They'll be too scared."

"Well then, let's do it."

They turned back to the forest. Maksheyev fired a shot and a few minutes later Kashtanov fired too. Then they returned to the edge of the clearing.

The camp was in an uproar. Several adults, mostly women, and children of all ages stood in a group near the tents. They were all looking towards the forest and talking excitedly. Near the camp-fire were Igolkin and Borovoi, naked to the waist and wearing ragged trousers; they were very tanned, and their long hair and beards were matted.

They were also facing the far edge of the clearing and their faces were jubilant.

Suddenly, apparently at the word "Now!", they both raised their arms and instantly all the savages fell on their knees and bent their faces to the ground. It became very quiet. Then Igolkin cupped his hands at his mouth and shouted:

"Most of the men went hunting early this morning. They've gone far away. The women will follow tomorrow to help to bring back the spoils. Only the children and old people will be here. Come and get us then. Bring us some clothes. Is everything all right? Are you all safe? Fire once if everything is all right, and twice if anything has gone wrong."

Maksheyev immediately crawled back a little and fired once. At the sound of the shot Igolkin raised his arms again, and the people who had got up to watch in amazement while he was shouting, fell on their faces again.

Igolkin let them lie there for a while; then he turned to the fire and began to sing a spirited sailors' song in a very loud voice. The savages crept up and settled in a large circle around the fire, each face showing surprise. Apparently, their captives had never done anything like this before.

Maksheyev counted fifty adults. There were many more

adolescents and children who sat apart from the grown-ups and were obviously enjoying Igolkin's singing, whereas the adults were startled and even frightened by it.

Igolkin went on singing for about ten minutes. Then he raised his arms again and Borovoi, who had been sitting motionless by the fire all the time, rose, and they both vanished inside their tent. The audience began to drift back to their own tents, but two women went to the small tent and sat by the entrance to guard the men's sleep.

The camp soon quieted down, and the last embers of the fire glowed in the empty circle.

Kashtanov and Maksheyev went back to tell the others what had happened; they all sat down to discuss plans for freeing their friends.

## FREEING THE CAPTIVES

Next morning, after a good night's sleep, they packed everything on the sledges and made them ready for going back. Then they set out for the savages' camp, taking clothing, boots, and rifles for their friends, and gifts for the primitive people. Near the clearing they heard shouting and dogs barking: evidently, the hunters had not yet left. The men crept up and watched from behind a clump of bushes.

The whole camp was bustling with activity; the central circle was full of hunters ready to leave. Men and women were carrying spears, darts, scrapers, and bundles of leather thongs from the tents. The children were everywhere: they kept touching the weapons and getting cuffed, which made them screech and howl. The adolescents were testing the sharp edges of the darts and spears, and pricking each other for fun. Beyond the circle were about fifteen half-wild dogs that had once belonged to the expedition. They seemed to be waiting for the hunters to get started and were snarling and fighting each other in the meantime.

At last the savages got their weapons ready. The adults took up their spears and set off in a group towards the east, with the youths behind them, carrying darts, knives, and thongs; they seemed to be the weapon-bearers and the porters for bringing back the spoils. The children ran shouting and screeching after them: some on all fours and some upright. The dogs followed at a distance. The children turned back at the edge of the clearing, and the band of fifty hunters stretched out along the path in single file and disappeared in the woods.

There were only old people left in the camp. A few crones crept out of some of the tents and sat near the entrances. Toddlers crawled out and infants were laid on skins on the ground.

Three young women were left to guard the prisoners' tent and sat outside, busy at their tasks. One was cutting a skin into thin strips with a bone knife, another was making wooden shafts for arrows, and the third was cracking large bones, to use the sharp pieces as arrow-heads and spear-heads.

Soon Igolkin came out of the tent. He tossed some sticks into the fire and squatted down near the women. He said something to one of them, then took out his big hunting knife and began cutting strips of leather too; the pile of thongs grew quickly with his help. Borovoi appeared. He did not offer to help, but stood facing the woods where the rifle shots had sounded the night before.

The picture of a twentieth-century sailor helping Stone Age women with their work made them all smile. The camp was nearly empty, and in view of the primitive weapons of the remaining adults they had no doubts of being able to free their comrades peaceably—or by force, if necessary. But they decided to wait another hour or two, to make sure the hunting party was out of earshot of any commotion or rifle shots, and that the three body-guards could not catch up with the hunters and bring them back quickly.

The children drifted back to the camp and began to play. They wrestled, tumbled, fought, and the older ones practised throwing darts into the air, or at the hides on the tents.

When Igolkin had cut up the whole skin he went back to the tent and brought out a chunk of raw meat which he cut into cubes. He stuck these on small arrow shafts and placed them round the fire to roast. Apparently, the captives had not yet breakfasted and intended to have a hearty meal before their flight. When the meat was ready they both sat down near the fire and began to eat with relish. At times Igolkin would offer a bite to the women sitting beside them, but they would laugh and turn away. Then one of the women went over to her own tent and brought back a big piece of raw meat. All three began to cut off long thin strips which they ate with pleasure. Whenever a child came over, they would cut him a thin strip too.

After the two men had finished eating, the rescue party decided it was time to begin.

They formed a straight line and advanced rapidly towards the tents, firing blanks from their raised rifles.

At the sound of the first shots everything came to a standstill in the camp. The people froze as they watched the approach of those who could make such terrible thunder-noises.

As the men entered the circle of tents the savages fell face down on the ground, and the smallest children howled with fright.

The men approached their friends and gave them the warm clothing. As they dressed the others kept firing into the air. Maksheyev said to Igolkin:

"Tell them that you've been with them for quite a while

and that now more powerful medicine-men have come for you. We've brought them gifts to show that we appreciate the way they treated you and to remind them of the strange ones who came from the land of Eternal Ice. Tell them that they shouldn't dare pursue us, or they will be severely punished. Tell them the Ice Gods know how to make terrible lightning to strike down their enemies, as well as loud thunder."

When the men had dressed, their rescuers stopped firing, and Igolkin addressed the prostrate savages, repeating what Maksheyev had said to him. Then he turned to the three women who had been their bodyguards and said:

"Give these gifts to your chiefs when they return from the hunt and let them divide them. We are leaving you this fire to use. Never let it go out, feed it with twigs and branches as we did. Again I order you: do not try to follow us. We are going back to the land of Eternal Ice and will return when it is warm again."

Then he placed the gifts outside the little tent, and the six of them walked across the circle, firing their rifles into the air continuously.

Not one of the prostrate savages had dared to move.

As soon as they were well hidden behind the trees at the edge of the forest, the men stopped to see what the savages would do. When the last shots had died away, the people began to get up and discuss what had happened. Some had gathered round the camp-fire and were looking at the flames in bewilderment. Then two of the three women took up their spears and ran off after the rest of the tribe. The third woman remained to guard the packages from the inquisitive children, but she herself did not dare touch the objects.

Having reached the sledges they had left in the forest, the men started back, dragging the sledges along the dry leaves on the narrow path.

Igolkin whistled shrilly now and then as they moved away from the camp. He had trained the dogs to obey that whistle and had kept them near the tribe all the time he and Borovoi had been captives. Although he had been giving them scraps constantly, the dogs had become half-wild, as the savages were afraid of them and would not have them in the camp. A few of the dogs had been killed by wild beasts, and most of the others had followed the tribe when it left to go hunting, so that only five dogs that had remained near the camp responded to the familiar whistle. They followed some distance behind the sledges, but would not let the men come near and snarled at General when he ran up to them. They would have to be tamed by feeding them regularly during the next few days, so that there would be at least one dog team.

They didn't stop until, after twelve hours of walking and pulling the sledges, they had put about thirty miles between them and the camp. Then, convinced that they were beyond reach of the tribe, they stopped for the night.

## THE PRIMITIVE PEOPLE ATTACK

They chose a large open space, put up the hut in the middle of it—as an extra precaution, to make sure they would not be ambushed—and took turns to keep watch. The dogs seemed to have recognized the hut and settled down in the snow near by, as General would not let them come too close.

While Kashtanov was on watch, General began to growl and then to bark unceasingly. Kashtanov noticed that all the bushes round the clearing were swaying and rustling slightly. He woke the others and they jumped out with their guns ready.

The savages saw that their original plan of a sudden attack had failed; they came out of the forest, surrounded the clearing, and began moving slowly and hesitantly towards the hut. They were women armed with spears, with knives between their teeth. Behind came young girls carrying darts. They seemed reluctant to use their weapons, because they apparently hoped to capture the medicine-men alive, as they had done before, and force them to come back to their camp. Igolkin told his friends to hold their fire while he spoke to the savages, but suggested replacing one of the bullets in the double-barrelled guns by a charge of buck-shot.

"I think a couple of rounds of buck-shot aimed at their legs should be enough," he said, "but if that doesn't work, we'll have to use bullets."

When the women were about thirty feet away, Igolkin waved his arms and shouted:

"Stop! Listen to me! I forbade you to follow us. You disobeyed my orders. Our fiery arrows are ready. If you move any closer, we'll throw the arrows at you! Go back!"

The women had stood still while he spoke. They began to consult each other and then one of the women shouted something, while the others waved their spears in agreement.

"They want Ivan and me to go back with them, because they say the tribe can't live without us, but the rest of you can leave," Igolkin translated for his friends. Then he shouted:

"Medicine-men cannot live with people long. We are returning to our tents on the ice for the winter, but we'll come back when it gets warm. Hurry! Go away!"

Some of the women moved a few steps closer, and one rash young girl suddenly threw her dart at Kashtanov. It flew past his ear and stuck into the hut.

"We've no choice," Borovoi said. "We must shoot before they get too bold. Let them have the buck-shot—one, two, three!"

Six rifles barked, and there were screams and howls

of wounded women from different parts of the circle. The
savages turned and made a dash for the forest, many of
them limping. The girl who had tossed her dart at Kashtanov took a few steps and fell motionless on the snow.

"What now?" Gromeko asked as the last of the savages
disappeared. "Should we wait for them to attack again,
or won't they dare to?"

"I think they've had enough," Igolkin said. "But let's
go inside for safety. We don't want to be hit by some girl's
dart."

Their precautions were unnecessary, for the howling
horde kept running until it was beyond earshot. The dogs
stopped barking; they ran up to the wounded girl and
began to lap up the warm blood flowing from her wound.
The men went to chase off the dogs.

She had been wounded in her right thigh, which was
bleeding profusely.

"That's strange," Papochkin said. "Buck-shot could never have produced a wound like that."

"Someone must have fired a bullet by mistake."

"I aimed at her," Kashtanov said.

"The poor thing's alive, she's just fainted from pain and fright," Gromeko said as he examined the girl. "The bullet passed through her leg without damaging the bone, but it tore through the muscles."

"What'll we do with her? All the others have gone."

"We'll just have to take her as a captive, and when she's better we can let her go again."

"Let her go!" cried Papochkin in horror. "By no means! We'll deliver her on board the *North Star* as a perfect specimen of a primitive human being not far removed from the monkey family. What a find she'll be for anthropologists!"

Gromeko fetched his kit, stopped the bleeding, and bandaged the wound. As he was tying the bandage, the girl suddenly came to and opened her eyes. When she saw that she was surrounded by medicine-men she was panic-stricken.

The girl was of medium height and as yet she had not the massive build and over-developed muscles of the adult women. Her whole body, apart from her face, palms, and soles, was thickly covered with short black hair. The hair on her head was longer and slightly wavy. The soles of her feet seemed to be a cross between those of apes and human beings. The toes were well developed and the big toe was at an angle to the other four.

When Borovoi had had a closer look at the girl's face, he exclaimed:

"Why, this is my old friend, Katu!"

"Do you mean you could tell them apart? They all looked alike to me," Kashtanov said.

"That was only a first impression. There *is* quite a difference, and we knew many of them by name, especially the older girls and boys, and the children. Katu used to bring me meat, roots, and other titbits she considered most delicious, to show her fondness for me."

"That's why she dared throw her dart at one of her darling's kidnappers!" Maksheyev laughed.

"Two inches to the right and I'd have lost an eye," Kashtanov added.

When Gromeko had finished bandaging, they made to carry Katu into the hut, but she began to shriek and kick. Igolkin was able to make out that she was begging them to leave her to die on the snow instead of carrying her into the tent to be eaten.

"To be eaten?" asked Gromeko in surprise. "Are they cannibals?"

"Yes. They enjoy a good meal of their friends who were killed or badly wounded during a hunt or a fight."

"Tell her not to worry. We've no intention of eating her, and we only want her to sleep and rest in the hut. Tell her that as soon as she gets well we'll let her go back to her camp."

It took a lot of persuading, but when Borovoi finally took her hand she calmed down and let them carry her into the hut. They laid her on one of the bedrolls and she soon fell asleep, still holding on to Borovoi's hand.

Since the time they had allowed for sleep was nearly up, they began to prepare for the journey ahead; they started a fire, put on the kettle, and sat down to have breakfast. When Igolkin went out to get some snow to fill the kettle, he noticed more dogs roaming about the edge of the forest; they had evidently come with the tribe and stayed behind. Perhaps the hut reminded them of the tasty *ukola* they had once had to eat and they recalled their former owners. Igolkin whistled several times, and twelve more dogs ran into the clearing; with these twelve, General, and the five that had followed them from the camp, they could just manage three teams for the sledges.

"What can we give them to eat?" Igolkin asked. "The only way to keep them from running away and tame them again is by feeding them."

"We brought food for a month," Gromeko said, "and we should be at the ice-house in about a week. I'm sure we'll have enough ham for them."

"Don't give them too much!" Borovoi added. "They'll run better if they're hungry and know they'll be fed at each stop."

After breakfast they gave the dogs the scraps and bones that were left, and a small piece of meat each. Then they began packing. They put Katu on the sledge with the felt-covered planks of the hut and piled everything else on the other one. The snow was deep enough for them to use their skis and in spite of the increased load, they made better progress than they had done the previous day. When Katu saw that they were taking her away from the direction of her camp, she shrieked, jumped off the sledge, and tried to run off, but after a few steps, she fell. When they tried to lift her back on to the sledge she fought furiously and tried to bite them.

She had apparently understood Igolkin to say that they were taking her back to the tribe, where they would let her go, but instead, they were carrying her off to the land of ice. They had to bind her hands and tie her to the sledge to keep her from trying to escape again. Poor Katu sobbed with fright, and was convinced they were going to eat her after all.

They reached the river-bed after midday. The snow there was packed hard, so that their skis and sledges did not sink in as they had done on the forest path. That day they covered thirty miles again.

They took turns to keep watch that night, but everything was quiet. Katu had refused to eat anything during the day, and they had to keep her tied up at night. All through their dinner and supper she watched, rigid with fear, as the medicine-men cut pieces off the ham with their shining knives. Every flick of their wrists made her think it would soon be her turn to be cut up like the ham.

They continued northwards for another week, and on the eighth day they reached the tundra; by noon they were at the foot of the hill. Katu had gradually become resigned to her fate; she got used to the medicine-men and would eat raw meat, but the sight of cooked food repulsed her. They untied her hands on the third day of the journey and her feet on the fifth, after she had promised not to run away any more.

## THE CAPTIVES' STORY

Each time they stopped on the way back to the hill, Igolkin and Borovoi told the others something of their experiences during the time they had spent with the savages, and Kashtanov made notes of their story.

The day the others had gone south, the two men had begun to build a meteorological cabin for their instruments and a strong door for the ice-house, to protect the supplies from their own dogs and from wild beasts. These tasks completed, they began cutting a second tunnel, farther down the slope, to serve as a refuge for the dogs, because the temperature kept rising steadily and the animals were forced to seek relief at the ever-receding edge of the ice-field. While they were busy with these urgent jobs, they went hunting only when it was absolutely necessary, but afterwards they began to go out hunting every day to store up a large supply of meat for the winter ahead: dried for the dogs and smoked for the men. Every day, as they returned from their hunting trips in the forest, they piled the sledge high with dry branches so that they gradually built up quite a pile of firewood for the cold winter months.

They shot mammoth and rhinoceros, musk ox, giant and northern deer. On the river and in the tundra there were ducks, geese, and other birds which supplied most of their food during the summer. They dried and smoked the meat of the large animals and were so busy that often they didn't even get enough sleep.

Soon after the others had left, the weather began to improve, the solid mass of clouds parted, and Pluto shone for a few hours a day, so that the temperature rose to $68^0$ in the shade. At last it was summer in the tundra. But by the middle of August there were already signs of autumn in the air: the sky was overcast, sometimes it rained, and after the rain everything would be enveloped in a heavy mist rising from the earth.

The mercury kept dropping, going as low as $32^0$ on windy September days. Leaves turned yellow, and by the middle of September the tundra had lost its summer green and was barren and russet-brown. It snowed at times.

In preparing for the winter, the men rechecked all their supplies in the ice-house, and transferred part of them to the hut. On the second day of taking stock, after they had locked the ice-house and were about to have lunch, they were suddenly attacked by savages who had crept up the other side of the hill. Neither of the men had ever dreamed there could be human life in Plutonia, and they were unarmed, except for their knives. As their attackers had spears, knives, and arrows, it seemed useless and pointless to resist. When the savages looked at the white men closely, at their hut and the meteorological cabin, they seemed in awe of the strange, unknown beings whom they took to their camp about six miles away, in a sparsely wooded area (later the men found out that the tribe had migrated there from the east the day before).

The savages had long discussions as to the fate of their prisoners; the men wanted them to be offered up as a sacrifice to their gods, but the majority of women were against the idea. They thought the mere presence of the strangers in the tribe would make it all-powerful, would bring success in hunting and in battles with other tribes. Therefore, it was decided not to kill them, but to treat them well and keep them in a separate tent in the middle of the camp.

At the time of the men's capture, the tribe was collecting various berries and roots in the tundra for winter use, and had remained there for several days. A heavy snow-fall forced them to move about twenty-five miles southward, where they could shelter from the biting winds in a wooded area.

At first the men were very miserable. The only food they had was the raw meat, berries, and roots their captors gave them. They slept on reeking animal skins and had others to cover themselves with. They could sometimes make themselves understood by sign language, but had no idea of what was going to happen to them. There was no chance of escape, as they were closely guarded day and night.

When they moved to a large clearing in a dense forest, the primitive people began cutting down thin dry saplings to be used as tent-poles. The ground around the camp was littered with dry branches, bark, and chips of wood; Igol-kin suddenly realized he could now make use of the box of matches in his pocket which he had taken along to the ice-house that day to light a lantern. He gathered a lot of dry wood and started a fire. As the first flames flickered up, everyone in the camp came running to see this marvel. When they burned their hands trying to touch it, the fire became an object of worship to them, and the strangers who possessed it were regarded with still greater awe. From then on the prisoners kept a fire going all the time in front of their tent, and used it to roast little pieces of the raw meat they were given.

Soon they began to understand the very simple language of their captors. The savages' mental scope was very limited and included only hunting, eating, and a primitive way of life. Their language consisted of one- and two-syllabled words; there were no declensions, no verbs, no adverbs nor prepositions, and they supplemented their meagre speech by facial expressions and sign-language. They could only count up to twenty on their fingers and toes.

The men went hunting and fashioned chips of flint into spear-heads, arrow-heads, knives, and scrapers. The women went berry-picking and gathered roots; they cleaned and dried the hides and furs, and helped to hunt large animals, when the entire tribe had to pit its strength against some monster.

The savages hunted any beast they came upon and ate the entrails as well as the meat; their diet included raw worms, snails, caterpillars, and beetles. The hunters would gorge themselves on the still-warm flesh of an animal they had killed and drink the blood as it ran out; then they would take the rest of the carcass and the hide back to camp. They would surround huge animals like mammoths and rhinoceroses and force them into pits dug on animal paths in the forest, where they would stone or spear them to death.

They hunted in families, or two or three family groups would team up together; if the quarry was so huge that the whole tribe had to go after it, only two or three women would be left in the camp to guard the captives.

On the basis of what Igolkin and Borovoi had told him, and from what he himself had seen of their weapons and skill, Kashtanov was of the opinion that the tribe had much in common with the Neanderthal tribes that inhabited Europe in the Stone Age, when mammoths, long-haired rhinoceroses, primitive bulls, and other animals of the Glacial period were alive.

The savages thought the fire they worshipped was a little sun. As the cold drove the tribe farther south, they were forced to leave the tent-poles behind, since they were too heavy and cumbersome to carry. As it would have taken too long to cut new poles each time they stopped for the night, they slept on the ground, seeking shelter from the cold wind in the underbrush.

Whenever they approached their prisoners' fire, they felt the warmth of the flames, so that very soon the entire tribe was sleeping around it and gathering all the firewood they could find in the vicinity. It never occurred to any of them that other fires could be lit and the two men made no attempt to tell them, for they wanted to remain the sole possessors of the fire and the savages' admiration. They felt that through time, if for some reason their friends could not free them, their situation would grow much more difficult.

They counted the fleeting days of autumn with ever-mounting concern and tried to guess how soon the four men would return from the south and come to their rescue.

Winter was setting in, and soon the tribe would move still farther south. And so the captives, hearing those first shots ring out in the forest, had felt joyful indeed.


## BACK ON THE HILL

They reached their hill at the edge of the ice-fields in the last days of December. They decided to rest and have a triple celebration: New Year, the success of the expedition to the south, and the freeing of the prisoners. There were enough provisions and firewood to make it unnecessary. to go out into the tundra or the forest for anything.

They cleared a square of snow, set up the hut, and dug

trenches through the three-foot-deep snow to the ice-house, the dog cave, and the meteorological cabin. They felt they had earned a rest. A small fire burned in the hut, making it warm and cosy. When they were not eating, sleeping, or out of doors, all six kept up a lively conversation, discussing their adventures and recalling various incidents.

Katu, the silent member of the party, was more than ever impressed by the white medicine-men who owned so many strange objects. Her leg was healing, and she was able to move about a bit. They often found her sitting on her haunches outside the tent, gazing longingly towards the dark strip of forest on the south horizon. She was very homesick for her people.

Igolkin tried to persuade her to stay with them and cross the ice to a warm country, where she would see all the wonders that white men had created. But she stubbornly refused, saying:

"Me forest, tent, meat, blood meat, hunt."

But they did not lose hope that in the end she would get used to them and agree to go with them. What a sensation that would be: an expedition that had brought back a living example of a primitive human being!

When the frosts set in she began to feel cold, but refused the clothing they offered her and wrapped herself in her blanket whenever she left the warm hut. She took no part at all in cleaning the hut, washing dishes, keeping the trenches clear of snow, or fetching in firewood. She wanted to know how many wives Igolkin had, whether they went hunting, how large their tribe was, and shook her head in disbelief when he tried to tell her about civilized life, about cities, seas, and ships. Her only occupation when she was not eating or sleeping was cutting arrow shafts and carving very crude little mammoths, rhinoceroses, bears, and tigers from the soft firewood. Soon she had a whole collection of these idols which she worshipped, and she kept begging Igolkin for some fresh blood to smear on them. This they could not give her, for the men did not go hunting and there were neither animals nor birds in the snow-covered tundra.

In January they began to go out for practice trips on the sledges to get the dogs used to the harness again. The dogs were quite tame now; they were well fed and lived in their ice cave, except for General, who kept close to the hut as a watchdog. When the dogs had got accustomed to pulling the sledges, they all went on longer trips across the tundra, towards the edge of the forest to gather much-needed firewood. Five of them would go on these trips, and one stayed behind to guard Katu.

One day, towards the end of January, it was Papochkin's turn to remain behind. Katu was always excited when they set out towards the woods, and she anxiously watched for their return, for she hoped they would shoot an animal and bring her back some of the raw meat she missed so much. But she was bitterly disappointed each time, as the men never came across any living creatures.

About two hours after the others had left, Papochkin dozed off in the warm hut. He slept for quite a while, and when he woke, Katu was gone. He ran out and saw a little black spot moving rapidly away, far off to the south. The girl had taken his skis, as she had learned how to use them, and he stood no chance of overtaking her on foot through the deep snow. She had taken her blanket, a ham that was hanging in the hut, a large knife, and a box of matches which she now knew the use of.

When the others came back they were quite angry, and for a whole unhappy evening Papochkin had to listen to their opinion of his carelessness. There was no chance of catching up with her by then; even if the whole expedition had given chase they might not have succeeded. Katu had nothing heavy to slow her down, and she was used to covering nearly sixty miles a day during a hunt, as compared with the maximum of thirty which the sledges might be expected to do. In any case, there was no sense in trying to take her away from her family by force.

By good luck they had made plaster impressions of her hands and feet and a mask of her face, and had measured her according to all the rules of anthropology; Papochkin had taken half a dozen shots of her.

In order to reach the outer world and the southern shore of Nansen Land by the beginning of summer, at a time when the polar day was very long, they had to begin their journey back across the ice at the end of March, or even the beginning of April. That meant they had nearly two months to wait, and they decided to train themselves and the dogs to cover greater distances at a time. Several times they had seen in the snow at the edge of the forest fresh tracks of deer, musk oxen, and wolves, and they hoped to shoot some game by travelling for a day or two from the hill. Both the men and the dogs felt the lack of fresh meat; they had grown tired of ham, and, thanks to Katu's gluttonous appetite, the supplies of smoked meat had greatly decreased. They had to save what was left of it for the journey back and try to feed themselves by hunting till then. They took turns to go on these hunting expeditions: one group of three would take two sledges and teams and the tent, and the other three and one dog team would stay behind to rest from the previous trip.

## ACROSS THE ICE

Towards the end of March the men decided it was time they started back across the ice. They left the meteorological cabin as it was and put a sealed metal box inside it, and another in the ice-house in the hill. These contained records of the discovery of Plutonia and of the major achievements of the expedition to the south. To prevent the primitive people from carrying off the sealed boxes and destroying the cabin when they returned north in the summer, some of the wooden idols which Katu had made were left on a shelf in the cabin and the floor was piled high with tins, bones, and other rubbish to suggest sacrificial objects. This was Igolkin's idea, for he had come to know the savages better than Borovoi had.

The sledges, heavily laden with the collections, provisions, and equipment sped across the snow-covered tundra to the edge of the ice.

The journey back across Nansen Land took a whole month; first they had to overcome the ice barrier, then came the long and difficult climb up the Russian Ridge and the descent down the northern slope over the ice-falls of the glacier. They were travelling against the wind, the sledges were overloaded, and there were not enough dogs; everything conspired to slow them down and exhaust their energy. The frequent blizzards were also a handicap, but at least they provided them with extra hours of rest. Beyond the ice barrier there were hours of daylight and hours of darkness,. something they had not experienced for a long time. They could not find some of the supplies of food they had left on their way to Plutonia, but on Cape Trukhanov there was a new store of provisions for a year which the crew of the *North Star* had left, with a note to say that the ship was anchored for the winter about ten miles to the east of the Cape. From the highest point they could see it lying at anchor in the distance, and when they were still two miles away, they were finally reunited with the others. Even Trukhanov had come out to meet them on a sledge pulled by young dogs that had been born aboard the *North Star*. There was no limit to their excitement and questions. Trukhanov beamed when he heard that his theory of the earth's inner space had been proved beyond a doubt.

# A SCIENTIFIC TALK

A terrible snow-storm began a few days after the return of the expedition. It was a normal occurrence for that latitude, but it brought their outdoor activities to a sudden end. They spent their time below decks, exchanging stories of the months spent in drifting among the ice-floes and the journey to Plutonia. Trukhanov was especially interested in the details of the descent into the earth which had been so full of strange and apparently unexplainable incidents.

"You know, we read your letter the day we saw mammoths in the tundra that had suddenly replaced the ice-fields, and although it explained where we were, it did not altogether satisfy us," Kashtanov told Trukhanov. "We wanted to know how you had come to the conclusion that the earth was hollow, and what the basis of your theory was, for it had been proved to be quite correct."

"Actually, it is not my idea, nor is it a new theory," Trukhanov answered. "Some West-European scientists formed the opinion over a hundred years ago, and I came across the theory in some old magazines I was looking through; I got interested in the problem and began to put it to the test, which convinced me of its accuracy."

"Won't you tell us about your work on the problem?"

"With pleasure. If you like, I could give you a detailed account of it this evening."

That evening the mess was the scene of an interesting scientific talk.

Trukhanov began by reminding them of the ancients' conception of the earth as a flat body in a primordial ocean, and of Aristotle's theory that the earth was a sphere. Then he continued with a more detailed description of the newer trends of thought.

"At the end of the 18th century, a scientist named Lesley declared that the earth was filled with air that was self-luminous as a result of the pressure upon it. According to his theory, there were two planets in the underground atmosphere, Proserpine and Pluto . . ."

"Pluto!" cried Borovoi. "Then we didn't give it an original name after all!"

"It was named so before we were born," Trukhanov said. "Some scientists even calculated the courses of the two planets, and suggested that when they were closest to the earth's inner surface they caused magnetic storms and earthquakes on the outer surface. According to Lesley, the inner surface was lit by a soft electric light; it was a world of eternal spring, and therefore luxuriant plant life and a unique animal world were peculiar to it . . ."

"And he was right!" Papochkin exclaimed in amazement.

"Lesley thought the passage into the hollow of the earth was somewhere in the region of latitude 82⁰ North."

"It's fantastic!" Maksheyev shouted. "How could he have indicated it so accurately? We found the southern edge of the passage at something over 81⁰!"

"Lesley determined it by observing the area of greatest intensity of *aurora borealis*, as he believed it originated inside the earth and was formed by the electric rays which illuminated the inside of the earth. He had many followers, and the question of sending an expedition into the inner surface of the earth was discussed at great length."

"Well, well!" Gromeko smiled. "We were almost beaten even in that!"

"The expedition did not take place, because the great scientists of the time—Buffon, Leibnitz, and Kircher—ridiculed Lesley's hypothesis and said it was pure fantasy. They firmly advocated the accepted theory that the earth's centre was a molten fiery mass with a multitude of secondary centres called pyrofiliations. Towards the end of the eighteenth century the convincing Kant-Laplace hypothesis that our whole solar system was created from burning gas became almost universally accepted so that all other ideas remained in obscurity.

"But in 1816 Kormuls tried to prove that the earth was hollow and that its crust was no thicker than three hundred English miles.

"Halley, Franklin, Lichtenberg, and Kormuls attempted to explain the earth's magnetism and the changes it had undergone through the centuries from the point of view of the possible existence of an inner planet. In 1817 a German professor named Steinhauser stated that there was practically no doubt as to the existence of such an inner planet, which he named Minerva.

"New plans of sending an expedition into the earth were discussed. In April 1818 a retired infantry captain named Simms, who lived in St. Louis, Missouri, sent a letter to the newspapers. He sent copies of it to many American and European universities. It was addressed 'To the Whole World,' and bore the motto 'Light brings light, to discover light to infinity.' Here's what he wrote:

*The earth is hollow and its inner surface is inhabited. It consists of a series of concentric spheres, one inside the other, and has openings of from $12^0$ to $16^0$ near the poles. I am ready to stake my life that this is true and propose to explore the inner cave if the world will help me. I have written a treatise on the subject, which is to be published soon, in which I produce evidence of the above statements, explain the various phenomena, and solve Dr. Darwin's golden secret. My one condition is that I should be the patron of this and the other new worlds. I will it to my wife and my ten children. I need only a hundred brave companions to leave Siberia at the end of the summer and proceed on reindeer-drawn sledges across the ice of the North Sea.*

*I guarantee that we shall find rich, warm lands abundant in useful plant and animal life—and perhaps even inhabited by human beings—as soon as we cross latitude $82^0$ North. We shall return the following spring.*

"And did the expedition take place?" Kashtanov asked.

"Unfortunately, or perhaps fortunately for us, it didn't. Simm's letter provoked a lot of discussion and magazines, newspapers, and well-known scientists were flooded with letters from intrigued readers. The proposal and the courageous captain—who was not afraid of leaving a widow and ten orphans behind—were given wide publicity in the press, but it didn't get him a hundred brave companions nor any money to finance the expedition. The scientists of his day regarded poor Simms as a dreamer or a madman. Although many people at the time believed that the earth was hollow and that a planet did exist there, they were by no means ready to accept a theory that supposed there was an opening in the earth's crust leading into it.

"A physicist named Chladni, writing in a scientific journal in response to Simm's letter, stated that such an opening was an impossibility: if one had ever existed, it would certainly have been filled up with water. Steinhauser had discovered that the inner planet moved extremely slowly, and Chladni explained this by the fact that all inner movement took place in a medium of compressed air, perhaps influenced also by the sun's and moon's power of gravity. Chladni had some other interesting theories, although he did not consider them indisputable: that since air under great pressure produces heat, and an intensely heated object begins to glow, then at the centre of the earth's hollow, where the pressure from all sides is greatest, the highly compressed air must logically be transformed into a light- and heat-giving mass, rather like a central sun.

"The inhabitants of the earth's inner surface, if they do exist, he said, always see the sun directly overhead, and the entire inner surface, lighted by it, around them.

"These theories of an inner planet were quite persistent. In the 1830's Bertrand also believed the earth to be hollow and he contended that there was a magnetic core inside which shifted from pole to pole under the influence of the comets.

"In the 19th century the Kant-Laplace theory that the earth's centre was a molten fiery mass was the most popular one. The advocates of this theory disagreed on one point only, and that was on the thickness of the hard crust of the earth; some said it was from twenty-five to thirty miles deep, others that it was more than sixty miles deep, and others again that it was from 800 to 1380 miles deep, i. e., from one-fifth to one-third of the earth's radius. However, the existence of volcanic and geothermic phenomena contradicts the possibility of such a depth of the earth's solid crust, as well as the theory that the earth is a completely cooled and hardened body. Therefore, the defenders of the theory of the earth's tremendous hard crust try to adjust it to these facts by saying that the volcanic centres are no more than isolated pools of molten matter which still exist within the crust.

"The second half of the 19th century saw a fourth theory come to light and displace the others; this was the hypothesis that the earth had a thin hard crust, a hard centre, and a more or less deep layer of molten ores between them, known as the olivine belt.

"The theory of the existence of a hard core inside the earth is understandable if we consider that the pressure close to the centre of the earth is so great that all bodies, despite the immense temperatures which are many times that of their melting point (under normal pressure), will remain solid.

"The earth's crust consists of the lightest elements, the olivine belt is made up of heavier ores rich in iron and olivine, and the core itself is the heaviest, consisting of metals, for instance. It is believed that the iron meteorites which consist, in the main, of nickeliferous iron are fragments of the cores of planets, while the stone meteorites which consist of olivine and other minerals rich in iron with pockets of nickeliferous iron give us an idea of the composition of the olivine belt.

"This theory has many followers to this day, but another one is competing with it. I mean Zöppritz's theory which has given new life to Lesley's ideas and those of the other scientists of the latter part of the 18th and the beginning of the 19th centuries.

"This theory has as its base the physical law which states that at extremely high temperatures—which, undoubtedly, must exist inside the earth—all bodies become gaseous, despite the great pressure.

"You are aware of the existence of a so-called critical temperature of gases, which point having been reached, they will neither compress nor turn into liquid, no matter how great the pressure is. There can be no doubt that the temperature at the centre of the earth is many times that of the critical temperature. Therefore, the core itself must consist of so-called one-atom gases which have lost their distinguishing chemical properties, as their molecules have dissociated into atoms under the influence of the high temperatures. This core is surrounded by a layer of overheated gases in a super-critical state, which are in turn surrounded by a layer of normal gases.

"That is followed by a liquid layer of molten matter, then a layer of thick liquid like lava or tar, then a layer intermediate between liquid and solid, matter in the so-called concealed-plastic state, which can best be compared with cobbler's wax.

"Finally, at the top we have a hard crust. Naturally, none of these layers is sharply defined, they blend gradually one into the other so that the earth's movement could not cause them to move at different rates or in different directions, thus influencing the tides or the shifting of the earth's axis. There is a difference of opinion as to the thickness of the earth's crust. The

Swedish geophysicist Arrenius believes that the gaseous core comprises 95 per cent of the earth's diameter, the fiery-molten layers four per cent, and the hard crust only one per cent of the diameter, that is, that it is about forty miles deep.

"Others consider it to be fifty, sixty, or even six hundred miles deep. However, the thinner crust of from forty to sixty miles is more in keeping with the phenomena of volcanism, orogenesis, geothermism, etc.

"So you see, this theory has revived Lesley's ideas, although minus the inner planets and outer openings; it has even corroborated Captain Simms's conception of concentric spheres. However, there was no question of the possibility of the existence of living matter inside the earth at temperatures that even dissociated the atoms of gases."

"All the same, it is inhabited!" Kashtanov exclaimed. "And when you organized the expedition you did believe in that possibility, didn't you?"

"Yes, I did," Trukhanov answered. "Now I'll tell you what my hypothesis was. I have long been a supporter of Zöppritz's theory and have calculated and observed the various phenomena in order to be able to further develop and corroborate it. My observations were mainly in the field of determining gravity, geomagnetic phenomena, and the courses underground tremors follow.

"It is a known fact that earthquake tremors are transmitted straight through the depths of the earth itself, as well as along the hard outer crust. Therefore, if an earthquake has taken place somewhere, sensitive instruments will record two series of shocks: first those that travel the shortest distance—along the earth's diameter—and then those that travel along the earth's crust, that is, along the periphery of the globe. The speed with which these tremors spread depends upon the density and the homogeneity of the medium, and the condition of the medium can in turn be judged by their speed.

"On the basis of many seismographic readings taken from stations all round the world, and especially from those recorded at my observatory on Munku-Sardyk, where I had the latest and most accurate and sensitive instruments at the bottom of a deep shaft at the foot of a mountain range, I discovered strange new facts which were in disagreement with Zöppritz's theory. It became apparent then that the earth's core did not consist of gases greatly condensed by pressure, but, in fact, nearly three-fourths of the core consisted of rarefied gases only slightly denser than the air we breathe. In other words, this gaseous core should have had a diameter of approximately five thousand miles, which would mean that there was no more than one thousand five hundred miles on either side that made up the liquid and solid layers, which meant there existed a solid or nearly solid body in the gaseous core. In other words, an inner planet with a diameter not more than three hundred and ten miles across."

"How could you determine the diameter of an invisible body?" Borovoi asked.

"Actually, it was quite simple. The body was in the path of earth tremors occurring at the direct antipodes of my observatory: that is, in the Pacific Ocean east of New Zealand; if, however, an earthquake occurred in New Zealand itself, or in Patagonia, there was never a solid body across the path of its shocks. A whole series of observations made it possible to determine the maximum dimensions of this body with sufficient accuracy.

"Therefore, I could prove that there was a large space filled with gases inside the earth and at its centre an inner planet with a diameter of no more than three hundred and ten miles.

"In general, these observations proved more in keeping with the theories of scientists living long before Zöppritz. In that case, however, one can doubt the accuracy of all the calculations concerning the distribution of heavy matter in the earth's core. We know that the average density of the earth is 5.5 and the density of rock formations in the surface layer of the crust is only 2.5—3.5 or even less, if we take the great masses of ocean water into account. Therefore, scientists believe that towards the centre of the earth the density of matter increases until it reaches 10 or 11 at the very core. However, if there is a great space inside the earth filled with gases of the same density as air and supporting a small planet, then we must completely alter our conception of the distribution of matter in the earth's crust surrounding the inner space filled with gases. I hold that the lighter surface of the crust is about forty-eight miles deep, the heavy inner part, consisting mostly of heavy metals, is about one thousand four hundred miles deep, and the inner space, including the planet, is about two thousand five hundred miles deep; when added up this will give us the earth's radius: 3,960 miles. If we take the average density of the heavy part of the crust as 7.8, then, according to the geophysicists, the density of the earth as a whole will be 5.5."

On a blackboard hanging on a wall in the mess Trukhanov did all the calculations to determine the volume and weight of the component layers of the earth, in order to prove his point of the distribution of matter. Having accepted Zöppritz's theory in this somewhat amended form, Trukhanov dealt with the origin of the opening which led from the outher to the inner surface of the earth and through which the condensed and overheated gases from the inner space must escape. His theory was that at one time an enormous meteorite had fallen to the earth, broken through its crust 1,476 miles thick, and remained inside, where it turned into the planet Pluto. As proof that such a thing could happen, he cited the huge depression, known as the meteorite crater, in the State of

Arizona in North America. This was a dent made at one time by a tremendous meteorite, fragments of which had been found in the depression. But that meteorite was unable to break through the earth's crust; it had bounced off and probably fallen into the Pacific Ocean, whereas Pluto had broken through the crust and remained within the earth.

"When did that happen?"

"Not later than the Jura, judging by the fact that you discovered plants and animals of that age at the most southerly point you were able to reach. The flora and fauna of the Jura penetrated into the inner surface after the opening had been made, the hot gases had escaped, and the atmosphere inside had cooled off. Afterwards, the flora and fauna of later periods gradually penetrated in the same way, the representatives of each successive period pushing the previous ones farther and farther into the interior. It is quite possible that there were even more ancient forms of animal and plant life in Plutonia, which you would have come across if you had been able to go farther south, beyond the Black Desert.

"As long as Nansen Land remains under ice, there is no possibility of our modern animals and plants reaching the inner surface.

"Twentieth-century man in your persons has been the first to brave the great ice barrier and reach the mysterious country that is a treasure-house of the living past of our planet. You have discovered a palaeontological museum whose existence I never dreamed of."

"You've given us a very vivid explanation of the things we found on the inner surface," Kashtanov said, "although palaeontologists may question you on some points of your theory. There's something I'd like to know: what happened to the fragments of the earth's crust that broke off when the opening was formed?"

"I believe that the smaller fragments were carried back

out of the opening by the escaping gases, and some of the larger ones might have become attached to the meteorite to form the luminous planet Pluto, while others might have fallen on the inner surface to form hills or even whole plateaux.

"Perhaps the olivine mountains, so rich in iron ore, that you discovered on the banks of the Maksheyev River were some of the fragments. Perhaps the entire Black Desert plateau is simply a gigantic fragment. These are all questions that cannot be answered without further study."

"And how can you explain the existence of the extinct and active volcanoes we came across on the plateau?"

"That's not too difficult. According to Zöppritz, there was a fiery-molten layer above the gaseous ones. Part of this layer turned to steam and gases and the rest remained as a boiling fiery sea after the opening had been made, forcing the gases to rush in through it and the pressure inside the earth to fall sharply. The steam and gases gradually escaped through the opening, causing the temperature and pressure in the inner space to fall accordingly and forming a hard crust over the sea of lava. At first this crust was thin and brittle and the steam and gases that were still rising up from the molten mass often broke through it. The crust kept getting harder and instances of such eruptions were becoming fewer and fewer, as was the case on the surface of the earth in the first period of its existence. These volcanoes merely indicate that there are still reservoirs of molten lava beneath this crust which are responsible for the eruptions, and the only difference we notice here is that the lava is made up entirely of very heavy ores full of iron that do not exist on the earth."

"You said that the inner surface was at first a molten sea," Maksheyev interrupted. "Wouldn't that mean that

21

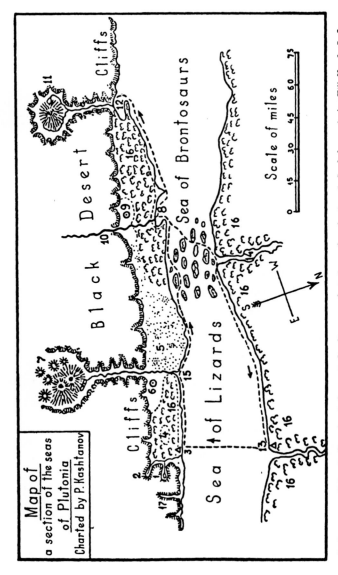

**Map of**
a section of the seas
of Plutonia
Charted by P.Kashtanov

Map of a section of the seas of Plutonia Charted by P.Kashtanov

1. Stegosaurus Lake; 2. Pterodactyl Gorge; 3. Landing ground; 4. Iguanodon clearing; 5. Sand dunes; 6. Ant-Hill No. 1; 7. Satan's Volcano; 8. Fish Bay; 9. Ant-Hill No. 2; 10. Ants' River; 11. Old Grouchy Volcano, Hermit Lake and Papochkn River; 12. Shelter Bay; 13. The mouth of the Maksheyev River; 14. Gromeko River; 15. The mouth of Sulphur River; 16. The forest of ferns, palms, and horsetail; 17. The Gorge of Billions.

fragments of the earth's crust that fell into it would have either had to sink or melt in it?"

"Not necessarily," Kashtanov countered. "The smaller fragments doubtlessly melt, but the larger ones—and they might very well have been up to several miles in diameter—melted only partially. And as far as their sinking in the fiery sea is concerned, that depended entirely upon their specific gravity. If they were lighter than the molten mass, which was quite probable, then they floated on its surface as icebergs in the sea, and, as icebergs in the sea, they melted from the sides and bottom only."

"I don't insist that my explanation is the only possible one," Trukhanov said. "It was merely the first one that came to my mind when you asked your question. This will all take a lot more study. So far, everything we know about Plutonia is limited to a narrow strip along the Maksheyev River and the shores of the Sea of Lizards. What is the enormous country like beyond the banks of the river? How far south does the Black Desert reach? What lies beyond the desert? Is it not possible there is life there too?"

"I don't believe there is," Papochkin said, "and this is why. There can be no life without moisture, and it is brought into the opening by the winds from the north. This moisture is, in the main, produced on the surface of the earth. We have seen that the rain does not reach farther than the southern shore of the Sea of Lizards. The winds deposit all their moisture in this comparatively small area near the opening, and the entire surface of Plutonia beyond the sea is a waterless, barren desert of hardened lava. I would even say that in the beginning the flora and fauna of the Jura were limited to a rather small area surrounding the opening, and that gradually, as the amount of water coming from the outside in the form of streams and lakes increased, this life was able to move

314

farther and farther south. Perhaps even the Sea of Lizards is a relatively new body of water and therefore it is not as salty as ocean water."

"I'll never agree with that," Kashtanov said. "If the sea is still as young as you would have us believe it is, none of the representatives of Jurrasic fauna, such as the fishes, ichthyosaurs, and plesiosaurs, would inhabit it. Neither the fishes nor the ichthyosaurs could have reached the sea over land like ants, nor could they have flown over, like pterodactyls. This points to the fact that the sea *did* penetrate into the opening—perhaps for a short while only and along a narrow channel, but it did, nevertheless."

"Wait a while, now!" Papochkin exclaimed. "How could the sea have penetrated into the opening on the heels of the meteorite? It would have met with flaming gases and a fiery surface, and all the fishes and lizards would have certainly made a colossal chowder, but would never have produced any progeny."

They all laughed at this last remark, but Kashtanov objected:

"You're jumping to conclusions, Semyon. I never said that the sea followed right in after the meteorite. Trukhanov believes it fell during the Triassic period, but the fauna of the sea belongs to the Jura. Therefore, the time that elapsed between the two periods was certainly enough for the gases to escape and the inner surface to cool off. Perhaps the Sea of Lizards stretches far to the north in another part of Plutonia, indicating the way in which the fauna of the sea once reached the inner surface."

"So many important and interesting questions arise as soon as we begin to discuss and analyze that strange phenomenon, Plutonia. Each one of us can think of a host of questions in his own particular field. Therefore, there will certainly have to be another expedition to Plutonia. Do you agree?"

# EPILOGUE

The month of May came and went, but did not bring in the long-awaited spring. The sun no longer dipped beyond the horizon in the evening, but its rays were not warm, so that the only places where the snow melted, were to the south of the ship and on the steep cliffs along the shore. There were many cloudy, windy days and sometimes snow-storms, so that it seemed as if winter had again set in. The new snow-fall would slow down the melting of the old snow, and it was not until the first part of June that spring finally came to the Arctic that year.

Countless streams rushed down the slopes; tiny flowers burst into bloom before their eyes on every spot that was free of snow; the sun-warmed puddles swarmed with strange water-bugs which seemed to have appeared from nowhere. But the sea was still frozen over. On calm days they could see from the crow's-nest a dark strip of water far to the south.

"I don't know what's happened to the spring this year!" the captain said one day as they all gathered on deck.

They were confined to the ship, as there was water on most of the ice round about.

"Last year at this time we were coming near this shore," Maksheyev said.

"There was a strong wind that broke up the ice then. It's been perfectly calm these past days, apart from a slight southerly breeze."

"Do you think we might have to spend another winter here?" asked Papochkin who was beginning to feel bored from lack of activity.

"No, of course not! In July, or August at the latest, the sea will be clear of ice—wind or no wind."

"July or August!" cried Gromeko. "You mean we'll be stuck here for half the summer?"

"That's something you can look for in the Arctic.

There's only about a month or six weeks of navigation in bad years and two or three months, at most, in good years."

The men on the *North Star* were getting restless. The second half of June was cold and dreary. The nights were frosty and it even snowed several times, making them feel as if the summer were over.

Finally, at the beginning of July, a heavy storm broke up the ice, and the ship, long since free of ice and ready to sail, fired a farewell salute to dreary Nansen Land and headed south.

The weather was still unsettled, with snow, rain, fog, and damp, and sometimes they had to wait hours for a fog to lift.

In the beginning of August the *North Star* was finally able to go on through the Bering Strait at full speed. The men's spirits rose, for they would be in Vladivostok in two or three weeks.

On a calm and balmy day in the middle of August, when the rough Bering Sea was as smooth as a pond, and the clear autumn air was so transparent that they could make out the peaks of Bering Island and the nearest of the Komandorskiye Islands to the south-east, they sighted a large ship steaming at full speed and seemingly headed for Nizhnye-Kamchatsk.

"It's probably a Russian cruiser patrolling the waters," Maksheyev said. They were all standing on deck and feeling cheerful because of the calm sea and their successful trip.

"What are they patrolling?" Kashtanov wondered.

"They're probably keeping an eye out for American and Japanese poachers. These islands are the best, if not the only, seal hatchery in the world, and the animals are being viciously exterminated. That's why our government has enforced certain restrictions on the duration of the hunting season and has limited the number of females and young that can be lawfully shot. But the profit-seeking sealers try to evade the law, and that is why navy ships patrol the islands with the right to stop any suspicious-looking vessels in these waters."

"It looks as if they might stop us!" Trukhanov exclaimed. "They're making straight for us."

Soon the large three-masted cruiser was close enough for them to distinguish the shiny guns and a group of men on the bridge. Suddenly a puff of smoke burst from one of the guns and the noise of firing thundered over· the water; simultaneously the cruiser ran up the order: "Stop or I'll fire."

The *North Star* stopped its engines obediently. At first sight of the cruiser the captain had ordered the Russian flag to be hoisted, in accordance with naval regulations, but the cruiser had not followed suit.

"It's not a Russian ship, it's the *Ferdinand,* and the name is in Roman lettering!" called the captain who had been looking through his spyglass.

"Then what right has it to order a Russian ship to halt in Russian waters?" Kashtanov asked.

"What's its nationality? *Ferdinand* sounds German."

"I'll find it in a minute," the captain answered as he leafed through his naval calendar quickly. "Here it is! *Ferdinand*—a cruiser of the Austro-Hungarian Navy, built in 1909 ... mm-m ... tonnage ... 10 guns ... mm-m ... a crew of 250."

Meanwhile the cruiser had come within a cable's length of the *North Star* and cut off its engines.

A few seconds later a boat was lowered, and they watched about twenty armed seamen and two officers climb down the ladder and get into it. The captain, the crew, and all the passengers of the *North Star* stood at the rail, watching the small boat come alongside. They had no choice but to let the ladder down for their unwelcome visitors.

Both officers and ten of the sailors came aboard.

"Is this a Russian ship?" the senior officer asked in broken Russian as he saluted.

"Yes, it's Russian. The *North Star* is a privately owned vessel," Trukhanov answered.

"Are you the captain?"

"No, I'm the owner."

"Is it a merchant ship or a whaler?"

"Neither. The *North Star* is taking the members of a scientific expedition back from a voyage through the Arctic Ocean. But I'd like to know by what right you have stopped a Russian ship in Russian waters and are cross-examining us?"

"In accordance with sea-war legislation and martial law."

"What martial law?" ... "What are you talking about?" ... "What do you mean?" demanded the alarmed passengers and crew.

The officer smiled.

"Haven't you heard about it? How long have you been sailing in the Arctic?"

"Since the spring of last year."

The officer turned to his companion and spoke in German, as the latter did not seem to understand Russian.

"I think these Russians have just fallen from the moon—they don't even know there's a war on!"

The other officer smiled too.

The spokesman addressed the Russians again:

"Please understand that the Austro-Hungarian Empire and the German Empire have been at war with Russia for the past year, and the Emperor's cruiser *Ferdinand* has claimed you as a prize of war. Is that clear?"

"But my ship is not a military vessel, it's a scientific and peaceful craft. Private property cannot be confiscated," Trukhanov objected.

"A peaceful craft? Then what do you call this?" The officer pointed to the little cannon on the bow, which was used for firing salutes and signalling. "That's a gun!"

Trukhanov smiled wryly.

"Any peaceful vessel can be armed," the Austrian officer continued. "It can carry a landing party, it can transport ammunition or military mail. We'll have to take you in, there's nothing else we can do."

"May I see your captain?" Trukhanov asked.

"Do you speak German?"

"No, but I know French and English."

"All right then! Come along with us."

The officer said something to his companion in an undertone; then he and Trukhanov went down into the boat, while the other officer and the armed sailors remained aboard the *North Star*.

Kashtanov spoke German fluently; the second officer was very obliging and answered all his questions about the war which had begun the previous year. Before long, Trukhanov was back, accompanied by two officers and several unarmed sailors.

"They'll put us ashore at Kamchatka," he said. "Let's go down to our cabins and pack while they take the *North*

*Star* in under escort. It's being confiscated with everything on board."

When they were in Trukhanov's cabin—the Austrians had all remained above to supervise the crew—he told them of his visit to the cruiser.

"The captain repeated everything the officer had said. At first, after consultation with his officers, he was all for taking us prisoner. My German is fluent, but I didn't want them to know, so that I could listen to what they said to each other. I discovered they're very short of supplies and they're counting on our stores to replenish their own. Therefore, they don't want any extra mouths to feed, which they would have if they took us prisoner. One of the officers insisted that they detain everyone under forty-five as being of military age, and I'm the only one of us who's over forty-five. The captain calmed him down by saying that by the time we get to Moscow from Kamchatka, the war will have ended in the utter defeat of Russia and France.

"And so," Trukhanov continued, "they've decided to put us all ashore, and we'll be allowed to take some extra clothing, food, and our personal money, but we'll have to leave the expedition's funds on board, as they are to be confiscated along with everything else on the ship."

"Do you mean they'll take our collections, all the results of the expedition?!" Papochkin demanded angrily.

"Yes, everything—to the last tooth and hair! We can stuff our diaries and notes into our pockets, but the photographs, skulls, hides, plants, and everything else will have to be left behind. They've promised that everything will be delivered safely to Vienna and returned to us after the war is over."

"On condition that they're not sunk on the way by a French or Russian submarine or mine!" Borovoi said indignantly.

"That's quite possible," Trukhanov replied, "especially as Britain has joined in the war."

"In other words, we've lost everything again, just like the time the ants robbed us," Maksheyev added with a wan smile.

"There's a chance of getting our things back," Trukhanov said. "I gathered from their conversation that they have a base somewhere near here, most probably on the Komandorskiye Islands, as the cruiser was coming from that direction. They'll take the *North Star* there. When we reach Vladivostok we can report it to the military authorities, and our ships will take care of the rest."

"It'll take us a long time to get to Vladivostok!"

"It's our only hope. Well, we'd better start packing."

They all went to their cabins. The *North Star* was proceeding at full speed under escort to Ust-Kamchatsk, the nearest coastal settlement from Petropavlovsk-on-Kamchatka. Soon the crestfallen passengers had gathered on deck with their suitcases and knapsacks. The Austrians examined their personal belongings very superficially and did not search them. Maksheyev was in luck, for he had transferred his gold from the leather pouch to a prospector's wide money-belt and felt very clumsy, as he had about fifty pounds of gold dust anchored round his middle. The Austrians paid no attention to the paunchy engineer in the wide native *kukhlyanka*. All the collections and instruments had long since been crated for the cross-country journey by rail and were handed over to the Austrians with a copy of the inventory. The explorers did not mention where they had actually been.

"We explored the Chukotka Peninsula and spent the winter on Wrangel Island," Trukhanov told the officer in charge of receiving the property. The man nodded understandingly and said:

"My father was a member of a Polar expedition to Franz Josef Land on the Austrian corvette *Tegetthoff*— you've probably read about it?"

"I have indeed!" Trukhanov said.

322

Towards evening both ships dropped anchor near a long sand-bar at the mouth of the Kamchatka River; the small fishing village was beyond it. Three boats took the passengers and their baggage ashore. Igolkin and the *North Star*'s captain went off towards the village to see what they could find in the way of transport. The others remained on the beach and sadly watched the three boats being hoisted up on deck and the two ships turn and set their course for the open sea again. When the two men returned with the only horse they could find in the village, the ships had disappeared in the twilight.

They spent the next ten days in the village, for there was no way of going south. The entire population was busy fishing, as it was the height of the autumn season, and nobody was prepared to spend time on taking so many men by dug-out to Petropavlovsk at the risk of having nothing to eat for his family or dogs for the whole winter. Igolkin took General and set out in a dug-out for his home in Petropavlovsk. Trukhanov gave him a letter for the governor, informing him that there was an enemy base on the Komandorskiye Islands, that the *North Star* had been confiscated, and asking for his aid in the matter.

Towards the end of August a Japanese fishing boat docked in Ust-Kamchatsk and agreed to take them to Japan for a payment.

The voyage, which took three weeks, was far from pleasant. Some of the men found themselves a place on deck, and others in the hold among the barrels of fish. They ate fish, rice, and drank tea; the sea was very rough and there were constant fogs, rain, and storms. They nearly went down on the reefs near the Kuril Islands during a storm; when they reached Terpeniya Bay the Japanese wanted to make them leave the ship, saying that the southern half of Sakhalin was Japanese soil, and consented to take them the rest of the way for an additional payment.

When they reached Wakkanai, on the northern tip of

Hokkaido Island, the exhausted passengers were glad of the chance to leave the schooner, as they could reach the port of Hakodate more quickly and comfortably by train.

There was a frequent and regular steamer service between Hakodate, on the southern tip of the island, and Vladivostok, directly across the Sea of Japan. They had to go through certain formalities and questioning, as Japan had joined the Entente, and then they took the first packet boat out and were soon in Vladivostok.

They were overjoyed and amazed to see the *North Star* at anchor among the other ships as they came into harbour. There was a sentry on board. It transpired that the Governor of Kamchatka on receiving Trukhanov's letter had sent a wireless message to Vladivostok, for he had no ships large enough to attack the Austrian cruiser. A Russian cruiser left Vladivostok and headed for the Komandorskiye Islands where it found the *North Star.* Unfortunately, the Austrians were able to escape in good time.

The commanding officer of the port, who told them all this, soon dashed their hopes of getting their collections back. It seemed that the Austrians had taken everything movable off the ship: the collections, equipment, provisions, and even the cabin furnishing and most valuable parts of the engines, so that the *North Star* had had to be towed back. Extensive repairs would be needed to make it seaworthy, and Trukhanov had to agree to the Navy's suggestion that he leave it in Vladivostok as a signal ship for the duration of the war.

A quiet and disheartened group of men boarded the Siberian Express for their journey home. They discussed the situation at length and finally agreed that it would be better to say nothing of their trip to Plutonia until the end of the war—which they expected would be soon—and the return of their collections and photographs. They had no tangible proof that a country full of wonders named Plutonia existed and could be reached by man. Any sensible person would say their story was pure fiction and would regard them as fakers or madmen.

The war dragged on for three more years. It was followed by the Great October Revolution and then the Civil War. The members of the expedition lost contact with each other. The whereabouts of the collections and documents is unknown. Trukhanov, who returned to a hermit's life at his observatory on Munku-Sardyk, lost all hope of ever getting them back.

By chance, the author came upon Papochkin's diary and sketches. This book was compiled on the basis of these documents.

# A WORD ABOUT THE AUTHOR

Academician Vladimir Afanasyevich Obruchev was born in 1863. He was the most outstanding Soviet geologist and is widely known for his scientific works on the geology and geography of Siberia, Central Asia, and China. He is the author of three very popular science-fiction novels for young people. They are: *Plutonia* (1924), *Sannikov's Land* (1926), and *In the Wilds of Central Asia* (1950).

V. A. Obruchev was an enthusiastic reader of popular science-fiction since his childhood. He wrote: " . . . I was fascinated by the accounts which I read of adventures in far-away places. I listened eagerly to stories told by people who had travelled about the world.

"The books of James Fenimore Cooper, Mayne Reid and, later, Jules Verne, all had a great influence on me. My brothers and I would make-believe that we were conquering the Arctic wastes, climbing high mountains, roaming the ocean bed, hunting lions, tigers, and elephants. We pretended to be explorers and would cut out pictures of people and animals to use in our wild animal hunts, our wars against the Indians, and our shipwrecks. I liked the hunters and sailors, and Jules Verne's scientists who were sometimes funny and absent-minded, but always knew a great deal about nature. I too longed to be a scientist, a naturalist, and an explorer when I grew up."

Obruchev graduated from a Mining Institute in 1886 and worked on the construction of the Transcaspian railway in Turkmenia, where he explored the Kara Kum Desert, the shores of the Amu-Darya River, and the old riverbeds of the Uzbois; he crossed the sands and mountains on the Afghan border and entered Buchara and then Samarkand with the railwaymen; from there he journeyed to the Alai Mountains. When the railroad was completed Obruchev went to work as a geologist in Siberia: on the shores of Lake Baikal, on the Lena River, and in the gold-fields near the River Vitima. In the years 1892-94 he was a member of the famous explorer Potanin's expedition into the deserts and steppes of Mongolia, to the mountains of Nanshan and Northern China. Later he explored the Transbaikal area and took part in expeditions to Dzhungaria and to the Altai. He spent many years teaching and was the scientific mentor of several generations of geologists and mining engineers.

In 1929, V. A. Obruchev was elected to the Academy of Sciences of the U.S.S.R.

V. A. Obruchev is the author of over a thousand scientific works, among which are a most extensive geological study of Siberia and a five-volume history of the geological exploration of Siberia, which have been awarded the V. I. Lenin Prize as well as the prizes and medals of several scientific societies. In November, 1954, he completed a detailed geographical study of the Nanshan mountain chain in China, based on his own observations and those of every other traveller who had ever explored these mountains. He spent his last years working on a geological study of the Nanshan Mountains.

Vladimir Afanasyevich Obruchev died on June 19, 1956, at the age of 92.

Lightning Source UK Ltd.
Milton Keynes UK
UKOW04f1854070115

244170UK00001B/24/P